Only once had she known the deep silence of the countryside at night. Her early childhood had been spent in cities, much of it under the roar of aircraft and what seemed, in memory, to be an incessant pandemonium of bombing. There had been that brief period in a small village, not so very different from Burracombe and sharing the same deep quiet under the starlit nights – and then the sudden wrench as she was torn away from the contented home she had found and taken to an orphanage on the other side of the county.

She stood now with her hand on the gate, looking up at the stars. It was her first New Year's Eve away from the Home. 1951: a new year, a new start.

I haven't made a resolution, she thought suddenly, and closed her eyes. *Let me make a success of this job – of this whole year. And let me, somehow, find out what happened to my little sister.*

It wasn't a resolution so much as a prayer, but it said everything that was in her heart.

Lilian Harry's grandfather hailed from Devon and Lilian always longed to return to her roots, so moving from Hampshire to a small Dartmoor town in her early twenties was a dream come true. She quickly absorbed herself in local life, learning the fascinating folklore and history of the moors, joining the church bellringers and a country dance club, and meeting people who are still her friends today. Although she later moved north, living first in Herefordshire and then in the Lake District, she returned in the 1990s and now lives on the edge of the moor with her three ginger cats and a black miniature schnauzer who has a fan club bigger than that of her mistress. She has a son, a daughter and two grandchildren, is still an active bellringer and member of the local drama group and loves to walk on the moors. Visit her website at www.lilianharry.co.uk.

The Bells of Burracombe

LILIAN HARRY

An Orion paperback

First published in Great Britain in 2006
by Orion
This paperback edition published in 2006
by Orion Books Ltd,
Orion House, 5 Upper St Martin's Lane,
London WC2H 9EA

An Hachette UK company

A CIP catalogue record for this book is available
from the British Library.

Printed and bound in Germany
by GGP Media GmbH, Pößneck

The Orion Publishing Group's policy is to use papers that
are natural, renewable and recyclable products and
made from wood grown in sustainable forests. The logging
and manufacturing processes are expected to conform to
the environmental regulations of the country of origin.

www.orionbooks.co.uk

Dedication

To the Bellringers of Devon – the 'Ringing County' –
especially my good friends in Peter Tavy and Tavistock

Author's Note

Readers just setting off to explore Dartmoor and South Devon may be disappointed to know that the villages of Burracombe and Little Burracombe do not actually exist. However, you may think of them as being somewhere in the triangle produced by Tavistock, Princetown and Plymouth. The other villages mentioned, and whose church bellringers take part in the Bellringing Competitions, do exist in this lovely part of Devon and are each worth a visit. You can even find the Watchmaker's Tomb in Lydford Churchyard, and although the inscription itself is now faint, it has been transcribed so that visitors can read the full text.

The villagers of Burracombe are like those of any other village in the 1950s, or indeed at any time – a mixture of human beings: some friendly, affectionate, humble and hardworking; some snobbish, self-important, misguided or slovenly; and yet all, I hope, entertaining.

This is the first story about Burracombe. I hope you will enjoy reading it, as I have enjoyed writing it, and that we will all enjoy those yet to come.

Lilian Harry

Chapter One

'You must be the new teacher!'

Stella Simmons turned quickly. The little bus, that had trundled around several villages on its way from Tavistock where she'd got off the train, was already departing down the narrow lane. There was nobody on the village green apart from herself and the young man who stood a few yards away, watching her with dark blue eyes. Tall, very thin and loose-limbed, wearing what appeared to be an old gardening jacket and trousers splashed with paint, he looked rather as if he'd been thrown hastily together from spare parts. Yet there was an attractive friendliness in his face and the grin that showed white, if slightly crooked, teeth. He was carrying a large, flat book.

'Are you the vicar?' Stella asked doubtfully, and he burst into delighted laughter, his wavy black hair flying around his bare head.

'Do I look like a vicar?'

'Well, no, but he was supposed to meet me here. And I'm not the new teacher – not yet. I've come for an interview. How did you know about me, anyway?'

'In a small place like Burracombe,' the young man said, 'everyone knows everything. We all knew that someone was coming today, and I guessed it must be you as soon as I saw you get off the bus. You're the only stranger here, you see.'

I

Stella met his bright blue glance and then looked away. The October sky was a hazy blue, with the jewelled colours of the woods shimmering as if through a delicate silvered veil. Her journey had brought her through meadows that dipped and dived, across wide, flat fenland and fields of sunburned stubble, and then between the brown folds of the moors. Even as she stepped off the bus into this village, tucked into a soft valley clothed with oak and beech trees, she had felt as if she were coming home. Oh, she thought, I hope I get this job . . .

The village green still seemed deserted, with the church tower tall and grey above the cob cottages clustered around it, but as she gazed about she began to see signs of life. Along the lane was a forge with a big Shire horse being shod by a brawny, bald-headed man. A young woman a few years older than Stella, wearing breeches and a yellow jumper, was holding the horse's head. A cottage door opened and a woman in a crossover pinafore stepped outside and began to shovel up some dung that had obviously been deposited there only a few minutes before by the horse; she gathered it into a bucket and disappeared round the side of her cottage, but not before giving Stella a quick, sharp glance. And then hasty footsteps coming down the church path announced the arrival of the vicar, and the young man murmured in Stella's ear: 'Here he comes. He's just like the White Rabbit in *Alice in Wonderland* – always terrified of being late!'

The vicar opened the wooden lych gate and hurried across to them. He grasped Stella's hand and shook it vigorously, talking almost before he was within speaking distance. 'My dear young lady, I'm Basil Harvey. So sorry to keep you waiting. I'd intended meeting the bus but I was asked to give an opinion on marrows – not that my opinion's worth anything. All I could say was that they're very big!' He let go of her hand and stepped back a little.

'It's so kind of you to come all this way. I hope you had a good journey?'

'Very good, thank you,' Stella said, smiling at him. He did indeed look a little like the White Rabbit, with a halo of silver hair and a pink face that looked as if it had been scrubbed. 'I came on the train as far as Tavistock, just as you said.'

'Ah yes. A pleasant journey. And when you're settled you must try the branch line, from Whitchurch to Plymouth. Or in the other direction, to Launceston. One of the most beautiful railway lines in the country, to my mind. Railways are something of a hobby of mine,' he confided a little sheepishly. 'But I mustn't keep you standing here. The other governors are meeting at the vicarage at twelve-thirty, so I thought it might be nice for you to see the church before going on to the school. And there'll be lunch afterwards.' He glanced at the young man, who was watching them quietly, an amused twinkle somewhere deep in his bright eyes. 'I see you've met our other recent newcomer to the village.'

'We've had quite a conversation,' the young man said easily, 'but we haven't actually introduced ourselves.' He held out his hand. 'Luke Ferris, at your service.'

'Oh.' Stella took his hand, feeling unaccountably flustered. 'And I'm Stella Simmons. But of course, you know that already.'

He laughed. 'I had the advantage of you, didn't I! But to be honest, I've only been here a week or two myself. I'm renting a cottage on the estate. I'm an artist – or like to think I am,' he added a little ruefully. She realised that the book he was carrying must be a sketchpad. 'Trying my hand at the Devon landscape.' He gestured at the vicar. 'It was Uncle Basil here who suggested it. Thought I needed a change from smoky old London.'

'And so you did. I'm not really his uncle,' the vicar told

3

Stella, 'but his father and I have been friends for many years. Anyway, we mustn't stand here gossiping. Miss Simmons will be getting cold. Come along and look at our church, my dear.' He turned to Luke. 'Why don't you join us for lunch? I'm sure Grace can stretch the rabbit pie to another plate.'

At the mention of rabbit pie, Luke shot a swift glance at Stella, who shyly looked away. 'I won't, thanks.' I want to go over to Little Burracombe and catch the afternoon sun on Cuckoo Wood. The colours are magnificent now, but if we get a wind the leaves will be gone overnight and I'll miss the chance.' He said goodbye and loped away along the lane, his jacket unbuttoned and flapping round his lean body. The vicar looked after him and then turned to lead Stella up the path.

'Luke's been rather ill for the past two or three years – Grace and I do worry that he doesn't feed himself properly . . . However, that's not why you're here.' He bustled up the flagstone path and Stella followed him, peering at the leaning gravestones on either side. *Robert Tozer, Beloved Husband of Alice . . . Fell Asleep January 14th 1842; Albert Tozer, 1796–1875, Gone But Not Forgotten; Jemima Tozer, 1800–1879, Wife of the Above; William Tozer, 1833–1835; Susannah Tozer, 1834–1840; Eliza Tozer, 1836–1880.*

'There are a lot of Tozers here,' she said. 'Are they a local family?'

'Oh yes, and there are still plenty of them about.' Basil Harvey looked at the gravestones. 'Many of them died young, as you can see, especially during the 1830s. Cholera, you know.' He hurried on and opened the big wooden door. Stella followed him into the dim church and stood still for a moment, letting her eyes adjust.

'It's lovely,' she said, looking up at the wooden beams on the vaulted roof and the sturdy, tree-like pillars of the nave. The soft grey of the stone was lit and coloured by sunshine pouring in through a stained-glass window, while the deep crimson of the altar cloth glowed like a winter bonfire behind the carved railing of the chancel. The stone floor was cold but the dark wood of the pews seemed to give out its own warmth as if extending a welcome that had been sustained for centuries past.

'We're very proud of it,' the vicar admitted, standing beside her. 'As you see, we're preparing for our Harvest Festival service on Sunday – that's why I was asked to choose which marrow should go at the foot of the pulpit.' He moved up the aisle towards a young woman who was arranging fruit and flowers around the pulpit and chancel steps. Two enormous marrows lay like slumbering green hippos on the floor, with a pile of scrubbed orange carrots beside them and a great sheaf of golden chrysanthemums thrust into a bucket of water. There were boxes of other vegetables and fruits as well – potatoes, swedes, scarlet apples, gleaming bronze onions – all in glorious disarray at her feet, while Stella now noticed two or three other women busy arranging more produce on the wide windowsills.

The young woman looked up as they approached. She was about thirty and was wearing an old jumper and skirt, yet still managed to appear elegant with her slender figure and long, artistic hands. Her fair hair was loose, in a long page-boy style, and her grey eyes were cool but friendly as she surveyed the vicar and his companion.

'You must be the new teacher.' She wiped her hand on her skirt. 'How do you do? I'm Hilary Napier. Sorry, I'm in a bit of a mess – perhaps we'd better save the handshake for later.'

Stella smiled and shook her head. 'I'm not the new teacher – not yet, anyway. I haven't even had my interview yet. Mr Harvey's just showing me round.'

'Well, that won't take long – Burracombe's not much more than a handful of cottages and a dog. I hope you're not a city girl. You'll find it very dull and quiet here if you are.' She eyed Stella assessingly. 'You look very young to be applying for a teacher's post.'

'I'm twenty-one. I've done all my training, and worked as a pupil teacher where I used to live.' Stella felt a twinge of anxiety. She had done her best to make herself look older before setting out on the journey that morning – trying to brush her short, dark curls flat, putting on a brown hat and coat that had been passed down to her by one of the other girls, wearing lace-up shoes and thick stockings. But nothing could disguise her fresh, smooth complexion, nor the brightness of her hazel eyes. She had an uneasy feeling that she just looked like a little girl, dressing up in her mother's clothes.

'Well, we want someone young and lively for our children, don't we,' the vicar was saying cheerily. 'Miss Morgan was an excellent teacher, I'm sure, but I did sometimes feel that the little ones were getting a bit too much for her. There were times when she didn't even seem to *like* them very much, but I'm sure she did really. It was just that she was tired.'

'It wasn't that at all,' Hilary Napier said. She had a brisk way of speaking, in a clipped voice that Stella guessed indicated an upper-class background and private education. 'She *didn't* like them. And it wasn't just her age, either – she never did like small children. Totally unsuited to be a teacher, if you ask me.' She bent and picked up one of the marrows.

The vicar protested. 'Oh, I'm sure you're wrong about that, Hilary. She was an excellent woman. Every child who passed through her hands went on to the junior class able to read and write and do sums.'

'Too frightened not to.' Hilary balanced the marrow in both hands and flicked her eyebrows at Stella. 'It was a good day for Burracombe when she retired. And not a

6

moment too soon, either – she must have been well over age. Eighty in the shade.'

Mr Harvey gave her a reproachful look. 'If I weren't accustomed to your sense of humour, Hilary, I might be cross with you. You shouldn't be talking like that, even if you don't mean it. You'll be making poor Miss Simmons wonder if she really does want to come to Burracombe.' He glanced suddenly at the watch on his wrist. 'Goodness gracious me! Where does the time go? We ought to be making our way to the school. And I haven't shown you the church properly at all. Never mind, there may be an opportunity later.' He whirled off down the aisle towards the door and Hilary Napier laughed.

'You'd better go,' she said. 'If Basil thinks you're late, you must be!' She gave Stella a friendly smile. 'I hope you get the job. Burracombe's quiet, but it's a nice enough place to live, provided you don't hanker for city streets and big shops.'

'I don't,' Stella said, smiling back. 'I lived in the country for a while when I was a child – evacuated, you know.' The usual shadow touched her heart, but she was so accustomed to it by now that she could ignore it – almost. 'I hope I'll see you again, Miss Napier.'

'Oh, I expect you will.' Hilary clasped the marrow to her chest as if it were a baby and carried it over to the altar. 'You'll be meeting my father, anyway – he's one of the school governors. Enjoy your visit to Burracombe. At least you've got a nice day for it. I warn you, it can be a bit bleak around here in winter.'

She turned to arrange the vegetables in a row along the chancel rail, and Stella followed the vicar out of the church.

The October air was as sharp as a russet apple as they trotted back down the church path. Stella looked about at the cluster of cottages and tried to imagine herself living here, in this tiny village on the edge of Dartmoor. A narrow

7

stream ran along the side of the road, and beyond the cottages the hills were clothed in woods, bronzed with autumn colour, with occasional splashes of deep purple. Above the woods she could see the moor itself, golden-brown with the dying bracken and scattered with the bright yellow of gorse flowers. *When gorse is out of season, kissing's out of reason* . . . Someone had told her that once, years ago. It never was completely out of season.

Luke had disappeared but there were a few more people about now. The Shire horse had finished being shod at the forge and was coming along the green. He was a huge beast with chestnut-brown sides, a creamy white blaze down his nose and feathery blond hairs covering his enormous feet. The young woman leading him paused as Stella and the vicar came down the church path, and the horse leaned his big head against her arm.

'Valerie!' Basil Harvey greeted her. 'Come and meet Miss Simmons. We're hoping she may come to be our new infant teacher.' He rubbed the horse's nose absently and felt in his pocket. 'I'm sure I've got a peppermint somewhere here . . .'

Stella smiled shyly. She was beginning to wonder how she would ever be able to remember the names of all these people. This young woman looked about the same age as Hilary Napier – a year or two under thirty, perhaps – and was about the same height, but her hair was dark and tied back from her face with a blue ribbon. She had a rather long face and her smile seemed tinged with sadness. She nodded at Stella.

'Nice to meet you.' She was the first person Stella had met who spoke with a Devon accent, although it wasn't very strong; perhaps she'd been out of the village for a while. She gave the vicar an apologetic glance as she added, 'Sorry, Mr Harvey, I can't stop, Dad needs Barley back on the farm. He cast a shoe in the night – got it caught up on the fence – and it's put us all behind.' The horse had his nose down in the grass and had begun munching, and she gave the head-collar a gentle tug. 'Come on, Barley, it isn't dinnertime yet. We've got work to do.'

She walked on and Stella saw the vicar look after her thoughtfully. Then he turned back to Stella with a cheerful smile on his rosy face.

'A nice person, Val Tozer. She lives at the farm just over there. Still with her parents – ought to be married with her own home and family, but she lost her fiancé in the war – a sad story. Right – the school's just along here and if we're lucky we'll get there while the children are still in class.' He gave Stella a conspiratorial glance. 'I'm afraid you won't meet the redoubtable Miss Morgan, though. Since Dr Latimer ordered her to retire, we've had the assistance of another of our old teachers, Miss Perriman – a very different kind of person. The children love her.'

He hastened on along the village street with Stella almost having to run to keep up with him. Her heart was beginning to beat fast and she felt again the tinge of apprehension that had accompanied her all the way on the train from Hampshire and then on the bus from the little market town of Tavistock.

I want this job so much, she thought. I don't know what I'll do if I don't get it . . .

Val Tozer strode along the lane, her hand stroking the soft skin under Barley's neck. The big, gentle horse nuzzled her as she walked but her mind wasn't with him. Nor did she notice the colours of the hedgerows, their summer green fading now to the browns of autumn with a few black-berries still glistening above the gateways, and the grey, spiky twigs of a sloe-tree in contrast with its purple fruits. Familiar as they were to her, they were far from her

9

thoughts as she walked between the steep Devon banks towards her father's farm.

'Val!'

Even before she heard the voice, the sound of footsteps behind her had brought a prickle to her spine. Her back stiffened and she quickened her pace.

'Val, wait. Please. Look, you can't go on avoiding me all the time.' The voice was closer. 'Please talk to me, Val.'

Val took a deep breath, squared her shoulders and stopped. Barley came to a halt and turned his head enquiringly. Stubbornly, she stared straight ahead.

Luke Ferris came beside her and touched her arm. She shook it off and stepped away from him.

'Don't do that.'

'Val,' he said despairingly. 'Val, please. We can't pretend we don't know each other.'

'I don't see why not.' Her breath felt tight in her chest, like a hard lump, and her heart was thumping painfully. 'I don't see why we have to have anything to do with each other.'

'But I'm living here now. We're bound to meet—'

'No, we're not. Not if you keep out of my way.' She faced him at last. 'I'm perfectly prepared to keep out of yours. And why did you have to come and live here anyway? Couldn't you have gone somewhere else?'

'I didn't know you lived here,' he said quietly and, at the flash of angry disbelief in her eyes, added, 'I *didn't*. You never told me – or if you did, I'd forgotten. It was all a long time ago.' He hesitated, but she didn't speak, and he went on, 'Look, I really didn't come here to make trouble. I needed to be in the country and Uncle Basil – the vicar – knew of the cottage and asked Colonel Napier if I could rent it. It was as simple as that. It never occurred to me that you'd be here.'

She looked at him. His face was thinner than she

remembered, and rather drawn. Yet he was still sunburned, as if he spent a good deal of time in the open air. She wondered briefly what he'd been doing over the years since they'd last met.

'Well, you know now,' she said brusquely. 'And if you don't mind, I'd rather we didn't talk to each other. We've got nothing to say.' She lifted her hand to push Barley's damp nose off her shoulder. 'I've got to go now.'

Luke's eyes went to her fingers and a frown gathered between his brows. 'You're not wearing a ring.'

'No,' Val said shortly. 'I'm not.'

'But . . .' He seemed to be feeling for words and when he spoke again it was uncertainly. 'You – you didn't get married, then?'

'I couldn't,' she said. 'He was killed in the D-Day landings. We didn't have a chance to get married.' Her eyes met his again and she added bitterly, 'Not everyone had a soft job drawing pretty pictures.'

'They weren't pretty,' Luke said quietly. 'You know that, Val.' He paused. 'I'm sorry to hear about Eddie, though. And – there hasn't been anyone else?'

Val's eyes filled with tears. She turned away and jerked at Barley's head. He gave a whicker of protest and she rubbed his nose in apology, but was already striding on along the lane.

'No,' she said over her shoulder, 'there hasn't been anyone else. There never will be.' She stopped and turned again, facing him. 'Go away, Luke. You've done enough damage. Go away and leave me alone.'

Together, she and the big horse marched away down the lane. Her shoulders were stiff, her back straight, but Luke knew that if he could see her face he would find tears pouring down her cheeks. He started after her and then stopped again, knowing that it was no use.

He watched until she disappeared from sight round the

bend in the lane. Then he walked slowly back through the village, past the green with its huge ancient oak tree, past the grey stone church, past the Bell Inn with its thatched roof and benches outside, past the school where the children were spilling out into the playground. Almost without seeing them, he passed the vicar and Stella Simmons, standing at the door and talking to Miss Kemp, the headmistress, and then he turned up the narrow lane that led to his own cottage, on the edge of the Barton estate.

He had spoken the truth when he'd said he hadn't realised that Val Tozer lived in Burracombe. But he couldn't, in all honesty, say that he wouldn't have come to live here if he had known.

Chapter Two

Basil Harvey, standing in the playground of Burracombe School, saw Luke walk by and lifted his hand. But Luke didn't seem to notice him. He appeared to be deep in thought, his long face furrowed with creases that had come too soon for his age, and there was a droop to his thin shoulders as he passed the school railings. He turned up the lane without acknowledging Basil, and the vicar watched him thoughtfully and with a touch of anxiety.

Basil Harvey was more than a family friend; he was Luke's godfather and took his responsibilities seriously. He had been as worried as the rest of the family when Luke had developed TB, but the sanatoriums seemed to have worked a cure at last, and now all the young man needed was peace, quiet and fresh air to build up his strength. Basil had hoped that in Burracombe he would find all of these, together with the chance to build up his reputation as a landscape painter.

Miss Kemp and Stella had seen Luke as well.

'Isn't that the man you introduced me to on the green?' Stella asked. 'I thought he was going to paint some trees.'

'Yes, he was. He wanted to catch the colours. I hope he's all right.' Luke disappeared along the lane and Basil turned back to the others. 'Well, I dare say he just changed his mind. You ought to get him to come into the school and talk to the children sometime, Miss Kemp. He's rather a good artist.'

'Perhaps we will.' The headmistress glanced at her watch. 'We'd better go over to the vicarage. I expect Colonel Napier and Miss Bellamy will be there by now.'

Stella followed them across the playground. The children had either gone home for their midday meal or were crowding into the tiny canteen where she had met the school cook, Mrs Dawe, who was serving shepherd's pie for those who lived too far away to go home. She had seen both classrooms – the large one for the 'big' children of seven to eleven years, and the smaller one, which would be hers (if she got the job) for the infants. There were usually about nine or ten of them, Miss Kemp had explained, although it would probably go up next year when the Crocker twins arrived.

'Twins!' Stella exclaimed. 'Are they identical?'

'Well, they're certainly very alike.' The headmistress glanced at Basil Harvey. 'I'd say that George and Edward were identical, wouldn't you, Vicar?' She folded her lips wryly. 'I'm afraid there'll be fun and games when those two arrive in school!'

'Now, we mustn't put Miss Simmons off,' the vicar said hastily. 'Anyway, they're only four years old now and there's almost a whole year to go before they start. They'll probably change a lot in that time . . .' As if feeling that even this statement had a certain ominous sound to it, he opened the school gate with something of a flourish. 'What do you think of our little school, Miss Simmons?'

'I like it very much.' Stella had spent most of her life in larger schools, with up to forty children in each class. Even when she had lived in the country, as an evacuee, schooling had been difficult, with the village school shared between local and evacuee children, taking turn and turn about in the mornings and afternoons. The prospect of having only ten or a dozen children to teach, in quiet and ordered surroundings, seemed like a glimpse of heaven.

Burracombe School and its playground were situated at the edge of the village. The headmistress's cottage stood to one side and beyond it were fields, a wood and then the moor where Miss Kemp had explained that the children were sometimes taken on nature walks. 'There's a pretty stream and a pond where they can catch tadpoles for the nature table.' It was near enough to the green and the church for the school to feel very much a part of local goings-on, and the children were taken to church every Wednesday morning for their own service.

'I'm in and out a lot too,' Mr Harvey told Stella as they walked back towards the church. 'I hope you won't mind my popping in. I like the children to get to know me and feel that they can come to me with their problems even after they've left school and have gone out into the world.'

'Yes, we encourage several of our friends to drop in and talk to the children,' Miss Kemp agreed. 'Mr Tozer, the farmer, comes in when he brings our logs for the fire, and tells us all about what's happening on the farm—'

'You met his daughter, Val, with the horse,' the vicar interrupted. 'And Hilary Napier, whom you met in the church, came in once to talk about her time in the ATS during the war. She was a driver, you know, and met some famous people – Mr Churchill, Mr Eisenhower, Lord Montgomery . . .'

'Colonel Napier, the chairman of the governors, is her father,' Miss Kemp continued. 'The other governor is Miss Bellamy. She's from a very old Burracombe family and quite a character.'

They passed the church to go through the gate to the vicarage, a large house set back from the road in a big, untidy garden. Rhododendron and azalea bushes fringed the path and a few tall trees were shedding coloured leaves on the lawn. The vicarage itself had a verandah running all the way around three sides, and the front door stood invitingly open. Mr Harvey ushered them through and called out to his wife.

'Grace! We're here.' He sniffed appreciatively. 'Mm, that smells good.'

A tall fair-haired woman emerged from the kitchen, wiping floury hands on a cloth. She smiled at Miss Kemp and held out her hand to Stella. Her grasp was firm and her eyes intelligent. 'It's good to see you, Miss Simmons. I hope you had a pleasant journey.'

'It was lovely. I had such good views of the moors. I like wild countryside.'

Grace Harvey nodded and turned to her husband. 'Colonel Napier and Miss Bellamy are here. I put them in your study.'

The vicar led the way down the hall. Over his shoulder, he said, 'Grace wanted to put us into the drawing room but I knew Colonel Napier would prefer the study – it's more formal. He's our Squire, you know. We had to bring in another chair, but I think we'll be comfortable enough.'

He opened a door and the two women followed him into a large room lined with bookshelves. There was a French window opening on to the verandah at the side and looking out into the shrubbery, and a large desk littered with papers. A small fire was burning in the grate with a leather armchair on each side of it, one occupied by a large man in his mid-fifties wearing a tweed suit, and the other by a small, stocky woman with a face so creased by tiny wrinkles that she looked as if she had been crumpled up in a giant fist. She was dressed in a shapeless purple jumper and a sagging brown skirt.

'Ah good, you've made yourselves at home.' The vicar beamed at them as the man got up and held out his hand. He was the sort of man, Stella thought as she took it, who would dominate any situation – solidly built, with confident bearing and a head like a lion's, certain of himself and his

16

position and probably rather arrogant. She decided not to be intimidated by him and lifted her chin to meet his eyes.

'So you're hoping to be our new infant teacher,' he said. His voice was strong and deep, just as she'd expected it to be, and carried a slight undertone of warning. It was as if he were saying, *Don't expect it to be a foregone conclusion, whatever the vicar might have said*, and she felt a small thrill of challenge run through her.

'I hope so,' she replied steadily. 'I like what I've seen so far.'

There was a small change in his eyes, as if he had registered that she wasn't here to beg, and that it was as important that Burracombe should make a good impression on her as the other way about. They regarded each other for a moment and then the vicar said, 'And this is Miss Bellamy, whose family endowed the school almost a hundred years ago.'

Stella turned to greet the old woman, who was now standing up. She was little more than five feet tall, with iron-grey hair and eyes as black and lively as tadpoles. Her face was as red and wrinkled as a Cox's apple and she seemed to bristle with energy. She shook Stella's hand vigorously. 'You'll find us pretty quiet down here in the West Country.'

Stella smiled. 'I lived in a village for a while, as a child. I think I'll like being in the country.' She felt something nudge her foot and looked down at the rug to see the elongated body of a dachsund. 'Oh – a dog!' She bent quickly to pat him and he lifted his long nose and licked her hand. 'Is he yours, Miss Bellamy?'

'He is. He's called Rupert.' The little woman bent and rubbed his back and he rolled over and stuck four short legs in the air. 'And a shameless beggar he is too. No dignity at all. Make yourself decent, Rupert! The idea! And in the

17

vicarage, too. Sorry, Vicar, but boys will be boys, as I'm sure you know.'

The Squire looked impatient and moved towards the desk.

'Let's get this interview started,' he said. 'I'll take your chair, Basil, if you don't mind.' The other three governors took the seats beside him and Stella sat in front of them, her brief moment of confidence deserting her as nervousness returned. 'Now then, Miss Simmons . . .'

At the farm, the Tozers were sitting down to their midday meal. Val, still feeling shaken after her meeting with Luke, was quieter than usual, but there was enough family chatter going on to conceal her silence, at least for a while.

'Well, it's been a warm start to the month,' Ted Tozer remarked, accepting a large plate of sausages and mashed potatoes from his mother Minnie. At eighty-two, she still cooked dinner for them every day, although once that was done her duties were over and she was content to sit by the kitchen fire in winter or potter in the garden in summer. Just now, she was beginning to think about Christmas and had already begun knitting new gloves and mittens for presents and for the church bazaar.

Ted was still talking about the weather and hoping it meant a mild winter. 'Don't speak too soon,' his wife advised him, helping herself to another sausage. 'Plenty of time yet, there be, for the weather to change. Just you remember 1947 – the snow didn't really start till halfway through January but once it started it didn't know how to stop. Us don't want that lot again.'

'No, you'm right, there, Alice.' The blizzard across the south-west of England at the end of January that year had cut off Burracombe for a fortnight. They'd lost any number of sheep up on the moor, and those that didn't freeze starved before the men could get fodder up to them. Work in the fields had been impossible too, with the ground like iron for weeks on end. The snow lying in the fields and on the moors and piled along the hedgerows became solid ice, impossible to shift, and had then melted all at once when the temperatures rose at last, and turned into floods. It was the worst winter yet, after years of severe winters all through the war, and they said that February itself had been the coldest since 1814.

'Still, we got a good summer to make up for it,' Joanna said cheerfully. She was sitting at the end of the table, with Robin in his high-chair opening and shutting his mouth like a goldfish as she spooned in potato and gravy. 'It was a lovely summer, 1947.'

'You only think that because you had the luck to marry me then,' Tom said, grinning at her. 'It could have rained the whole year and you'd still have thought it was lovely.'

'It's us who were the lucky ones,' Alice told him. 'The thought of our Joanna going back to London was as bad as – well, as our Val leaving home. Proper wound herself round our hearts, she had – just like this little one here,' she added, leaning forward to poke her grandson's tummy and make him squeal. 'It were a good day for the Tozers when you came home and had the sense to ask Jo to marry you.'

Joanna smiled, but her smile had a touch of sadness about it. She had lost both her parents in the Blitz in 1941, and when the war ended and she'd been demobbed from the Land Army, she had felt like a lost soul, cast adrift on an open sea. She'd been glad to stay on until Tom came home, and when he finally arrived, everything had changed. With one look, they both knew what their future must be, and Joanna had settled down as a farmer's wife as easily as if she'd been born to it.

'Mrs Warren was in the shop this morning, talking about this big Festival they're having in London next year,' she said, wiping Robin's chin. 'She's going to get up a coach-party to go and see it. D'you think you'll go, Mum?'

'Me, go to London?' Alice said. 'Oh, I don't know about that. I went once when I was a little girl, to see the old King's Coronation, but I didn't really like it. It was so busy! And I dare say it'll be even worse now.'

'I expect it will,' Tom said with a grin. 'They've got cars now, Mum. It was all horses then, wasn't it.'

'Well, there were cars about,' Alice said, 'but not very many. I don't think I could get used to all the traffic these days. I don't even like going to Plymouth or Exeter all that much. Tavistock's good enough for me, and the Goosey Fair's as good as any big festival in London.'

'Yes, but we won't have to worry about traffic,' Joanna said. 'The coach will take us right there and bring us home afterwards. You'll go, won't you, Val?' she asked her sister-in-law. 'You'll go on the coach trip to the Festival?'

'Haven't really thought about it.' Val's thoughts had been far away, further even than London. 'I might. It'll be something to do.'

Alice glanced at her sharply. 'Is something the matter, Val? You've hardly eaten a thing. You're just picking at those sausages.'

'Sorry, Mum. I'm not very hungry.' Val moved her plate away. 'I'll go out and start filling up the racks in the milking parlour, Dad. It'll save time later.' She pushed back her chair and left the table, and they heard her pulling on her boots in the outer kitchen.

Alice looked at her husband in consternation. 'Well, and what's that all about, d'you know, Ted? Our Val enjoys her food so much as a rule. And your mother's made a nice bread-and-butter pudding for afters, too – it's her favourite.'

Ted shrugged. 'You know what these young girls are like, never the same two days running. Look at our Jackie –

all smiles one minute, but you just got to say the wrong word and she's flouncing out and slamming doors till the house shakes. Val'll be all right when she's worked it out of her system, whatever it is.'

'Yes, but Val's not a young girl,' Alice said sharply. 'She's a woman of twenty-eight and she ought to be married with her own home by now. As she would have been, if Eddie hadn't been killed.'

'That was six years ago,' Ted said. 'She should have got over that by now. She met plenty of other young men while she was away nursing, you'd think there'd have been someone to take her fancy.'

'Valerie's like me,' Minnie said, sitting down at last with her own plate. 'A one-man woman. I never wanted to look at another man after your father died, God bless him.'

'Mother!' Ted exclaimed. 'You were sixty-nine when Father died. There weren't likely to be many other men for you to look at.'

Minnie wagged her fork at him reprovingly. 'That's all you know, Ted Tozer. There was Arthur Dawe for a start, him that farmed over to Shaugh. He asked me often enough. And I could have had George Crocker, any time I liked. He threw out enough hints about my cooking.'

Ted spluttered with laughter. 'Arthur Dawe! He's ninety if he's a day. And as for George Crocker – well, he was just looking for a housekeeper with her own bit of money. Mean old toad.'

Minnie sniffed. 'Never mind that, all I'm saying is I had my chances. Those weren't the only two. It's a good job I could run fast, that's all.'

'Good job they could run faster,' Ted muttered, and ducked sideways as she aimed a slap at him. 'Good job for us, I mean,' he added hastily. 'I don't know what we'd have done without you to cook our dinners for us, Mother.'

'You'd have had Alice to cook them instead, and she'm just as good a cook as me.' Minnie cut up one of her sausages. 'Anyway, all that's by the by. What us wants to know is what's eating our Val. You're right, Alice, there's something the matter there. Pale as a ghost she was, when she came in from taking Barley to the forge. Pale as a ghost.'

'I don't know, I'm sure.' Alice passed the cabbage over to Joanna. 'Take some more of this, maid, you've got hardly any . . . I tell you what, I've been worried about that girl for a long time now. Whatever you may say, she's not getting over that business with Eddie as she should. It's not natural for a girl of her age to grieve for ever. It's as if she's got stuck somewhere.' She looked round the table at them all and said, 'It's my belief something else happened to her – when she was out in Egypt during the war, most likely. She never talks about it much, but she must have seen some nasty sights, nursing out there.'

'I don't see what she could have seen that'd turn her off marrying,' Ted objected, swallowing the last of his sausage. 'Anyway, that was before Eddie was killed. What difference could anything that happened out there make?'

'I don't know, but she seemed different when she came back. Why, she was a real ray of sunshine when she was a girl and even after she joined the VADs she was always bright and cheerful. But when she came back from Egypt, she'd changed. That's all I'm saying.' Alice got up and began to collect the vegetable dishes and take them over to the sink.

The rest of the family finished their meal in silence. Minnie served out the bread-and-butter pudding and then Joanna said, 'I think Mum's right. I didn't know Val before the war, but I think she looks really sad sometimes, as if she's thinking about something she can't talk about. I don't know what we can do about it, though.'

22

'You can't do anything,' Tom declared, scraping the crispy bits off the pudding dish. 'Val's a grown woman and she's got to sort out her own problems. I don't know what you're all worrying about anyway – she seems all right to me. Just because she didn't want her dinner . . .'

The women looked at him and then at each other in exasperation, but Ted was nodding in agreement. 'Leave her alone. Everyone feels a bit down in the dumps now and then.' He scraped back his chair. 'Time you and me were outside, Tom. Can't leave the maid to do the work all on her own.'

'That's right,' Alice said. 'This is supposed to be her day off. She works all hours at the hospital, and then has to come home and do your work as well!'

The two men went outside. Minnie settled in her rocking-chair and Alice started the washing-up while Joanna cleaned her son's face and set him on the floor to play with some wooden bricks. She went over to the sink and began to dry the dishes.

'I shouldn't worry too much about Val,' she said quietly. 'Whatever it was that happened to her, she's as happy here as she'll ever be. She's got her family around her and a job she loves at Tavistock Hospital, and she's happy helping out on the farm in her spare time. There are plenty of people a lot worse off than Val.'

Alice paused and stood with her hands in the hot, soapy water, gazing out of the window at the yard where Val was disappearing into the cowshed.

'I know, maid,' she said, 'and most of the time she does seem happy enough. But you know what it is with your own,' she glanced down at the toddler playing at their feet. 'You want everything to be right for them. And it's not right for Val. I know it isn't.'

She sighed and went on with the washing-up, then

added so low that Joanna could barely hear her, 'But Tom's right. Unless us knows what it is, there's nothing any of us can do about it.'

Chapter Three

As far as Stella could tell, the interview had gone quite well. They had asked her a lot of questions and she'd answered them honestly: how she'd been orphaned during the war, then sent to a Children's Home in Hampshire. She looked at the four governors, hoping that she hadn't sounded self-pitying. She thought they probably knew most of her story anyway, from her letter of application and from the references they'd asked for from the Home.

'They were very good to me at the Home,' she said now. 'They let me stay on and work as a pupil teacher, and while I've been at college they've let me go back and live there during the holidays. Otherwise, I'd have had nowhere to go.'

'So you've had quite a lot of experience already, of working with children,' the vicar said with an understanding nod of his silver head.

'Yes,' Stella replied. 'I worked mostly with the infants – that's why I applied for this post.'

'And you'll be happy to come and live in Devon?' Colonel Napier asked, his voice gruff.

As local Squire, he must own a good deal of the land hereabouts, and Stella knew he would have a lot of influence. She could see too that he was a dominating man, used to being obeyed, but she didn't think he was a bully. He would appreciate someone who was ready to speak up for herself.

'Yes, I will,' she answered him. 'I love the countryside – I'd hate to live in a city.' She shivered a little, remembering the narrow streets she had lived in as a child.

'Hmph.' He glanced at the two women, Miss Kemp and Miss Bellamy. Miss Kemp began to ask about Stella's teaching experience and training, and the lines she would take with the children: how did she feel reading and writing should be taught, was she good at teaching crafts and handiwork? Then it was Miss Bellamy's turn and she leaned forward, her little black eyes bright.

'You say you've no other home now. Does that mean you'd like to stay in Burracombe during the holidays as well as termtime? You'd want to be part of the village – join in with the other things that go on here?'

'Yes, I would. I want somewhere to settle down – somewhere I can call home.' Stella thought of the village, its centre clustered about the green with the pub and the church close by, and the school only a little way down the lane. Although its centre was small, Burracombe was quite a large village, with its own shops and Post Office, its bakery, its butcher, and the little hardware store tacked on to the garage. And although she hadn't had time to read them, she'd seen several notices pinned to the board by the village hall. There'd be a Women's Institute, a Mother's Union, whist drives, dances – perhaps even an amateur dramatics group or a church choir. 'I'd really like to join in things,' she said, unaware of how wistful her voice sounded.

The interview had ended soon after that and they'd all gone to the dining room for lunch. Mrs Harvey had made a rabbit pie, with plenty of onions, fresh vegetables and a thick gravy. The mashed potato to go with it was light and fluffy. Afterwards, there was blackberry-and-apple crumble and, to Stella's amazement, clotted cream.

'I've never seen cream like this,' she said, spooning some

of the crusty yellow mound on to her plate. 'In fact, I've hardly ever seen cream at all!'

'Good Devonshire cream, that is,' Miss Bellamy asserted. 'You won't get it anywhere else. Well, they do make it in Cornwall, but then it's Cornish cream – not as good, is it, Gilbert?'

The Colonel, who had spooned a generous helping on to his own bowl of crumble, shrugged. 'Can't see any difference myself.'

Constance Bellamy snorted. 'Try telling that to Ted Tozer or Alice! Our cream's got to be richer, it stands to reason – look at the fields. You don't get that green down in Cornwall.'

'And it all comes from the rain,' the vicar told Stella with a smile. 'Plenty of rain means lush grass, means rich milk, means cream. Have some more, my dear.'

'Yes, you mustn't believe too much talk about sunny Devon,' Mrs Harvey said. 'We do get lots of sunshine, and of course it's generally milder here than in the rest of the country, but we get plenty of rain as well. You'll need a good mackintosh when you come here.'

'*If* Miss Simmons comes here,' her husband corrected her gently, and she looked startled.

'Oh dear! Have I spoken out of turn? I thought it seemed as if you'd decided.'

Colonel Napier and Miss Kemp glanced at each other, and then at the other two governors. Then the Squire cleared his throat and said, 'Well, since we've come to this point, perhaps we'd better say that I think we have.' He addressed Stella. 'We had a talk while you were out of the room, and we'd like you to know that if you're still interested in taking the post of infant teacher in our school, we'll be delighted to have you. We're in complete agreement over this.' He paused, while Stella's heart suddenly thumped. 'Welcome to Burracombe.'

Stella stared at him. She looked round the table at the others. Miss Kemp was looking pleased and encouraging, the vicar's pink round face was glowing and Constance Bellamy was nodding. She felt a sudden surge of joy and, at the same time, a prickling of tears in her eyes.

'Do you really mean it?' she asked, almost afraid to believe what she had just heard. 'Have I really got the job? I thought you'd need longer to think about it. I thought there must be other applicants.'

'There have been two other applicants,' Miss Kemp told her, 'but we've all agreed that you're the one we think most suitable. So if you can make your own decision and let us know . . .'

'Oh, I've already decided,' Stella said instantly. 'I'd love to come to Burracombe. I knew I wanted to, the minute I got off the bus.' She thought fleetingly of Luke Ferris's wicked grin and twinkling blue eyes, of the village with its beautiful surroundings and then of the school itself with its two classrooms and bright, active children. 'It's just what I wanted,' she added sincerely.

'Then that's settled. We'll go into details later, but we'll take it that you'll come to us immediately after Christmas. You'll start the New Year with us. We've already arranged lodgings with Miss Friend – known to the village as Dottie.' Miss Kemp beamed at her and then turned to Mrs Harvey. 'Grace, I'm sure Miss Simmons would like another helping of this delicious crumble to celebrate.'

Stella looked at her plate, sure she wouldn't be able to swallow a morsel. She felt dazed by the news, hardly able to take in the headmistress's words, and so full of joy that there seemed no room for food. Nevertheless, she spooned on more cream and found that she was able to eat it after all. The crumble was light and crisp, the blackberries and apple an ideal combination, and the clotted cream rich and buttery. She thought of her wartime childhood, with only a few sweets a week – and not that many more even now. Five years on and we've still got rationing, she thought. Not that you'd believe it, to look at the meal they'd just eaten.

'I hope I'm not taking your rations,' she said, looking again at the bowl from which they'd all helped themselves so liberally. 'I really didn't expect such a lovely meal.'

'Bless you, you're welcome,' the vicar's wife said, smiling. 'We do have to be careful, of course we do, but things are easier here than in the towns. We've all got space to keep a few hens, you see, and we're allowed to use our own eggs, so long as we don't have too many. And the milk's so rich it would be a crime not to make cream from it. I make my own – just pour the milk into a pan and simmer it very gently for two hours or so, and then let it cool. The cream comes to the top naturally, you see, and we can still use the skim. None of this came from a shop.'

'No, indeed,' Miss Kemp agreed. 'The apples are from the vicarage orchard, and I picked the blackberries myself on a nature walk with the children. They all took a basketful home. There are mushrooms in the fields too, but you have to be out early in the morning to pick them.'

'Why?' Stella asked. 'Don't they last long enough in the day?'

The vicar laughed. 'Well, if it's a hot day they might shrivel up a bit, but mostly it's just because people *do*, pick mushrooms early in the morning, so if you're not out there too, they'll all be gone! It's like a kind of silent race.'

'You'll soon learn country ways,' his wife said. 'You can't live long in a place like Burracombe without hearing all the old country lore.'

'Not that you have to believe it,' the Colonel remarked. 'Lot of mumbo jumbo . . .' He began to rise to his feet. 'Basil, I must be going. Plenty to do. Grace, the lunch was delicious. Miss Kemp – better get back to your class.' He gave Stella a nod. 'Welcome again, Miss Simmons. I hope you'll be happy in Burracombe. I'm sure we've made the right decision.'

'Yes, I must go too,' Miss Kemp declared. 'As the Colonel says, the children will be waiting. I left Mrs James reading to them all but I mustn't presume on her good nature any longer.' She turned to Stella. 'I'll be writing to you, Miss Simmons, and of course you'll be hearing officially about your appointment. I look forward very much to meeting you again in the New Year.'

She and the Squire departed together and Stella was left with her host and hostess and Constance Bellamy. She hesitated, not sure what to do next, and the vicar came to her rescue.

'What time is your train back to Hampshire? You must be sure not to miss the Tavistock bus – it goes at three-fifteen.' He smiled. 'You'll meet a lot of your new charges again – those who live too far away to walk use that bus to go home.'

'You'll be very late home tonight, I'm afraid,' his wife said, looking worried. 'Really, we should have asked you to stay the night. Shouldn't we, Basil?'

'Oh, there's no need,' Stella said quickly before they could offer her an invitation. 'I'll be back by ten. And I promised I'd be there in the morning, to get the little ones up.'

The vicar looked at the tall grandfather clock in the hall. 'Well, it's two o'clock now. What would you like to do? I could take you over to the church again – they'll have finished the harvest decorations by now. Or—'

'Well, if you don't mind,' Stella said, 'it's such a lovely afternoon, I'd quite like to walk round the village by myself. Just to get the feel of it, you know, and have something to think about before I come back again. I'll go into the church as well,' she promised hastily in case he was offended. 'I'd like to see the decorations.'

'Of course,' Mrs Harvey said, and added hospitably, 'You must come back here and have a cup of tea before catching the bus. We'll expect you in about half an hour.'

Stella put on her jacket and gloves and walked out into the afternoon sunshine, turning away from the village street with its small shops interspersed between the cottages, and walking along a lane that led into the countryside. I really am seeing Burracombe at its best, she thought, gazing at the green and gold tapestry of the hedgerows. A narrow stream glittered beside the road, and blackberries hung full and glossy over her head. The high, grassy Devon bank would be sprinkled with primroses in the spring, she thought, and perhaps violets too, and later there would be foxgloves and dog-roses and honeysuckle. But now the year was winding down, the trees and hedges getting ready to close down for the winter. The grass was fading to a pale, dusty fawn and the leaves on the hedges were turning brown, lit by the tiny red lanterns of hips and haws, and the more sinister purple of honeysuckle and deadly nightshade.

Stella loved the autumn. The rich golds and scarlets of the trees were like a huge damask quilt flung over the countryside, and the swelling moorland above the valley glowed auburn against the tender blue of the sky. A smell of fresh air and damp earth and woodsmoke tingled in her nostrils, and somewhere nearby she could hear a bird singing – a pretty, liquid song like the sparkling drops of the stream translated into music. Stella stopped for a moment and looked about, and then caught sight of the orange breast and bright black eyes of a robin, its brown body camouflaged by the tawny leaves.

By the time she came back after Christmas, the year would have turned and the leaves gone, leaving a tracery of grey, brown and black twigs. The birds would have eaten the red rosehips and the fruits of the hawthorn hedge, and even the bryony and deadly nightshade berries would have shrivelled and cast their seeds. The blackberries would be long gone and the flowers of spring still huddled beneath the cold earth.

Stella didn't mind winter. She liked the cold bite of a bright January morning and the full-bellied bruises of clouds that promised snow. She loved the occasional mild day when it seemed as if spring had arrived early, and enjoyed a walk in a clean, scouring wind as long as she was well wrapped up against it. She wasn't so keen on rain and hoped that the vicar had been exaggerating when he said what a wet county Devon was, but everywhere had rain and you just had to put up with it. And the little streams and rivers that abounded in this area would look all the better after a downpour.

She came to a small wooden gate which led into a wood and hesitated for a moment; then, as there was no *Private* sign forbidding her to enter, she opened the gate and walked along a narrow footpath between the trees. They were spaced quite wide apart, tall, thin oaks and beeches, and their brown leaves, mast and acorns crunched beneath her feet. Rocks and boulders lay scattered between them and everything was covered in thick green moss. It even grew up the trunks of the trees, well above her head. The tinted leaves rustled in the soft breeze and as she looked up, she could see that a few were already falling. Somewhere amongst the branches a bird screeched, and she heard the scuttering sound of small feet.

The path led her up a short, steep hill. The sun slanted down into her eyes and she climbed almost blindly, emerging at the top to find herself on the edge of the moor. A tumbled wall bordered the wood and she clambered through a gap and stood on brown, dead bracken, catching her breath.

'So we meet again.'

Stella gasped and turned quickly. The man who had first spoken to her when she got off the bus was sitting on a large rock, a sketchpad on his knee and a pencil in his hand. His mouth quirked in a grin and she laughed with relief.

'You startled me.'

'Sorry. I seem to be making a habit of it. I'll try not to do it again.' His dark brows gathered together in a small frown. 'What are you doing up here? I thought you were being interviewed.'

'I was. We've finished now and I'm just having a walk before I catch the bus.' She hesitated, then said rather shyly, 'I've got the job.'

'You have?' His grin widened. 'That's really good. I'm very pleased. When do you start?'

'After Christmas. I had promised to stay on at the Home, where I'm teaching now, until then.' She stumbled with her words, feeling suddenly unwilling to admit that she lived in an orphanage. 'I'll probably come and settle in some time in the New Year.'

'Come earlier, if you can, and I'll show you around a bit. Not that I know much myself, but I'll know more by then.' He laughed and Stella smiled. 'Do you know where you'll be living?'

'Miss Kemp says they've found somewhere for me to lodge. A friend, I think she said – or maybe a Miss Friend – but I'm not sure. Is that a surname?'

Luke laughed again. 'It certainly is! Half the village is called Friend, and the other half are either Pettifer or Tozer. And they're all related, one way or another. You have to be *very* careful what you say. The Burracombe village grapevine is extremely efficient.'

'I will be,' she promised, and then glanced at her watch. 'I'd better go. I said I'd go back to the vicarage for a cup of tea.'

'That's a pity,' he said, unfolding his long legs and standing up. 'I was going to suggest you come and have one with me in my cottage. Never mind, there'll be plenty of time once you're here. Anyway, I'll walk back with you.'

'I don't want to interrupt your work—' she began, but he waved a hand.

'The light's going anyway. I was just about to pack up.' He closed his sketchbook and led the way along the wall and through another gap where a broader footpath took them down through the wood, passing a tiny cottage on the way. 'This is my abode,' he said. 'It used to belong to a family of charcoal-burners, so I've been told – they lived here until the end of the war. Then the old man died and his son didn't come home from the war, and the old lady went to live with her daughter in Horrabridge. It had been empty for a couple of years when I moved in.'

'It looks very cosy,' Stella said, wondering what it must be like to live in such an isolated cottage in the middle of a wood.

'It is, when I've got the fire going, and there's certainly plenty of firewood around.' He gestured at the fallen branches and trees lying on the moss-covered earth and rocks. 'I can live quite cheaply.'

'It must be lonely, though.'

Luke gave her a swift glance. 'Not at all. There are plenty of birds and animals about – rabbits, foxes, badgers, they all come past my door, and if I sit quietly on that log there for a while, the birds forget I'm about. Listen to that.' Stella tilted her head slightly and heard a drumming sound somewhere in the trees. 'That's a woodpecker. You'll see him if you look hard enough – leaning out from the trunk and drilling at it with his beak. And look, there's a squirrel.' He put his hand on her shoulder and turned her. She caught a flash of red disappearing behind a tree-trunk and then spotted the animal itself, scurrying along a branch. It

34

ran right to the end and then took off, almost flying across the wide gap to land in another tree and disappear amongst the leaves. Stella caught her breath with delight.

'Oh, that's lovely! They're really red, aren't they.'

'They are, but we've got greys moving in and I've heard that when they take over an area, the reds disappear. It's a shame because the red squirrels are the ones who really live here – the greys came over from America. Look, there he is again. He's collecting chestnuts from that tree and burying them for the winter.'

'They hibernate, don't they?' Stella asked, but Luke shook his head.

'No, they just spend a lot of time asleep in their dreys while the weather's bad. Then they come out and find as many nuts as they can and gorge themselves, ready for the next bad spell. You can see them when there's snow on the ground and the sun's out, scampering about looking for their hiding places. Half of them are lost, of course, and that's one of the reasons we get new trees – the squirrels have planted them!'

Stella laughed and then jumped as she heard the same screech as she had heard before. 'What's that?'

'A jay.' Luke pointed and she saw a brightly coloured bird almost as big as a rook flash between the trees. 'There are loads of them round here. They like woodland.'

'You seem to know a lot about birds and animals,' she said, watching the squirrel as he sat on a branch, a nut held between his tiny paws, chattering crossly at the noisy jay.

'I spent a long time in the country,' he said briefly. 'I had plenty of opportunity to learn. Right, how about that cup of tea now you're here?'

'Oh no, I mustn't. Mrs Harvey's expecting me. It would be rude not to go back.' She looked up at him and smiled. 'It's been really nice to meet you, Mr Ferris.'

35

'Luke, for heaven's sake. And your name? I can't call you Miss Simmons, as if I were a mixed infant.'

'Stella,' she said, and put out her hand as if they had only just been introduced.

He took it and held it in his, and once again she felt the warmth of his long fingers. 'Stella,' he repeated softly. 'A star. A nice name – it suits you.'

Stella felt her cheeks colour. She drew her hand away and gave a little laugh. 'I really must go. I've got a long journey – I mustn't miss my train.'

'No, of course. Look, if you take this path down to the road you can cross the field and come out just opposite the vicarage gate.' He walked with her, his long strides covering the ground swiftly so that Stella, who wasn't particularly short, had to move quickly to keep up. The wood opened on to a meadow grazed by a flock of white sheep with black faces, who glanced up as they came into view and then went back to their munching. In a few moments, Luke and Stella were at the road and she waved him goodbye and crossed to the vicarage.

Luke leaned on the gate and watched her go. The sun was lower in the sky now, dipping towards a band of purple cloud coming in from the west. It would almost certainly rain before morning. He had lost the light on Cuckoo Wood and before he got another chance like this, all the leaves might have been blown off the trees. But there would be something else to paint, some scene or trick of light he had never seen before, something new to try to capture on his canvas.

He glanced along the lane leading to the Tozers' farm, where he had met Val that morning. He sighed, straightened his shoulders and turned back towards the woods.

That was an artist's life. Leaving one lost chance behind and moving on to the next.

Chapter Four

Gilbert Napier got into his car to drive back to the Barton. It was a new car, bought when petrol came off ration, and he'd celebrated by treating himself to this smart-looking Armstrong Siddeley, selling the old Hillman Minx and handing on Isobel's boxy little Austin to Hilary. It looked pretty old-fashioned now, he had to admit, and she'd been murmuring about getting something more up-to-date – one of those little Morris Minors, perhaps, or an estate car. But there was Stephen to think of too; recently home from Cambridge, he ought to be provided with a decent motor-car.

Napier frowned a little. It was only natural for a young man of his age to want something sporty, but if anyone had an estate car it ought to be him, since he'd be working with his father learning to run the Burracombe estate, ready to take over when the day came. Not that that would be for a long time yet. At fifty-five, Gilbert Napier still had a good many years left in him – years in which Stephen could be trained to become as good a Squire as his brother Baden would have been.

The familiar pain washed over him. Nobody could be as good a Squire as Baden would have been. The boy was cut out for the job right from the start. You could see it in his bright eyes, his interest, his courage and determination. Napier could remember the way he'd stumped round the stables, only two or three years of age, clamouring to be lifted into the saddle. And the pretty little skewbald Napier had bought for the children to learn on wouldn't do – no, it had been Napier's own black mare, fiery Trespass, that the boy wanted to ride. He'd been persuaded in the end to accept a pony of the same colour, but the minute he could handle him he'd wanted to go on to something more lively, and so it had been throughout his childhood. Fearless, venturesome, intelligent and popular, he had been all Napier had ever wanted in an eldest son and heir. In his hands, the Burracombe estate would have been safe.

And it had been just those qualities that had killed him.

The sleek car never even reached fourth gear on the short journey from the vicarage and along the drive to the Barton. It was a car for the open road, like that TR3 that Stephen kept talking about. Well, maybe he should let the boy have his way after all. You were only young once, and the war had messed around with his life as well. He'd been only eleven when it had started, and it had curtailed any chances he might have had of going abroad, as Baden and Hilary had done, and he hadn't even been able to live in his own home during the holidays. The estate house where they'd had to stay while the Barton was being used for a school wasn't bad, but it had been pretty cramped when they were all at home. He wouldn't be surprised if the difficulties of living there had played quite a large part in Isobel's death.

Another pang struck at his heart and he gave an impatient shrug and brought the car to a halt outside the front steps. Crocker, the gardener and stableman, could put it away. Napier never allowed the man to take the car out on to the road, but he liked to give him the small pleasure of driving it in the grounds.

Hilary was making pastry in the kitchen. She looked round as he came through the door. 'Hello, Dad. How did it go? Will she do?'

'I think so.' He sat down at the table. He would never have sat in the kitchen in the old days, barely knew where it was, but then Isobel wouldn't have been in here making pastry then either. The war had changed a lot of things and he still hadn't got used to half of them. All the same, he had to admit that it was pleasant here with the Aga giving out a gentle warmth and Hilary standing there with her sleeves rolled up and her hands covered in flour. 'She seems a pleasant enough woman, and has had plenty of experience with children. We've given her the job, anyway. See how she goes on.'

'That's good. I met her in the church. She seems rather young.'

'Twenty-one. I just hope she doesn't up and get married when she's only been here five minutes. That's the trouble with young women.' He caught his daughter's eye and reached out hastily for the newspaper. You couldn't say anything in this house without putting your foot in it, but it was time Hilary found herself a husband. Twenty-eight and still not married! That was another effect of the war.

'Want a cup of tea, Dad?' she asked after a pause. 'The kettle's simmering. I'll just finish this first.'

He glanced at the pastry she was rolling out. 'What are you making?'

'Blackberry and apple pie. Your favourite.'

'Had pie at the vicarage,' he said before he could stop himself. Hilary stopped abruptly, the rolling pin poised above the flattened dough. 'Doesn't matter,' he added, knowing what she was thinking. 'Don't mind having it twice. As you said, it's my favourite.'

'Yes, but you need variety. It's not good for you to have pastry two meals running.' She looked at the bowl of blackberries and apples, sliced and ready to go into the dish. 'I'll just stew them and use the pastry tomorrow for a meat pie.'

'I'll still have pastry two *days* running,' he began, but she was already rolling it up and slapping it between two plates. She took it into the big larder without answering, and he sighed. I never used to have this problem with Isobel, he thought. I never knew what was for dinner until it was put in front of me, and it was always good. Of course, we had Mary to cook for us then and I wouldn't have been sitting at the kitchen table like a farmer, I'd have been in the drawing room or in my study, where a gentleman ought to be.

Hilary came back and tipped the fruit into a saucepan, ready to stew. They didn't have a permanent cook any more, but Dottie Friend came in and helped when they had guests or a dinner-party. Dottie was a village treasure – she cooked for the doctor's family occasionally, she worked at the pub and she helped out in the school if Mrs Dawe, who cooked the school meals, was ill. And since she sometimes took in paying guests, Basil Harvey had asked her if she would let her spare bedroom to the new teacher.

'Did you say you met Miss Simmons in the church?' he asked as Hilary came back into the kitchen and moved the kettle on to the hotplate of the Aga. 'What did you think of her?'

'I only spoke to her for a few minutes. She seemed just as you said – a pleasant person. We shan't know what sort of teacher she is until she starts at the school. Are her references all right? Or is this her first job?'

'It is, but she's worked as a pupil teacher in the Children's Home where she grew up. Got more experience than most in handling young children, I should think. They sent a good reference anyway.'

'A Children's Home?' Hilary turned from the Aga where the kettle had boiled almost at once. She swilled hot water in the teapot and tipped it into the sink, then put in two teaspoonsful of tea. 'You mean she's an orphan?'

'That's right. Parents killed in the war. Sad story, but only one of many. At least she's been looked after, given an education. And now she can earn her own living at a decent career, which is more than plenty of other young women can do.'

'Yes, it is.' Hilary heard the tinge of bitterness in her voice and glanced at her father, but his big, leonine head was bent over the newspaper and it seemed to have passed him by. She went back to the larder for the milk and poured a little into two cups, then stood gazing out of the window as she waited for the tea to brew.

I probably had a much better education than Stella Simmons, she thought, remembering her years at boarding school learning Latin, French and mathematics as well as English, history and geography. Yet there had never been any question of a career for her. When she left school, she would go to a 'finishing school', probably in Switzerland, be presented at Court and embark on a social whirl of parties and dances, then marry a wealthy and well-born young man and spend her life just as her mother had, having a family, running a home and, above all, being a good wife to her husband.

The war had changed all that. Aged seventeen when Mr Chamberlain had made the dreaded speech that announced that Britain was now at war with Germany, she had felt a great leap of excitement. Now women would come into their own, just as they had done during and after the Great War of 1914–18. Then, they had ridden motorbikes, driven buses, run farms and generally proved that they could do many of the jobs that men had always considered their own province. Hilary had seen her chance of escaping the chains that bound her, and leading her own life – a life of challenge and responsibility. She had applied to join the ATS, the women's branch of the Army, as soon as she left school. 'I won't accept any favours, though,' she'd warned her father. 'Whatever I do, I want to do on my own merit.'

To her delight, and because she could already drive her mother's little Austin and her father's Hillman Minx, she was given a job as a driver and found herself chauffering Generals, Brigadiers and – once – her father himself. By the time the war ended, she had the satisfaction of a job where she had authority and the respect of others, a job that was vital to her country.

But when she returned home to Burracombe Barton to consider what to do next, she had found herself chained all over again, first by her mother's long illness and then by her death. Hilary had taken over the running of the house and it seemed now as if it would be impossible for her ever to leave, unless it were by marriage. And that, she thought, was unlikely. Her years of independence had made her reluctant to hand her life over to any of the young men she was likely to meet in her circle.

'What's happened to that tea?' her father asked, jerking her out of her thoughts, and she turned quickly.

'Sorry. I was miles away.'

'I could see that.' He watched her pour the tea. 'Any word from Stephen, by the way?'

Hilary brought the cups over to the table and sat down. 'No. I imagine he's still in Italy. He was talking of going to Switzerland for some skiing when the snow starts, but that won't be for a few weeks yet. I dare say we'll get another postcard soon, when he remembers us again.'

'When he runs out of money, you mean.' Napier drew his brows together. 'Time that boy stopped gallivanting and came home to learn his job.'

'Well, it is supposed to be a cultural tour,' Hilary reminded him. 'And I think he feels he needs some time off after coming down from Cambridge.'

'Maybe he does. Doesn't mean he can gad about the

world like some rich playboy. There's work to be done at home – an estate to run – and as far as I can see, he hasn't the first idea how to go about it.'

Hilary bit her lip. 'I'm not sure whether Stephen will want to take over the estate,' she began, and the big head came up with a jerk.

'Not want to? Why the devil not? He ought to thank his lucky stars he's got such an opportunity. Fine estate, handed to him on a plate – all he has to do is learn to manage it. And it'll be a few years yet before he has to take on full responsibility. Of course he'll want to. Be a fool not to.'

'But do you think he's really suited to it?' Hilary said, feeling her way. There was no point in annoying her father unnecessarily, but she and her brother had had a long talk before he went off for his trip on the Continent, and she'd promised to pave the way for him if she could. 'I mean, he never expected to inherit, and—'

'You don't have to remind me of that,' Napier said harshly. He drained his cup and stood up. 'If it hadn't been for the damned war, I'd have had Baden here now, running the place with me. But since I haven't, it's up to young Stephen, and if you ask me, he's had more than enough time to come to terms with it. I dare say he *would* rather spend his time jaunting about Europe, but he's over twenty-one now and it's time to settle down to a job of work. And I don't know what other sort of work he might think he's capable of doing!'

'That's a bit unkind, isn't it?' Hilary said. 'He's capable of lots of things. He worked hard at Cambridge, after all, and got a good degree.'

'A good degree!' Napier snorted. 'In mathematics! What use is that going to be to him? Don't know why he wanted to bother about a degree anyway. The purpose of going to Cambridge was to get to know the right people, same as at

Harrow. Didn't want him to fail, naturally, but he wasn't supposed to spend all his time with his head in a book.'

Hilary suppressed a smile. She had been to visit Stephen a few times at Cambridge and knew that he hadn't by any means spent all his time with his 'head in a book'. He had played hard as well as worked hard, and was probably playing equally hard now, on his supposed 'cultural tour' of Europe. Well, she had done her best and would continue to support her brother in his desire to lead his own life, but it was going to be an uphill struggle.

Her father stamped out of the kitchen and she went back to her preparations for dinner that night. Dr Latimer and his wife were coming and she needed to get the meat into the oven to roast. They were having leg of lamb – the first of the year – with roast potatoes and vegetables from their own kitchen-garden. It was a pity about the fruit pie, but there was a piece of Stilton cheese that she'd managed to get from Creber's, in Tavistock, to go with the port. Like most dairy foods, cheese was still on ration but you could occasionally get a treat.

As she worked, she thought again of Stephen and his plans. He was going to have to come home and confront their father at some point. She wished that she could do the same.

I'm going to be here for the rest of my life, she thought, standing at the sink with a potato half-peeled in her hand. I'm never going to get away.

Val Tozer finished her jobs in the yard and decided to walk over to the Barton to see if Hilary had time for a cup of tea. Strictly speaking, she didn't have to work on the farm as she was a Sister at the Cottage Hospital in Tavistock, but she liked to occupy herself on her day off and enjoyed being with the animals. This afternoon, though, she needed to be away from the family.

44

Val and Hilary had known each other since childhood but had only been friends ever since they'd met, unexpectedly, in Egypt during the war. Val was an Army nurse at a military hospital and Hilary had been sent out with the regiment to which she was attached, as driver to the Brigadier. They'd encountered each other at a dance and stared in astonishment as they recognised each other. A meeting to catch up on village news and gossip had followed next day, and they'd discovered a rapport which had lasted ever since. Now they met at least once a week.

There were several ways to reach the Barton from the Tozers' farm. You could either go the short way, straight up the lane to where it joined the estate drive, or you could walk through the village past the shops and vicarage. Val chose to take a meandering way across the fields and through the trees to the top of Cuckoo Wood. From there, she could walk along the edge of the moor to drop down behind Barton House and walk through the grounds.

As she opened the gate into the meadow, she noticed a bent figure half in and half out of the ditch that ran beneath the hedge. It straightened as she came through and she saw Jacob Prout's weatherbeaten face. He was wearing the battered wax jacket that he was rarely seen without, his wispy hair stuck out at all angles round his head and she had the thought that he would only have had to stand in the middle of the field with his arms outstretched to be mistaken for a scarecrow. Scruff, his Jack Russell, emerged from a rabbit-hole and ran over to her, rubbing his muddy snout against her legs.

'Hello, Jacob. How are you?'

He squinted up at her against the afternoon sun, his eyes almost disappearing in a mass of wrinkles. Out in all weathers as he worked around the village, sweeping the lanes, clearing ditches, trimming and layering hedges, looking after the churchyard and digging graves, and doing any other odd jobs that might be asked of him, his face was the deep reddish-brown of cured leather. He lived alone in a tiny cottage at the end of the village street, keeping it as immaculate as he kept the village itself and maintaining a constant feud with his next-door neighbour Jed Fisher. Nobody knew quite how old he was, since nobody could remember exactly when he was born.

'Afternoon, Val. How be you?'

'I'm all right, thanks.' She leaned on the gate and watched as he swished at the brambles with his sickle. Scruff went back to the rabbit-hole and began to dig furiously. 'I expect you've been busy getting ready for the Harvest Festival. Are those your marrows I saw by the altar rail?'

Jacob snorted. 'One of 'em is. T'other's that Mrs Warren's. Took up vegetable gardening now, she has. Thinks because she've growed a marrow she'm an expert. I told her, "Wait till you can show me a basket of good red tomatoes with a proper flavour, then I'll take a bit o' notice".'

Val smiled. 'She's talking about starting up a Gardening Club.'

'Gardening Club!' he said contemptuously. 'What do us want a club for? Take up val'ble gardening time, that's all that'll do. I got too much to do in me own garden to be messing about with clubs.' He gave her a narrow look. 'Did I see you talking to that young artist feller down the lane this morning? Ferret, or something?'

'Ferris,' Val said, thinking that she might have known someone would have seen them. You couldn't sneeze in Burracombe without someone sending round beef tea. 'Yes, we did have a few words. He's renting the charcoal-burner's cottage, isn't he?'

'That's right.' Jacob wiped the back of his hand across

46

the end of his nose. 'Seems a decent enough young chap. Been in the Bell a time or two.'

Val was pretty sure that Jacob was hinting at something. It had probably been obvious that she and Luke weren't exchanging a few commonplace pleasantries; he might even have overheard them talking. 'Where were you, then? I didn't see you.'

'Oh, I were just over in the field,' he said vaguely and her suspicion grew stronger. He turned back to the ditch. 'Anyway, better get back to me work. If it comes on to rain before this lot's cleared we'll have a flood over the road, and I got me own garden to see to as well.'

Val walked on across the field, still thinking about Luke Ferris. She'd seen him speak to the young schoolteacher by the green and watched as she and the vicar went into the church. Luke might have turned towards the forge then, but instead he had wandered off along the lane and she'd hoped that he'd gone to do some sketching or painting. It had been a shock to hear his voice behind her, as she led Barley back along the farm track, and it had taken her a moment or two to gather her composure before she could turn and face him.

She climbed the footpath leading through Cuckoo Wood. The charcoal-burner's cottage where Luke was living was on the other side, but she was uncomfortably aware that she might run into him at any moment. At the top of the hill, she paused for breath and then looked around.

Luke was sitting on a rock at the edge of the wood. He was holding his sketchbook and talking to someone, and as she watched, Val realised that it was the young school-teacher, Stella Simmons.

She turned abruptly and plunged down the hill towards the Barton.

Chapter Five

Stella arrived in Burracombe a few days after Christmas. She had spent the holiday period with a friend she had made at college, after saying goodbye to the Children's Home and the local primary school where she'd worked as a pupil-teacher at the end of the term. Now, at last, she felt that she was beginning her own life.

The vicar had come to Tavistock in his rattling pre-war Ford Popular and packed her few possessions into the boot. It was early-closing day and the little town looked grey and quiet as he drove down the steep hill into the big square. Stella hadn't had time to look around on her visit in October, and she gazed about her with interest.

'It looks nice. Do they have markets in the square?'

'No, there's a pannier market – that's an enclosed market, in a big building – behind the Town Hall. That's the Town Hall there, opposite the church. This river we're crossing now is the Tavy. It starts up on the moor and joins the Tamar estuary above Plymouth. It's supposed to be the second fastest-filling river in the country, but don't ask me which the fastest is!'

They drove on through Whitchurch and then across open moorland. The sky was clear, with the cold paleness of winter, and the sun was sinking behind them, throwing a soft light across the coppery dead bracken. Sheep were grazing beside the road and the vicar had to slow down twice for ponies which lifted their heads and ambled across just in front of him.

'Wild ponies!' Stella exclaimed. 'They have those in the New Forest too. I was evacuated there for a while, when I was little.'

'Well, they're not quite wild – they belong to the farmers. But they roam like wild animals, except when they're gathered up in the autumn.' He slowed down for another one. 'Won't be long now, and you'll be in the warm. Dottie Friend will look after you – she's looking forward to having you as her lodger. You'll like her – a real Burracombe character. Of course, she's out a lot – works at the inn, and cooks for the Squire too – so you'll be a bit like ships that pass in the night. But she's a good soul. She'll make you very comfortable.'

He had been quite right. The sky was dark by the time the car nosed its way down the village street, but little squares of golden light spilled from all the cottage windows and there was a blaze of fire from the open door of the blacksmith's forge. The vicar drew up outside a cottage standing back from the lane, behind a picket fence and a tangle of wintry bushes, and as he did so the door flew open and a woman hurried out.

'Be that you, Vicar?' she called, peering out into the darkness, and then came down the path to the gate. 'Come you in, my dear. You must be wanting a cup of tea after all that journey.' She reached out and caught Stella's hands, rubbing them between her own. 'Why, you'm frozen stiff. Come and sit yourself down by the fire, do.'

'I've got some cases,' Stella began, but Dottie Friend was already urging her towards the door and she found herself pushed into a warm, square room with two chairs set on either side of a blazing fire. The stone-flagged floor was brightened by a mixture of coloured rag rugs and faded carpet runners, and there was a table to one side covered by

49

a green baize cloth, with a ruby lustre glass bowl of oranges and small apples with wrinkled red skins in the centre. Festooned from the low wooden beams across the ceiling were strips of home-made paper-chains of scarlet, green and yellow paper, and a small Christmas tree stood in one corner.

'Come over to the fire,' Dottie urged hospitably. She was shorter than Stella, with a plump, rounded figure and a mass of yellow curls. Her eyes were brown and warm. 'Vicar and me'll bring in your bags. Kettle's on and there'll be a cup of tea ready in just a minute or two. I'll make a bit of toast as well. Nothing like a bit of toast when you'm cold and hungry. There's a nice casserole in the oven, for supper.'

Stella found herself pressed down into one of the armchairs while the vicar and Dottie brought in her shabby suitcase and shopping-bag. Basil Harvey carried the case straight upstairs and Dottie looked enquiringly at the shopping-bag.

'Oh, it's just a few things I couldn't get into the case,' Stella said hastily. 'And for the journey. Don't bother to take it up now.'

'Might as well get it out of the way,' Dottie said, and her round little bottom and stumpy legs disappeared up the narrow stairs.

The cottage was quite roomy, with three rooms downstairs – one the parlour, kept for 'best'; one the big, cosy living room and kitchen, and one the scullery with a lavatory tacked on to the back – and three bedrooms above. Stella's room had a colourful rag rug on the polished floorboards, a faded patchwork quilt on the iron-framed bed, and curtains patterned with spring flowers at the window. She had a bookcase, a dressing-table, a washstand, a cupboard let into the wall where she could hang her clothes, and a small table to serve as a desk. The room would have been cold, had it not been above the kitchen with the range that was kept stoked all night but, as it was, it was cosy enough for Stella to sit in, in the evenings, and prepare her lessons for the next day. Dottie made it clear, however, that she was to use the house as her home, and come downstairs whenever she pleased.

'You don't have to spend all your time in your room, my flower – I like a bit of company. In any case, I'm out most evenings, working at the pub, so it'd be a waste if nobody was here to enjoy the fire.' She beamed at Stella. 'I dare say you'll have schoolwork to do, so you can do it down here. Not that you look old enough to be out of school yourself, hardly!'

'I'm twenty-one,' Stella said. 'This is my first real post. I was a pupil-teacher at the Home and in the local infants' school, and during my training we went out to schools and did practice teaching. I haven't ever had a class all of my own, though.'

Dottie looked at her thoughtfully. 'They'm not so bad, Burracombe tackers, the little ones, anyway. Some of they bigger boys are little monkeys. And there's no more than a dozen in the Infants – just three or four babies, and three coming up to seven, and the rest are in between. You'll manage them well enough.'

'I think you'll be very comfortable,' the vicar said to Stella as Dottie bustled about making tea from a huge kettle which was whistling gently on the range. 'Now, if you'll forgive me, I'll be off – I've got a Parochial Church Council meeting this evening. We're starting to think about the Festival,' he said to Dottie. 'Mrs Warren's very keen for everyone in the village to become involved. I think she wants us to do something in the church.'

'I dare say I'll hear all about it in the pub,' Dottie said dryly as he departed. 'There's more decided there than in any of these blessed meetings. But there, they like to go

51

through the motions, makes them feel important. Now, my dear,' she poured a cup of tea and handed it to Stella, 'you get that inside you and you'll soon feel better. You've come all the way from up-country, the vicar tells me.'

'Hampshire,' Stella said, raising the cup gratefully to her lips. It was too hot to take more than the tiniest sip but the warmth in her hands and the heat of the fire were already spreading through her body. 'It did take a long time. I started off quite early this morning. There were changes, you see, but the waiting rooms all had nice fires so it wasn't too bad.'

'Well, you'm here now.' Dottie sat down opposite. Her rosy face shone with goodwill, and as Stella looked at her she felt another kind of warmth spread through her body and her heart. She's really pleased to have me here, she thought in wonder. As if I weren't just a lodger but someone she already knows and likes.

She felt the prickle of sudden tears in her eyes, remembering the time when she'd been part of a family, with a mother, a father, a sister and a brother. Only when they were taken from her had she realised what she had lost; she felt as if half of herself had been wrenched away, leaving a gaping wound that had never properly healed; there always remained that aching loneliness.

Here, in Dottie Friend's cottage at Burracombe, where she had only been for a few minutes, her memory stirred with a glimmer of the warmth she had known as a child, and to her dismay, one of the tears that had pricked her eyes welled up and rolled down her cold cheek in a sizzling bead.

'There, you'm worn out!' Dottie exclaimed. 'Now, don't you worry about me, my pretty, I'll just get on with a few jobs while you drink your tea, and then we'll have supper all cosy together. And afterwards I thought you might like a bath.' She indicated the scullery door with her head. 'We'll bring it in and fill it up with nice hot water, and you can have it in front of the fire, which is the only way to have a bath, if you want my opinion. None of those nasty cold bathrooms like they got up at the Barton! And you needn't worry – I've got to go up to the pub about eight o'clock, so you can be nice and private and we'll empty it out in the morning.'

Stella had not had a bath in front of the fire since she was a small child. At the Children's Home they had had a large bathroom with two enormous baths in it, filled by a long tap from a large geyser. The children had had to queue up to have their turn at being dipped into the hot water, softened by gritty lumps of washing soda, and scrubbed with slabs of green carbolic soap. Girls were bathed on Fridays and boys on Saturdays so that they would be clean for church on Sunday.

Later that night, after a supper of rabbit casserole with floury jacket potatoes and mashed swede and carrots, Dottie had dragged in the long tin bath and set about filling it with buckets of hot water. It had taken some time to do this and Stella protested at the amount of water being used but Dottie shrugged her objections aside. 'Plenty of fuel hereabouts,' she said, nodding at the stack of logs in the big inglenook fireplace. 'And 'tis your first night. Us wants you to feel welcome here in Burracombe, Miss Simmons.'

Stella smiled at her, feeling the prick of tears again. 'I do. It's very kind of you, Miss Friend.' She hesitated, feeling sure that this comfortable little woman must have been married. 'Is that right? Should it be Mrs?'

'No, it's Miss, but if we're going to shake down here together we'd better get this straight from the beginning.' The little woman looked quite fierce as she shook a piece of wood at Stella. 'Dottie's my name, and everyone calls me by it, and you'd better do the same, maid. Otherwise us'll never be easy together, now.'

'All right,' Stella said, wishing that she wouldn't keep feeling like crying. It's because I'm so tired, she told herself, because I'm tired and cold and because she's so kind. It's a long time since anyone was as kind to me as this. 'And you must call me Stella. Please,' she added, seeing the objections already rising to the rosy lips. 'There – there aren't many people to call me by my name now, you see. I'd really like it if you would.'

Dottie gazed at her for a moment and there was an odd expression in her eyes. Then she nodded and stepped forward, putting one hand on Stella's shoulder and reaching up to give her a quick kiss.

'That's settled then,' she said rather gruffly, and turned away, reaching out for the coat that hung on the back door. 'Now I'd better be going. Don't you wait up for me, mind. The pub closes at ten but there's always the clearing-up and all to do, ready for tomorrow, so I won't be back much before eleven. You have your bath and make yourself a cup of cocoa if you want one – and there's a hot-water bottle in your bed already, so 'twill be warm for you to get into. I'll see you in the morning.'

'What time would you like me to get up?' Stella asked, and Dottie shook her head.

'Bless you, maid, you get up just whenever you want. 'Tis holidays, isn't it? Plenty of time for you to think about getting up early when school starts again.' She pulled on a shapeless grey coat and tied a belt round her middle. 'Now, you just help yourself to anything you need, and have a good rest. That's all you got to do.' And with a blast of cold air through the door, she was gone.

Stella did as she was told. Making sure the curtains were all securely pulled, she undressed and got into the bath, lying back and luxuriating in the feel of warm water and the heat of the fire on her bare skin. She stayed there a long time, half asleep, letting her mind wander over the events

54

of the past days – her last Christmas term at the Home, the journey here, the nervousness of beginning her first job . . . and then drifting further back to the days when she had had a family. To memories of a warmth and cosiness just like this – baths in front of the fire, her mother's gentle hands as she soaped her body, herself and her sister wrapped in towels and sitting on the rug with an orange each, feeling cherished and safe.

They hadn't been safe, though, had they. The war had started and everything had changed. Everything had been spoiled. Daddy going away. The bombing – their house destroyed and everything lost – their clothes, their furniture, her little sister's favourite dolly Princess Marcia, and the little donkey with the straw panniers that Daddy had brought back from one of his sea-trips and which Mummy had kept on the mantelpiece. All gone. You could never really be safe.

The water felt suddenly cold. Stella shivered and got out of the bath, reaching for the towel Dottie had left hanging over a clothes-horse at the side of the fire. She dried herself and wished she could empty the bath. It didn't seem right to leave it for Dottie to find when she came home tired from her evening's work.

Forgetting about the cocoa, she lit a candle and went upstairs to the bedroom that Dottie had shown her before supper, and pulled on her long flannelette nightdress. The stone hot-water bottle made a lump in the middle of the bed. She got in and touched it cautiously with her feet, finding it wrapped in what appeared to be a specially knitted pullover of its own.

Stella blew out her candle and lay down. She felt almost too tired to sleep and her mind was a bewildered jumble of thankfulness and the sorrow that accompanied her every- where, sometimes dull enough to be ignored but sometimes sharply painful. The pain briefly touched her heart and then she fell asleep, and didn't stir again until morning.

In the two days that had passed since then, Stella had found herself settling down in Dottie's cottage almost as if she'd always lived there. Dottie was hospitable without being overpowering and because she had several jobs around the village, she was out as much as she was in, giving Stella plenty of the solitude that she craved. Living in a Children's Home, she had scarcely ever been alone, and she revelled in the quiet peace of the cottage when she had it to herself. Dottie's fat tabby cat, Alfred, kept her company, slumbering beside the range on an old brown cushion and occasionally waking to stroll ponderously over to his food bowl or go outside to fossick in the hedgerow and return with an air of satisfaction for a job well done. He rubbed himself against her legs when his bowl was empty, and clambered on to her lap when she sat in the armchair and picked up a book, settling into a large, furry mound and apparently growing heavier as the time went on, and when she eventually pushed him gently to the floor he turned and gave her a look of indignation.

'He thinks he's died and gone to heaven,' Dottie said when Stella apologised to him for her temerity in wanting her lap to herself. 'It's years since he had anyone to boss about like this. Don't you take no notice. You don't want to let him get the upper hand.'

Before she went to the pub in the evenings, Dottie made supper for them both. They listened to *Luscombes*, a radio serial about country families in Devon, to *Henry Hall's Guest Night*, and the six o'clock news; they chatted about the village, its inhabitants and their ways, and about their own lives. Dottie hadn't always lived in Burracombe; she'd gone off to London as a girl and worked in the theatre, backstage, as a dresser for a well-known actress.

'It started when she came to the village for a rest,' Dottie explained one evening. 'The doctor had told her she was overdoing it – always highly strung, she was, lots of those sort of people are – and she had to have peace and quiet. She was friendly with Mrs Gilbert – the Squire's wife, what died a few years ago, poor lady – they'd known each other at school – and she came to stay at the Barton. I was working as a maid there at the time, not long left school myself, and I did some sewing for her. She took a fancy to me and asked me to go with her when she started work again.'

'It must have been very strange for you,' Stella said, swallowing a piece of gravy-soaked dumpling. Dottie had made a stew and the dumplings were as light as balls of fluff. 'Going to London – not many young girls would have done that in those days.'

'No, and my mother and father weren't keen at all, to begin with. But she was a lovely lady, my actress, and she promised she'd look after me, and so she did. And I came home in between, when she was "resting" as they call it. But as time went on, she didn't rest very much. Always in demand, she was, you see. Some of her plays went on for years, and when one finished they were after her to do another one. But in the end I had to leave her.' Dottie's brown eyes were moist. 'My old mum died, you see, and I came back to Burracombe to look after my dad. But I always kept in touch with my actress and she used to come to Burracombe all through the war. Still does, from time to time, but she's getting on now, I don't see her so much these days.' The plump little woman got up and put their empty plates together, and went on briskly, 'I liked being in London, but it's no place to be now. I was glad to be out of it when the war started, I can tell you. And there was plenty for me to do down here. I started work at the pub and helped out at the Barton and the doctor's house, and that's what I've kept on doing. Now, there's some bottled plums for afters and some nice custard, will that be all right for you?'

'Yes, please.' Stella watched while Dottie spooned glistening purple plums from an enamel dish and poured custard on top. 'You're a wonderful cook, Dottie. And you do all that needlework too.' The patchwork quilt on her bed had, she had learned, been made by Dottie when she was a girl, and there were samples of her work all over the cottage – cushion covers, rag rugs, embroidered tablecloths, curtains – as well as the clothes she made herself. 'I don't know how you find the time, with all your other jobs.'

'Oh, I like to have something to pick up. Can't just sit doing nothing. Always got a bit of knitting or sewing to hand. If I'm not making something new or mending something old, I'm doing a bit of embroidery or knitting for the church bazaar.' Dottie leaned over and picked up a shapeless bundle of purple knitting from a chair. Stella gazed at it, wondering what it was. 'My favourite jumper, this was, but it was going under the arms so I unpicked it. I'm making a toy elephant.'

'A purple elephant?' Stella exclaimed, and they both laughed.

'Oh, I make all sorts of toys. The little uns don't care what colour they are.' Dottie finished her plums and jumped up again. 'Anyway, I can't sit here nattering all evening. I'll just get these few crocks washed and I'll be off to work.' She waved away Stella's efforts to help. 'No, you'm a guest. It'll only take me a few minutes and I know where everything goes.'

A little later, Dottie pulled on her old coat and woolly Fair Isle hat and whisked out into the night and Stella settled down by the fire with Alfred on her lap, feeling as if she had come home.

There was just one thing missing. That one person she

had longed for all through these past ten years. Where was she now? Where was her sister, torn from her side in the middle of a war that had wrenched apart so many lives. *Where was Muriel?*

Chapter Six

On the last day of the year, the old stone church of St
Andrew, with its tall tower rising from the centre of the
village, was filled with parishioners. Constance Bellamy sat
in the pew immediately behind Grace Harvey and her
daughter Erica. At seventy-six years old, Miss Bellamy was
one of the longest and most regular attenders at St
Andrew's, and took a proprietorial interest in all that went
on. There had been a break during the First World War
when she had volunteered her services as a VAD nurse and
left the village to work in Service hospitals, spending nearly
two years in Malta; but she had returned as soon as the war
was over and resumed her life at the Grey House, on the
edge of the village, almost as if nothing had happened. She
had never married and never, as far as anyone knew, even
had a sweetheart – although, as some murmured, you
didn't know what might have happened out there in Malta
– and when her parents died she had stayed on in the Grey
House, where she lived with her dachshund Rupert and a
cat called Malkin.

A tiny woman with a brown, weatherbeaten face, always
bustling about the village, she made Basil Harvey think of a
motor-powered walnut. In an earlier age, she would
probably have been persecuted as a witch – although, as
he'd remarked to Grace once, he wouldn't have given the
persecutors much chance, faced with her energy and
withering tongue. At the same time, he wouldn't have been

very much surprised if it had turned out that she *was* a witch. 'The way she looks at me sometimes with those little black eyes of hers, I'm always thankful to find I haven't turned into a toad or a black beetle.'

'Don't talk such nonsense,' Grace had reproved him. 'Miss Bellamy's the salt of the earth. The village wouldn't be the same without her. And for goodness sake don't let anyone else hear you saying such things!'

Basil smiled. It was funny how people expected vicars to be innocent souls who had never heard a swear-word or made a joke in their lives – yet if a churchman were to be any use at all, he had to be fully aware of human nature in all its many shades.

Opposite Constance Bellamy, in the pew behind the Napiers, sat Henry Warren and his wife Joyce, who was President of the Women's Institute and also ran the Gardening Club and the drama group. Basil had heard that she was currently trying to set up a Bridge Club, which he thought would be a good idea, being a bridge-player himself, but if she went on like this, Joyce would need a village hall all to herself. The whist drives, Mother's Union, country-dancing group and Local History Society all held their meetings there too, and the diary was getting rather crowded. He'd had Edie Pettifer, from the news-agent's, round only a few days before Christmas, complaining that there hadn't been a date free for the kiddies' Christmas party until two days before New Year's Eve; and where Edie Pettifer went, Bert Foster, the butcher next door, was sure to follow.

They were into the second hymn now and Basil chided himself for letting his attention wander. It was easy enough to keep his mind on the prayers, but he knew all the village's favourite hymns so well by now that he could sing them without really thinking about them. If the villagers only realised, he thought, that their vicar's attention was as easily distracted as was theirs! And although he tried hard to make his sermons interesting, he couldn't really blame them for drifting off to thoughts of their own concerns while he was talking. Perhaps it even did them more good. That twenty minutes of peace and quiet might be all they got in their busy lives.

Still, it wasn't his job to preach today. He'd handed over that part of the service to his new curate, young Felix Copley. Rather more cynically than was suitable for a vicar, perhaps, he wondered if Felix's presence was part of the reason for the church being so full this morning. There were certainly plenty of young women in the congregation – Nathan Pettifer's two girls, Gillian and Angela, for a start, Ginnie Nethercott from the pub, and that pretty young schoolteacher Stella Simmons. Or was he being uncharitable? Miss Simmons would be bound to come, and the other girls were surely too young and lively to take much interest in a curate.

Basil watched Felix climb into the pulpit, tall and well-built, his hair gleaming like corn ripe for harvest, his mobile face full of warmth and humour. A bishop in the making, he thought. He's got the bearing and he's got the charisma and the personality. He'll have the women at his feet and the men on his side. Maybe he was, after all, the reason why the church was so full.

Felix stood still for a moment, looking down at the expectant faces of the congregation. Then he spoke the introduction and began to talk, and Basil listened attentively. The curate's voice was deep, smooth and musical, the kind of voice its owner might himself get rather too fond of hearing, but there seemed to be no danger of that at present, as Felix spoke simply and naturally about the welcome he had received in the village. He talked of a stranger's shyness at finding himself in a closely knit community, and the warmth of Devon hospitality that had drawn him so swiftly to its heart, and he spoke of Jesus' words about entertaining angels unaware.

'I'm no angel,' he said with a grin that drew appreciative smiles from his listeners, 'but I can see that if ever angels do come amongst us, you will all be very well able to entertain them, for you've practised on many a lesser soul.' He paused, and his smile faded to leave his chiselled features suddenly grave. 'And I'm sure that angels *do* come amongst us. They may be here at this very moment. And I ask that you continue to extend, to all strangers, that same hospitality. For, angel or no, we are all God's beings and by doing so, we fulfil a part of God's own purpose. And now to God the Father, God the Son and God the Holy Ghost . . .'

Yes, the boy could preach a good sermon, Basil thought as the congregation rose to its feet for the last hymn and Felix came down from the pulpit. Not too long, not too short, lively enough to keep the people interested, and thoughtful enough to give them something to chew over. Basil gave him a nod of approval and went forward to receive the collection plates brought to him by Henry Warren and Dr Charles Latimer.

'Very nice service, Vicar,' Henry's wife Joyce said to him as they filed out through the south door. She looked at Felix, standing by Basil's side. 'Welcome to Burracombe. You did very well.'

The curate smiled his thanks. 'It's kind of you to say so. I'm looking forward to working here. It's a beautiful area.'

'Do you know Dartmoor well?' she asked, and he shook his head.

'I don't even know Devon well, I'm afraid. I grew up in Cambridgeshire. I hope the locals will accept a foreigner.' He crinkled another smile at her but Joyce Warren regarded him impassively.

'You must come to tea,' she commanded. 'Come on Tuesday. I have WI on Wednesday.' She spoke as if she intended to make a report on him at the meeting. 'Three o'clock at Tor House – the vicar will tell you where that is.'

She marched on through the door and Basil watched Felix having his hand shaken by a tiny woman with white curls and a birdlike face. The young man looked astonished when he saw that there were two of them – identical twins, each gazing up into his face with bright, eager eyes and nodding her head.

'Lovely sermon, Mr Copley.'

'Lovely sermon.' Their voices were like the twittering of sparrows in a hedge.

'Thank you,' Felix said, looking bemused. He glanced sideways at the vicar and Basil came to the rescue.

'These are the Misses Friend – Jeanie and Jessie. They run our Post Office and sell sweets and tobacco and stationery as well. And this is their brother, Billy, who lives with them.'

Felix turned to the rather podgy man standing just behind them; a smile of extraordinary sweetness broke out over the wide, flat face with its button nose and slanting eyes. The man held out his hand and Felix took it.

'I'm Billy,' the man said. 'I live at the Post Office. I help Mr Foster.'

'Mr Foster's the butcher,' Basil explained. 'He's a chapel man.'

Felix nodded. The vicar had already explained that the village had its own Methodist chapel, a sturdy grey building with a windswept graveyard overlooking the moor.

'I carry the meat,' Billy announced. 'Pigs and lambs and sides of beef. I carry things for Jeanie and Jessie too.' He lifted one arm. 'I'm strong, I am.'

'I'm sure you're very useful,' Felix said gently. 'It's good to be strong, and it's good to see you in church.'

64

'I like church. I like the music.'

'Come along, Billy,' one of his sisters said, taking his arm. 'Come along home, now. It's time for dinner.'

Billy nodded and smiled. 'Sunday dinner. I like Sunday dinner.' He ambled off down the church path, large and bulky between the two tiny women.

'Billy's a dear soul,' Basil said quietly. 'Quite a few years younger than his sisters. His parents were well into their forties when he was born, and they're both dead now.'

'He's lucky to have two good sisters to look after him,' Felix said, and turned to the next person who was waiting to greet him. Not all the parishioners had stopped to talk – many had hurried by with a smile and a greeting – and there were only a few left in the little group waiting to shake his and the vicar's hands.

'This is Miss Simmons who's come to take on the teacher's post,' Basil said, introducing Stella. 'Felix Copley, my curate. You remember, Felix – you met the headmistress, Miss Kemp, the other day. Miss Simmons lodges with Dottie Friend, whom you'll encounter all over the village and especially in the pub!'

'I keep encountering Friends wherever I go,' Felix said wryly. 'Friends and Pettifers seem to make up most of the village. Are they all related?'

'More or less,' Basil said vaguely. Even after five years, he had himself never quite got to grips with the ramifications of village relationships. 'But what a nice thing to be able to say – that you encounter friends wherever you go. And very true of Burracombe, I think you'll agree, Miss Simmons?'

'I certainly will,' she said, gently withdrawing her hand. 'I've only been here a few days, but it seems to be a lovely village to live in, Mr Copley.'

'Felix,' he said. 'I'd like everyone to call me Felix. I don't feel quite grown up enough to be called "Mr".'

'I'll be bringing our new curate round to the school as soon as term starts,' Basil said as Stella Simmons turned away. 'Sweet girl,' he added. 'Miss Kemp's very pleased with the appointment and I'm sure the children are going to love her.'

Constance Bellamy, the Latimers and Colonel Napier had all left the church, filing down the aisles immediately behind the vicar as he made his way towards the door. The last person to leave was George Sweet, the village baker, who always seemed to have a smudge of flour somewhere about his person. He stuck out a big, powerful hand and gave Felix a sharp look.

'Not a bad sermon, for a first time. Good to have you with us. Lodgings all right? Aggie looking after you?'

Felix nodded. He had already met George, who was one of the churchwardens and had found him lodgings with his widowed cousin Agatha Madge. He thought George looked more like a pugilist than a baker, but Basil had explained that kneading the huge amounts of dough that George Sweet made every night developed the muscles every bit as well as weight-lifting.

'Mrs Madge is like a mother to me,' he said. 'And we certainly don't lack the staff of life. Your bread's excellent.'

George nodded, as if this went without saying. 'Well, I dare say I'll be seeing you later on. I'm coming round to Aggie's for Sunday tea.'

'And he's coming to us for Sunday dinner,' Basil said, taking Felix by the arm. 'Come on, now. If you meet any more people today you'll be completely confused. That's one of the problems with this job,' he added as they went back to the vestry to remove their robes. 'Remembering all the new faces and being able to put the right name to them. It's not one of my strong points, which is one reason why I hope never to be moved from Burracombe. You'll meet them all again tonight, too, round the tree.'

'Round the tree?'

'Yes – to see in the New Year, you know. It's a tradition here – had to be stopped during the war, of course, but it was revived in 1945. The whole village gathers on the green. The bells are rung half-muffled to signify the death of the old year, and then the muffles are taken off and the tenor strikes the hour before they're rung out to celebrate the birth of the new year. And everyone dances round the tree – well, those who can – and there's a lot of hugging and kissing and good wishes. It's an excellent start, and I always hope that those who've spent the old year feuding will make up their differences then and be friends.'

'And do they?' Felix asked in amusement.

Basil Harvey sighed. 'Some of them do but I'm afraid most of them have slipped back by the end of the first week!' He hung his cassock on a hook and pulled on his overcoat. 'Anyway, we'd better get a move on or Grace will be worrying about the meal. Apparently it's very difficult to have everything ready at exactly the same moment, and if we're not there then it will be irrevocably spoilt.'

They closed the church door and set off along the path that led to the vicarage garden, each immersed in his own thoughts. On the whole, Basil thought, his new curate had shown up very well. The congregation seemed to have enjoyed his sermon and those who had stopped to talk had been pleasant and welcoming. The little exchange between the young man and the new schoolteacher had been interesting, but it was far too early in Felix's ministry for any complications of that sort.

Felix himself had no such reservations. He had had girlfriends before, but nobody serious. At almost thirty, he had begun to think it was time to settle down, and although he had no intention of rushing into romance on the promise of a pair of large hazel eyes, he was open to possibilities. He wondered if the new schoolteacher would come down to the village green that night and dance round the tree with everyone else.

As he followed the vicar through the front door of the vicarage and into the hallway, the smell of roast beef touched his nostrils and he drew in an appreciative breath. He was going to enjoy this new year in Burracombe.

Chapter Seven

'Nineteen-fifty-one,' Alice Tozer said as the six church bells rang out their joyful peal in the frosty midnight air and the villagers burst into cheers. 'A new year's like a new start, that's what I always say.'

She gripped her mother-in-law Minnie's hand in one of hers, and her daughter Val's in the other as the crowd began to circle around the ancient oak tree, and hoped it wouldn't be too much for the old lady. Minnie was a marvel, you had to admit that, but she was eighty-one when all was said and done, and there was a limit to how much dancing round a tree at midnight she could do, even if it was New Year's Eve.

'Let's hope it is.' Minnie had lived through two world wars, not to mention the Boer War that had taken her own brother at the turn of the century. 'And so it would be, if they'd just let us ordinary folk live our own lives. It's all this argy-bargying in Parliament as causes all the trouble, and always will be.'

Val, on the other side of her mother, said nothing. It had taken all Alice's powers of persuasion to get her to come out at all, and she was still wishing she had stayed indoors by the fire or, better still, in bed with her memories. 'It's time you got over all that,' Alice had said to her earlier, standing in the warm farmhouse kitchen and winding a long green scarf round her neck. 'Nobody was more sorry than me when Eddie was killed, but it's six years ago now, Val, and you've got to look forward. We all have our troubles in this life, and it don't do no good to give way to them.'

Val had been shocked. Her mother had never spoken to her like that before. Ever since the news had come of Eddie's death, on New Year's Eve 1944, Alice had been unstinting in her support. Tears had come to Val's eyes as she stared at her, and Alice's face had softened. Quickly, she came across the big kitchen and laid her hand on her daughter's shoulder. 'I don't mean to be harsh, maid, you know that. But there's a time for grieving and a time to be happy, isn't that what we're told? And it seems to me that your time for grieving is over now, and if a new year isn't a cue to be happy, what is? I know what New Year's Eve means to you – I'll never forget the day we heard about Eddie – but that makes it all the more a time to put it all behind you and look forward. So won't you come out with us tonight? Listen to your dad and the others ring in the new year, and wish everyone a Happy New Year?' She looked pleadingly into Val's brown eyes. 'Nobody would want you to be unhappy all your life,' she said quietly. 'Eddie wouldn't, I know.'

Val twisted sharply away from her. Then she bit her lip, reproaching herself for her unkindness, and turned back. Alice was standing quite still, the scarf still not completely wrapped around her neck and her brown tweed coat still unbuttoned. Val took a deep breath and gave her a wavering smile.

'All right, Mum. I'll come. It won't make any difference to Eddie whether I dance round the old tree or not. He's gone, and that's all there is to it.' She lifted her head and squared her shoulders, but as she went to the cupboard to fetch her own coat, Alice watched her with troubled eyes. It would take a lot more than a few words from her and a dance round the village oak tree to bring Val out of the cocoon she had wrapped round herself for the past six years.

She sighed. She'd always thought that boys were harder to bring up, with their wild ways, but it seemed now that daughters were the ones that gave you more worry. Look at her youngest daughter, Jackie. She'd gone off earlier, saying she'd see her mother at the tree at midnight, and goodness only knew what she might be getting up to in the meantime. It was true she was only going to supper with the Pettifers, and Alice didn't doubt that Freda Pettifer, whom she'd known since she was a baby in a pram, would keep a strict eye on things, but there was a long time between eight o'clock and midnight, and no doubt Jackie and young Roy would find some way of slipping out into the darkness together. To Alice's mind, those two were altogether too keen on each other, and she shuddered to think what Ted would say if there was any trouble there.

As she watched Val slide her arms reluctantly into the sleeves of her winter coat, Minnie came into the kitchen with Joanna. Val started to take her coat off again. 'You go, Jo – I'll stay home with Robin. You'll have a much better time than I will.'

'Don't be silly!' Joanna had taken the situation in at a glance. 'I've been every New Year's Eve since the war ended. It's your turn now. Robin's my little boy, after all – I'm the one who ought to be staying at home. You go and let your hair down, Val.'

'Is this a conspiracy?' Val asked, her voice trembling a little. She looked at her tiny grandmother. 'Are you in it too?'

'I think it's time you started to go out and about a bit, if that's what you mean,' Minnie retorted smartly. 'And I'd offer to stay home myself if I didn't think this might be my last New Year's Eve. I don't suppose I'll see another at my age.'

71

'Go on, Mother,' Alice said automatically, holding up Val's coat. 'You've been saying that for the past five years and you're still here to make a nuisance of yourself . . . Come on now, Val, put this on and let's be off or we'll miss the peal and your father and our Tom'll never forgive us.'

Val allowed her mother to slip the coat back on to her shoulders and pulled the collar high around her neck. She felt in the pockets for the gloves Minnie had knitted her for Christmas and turned towards the door.

'Well, let's get it over with,' she said. 'Happy New Year, Jo. See you in the morning, if you've gone to bed by the time we come back.' A blast of cold air surged in as she stepped out into the yard, and she shivered and pulled her coat closer around her.

Minnie caught Alice's eye and shrugged. ''Tis no use worrying yourself about the maid. She'll get over it in her own good time.'

'Will she?' Alice murmured as they followed Val outside. 'It's been six years, Mother. I wonder sometimes if she's ever going to get over it. Not everybody does, do they? Look at Auntie Flo. She grieved over her Albert till the day she died.'

'Flo was always an obstinate piece,' Minnie said. 'I know she was my sister, and you shouldn't speak ill of the dead, but it's true. She got it into her head that it would be wrong to look at another man after she lost Albert and nothing would make her see any different. And what good did it do? She could have been a wife and mother, same as me, and brought a family into the world, but no, she had to wear it like a hump on her shoulder till the day she died . . . You don't want young Val going the same way, Alice. A waste, that'd be, a proper waste.'

They stopped for a moment, closing the door behind them and looking up at the sky, peppered with stars. The sound of the bells, softly muffled as they rang their last peal of 1950, accompanied them down the track between Devon banks that would in just a few weeks be thickly clustered with primroses, and when they reached the village green it was to find gathered there all the friends and neighbours they had grown up with and known all their lives. Then the peal stopped and there were a few moments of silence before they heard the sound of the tenor bell, tolling the notes of midnight for the death of the old year. The deep tone seemed to echo the sorrow in Val's heart, but just before the thirteenth stroke, the other bells joined in, pealing open and joyous to welcome the new year, and everyone broke into cheers.

'Nineteen-fifty-one,' Alice said in Val's ear. 'A new year. A new start.' And Val turned impulsively and kissed her mother's cheek.

'A new start,' she agreed shakily and made up her mind that, although she would never forget the boy she had loved, she would start now to make something worthwhile of her life.

She glanced round a little nervously, wondering if Luke Ferris was amongst the circle round the tree. She hadn't spoken to him since that day in late October when he'd caught her up in the lane. The hospital had been busy and she'd spent her days off helping on the farm or going to see Hilary at the Barton, and had avoided the wood where the charcoal-burner's cottage stood. There'd been Christmas shopping, too, and the usual debate about whether to go to Plymouth or Exeter for the day out that she, her mother and Joanna usually had, and all the preparations to do at home. This year, they'd shared out the work – Val had made the cake, Joanna the mincemeat and Alice the puddings, with Minnie chopping onions, the handle of a fork gripped firmly between her false teeth to stop her eyes watering. What with everything, she'd hardly been into the village except to go to church for the Carol Service, and it had been so full then that even if he had been there she could easily have missed him.

Still clasping her daughter's hand, Alice too glanced around the ring of faces, lit by the lanterns hung from the spreading branches of the old oak. Laughing faces, all filled with the same hope for the new year that she was feeling herself. It won't all go right though, she thought with a sudden prickle of fear. Some things are bound to go wrong – people will fall ill or die, there'll be accidents and sadness. That's life, after all. But at least, please God, let there be no more wars. Let us have peace now. And for goodness sake let's get rid of this blessed rationing!

'Now, where be that maid to?' she asked, searching the faces for her other daughter. 'Slipped off with young Roy Pettifer, I wouldn't mind betting. That girl's growing up too fast. Well, I'm not going home without her. I'll get Val to take you back, Mother.'

'You will not. I'm capable of finding my own way.' But Minnie was only arguing for the sake of it and didn't demur when Val took her arm to guide her along the rough track back to the Tozers' farm.

'Come on, Gran. Let's get you back in the warm while Mum finds our Jackie. I'm ready to go myself now, anyway.' They started to walk slowly back along the track, Val's torch throwing a pool of light to show Minnie the way.

Overhead, the stars seemed almost close enough to touch, a glittering sprinkle of light that seemed to reflect the frost already riming the hedgerows. It had been dry since Christmas and there were no puddles on the roads, no ice to slip on. Alice watched for a moment as the two women set off down the lane, then turned back to the green to look for her younger daughter.

'Jackie!' she called, peering into the darkness. 'Come on

– everyone's going home now. You've got to get up for work in the morning, remember.'

There was a pause and then, as the last few people moved away from the green, Jackie and Roy emerged from a hidden corner. It was too dark to see them properly, even by the light of the hurricane lamp Alice had unhooked from one of the branches of the oak tree, but Jackie's fair hair looked dishevelled and Alice could guess that her face was flushed. She gave them both a quizzical look and took Jackie's arm.

'Roy could've seen me home,' the girl said in an injured tone. 'You didn't have to go shouting out for me like that, Mum, in front of everyone.'

'It's too late for you to be out with a boy,' Alice told her. She nodded at Roy. 'I know you'd have looked after her, but her father's strict over times, even on New Year's Eve. And I can hear the ringers coming down the church path now, so we'd better be on our way. He won't be pleased to see us still hanging about here. Off you go now, Roy.'

The boy shrugged and grinned. 'All right, Mrs Tozer. I've got to be up at six anyway. I promised to help Dad with the milking since it's a Sunday.' He strolled off down the lane and disappeared in the darkness.

'He's a nice enough boy, Jackie,' Alice said after a short silence, 'but I don't want you getting serious. You're only seventeen and he'll be away doing his National Service before long. There's plenty of time before you need to think about all that sort of thing.'

'He might not go away yet,' Jackie said. 'He could finish his apprenticeship first.'

'Whenever he goes, it'll still be for two years. Anyway, you haven't had time to look around. You don't want to take the first chap that comes along.'

'Like you and Dad did, you mean? It don't seem to have

done you any harm.' Jackie's voice was sulky and Alice's heart sank.

'Come on, love, don't let's get the New Year off to a bad start,' she said. 'You know your father and me only want what's best for you. And there's a lot to look forward to this year. There's the trip to London to see the Festival—'

'Me and Roy've been talking about that,' Jackie said quickly. 'We don't want to go on the coach with everyone else. We want to go on the train, by ourselves, and stay for two or three days.'

Alice stopped abruptly. She held up the lamp and stared at her daughter's face. 'You want *what*? Stay up in London – by yourselves? Don't be so silly!'

'It's not silly. It's what we want to do.' Jackie faced her mother defiantly. 'Why shouldn't we?'

'You know very well why you shouldn't. A young maid going away with a boy, not even engaged! Whatever would people say?'

'I don't care what they say. Anyway, who says we're not engaged?' Jackie tossed her head.

'*I* say,' Alice said firmly. 'And so will your father, when he hears about it. Engaged, indeed! Why, Roy's never even asked your father – and neither will he, if I'm any judge. He knows what the answer would be!'

Jackie tossed her head again and her fair hair flew round her face. She'd worn it loose tonight, rather than tied back as she had to wear it for her work in the Barton. She spoke in a quick, nervous tone.

'He's asked *me*, and that's what matters. And I've said yes, so we're engaged. Nobody can stop that and I don't need to wear a ring, so there's nothing you or Dad can do about it.' She turned and began to march along the lane. 'And in four years' time we'll be able to get married whatever *anyone* says, so you may as well get used to the idea.'

'*Jackie!*' Alice hurried after her, shocked by the sudden turn the conversation had taken. 'Jackie, how dare you talk to me like that. And on New Year's Eve, too, when—'

'New Year's Day,' Jackie said, walking fast. 'It's New Year's *Day*. That's what we were all doing out here at midnight, remember?'

'And there's no call to be cheeky!' Alice said sharply. Then she caught her breath and spoke more gently, taking her daughter's arm as she did so. She felt it stiffen like a piece of wood under her hand. 'Jackie, don't let's have words over this. It's not a good way to start a new year, now is it?'

Jackie said nothing for a few moments. Then she stopped abruptly and turned towards her mother. Alice's arms went round her at once and they clung together in the dark lane. 'I do love him, Mum,' she whispered. 'I do! And he loves me. We can't help it that we're young, can we? We can't help it that we've fallen in love. And – you weren't much older when you and Dad started courting, were you? You've often said how you were childhood sweethearts. So don't be angry with us. Please don't be angry.'

Alice sighed. ''Tis all right, my dear. I do understand. I just don't want you to do anything you might be sorry for later on, that's all. I don't want you to rush into anything.' She paused, then said, 'Your dad and I were childhood sweethearts, it's true, but it don't always work out so well. Look at your Auntie Nell. That was never a happy marriage.'

Jackie lifted her wet face. 'Wasn't it? But she seemed so upset when Uncle Fred was killed.'

'Oh, she was upset, of course she was. He was her man, wasn't he? But she weren't never happy with him, never. It was a good day for her when he was called up. Anyway, we don't need to go into all that. All I'm saying is, you've got

77

your whole life ahead of you, you and Roy, and things can change. People can change. Give it time, that's all, and don't go talking about engagements to your father. Not for a year or two, anyway.'

Jackie found a hanky and blew her nose. They began to walk on again and she said in a doleful voice, 'A year or two's a long time, Mum.'

'Not as long as a lifetime,' Alice replied. 'And these years are precious ones, Jackie. You want to enjoy them, not get tied down. I don't say you can't see Roy whenever you like, but just take it slowly, that's all. Like I said, there's a lot to look forward to now that the war's well and truly over and the country's getting back on its feet.' She hesitated and then said, 'But I can't see your father agreeing to let you go off to London with Roy, not to stay. You'll have to forget that.'

Jackie said nothing and it was too dark for Alice to see her face to know if she had accepted this or was still sulkily defiant. Jackie had always been strong-willed and determined to have her own way, and there was no reason to suppose she had changed now. It looked as if there were storms ahead.

I just wish our Val could find someone to fall in love with, Alice thought, turning her mind to her older daughter. Val was the sort of young woman who was cut out to be married. Warm and loving, she would make a good wife. But she seemed to have set her face against all ideas of marriage, and it looked as if she meant to stay at the farm for ever.

At least Tom and Joanna were settled and happy, and so were Ted and Alice's elder son, Brian, and his wife Peggy, over in Germany. Two out of four wasn't too bad, and the only real problem with Jackie was her wilfulness. And who knew what the year ahead would bring?

A new year, she thought as they came to the farmyard gate and Jackie unlatched it. A new year, with a Festival to give us heart. It's just what everyone needs.

Chapter Eight

Stella Simmons was hoping for a new start too.

Dottie had persuaded her to come to the midnight celebrations. 'You need to get to know village people,' she said, her rosy face beaming as she buttoned a cherry-red cardigan over her frilly blouse. 'And 'twill please them to see the new teacher joining in. That Miss Morgan was proper stand-offish – wouldn't even crack a smile. I don't think the children liked her much either. Good thing when she retired.'

'I hope they'll like me,' Stella said. As she'd said goodbye to the staff and children of the Children's Home before Christmas, she'd felt suddenly frightened at the thought of never going back again, except as a visitor. She knew they'd been good to her, allowing her to stay on during the holidays from college in return for working with the children, but now that was all over and she was on her own. Burracombe must be her home now.

'Why, my pretty, of course they'll like you!' Dottie found her Fair Isle hat and pulled it over her yellow curls. 'You don't have no call to worry about that. Now, you get your coat on sometime around ten o'clock or so, and come down to the Bell and I'll introduce you to a few folk. Us'll be having a little party there, see – Bernie and Rose always puts a few bits and pieces out for the regulars.' She scooped up a basket which Stella knew was filled with snacks prepared by her landlady earlier in the day – sausage rolls, mince pies, egg sandwiches wrapped in a clean teacloth, and an assortment of jam tarts. Dottie was a good cook and, as well as working as barmaid at the Bell Inn, made cakes and tarts for George Sweet's shop and helped out at the Barton House and at the doctor's house too, whenever they had guests. She had been baking all day and Stella had at last been allowed to help. She promised to come down to the pub later on.

Sitting by the fire, Stella hoped that Dottie was right about the children liking her. Despite having lived in an orphanage for so long and helping with the smaller children as she got older, she had found trying to control a room full of children she had never met before a daunting experience during her teaching practice. At the end of the first day, she was almost in tears.

'I'm not going to be any good at all. They won't do a thing I say.'

Miss Carter, the teacher whose class she was taking, had smiled sympathetically. 'They're trying you out. They always do it with a new teacher. I never intervene on the first day because you will come across children like these when you're qualified, and you need to know what they can be like. We'll sort them out tomorrow, don't worry.'

She had, too. The children had sat silent at their desks, some in tears, as Miss Carter had given them a tongue-lashing that almost had Stella weeping in sympathy. After that, she had had no further trouble with them; they'd even begun to enjoy the projects she had brought for them to do. At the end of the fortnight she was touched to receive a variety of posies of wildflowers, a small punnet of strawberries and even a jar of tadpoles, given her by the boy who had been her greatest torment in those first few days. His cheeky face split into a grin, he'd thrust them at her with the words, 'You're all right, miss. We wouldn't mind having you as our teacher all the time.' He'd nodded at the

81

tadpoles. 'They're out of our pond, they are. Turn into toads, they will.'

'Thank you,' Stella said, wondering how she could transport them back to the college and what she could do with them there, but Miss Carter solved that problem as well.

'I've got a pond in my garden. I'll tip them in there. Toads are always useful – they eat slugs, you know.'

Stella looked at the clock and realised that it was already after eleven. She had sat too long over the fire and fallen asleep. She put another log on the embers; Dottie had asked her to keep it stoked up, since they'd both be coming home late. Not that Stella really felt like leaving her comfortable armchair in this cosy little room and going out into the night, but she knew that Dottie would be hurt if she didn't put in an appearance.

She wrapped herself in her coat and scarf. Pulling on gloves and the hat that her college friend Pat's mother had knitted her for Christmas, she stepped out into the frosty air and heard the bells already ringing their muffled peal for the dying of the year. As she came down the lane, she saw the villagers gathered round the tree, torches and lanterns dancing as they moved about, and she paused. The only people she knew were Dottie, the vicar, and the other school governors, and even if she had been able to see them in the darkness she would have hesitated to join them. She felt suddenly isolated and lonely.

'Why, it's Miss Simmons!'

She turned quickly and saw Felix Copley. He was bareheaded, his fair hair gleaming in the flickering light, his teeth glimmering in a wide smile. He held out his hand.

'Good to see you. I was hoping you'd come. Let's stick together, shall we? Two "furriners" together!'

Stella put her hand into his and he drew her into the circle. She felt warmed by the contact and grateful for his

82

kindness in looking out for her. His hand was big and strong, more like a farmworker's than a clergyman's, she thought. But Basil Harvey was quite unlike the wispy little cleric who used to visit the Children's Home and take the services in the little chapel there. Then she remembered Mr Beckett, the vicar she'd been billeted with for a few months after the bomb had shattered her life, and tears filled her eyes.

The muffled peal faded into the darkness and the villagers fell silent, gripping each other's hands and waiting. It was as if, for a moment or two, the whole world held its breath. And then the tolling of the tenor bell struck the hour and they knew that another year had begun.

'Nineteen-fifty-one! Happy New Year!' someone called as the twelfth blow rang out, and then the rest of the bells pealed forth, their chimes as bright and clear as the stars above. The throng began to dance around the tree, skipping in a huge circle and then breaking away to greet each other and give their wishes for happiness and good luck in the coming months.

Stella and Felix found themselves standing together, a little apart as they had been at the beginning. They looked at each other and then he smiled again and shook her hand.

'Happy New Year, Miss Simmons.'

'Happy New Year, Mr Copley,' she said, and they both laughed, although Stella couldn't have said what they were laughing at. He was still holding her hand.

'A new year in a new place for both of us,' he said. 'When do you start school?'

'Not for another week, but I wanted to come early to settle in and get to know the village. And I've got to see Miss Kemp – we need to work out what I'm going to do. How I'm to organise my lessons and so on. I don't think there are any new children starting, so I need to find out how the little ones are getting on with their reading and writing. Miss Kemp says she expects them all to be able to read and ready to learn joined-up writing when they go up into her class.' She stopped. 'Sorry – this must be very boring.'

Felix laughed. 'It's not boring at all, but I think we ought to celebrate the New Year before you start to think too much about work. Come into the pub and I'll buy you a drink.' He grinned mischievously. 'I think the new curate and the new teacher can be allowed to be a little daring on New Year's Eve, don't you? There's just time before Bernie calls for last orders.'

He took Stella's hand again and pulled her across the green to the light spilling from the open doors of the Bell. Many of the villagers had gone back inside after midnight had been struck and were taking advantage of the extended licence to have another drink and finish up the supper that had been laid out on long tables. Felix pushed his way in and Stella caught sight of Dottie behind the bar, her yellow curls tumbling round her face and the frilly blouse she had put on 'for best' showing rather a lot of her plump chest as she leaned on the bar, laughing at something one of the farmers was saying.

'What'll you have?'

'Oh, I don't know.' Stella had been into very few pubs and the only drink she normally had at this hour of the night – if she were still awake and wanting a drink at all – would have been cocoa. You couldn't ask for cocoa in a pub though, especially not on New Year's Eve. Or New Year's Day, as she supposed it now was. 'A – a lemonade, please.'

'Really? It's rather a cold drink, isn't it? Why not have a ginger wine?'

'Yes, all right.' That didn't sound too alcoholic. She waited while Felix fought his way to the bar. People looked round at him, recognised who he was and made way, their eyebrows raised a little. He grinned back cheerfully and

Stella could see some of them pull down the corners of their mouths, as if to say 'he's all right', while others looked down their noses disapprovingly.

Dottie spotted her and waved cheerily, and several people turned to see who she was waving at. Stella felt her cheeks grow hot and was thankful when Felix battled his way back through the noisy throng and handed her a sherry glass filled with deep golden-brown liquid.

'Thank you.' She took a sip and gasped as the wine tingled against her lips, tongue and throat. 'Goodness me, it really is gingery!'

'It'll warm you up.' Felix was drinking beer. He glanced round and said, 'Look, there's a table and a couple of chairs – let's grab them.'

They made their way over to the corner which had just been vacated and sat down. Stella looked at Felix and felt a sudden sense of disbelief. I can't be doing this, she thought, sitting in a pub with a man I barely know. Whatever would Matron at the Home say? At the same time, she felt a warm pleasure that she had made a friend already, for she felt sure that Felix was going to be a friend. She smiled at him and when he lifted his glass to her, she raised hers in return.

'Happy New Year,' they said again, in unison; over at the bar, Dottie saw them and lifted the glass of stout that was standing by her side and shouted across, 'Happy New Year!'

'I don't think everyone approves of you being here,' Stella said, and Felix chuckled.

'They probably think clergymen shouldn't drink at all, and if they do they ought to do it privately, in their own homes and with the curtains drawn. But Mr Harvey comes in for a pint now and then, he told me, so they ought to be accustomed to it. And it's a good place to meet people – better than the church, in some ways.'

The bells had stopped ringing and there was a small commotion as the bellringers came in and good wishes were exchanged all over again. There was just time for one more drink and then Bernie, the tubby landlord, called 'time' and people began to head towards the door.

'Let me see you home now,' Felix said, putting his hand beneath Stella's elbow. 'It's the cottage just along the lane, isn't it?'

'That's right. But you don't need to bother – there are plenty of people walking that way. Besides, I can't imagine anything bad happening in Burracombe.'

'All the same,' he said, 'I can't let a lady walk home alone.' He kept his hand under her elbow, guiding her along the rough metalled road. As she had said, there were others going that way too, their torches making little pools of white light in front of them. The jubilation of the new year had quietened a little, and they were talking and joking. It was almost like a big family going home together, Stella thought, with sudden, sharp emotion that was half-pain and half-pleasure.

They came to Dottie's gate and Felix wished her goodnight. She gave him a final smile and stood for a moment looking up at the stars and listening to the silence.

Only once had she known the deep silence of the countryside at night. Her early childhood had been spent in cities, much of it under the roar of aircraft and what seemed, in memory, to be an incessant pandemonium of bombing. There had been that brief period in a small village, not so very different from Burracombe and sharing the same deep quiet under the starlit nights – and then the sudden wrench as she was torn away from the contented home she had found and taken to an orphanage on the other side of the county.

She stood now with her hand on the gate, looking up at

the stars. It was her first New Year's Eve away from the Home. 1951: a new year, a new start.

I haven't made a resolution, she thought suddenly, and closed her eyes. *Let me make a success of this job – of this whole year. And let me, somehow, find out what happened to my little sister.*

It wasn't a resolution so much as a prayer, but it said everything that was in her heart.

Chapter Nine

For Hilary Napier, that New Year's Eve had seemed to bring little promise of a new start. Even though her brother Stephen had come home just before Christmas, somewhat reluctantly and complaining that he hadn't done nearly enough skiing, nothing much seemed to have changed at the Barton. Her father was already beginning to make pointed remarks about 'still thinking you're on holiday' and 'work to do, even if it *is* Christmas', and Hilary could see that it was only a matter of time before the arguments began.

She had come in from walking the dogs to find her father already at breakfast with a copy of *The Sunday Times* beside him. 'Morning, my dear. Dogs behave themselves?'

She smiled at him and poured herself some coffee from the silver pot on the sideboard. Her father liked to have breakfast served in the old way, so Hilary prepared it all before she took the dogs out and left it ready in the breakfast room, for all the world as if they still had servants. 'Of course.' She glanced at the two black labradors, who had lumbered over to the fireplace and flung themselves down in front of it with huge sighs, as if this were all they had been waiting for. 'They're getting too old to do much else these days. They still enjoy their morning run, though.'

Napier nodded. 'I'll have to see how those youngsters Burley's been training are shaping up. Wouldn't do to be without the dogs. Selsey's showing signs of stiffness, and Bart was definitely tired after the last shoot.' He glanced at his newspaper.

Hilary helped herself to toast and a boiled egg. She sat down opposite him. 'What's the news?'

Napier frowned. 'It looks to me as if the Communists are going to take Seoul. This Korean War's a bad business. I thought we'd done with all that when we bombed the Japanese. Now here we are in the thick of it again.' He shook his head. 'And our own Government's no help. It's Churchill we want in charge now, not Attlee. That election last year was a complete shambles.'

Hilary had heard all this before. She remembered the election fever of a year ago, the campaigning and canvassing. Her father had been chairman of the selection committee for the local branch of the Conservative Party and, although their own candidate had won his seat, the return of Labour to Government had been a bitter blow.

He folded the paper and dropped it on a chair, then reached out for a slice of toast. 'Where's that boy? Still lolling about in bed?'

'I expect so. He was going to the Bouldings' party at Little Burracombe. I was invited too, but I'm going to the Latimers' tonight, so I passed.'

The Squire grunted. He'd been invited to the doctor's New Year's Eve party as well, but somehow he didn't have the heart for that sort of thing these days. The dogs stretched out in front of a smouldering log fire, a glass of malt and his memories would help him see in the new year, and then he'd shut the two labradors in the gunroom and gone to bed, hearing the last peal of the bells as he slipped between the sheets.

He glanced at his daughter, struck as he always was by her resemblance to her mother. Isobel had been just the same age as Hilary was now when he had inherited the estate in 1926, and Hilary had been four. Baden, the eldest of their three children, had been a sturdy boy of six, and young Stephen hadn't even been thought of yet. They'd had everything before them then, he thought – a growing family, a good, solid house and an estate to run which would take all his energies and give him the life he'd been bred for. They'd looked forward to a lifetime together, growing old in this place where he had been born, with Baden taking the reins when the time came and grandchildren playing round their feet.

And now both Isobel and Baden were gone. Stephen, the youngest, had only just finished with Cambridge and Hilary, still unmarried at twenty-eight, was old before her time. He still had the estate, of course, still had his positions as a magistrate and Master of the Hunt, still had his finger in all the appropriate pies – but life was an empty affair without his wife and the son who had seemed like another part of his own self. As for Stephen . . . He shook his big head.

'Time he stirred himself,' he said. 'Church at eleven, and then he could come round the estate with me, see what's what. He'll have to start taking an interest soon, make himself useful now he's finished with Cambridge. I'll need someone to hand over to eventually, and there's nobody else.' He looked down at his plate, frowning.

Hilary said nothing. She buttered her toast and cut it into narrow slices. Her father's eyes strayed back to the newspaper again.

'D'you think there'll be another election this year?' she asked. It had been talked of ever since Labour had got back in with their slim majority. A coalition was out of the question – the country had had six years of that during the war and, although it had worked well in those circumstances, neither of the main parties wanted it now. They wanted to work to their own policies.

90

'It's to be hoped so. Ridiculous, getting in with a majority like that – virtually a hung Parliament. Bad enough that they should have been brought in after the war. Gross ingratitude, that's what it was, after all Churchill had done for the country.'

'Well, Labour haven't been that bad,' Hilary said. 'They've brought in quite a few good measures – National Health insurance, pensions, better education for everyone. And I think people just wanted a change, after the war.'

'A *change*! For heaven's sake, Hilary, Government's not a suit of clothes or a strip of wallpaper, to be changed just because people are bored or there's a new fashion.' He folded his newspaper irritably. 'I dare say some of the steps they've taken – health and pensions – have been good enough, but they were on the cards before the war started. It was just a matter of waiting for the right time. As for education, I'm not so sure. What use would a grammar-school education be to a boy like Roy Pettifer, for instance, who's just going to take up an apprenticeship in a garage and work with his father? Or to a girl like young Jackie Tozer, working as a maid in our kitchen? It doesn't make sense.'

'It docs if they've got the intelligence to pass the scholarship examination,' Hilary argued. 'If a bright boy like Roy had a grammar-school education he might not take up an apprenticeship. He could go on to college, even university. There's no knowing what he could do. And Jackie's intelligent enough to do something far better than kitchen work. She could become a teacher, or even a doctor like Felicity Latimer.'

Her father stared at her. 'Teacher? Doctor? What nonsense is that? Girl like Jackie will get married before she's twenty and settle down with half a dozen babies round her feet. What's the use of the country paying for an education for that, hey? And what's this about young

Felicity? I'd have thought her parents would have more sense. She's far too young to be thinking of a career, anyway.'

'Well, her father's a doctor,' Hilary pointed out. 'He might be pleased to have Felicity following in his footsteps. Women doctors aren't unknown, after all.'

Squire Napier grunted. 'Doesn't mean they're a good thing. Doesn't make any difference what class a young woman is, anyway – she's still going to get married and have children, and then she's got to stay at home and look after them, no matter who she is. Same for Felicity as it is for young Jackie.'

Hilary was silent for a moment or two. Then she said quietly, 'Not every young woman gets married.'

Napier drew in a deep breath. He coughed a little and said gruffly, 'I'm sorry, my dear. I wasn't thinking. Although you would have been married by now, and had a youngster or two as well, if it hadn't been for – for . . .'

'For Henry being killed?'

'I wasn't going to say that. I was going to say "if it hadn't been for the war".'

'It comes to the same thing, doesn't it,' Hilary said, and struck her egg with the back of her spoon.

The door opened and they both looked up with some relief, tempered in the Squire's case by an immediate irritation, as Stephen Napier came in, wearing his dressing-gown and with his fair hair rumpled. He gave his father an abstracted smile and touched his sister's shoulder lightly as he passed behind her. Hilary's features softened and she dipped her spoon into the yolk of her egg.

'Any coffee left?' Stephen cupped his palm around the pot to feel the temperature and then poured himself a cup. 'Mm, that's the stuff to give the troops.' He brought the cup to the table and sat down opposite Hilary.

'I'm not sure how you'd know that,' Napier said acidly,

helping himself to more bacon. 'Since you've never been in any of the Services.'

'Well, that's hardly my fault. I was only seventeen when the war ended and I've been up at Cambridge since I left school. I dare say my call-up papers will come through soon enough.' He winked at Hilary and put on a passable imitation of his father's voice. 'Few months' square-bashing, soon make a man of me.'

Napier raised his head abruptly. 'And that's enough of your impertinence, my boy! Not that it isn't true. Discipline's what you need, and discipline's what you'll get once you're in the Army. And while we're on the subject—'

'While we're on the subject,' Stephen said, reaching for the toast, 'I don't want to go into the Army. I'm hoping for the RAF.'

'The *RAF*?'

'Yes. Why not? Much better fun than tramping round muddy fields covered in leaves. In fact, I'm thinking of signing on as a Regular and training to be a pilot.'

'A Regular? A *pilot*?' Gilbert Napier stared at his son and snapped, 'Don't talk such nonsense! You'll do your two years in my old regiment – I've put in a word already – and then come back here and start learning to run the estate.' His face darkened a little and Hilary knew that he was thinking of Korea. Not all the British regiments were being sent to the Far East, but the way things were going there was a chance. There must be people all over Britain who had already lost one young man in the Second World War and were dreading losing another.

Stephen spread home-made marmalade thickly on his toast. 'I'd rather go into the RAF.'

'Rather? *Rather*? What in God's name does that have to do with it? You've got a job to do here, don't you understand? You're going to inherit. What use will you be if you've spent all your time on an airfield? What sort of a job is a pilot anyway?'

'A pretty good one, I think. More comfortable than being in the Army, anyway. No mud, and you get back to your own bed every night.'

Napier stared at him. 'Is that all you can think about? Being *comfortable*?'

'No.' Stephen met his father's eye. 'I think about what I'd like to do with my life. And what I'd like to do, since I have to do National Service of some sort, is take the chance to be a pilot. I don't think I've got much chance of that by going as a squaddie for two years.'

'You wouldn't be a squaddie. You'd go in as an officer.'

'Jumping over the heads of other men. Sorry, Dad, I'd rather do things on my own merit than because of your influence.'

Napier stared at him, his face reddening with anger. Stephen continued to spread his toast but Hilary, watching them both, could see that his hand was trembling slightly.

'*My influence*? Don't you realise how fortunate you are to have the background you do? The family, the education, the *money*, behind you? I've never noticed you refusing any of these things before. Where do you think you'd have been without them, hey? D'you think you'd have gone to Cambridge, got that degree of yours, if you hadn't had *my influence* and all that goes with it?'

Stephen looked up. He too had noticed the tremble and laid his hand on the table. He spoke quietly, afraid that his voice would betray him as well. 'No, Dad, I don't suppose I would. And that's not fair, is it? As it happens, I do have a brain of sorts and I worked hard and got a First in Mathematics, but there were plenty of undergrads who didn't bother, men who were there because of *their* fathers' influence and would never have got to Cambridge otherwise. And there are people who ought to be there but don't have the chance, because their fathers *don't* have influence.' He paused, then said quietly, 'I'm grateful for everything I've had, Dad, but now I want to live my life on my own, without any help or influence. That's all.' He lifted his cup to his lips, his hand determinedly steady.

'It *isn't* all. Not as far as I'm concerned. You've got a job to do here, at Burracombe. You'll do your National Service, naturally, it's your patriotic duty, but once that's done you'll be needed here. Get that out of the way and you can come home and get on with your real job.'

'But that's just it!' Stephen exclaimed. 'It's *not* my real job. I was never intended to take over the estate. I never expected it – I'm not *suited* for it. Hilary would be better at it than me.'

Hilary opened her mouth quickly, but the Squire forestalled her. '*Hilary?* Don't be so ridiculous! She's got enough to do, running the house. As for not being suited to it, that's nonsense. Put your mind to it, you can do anything. And you don't have to remind me that you never expected to inherit.'

Napier's voice dropped on his last words and his eyes went to the mantelpiece where a portrait of his elder son hung. It had been painted when Baden had first joined the Army, at the beginning of the war, and showed him looking proud and smart in his uniform with the badge of the Devons on his lapels, his captain's three pips on his shoulder and his cap held under one arm. His ice-blue eyes, so like Gilbert Napier's, looked out steadily from beneath his smooth, dark hair and his lips were firm above a firmly set jaw. He had been killed in action less than six months after the portrait had been hung.

There was a silence. Hilary and Stephen stared at the portrait and then at each other. Stephen looked awkward, embarrassed and irritated. He put down his cup and said, a little too loudly, 'Father, you can't expect me to take on everything that Baden would have done. I can't *be* Baden.'

'Of course I know you can't "be" Baden – ridiculous suggestion. But you can be a very good substitute for him. You can do the job he would have done, if he'd been spared. It's what you *ought* to be doing – ought to be proud to do.'

Stephen shook his head violently. 'No! I'm not a substitute. I can't live his life for him. I keep telling you, I've got my own life to live – doesn't that count for anything?'

'Your *own* life? Isn't that just what I'm trying to tell you?' Gilbert Napier thumped his fist on the table. 'This *is* your life now. And you're damned lucky to have it, let me tell you.' The blue eyes, which could look like chips of ice, had darkened almost to black and his voice was low and tight. 'Your brother gave his life for his country – for this estate, this village. For me, for your mother, for you and your sister, for everything we've ever lived for. He gave his life so that our way of life could continue. So that England – oh yes, and Scotland and Wales and Ireland too, if you must have it – could go on being the England it's always been. And it's you, and men like you, who for one reason or another were fortunate enough to survive the war, who have to make sure that it does continue. Not by playing at being pilots. Not by messing about in punts up and down the Cam. But by getting your National Service done, learning a bit about what it means to be a man, and then coming back here and getting on with the job – the job of maintaining the style of living that made this country what it is. And you ought to think yourself privileged to do it,' he finished, his voice cracking a little. '*Damned* privileged.'

There was a short silence. Hilary and Stephen stared down at their plates. Then Hilary looked up at her father, but before she could speak, the Squire got up abruptly and strode towards the door.

'Going for a walk,' he announced, and the two black labradors scrambled to their feet from their place in front of the fire and dashed across the room. 'Be back in time for church.'

He shut the door hard behind him and Hilary met Stephen's eyes. 'You've really upset him, Steve.'

'I've upset *him*!' Stephen exclaimed. 'What about him upsetting me? It's my life he's trying to order, Hil. Look, I'm as sorry as anyone else about Baden, but it wasn't my fault he got killed. And it's not my fault it was him and not me,' he added in a lower tone, dropping his eyes again.

'Stephen! That's an awful thing to say. As if Daddy wished it had been you instead!'

'Well, doesn't he?' Stephen lifted his head. 'Don't you think he'd rather Baden had lived? If he'd been told he had to lose a son, which one d'you think he'd have chosen? Not Baden, that's for sure. Not the golden boy who never put a foot wrong – the son who was going to follow in his footsteps and be Squire one day. No, I'd have been the one he could do without – I've *always* been the one he could do without.'

'That's not fair, Steve.'

'Well, there's a lot of truth in it.' He looked squarely at his sister. 'You know that, Hil. And you know what it would be like for me if I had to stay at home and learn to run the estate. I'd hate it. I'd make a complete mess of it. And Dad would hate me for it.' He pushed his cup away and leaned his elbows on the table, resting his head between his palms. 'I'm just not suited for it.'

'Well, someone's going to have to do it,' she said.

'Why?' he demanded. 'Why does someone have to do it? Why, just because we happen to be born here, does it have to rule our lives? Look at you, Hil – you could be doing

97

something really interesting, something worthwhile, but you're trapped here, running the house for Dad just because Mother's not here. You could be married, have your own home and family—'

'No,' she said quietly. 'I don't think that's ever going to happen now.'

'Not while you're cooped up here, perhaps. But it could. And anyway, you could be doing something else with your life. It doesn't have to be given up for the estate. Same for me. Baden's not here, so I've got to give up my life. Why? What's so important about the estate that we have to sacrifice our whole lives to keep it going?'

'Because it's part of our family. Because it's been ours for generations.'

Stephen shook his head. 'That's no reason. Some other family could take it over if they wanted to. It could be sold. The farms could be sold – the tenants themselves might like the chance to buy them. It doesn't even have to be an estate.'

Hilary stared at him. 'Stephen, think what you're saying! That's exactly what Daddy *doesn't* want to happen – the estate being split up and sold. He wants it to stay as it is, as it's always been. He wants to preserve the English way of life. What you're saying would destroy it.'

'No,' he said. 'What I'm saying would change it. But it's changing anyway, Hil. It has to. The war's changed it. You know yourself, people aren't the same any more. I heard you and Dad talking just before I came in, about education. Girls being doctors, like Felicity. Boys like Roy Pettifer wanting to go to college. That's one of the things that the war has done – yes, and the Government too. The war showed ordinary people what they can do, given the opportunity, and the Government is giving them that opportunity. People don't want to be servants and slaves any more, they want to go further. And this Festival of

Britain that Dad's so keen on will change things even more.'

'How? How will it do that?'

'It'll show them what's out there,' he said. 'There'll be things at the Exhibition that will open your eyes, Hil. New scientific advances. Machines that can do all sorts of things. Factories are going to change. Homes will change. Farms will change. In a few years' time, we'll all be using tractors and machinery – there'll be no more horses on the land at all.'

'No more horses? But—'

'Not for work. There'll be horses for riding on, of course, and there'll still be hunting. But the carthorses and the big Shire and Clydesdale plough-horses – they'll be gone.' He reached out again for his coffee, sipped and wrinkled his nose. 'This has gone cold.'

'There's some more here.' Hilary reached absently for the pot and refilled her own cup as well. She stared into it for a minute or two. 'Steve, if you're right and there are all these changes, what d'you think will happen to the country? Will we lose our farms and countryside altogether? I don't think I could live here if that happened.'

'I don't know,' he said soberly. 'But it's not been much of a place to live since the war ended, has it? All the rebuilding, the shortages, the rationing . . . still going on years later. I tell you what, I'm not sure we're ever going to get over it all. This Festival, it's a good try. But will it work?'

'So, if you don't want to run the estate when you finish your National Service, what will you do?'

He looked up at her, his expression more serious than she had ever seen it. He seemed to consider for a moment, as if debating whether to tell her. Then he said, 'I meant it when I said I wanted to learn to fly, Hil. But after I've done my National Service, I'm thinking of emigrating. America,

Canada – somewhere like that. That's where the future is now. Not on some tinpot little estate, buried in Devon.' He nodded slowly, and then gave her his old, familiar grin. 'Tell you what, you could come with me. How'd you feel about that? Come and keep house for me if you like. It'd be a darned sight more interesting than keeping house for Dad.' He gripped her wrist and his eyes blazed suddenly into hers. 'Think about it, Hil! Just *think* about it.'

Chapter Ten

On New Year's Day the local Hunt assembled, as it did each year, in front of the Bell Inn. The shops were open, the scent of fresh bread issuing across the green from George Sweet's bakery, and hounds milled about, already eagerly sniffing the ground while members in both black and hunting-pink jackets sat tall and straight on their smartly clipped horses. Bernie Nethercott, his wife Rose and Dottie Friend were coming out of the inn bearing trays of glasses which they offered to the riders, and Constance Bellamy was standing by with a shovel and bucket ready to pick up any droppings.

'I pile 'em up in a corner and let 'em rot down, ready for the roses,' she explained to Stella Simmons, who was standing nearby. 'Best manure there is. Settling down all right, are you?'

'Yes, thank you.' Stella hesitated, not sure what to say next, but Constance was already speaking again.

'Time I came and had another look at the school,' she stated in the deep and forceful tones which seemed so incongruous in such a small woman. 'Grandfather endowed it, y'know. Take a personal interest, always have. Usually pop in sometime during the term – missed the Christmas party, touch of bronchitis.' She darted forward with her shovel as a large black horse deposited a heap of steaming dung on the road. 'Thank you, Sultan. Morning to you,

Gilbert,' she added, beaming up at the rider. 'Fine morning for it.'

Gilbert Napier nodded at her as his horse tossed its head and stamped one forefoot with impatience. 'Should have a good day.' The church clock struck eleven and he lifted one hand to the huntsman. 'Time to be off, Roger. Call 'em in.'

The huntsman, smart in his bright red coat and black hat, lifted his horn to his lips and blew. The scattered hounds immediately came together and set off along the lane, their tails like waving banners above a shifting kaleidoscope of black, yellow and cream bodies. The horses followed, their hooves clattering on the road and the riders lifting rhythmically up and down in the saddle. Stella, Constance Bellamy and the others stood watching and Dottie Friend heaved a sentimental sigh.

'Lovely, isn't it? I always like to see the Hunt. Real old country tradition, that is. Missed it during the war.'

'Foxes didn't though, did 'em!' Bernie Nethercott said. 'Anyway, it didn't stop altogether. Roger could still take hounds out.'

''Twasn't the same though, with no hunting pink and all the horses and riders.' Dottie turned to Stella. 'See, most of the younger men and women that were riding to hounds then were off serving somewhere. There were only Roger and a few farmers left, and they didn't have time for hunting. They kept the hounds and took 'em out when they could, but it were never like a real Hunt.'

Stella nodded and smiled, but in her heart she wasn't at all sure that she liked the idea of a fox being chased across fields and moorland by a pack of hounds, urged on by men and women on horseback. It seemed rather unfair – wouldn't just one or two dogs be enough? But there had been no fox-hunting in the village she'd lived in so briefly during the war and she was still learning about country ways. The first thing she had learned was not to question them, but simply to keep quiet and observe.

She turned and found Felix standing beside her, his corn-coloured hair shining in the January sunlight. He smiled down at her.

'Hello, Stella. We meet again. Happy New Year.'

'Happy New Year,' Stella said, feeling suddenly shy. It had taken her longer than she'd expected to get to sleep last night. The late hour, the gathering round the tree and the drink in the pub had all been unusual enough to keep her mind buzzing until after Dottie had come home, creeping about downstairs and tripping over the cat. She wasn't sure how to respond to the friendliness this young curate was showing her. He had to be friendly to everyone, it was his job, and he'd probably been as pleased to have her company as she'd been to have his. That was all it was.

'I'll be meeting you in a professional capacity soon,' he remarked. 'The vicar tells me we visit the school regularly to talk to the children.'

Stella nodded. 'It's hard *not* to meet people here anyway. I've only been here three or four days, and already I can't walk down the village street without running into half a dozen people I know.'

'And if you don't know them the first time, you will the second time,' he agreed with a grin. 'At least, they'll know you! Not that they wouldn't already. In my experience of villages, word gets round faster than lightning, and a new face stands out like a sore thumb. I don't mean that you look in the least like a sore thumb,' he added hastily.

Stella laughed. 'Did you grow up in a village?'

'Yes, in Cambridgeshire.' He glanced around the village green with its huge old oak tree, the cottages clustered around, the Bell Inn with its thatched roof and the church behind it. Beyond the fields and lanes the slopes of Dartmoor rose smooth and brown, frosted with white. 'It's rather different from this. You see, it's quite flat there, with the Fens and the ditches. The fields aren't hedged like they are here, so you can see for miles.'

'It sounds rather dull,' Stella observed, and immediately wished she hadn't. 'I mean, I'm sure it's very pretty really, but—'

Felix smiled. 'Actually, it is rather dull in comparison with Devon scenery, but the villages are attractive, and there's something about the wide expanse of sky . . . I suppose every part of the country has something to be said for it. Its own character.' They began to walk slowly along the lane, away from the green. 'Are you comfortable in your lodgings? You're living with Dottie Friend, aren't you, the barmaid at the pub?'

Stella nodded. 'That's right. She's a lovely person. I grew up in Hampshire.' She hesitated. There was nothing to be ashamed of in having been orphaned and grown up in a Children's Home, yet she knew that it sometimes embarrassed people when she spoke of it, and it was too complicated to explain anyway. 'I saw this job advertised and applied for it, and here I am.'

'And do you like it?'

'Well, I haven't started yet,' she said, raising bright eyes at him. 'The new term starts next week, remember. But I'm sure I will, once I can understand what the children say. The local dialect seems a bit like a foreign language at the moment.'

'The vicar keeps introducing me to people and I haven't the faintest idea what they're saying, either,' he confessed. 'I just wonder if they understand *me*.'

'Oh, they don't have any problem. They're used to listening to the radio, you see, so they hear ordinary speech all the time.' They arrived at the gate to Dottie Friend's cottage, and Stella laid her hand on the latch. 'It's been nice to meet you again, Mr Copley.'

'Felix,' he said, looking into her eyes. 'I told you yesterday, I'm hoping everyone will call me Felix.'

Stella looked back at him, a little nonplussed. She'd been taught that you called people by their surnames until you knew them well, and she'd been surprised when he'd called her Stella just now. She said doubtfully, 'I'm not sure that they will. Not till they know you better, anyway.'

Before Felix could reply, Dottie herself came panting up the lane, a laden shopping-basket hooked over her arm. She gave them both a beaming smile and Stella hastily opened the gate to let her through.

'What a morning! 'Tis always busy when the Hunt meets, but I think the world and his wife must have been there today. Bernie let me off to do a bit of shopping but I've got to go back straight away. I just thought I'd put some dinner up for you, my pretty, before I go, that's if you'm ready for it. 'Tis early, I know.' She gave Felix a quick, friendly nod. 'You'm the new curate. Heard you preach yesterday – not up to Vicar's standard, of course, but nice enough. Well, sorry I can't stop now, but I've to go up to the Barton when the inn closes, and I'm all behind like a duck's tail as it is. So if you'm ready for your dinner, Stella?'

'Oh – yes, of course.' Stella followed her through the gate and turned to smile at Felix. 'I'll see you again, Mr Copley. It's been nice to talk to you.' She followed Dottie into the cottage and the door closed behind them.

Felix turned away. It was his free day and he'd rather hoped to persuade the pretty young schoolteacher to join him for a walk. He might even have coaxed her into calling him Felix.

Never mind – there was plenty of time yet. All the time in the world, in fact.

It was gone three when Hilary clattered into the stableyard

on Beau, her bay gelding. She slipped off his back, rubbed his white nose in gratitude for a good day out, and fastened him to the ring outside the stable door, ready to wash him down. They were both exhausted and covered in mud, but Beau's needs came first. Once he was in his stall, munching at his feed, Hilary could go indoors and soak in a hot bath.

Her father had not yet come home, and she was grateful for the peace and quiet of the yard. She began her tasks of making Beau clean and comfortable, feeling the satisfaction of hard exercise.

They hadn't killed a fox; it didn't much matter whether they did or not, as far as Hilary was concerned, and she suspected that quite a few of the other Hunt members felt much the same. The unpredictability of the ride was what they enjoyed, the chase across fields and moorlands, never knowing where they would go next, taking hedges and ditches and streams as they came; the wildest way there was of riding horses in England these days, and the most exhilarating.

As she worked, she thought of her brother's outburst yesterday morning. He had gone off after breakfast and spent the day at Little Burracombe with his friend Jeremy Boulding. Their father had also been uncommunicative, coming home from church to shut himself up in his study, and Hilary had found herself alone, without even the company of Jackie Tozer, who came in every day except Sunday. Jackie and the gardener-cum-stableman Josh Crocker, with the occasional help of Dottie Friend, were all that remained of the staff of twelve kept before the war, and Hilary spent her days doing work her mother would never have dreamed of doing. Riding Beau was all the time she had off from the house.

How had this happened, she wondered as she rubbed down the horse's legs. How had she become what wasn't much more than a skivvy? She thought of her years in the

ATS – years when she'd had a responsible job, when she'd been expected to use her initiative, driving important people in a car that was better than any her father had ever owned, respected and accepted for who *she* was and what she could do, not who her father was or where she came from. I was myself during the war, Hilary thought, combing the mud from Beau's coat. I've never really been myself since.

Even Stephen, who had talked so excitedly about his plans to emigrate, who had seemed to want to include her in those plans, had seen her as no more than a housekeeper. In truth, he was no better than their father; whatever he wanted to do with his life, it hadn't occurred to him that Hilary might have a life as well, that she might want to spend it in her own way, be just as adventurous.

I meant to do something, she thought, brushing clots of mud from the horse's long black tail. When the war ended and I was demobbed from the ATS, I meant to look for something else, for some real work. The other girls had – her friend Rosemary, for instance, had become a stewardess on one of the new airlines and now flew all over Europe. I could have done that, Hilary thought. But when she thought honestly about it, she knew that most of the young women she had known during the war had simply done what was always expected of them – they'd got married, started families and settled down.

Perhaps they were happy with that. But a tiny worm of doubt moved in her mind. Would she really have enjoyed such a life? Or would she have come to feel just as frustrated and unfulfilled as she did now?

Beau whickered and she realised that she had been scrubbing the same flank for several minutes. She apologised and put her arm under his neck to hold his big warm head close to hers. They stood cheek to cheek for a moment, then she moved away and unhooked his rein to lead him into the stable. His feed – a mixture of oats, bran, maize and linseed – and haynet were already in place and he began to eat at once. Hilary closed the door to his stall and stood for a moment watching him and listening to his satisfied munching. Now for that hot bath, and then it would be time to think about dinner. And Val Tozer was coming over afterwards so they could have a good gossip over a glass of ginger wine or home-made sloe gin.

'I suppose I ought to be grateful that I've got a nice place to live and don't have to slave in a factory or an office,' she said later, when the dishes were cleared away – Val had arrived just in time to help, despite Hilary's insistence that she sit at the kitchen table and watch. Then Hilary got out the bottles and held them up enquiringly, and they settled down in two old armchairs by the Aga with a glass of sloe gin each.

'Or give farmers blanket baths,' Val said. 'You know Olly Sedge? He's just had his appendix out. Sometimes I think it would be better if I worked in Plymouth or Exeter in a hospital where I wasn't likely to know all the patients. It didn't bother me, I'm used to it, but the poor man didn't know where to look so he just shut his eyes and we pretended we'd never seen each other before.'

'Did you have to manage all by yourself?' Hilary asked. 'He must weigh twenty stone if he's an ounce.'

'He does. He nearly broke our scales when he came in. Well, he might lose a few pounds now. He's on a light diet and I can tell you, he doesn't like it much!'

Hilary smiled. 'That's another career I can cross off my list, then. I don't think I could give blanket baths to people like Olly Sedge. Or anyone else, for that matter.'

'What would you really like to do?' Val asked curiously. 'I mean, if you hadn't had to come home when you did, what would you have done?'

'I don't really know. That's part of the trouble. All my upbringing was aimed at fitting me for the sort of life I'm leading now – running a house, looking after men. Only I was supposed to be married and have my own family. Perhaps it would be all right if I had. If Henry hadn't been killed . . . What about you, Val? You lost your fiancé too. You wouldn't be nursing now if Eddie had lived.'

Val said nothing for a moment or two. She gazed at the purple liquid in her glass and finally said, 'I don't know, Hil. I don't know what I'd have been doing.'

Hilary glanced at her in surprise. There had been an odd note in Val's voice. She said, 'Well, you'd have been married, wouldn't you? And Eddie would have come out of the Army and gone back into farming, I suppose. That's what he was doing before the war, wasn't it?'

'Yes, but I don't think he'd have gone back to it. He was a mechanic in the Army, working on tanks, and I think he'd have stayed on. He liked the life. He liked seeing different places, and he liked working with engines. I don't think he would ever have gone back to farming.' She sipped her drink and added, 'There might not have been any jobs for him anyway. You know what an awful time farmers had during the war, with all those restrictions and everything. They couldn't make their own decisions any more, over their own land that they knew better than anyone.' Her voice rose in indignation. 'Look at Arnie Betterswell, he'd built up a lovely dairy herd and he was told to sell them all off and grow potatoes instead! Where was the sense in that? Didn't we need milk any more? Couldn't someone with decent arable grow potatoes?'

'I know.' Hilary had been away when most of this was happening although, like Val, she'd heard all about it. But Val went on as if she hadn't spoken.

'And there was that poor man over at Buckland. They told him he had to plough up two fields and put them down to wheat, and if he didn't do it he'd be evicted. He was *dying*, Hil, and Dad and some of the others wrote to tell them so, but did they take any notice? No, they didn't. They wrote back a pompous letter about their decision "not being reversible" or some such nonsense. It was cruel.'

'What did he do? Surely they didn't actually turn him out?'

'Oh yes, they did. I saw it myself – it was heartbreaking. He was out in the lane himself, looking as if he was at death's door, which he was, and his wife crying her eyes out. All their possessions were just dumped out in the lane and they had nowhere to go, nowhere. In the end the other farmers got together and brought their carts round to take the stuff to any barns where they had a bit of space, and the couple went to relatives in Plymouth. The man died a few weeks later. I don't know what happened to his wife but someone told me that some of their things are still in the barns; she just never came back to collect them.'

Hilary stared at her. 'That's awful. I didn't realise it had been that bad.'

'Oh, he wasn't the only one. Some people actually went and lived in shacks – *henhouses* – because they had nowhere to go. And they didn't get any compensation, you know, not a penny. It didn't make any difference whether they owned their farms or were tenants, or how much money they'd spent to improve them. They had nothing. And they couldn't even appeal. The "War Ag" – the Ministry of Agriculture – was above the law.' She leaned forward a little. 'And who do you think got the farms when the poor farmers were thrown out, Hil? I'll tell you. As often as not, it was friends of the War Ag men themselves. They put their sons in, some of them, so that they would be exempted from military service.'

'That's terrible,' Hilary said, shocked. 'It's corruption.' She thought for a moment, then said a little doubtfully,

'How do you know all this, Val? I mean, are you really sure it's true?'

'Oh yes! They formed a union, you see, and Dad went along to the meetings in London. Actually, the ones who owned their farms were offered them back at the end of the war, but a lot of them had lost heart by then. Some of them were dead, anyway. Some had even killed themselves. There was one poor man in Hampshire who refused to plough up four acres – four acres, Hil – and he ended up under siege in his house, surrounded by police. They put gas down his chimney but he had his gas-mask on so that was no good. And then he shot a policeman and injured him so they shot him dead. All over four acres!' She took a bigger sip of her drink and added bitterly, 'Who'd want to come back to farming? We kept the country fed during the war, but it was because people like Dad and the other farmers worked all the hours God sent – no thanks to stupid men from London who didn't know one end of a pitchfork from another. I'd soon have shown them which end was which, if I'd had the chance!'

Hilary laughed, and Val smiled a little unwillingly. 'It's true, though, isn't it,' she went on. 'It happened here as well. Your father had to plough up all those beautiful lawns and grow what he was told to grow, and they're only just getting back to what they were.'

'Well, Dad wasn't actually here much then,' Hilary said. 'He was away for most of the war and we had that estate manager looking after things, and the house was requisitioned. But you know, Eddie could still have worked in the country – farms are going to need mechanics when everyone stops using horses and goes over to tractors. Your sister told me the other day that young Roy Pettifer thinks there'll be more work than ever.'

'Yes, I suppose so,' Val said without much interest.

'Anyway, Eddie got killed, didn't he, so that was the end of that.'

Hilary looked at her. 'You do think you and Eddie would have got married, don't you?'

Val gave her a quick glance, then looked down at her drink again. 'Yes, of course. Why?'

'I don't know, it's just that sometimes when you talk about him – well, it's as if there's something else on your mind. And when we were in Egypt . . .'

'Well?' Val demanded when Hilary hesitated. 'What about when we were in Egypt?' She met Hilary's eyes, and Hilary saw something in them that disturbed her. 'What about it?' Val repeated. 'What do you mean? What are you hinting at?'

'Nothing! I didn't mean anything. Really I didn't. It's just that – well, sometimes I wondered if you were really as much in love with Eddie after all. Look, it *happens*,' Hilary went on desperately, trying to take that anger out of Val's face. 'It happened a lot then. Girls got engaged and their fiancés went away, and they realised they didn't really love them after all. Everything was so *hurried* in those days. And sometimes they met someone else, and—'

'Well, it didn't happen to me,' Val said tersely. She put down her glass, still with some sloe gin in it. 'I think I'd better be going. I've got an early start in the morning.'

'Val, no!' Hilary put out her hand. 'Don't go like that, please. I didn't mean anything by it. I wouldn't have blamed you anyway. But there were times when you – well, you just weren't around so much and I couldn't help wondering . . .'

'I was working. I was a *nurse*. We had busy times.'

'I know,' Hilary said. 'I'm sorry, Val. I shouldn't have said anything. Don't go, please.'

Val hesitated for a moment, then drew in a deep breath and picked up her glass. 'I could do with a drop more of this,' she said, and Hilary heaved a sigh of relief and poured more of the dark, glistening drink.

'You'd better not have too much. You won't be able to walk home.'

'I know. And I don't want a hangover in the morning.' Her tight face softened and she gave Hilary a wicked grin. 'You're a fine one to talk, anyway. Remember that night we went to a ball in the Officers' Mess? *I* saw you, with that blond Subaltern! If I'd had a camera with me, I could have blackmailed you for years.'

They laughed together and went off, as they often did, into a stream of reminiscence about their days in Egypt. Val relaxed and Hilary made a mental note not to suggest again that her friend hadn't loved the man she'd been engaged to marry. It was odd, though – they'd often talked just as frankly, and Val had never taken offence before. Her reaction had been quite unexpected.

But for the rest of the evening Val seemed cheerful enough, and it wasn't until after she had gone and Hilary was filling her hot-water bottle that her thoughts returned to her friend's moment of anger.

I was a tactless fool, she thought. How would I have felt if someone had suggested that I didn't love Henry? It would have been like suggesting I was glad he'd died and that I didn't have to marry him.

She stood for a moment, staring at her reflection in the dark, uncurtained window, and felt the chill of guilt creep into her heart.

Chapter Eleven

'Attention, everybody!'

Dr Latimer rapped the small wooden gavel that had been presented to the village hall by Gilbert Napier's father, the 'old Squire', and the hubbub died down a little. He waited until everyone had fallen silent and then began, in the pleasant voice that had asked most of them, at one time or another, to put out their tongue or say 'aah' or tell him how they felt this morning.

'Right. Good evening, everyone, and let me take this opportunity of wishing you all a rather belated Happy New Year. Thank you all very much for turning out on such a cold evening. I'm very pleased to see so many of you and hope you have lots of ideas for celebrating the Festival of Britain here in Burracombe.'

The audience, numbering about twenty, gazed back at him with stolid expressions. You would never have thought they'd been chatting with animation only minutes ago. The doctor waited for a moment, then said, 'Perhaps I should run through the official plans for the Festival. As you know, it was the King's idea, to give the country a chance to show the world that we're picking ourselves up after the war and are ready to build a new world in the peace. So some of us thought it would be a good idea to get together and decide what we want to do about it.'

He paused again and once more there was silence. Then Ernie Crocker, who was churchwarden and the oldest of

Ted Tozer's farr
but that be all ha
do with us dowi

'And I might ¡
doing something.
visit the Exhibiti

'Yes, but you'r
you?' Jackie Toze
with Roy Pettifei
cover of folded ar
dreary old Exhibit

'Dreary? It we
indignantly and he
will be highly educ
with interesting exh

'Well, I don't mind going to see that,' Jack
'and that Skylon they're talking about, but I don't see w
we can't go to the Fun Fair as well. They're going to have a
treetop walk and a Rotor, and all sorts of rides and
roundabouts.'

'Roundabouts!' Ernie snorted. 'That's all you youngsters
thinks about. Bain't Tavistock Goosey Fair enough for
you? Plenty of roundabouts there. Mrs Warren's right – it's
education you'm going to need in this brave new world they
keeps telling us about. Anyway,' he added, 'what's a Rotor
when it's at home? I've never even heard of it.'

'Oh, it's a new thing, Mr Crocker,' Roy Pettifer said
eagerly. 'It works by centrifugal force, you see. People go in
and stand against a wall built in a circle, and it suddenly
starts to whirl round and they all get kind of stuck against
it. They go right up in the air and the girls' skirts—' He
caught Mrs Warren's eye and faltered into silence. 'Anyway,' he mumbled after a moment, 'there's all sorts of
things there and I think Jackie's right. If we're going in a
coach we ought to go to the Fun Fair as well.'

Warren said after a frosty
ng Burracombe should be
e to attend.'

elix Copley, felt his elbow dig
ps quivered and she slid him a
ith Basil and Grace Harvey, Felix had
dinner at the Barton just after the New
had felt an immediate liking for the friendly,
g young curate. He had come into the church
e was arranging flowers and they had spent a
t quarter of an hour leaning against the ancient stone
, chatting and discovering a shared sense of humour.
ather a wicked one for a clerical gentleman, she had
reproved him, but he'd only grinned and twinkled his blue
eyes at her and told her that clergymen needed a sense of
humour. 'I'm sure God has one,' he said. 'Who was it said
that He must have had, to make ducks?'

'I've no idea,' she'd said, laughing, 'but I suppose you
must be right. Think of donkeys and kangaroos!'

'And elephants,' he said. 'They've got a sense of humour
too. And three-toed sloths – not that they've got one, but
they always make me laugh just to think of them. And—'

Hilary brought her mind sharply back to the discussion.
They were still arguing over the Fun Fair.

'But if it's the *King's* idea . . . ' little Jean Friend, who
ran the village Post Office and sweetshop, began timidly,
and her sister Jessie nodded her white head and joined in so
that their voices sounded like the twittering of birds. 'I'm
sure the King wouldn't agree to anything that wasn't quite
suitable.'

Joyce Warren opened her mouth and then closed it again
while the rest of the audience watched in fascination. It
wasn't very often that they saw their WI President and
doyenne of the Bridge Club, the Drama Group and the new
Garden Society at a loss for words and the fact that it was

the timid little twin sisters from the Post Office who had brought this about was something to treasure. There were a few chuckles, quickly muffled by gloved hands.

Charles Latimer decided that it was time to regain control of the meeting. 'Be that as it may, and it could well be a matter for discussion at another time, the purpose of this meeting is not to discuss what will be happening in London, but what will be happening here in Burracombe. Do we want to take part in the celebrations that will be taking place all over the country and put on some kind of event – or events – of our own here in the village? The Festival of Britain in Britain itself, rather than simply in the capital city.'

The small burst of animation caused by Jackie's complaint died away and once again the audience gazed at him with inscrutable expressions. He glanced towards Joyce Warren but she was looking straight ahead with her chin raised. He sighed.

'I'm sure some of you will have ideas. Some kind of village party, perhaps? A fête? The WI is always so good at putting on that kind of thing. A sports day for the children? The school might help there. Might the Drama Group perform an entertainment of some kind?' He glanced again at Mrs Warren, and this time she made a reluctant response, lifting one shoulder slightly and deigning to meet his eye. 'I was wondering about your idea of a pageant,' he said encouragingly.

Joyce Warren looked a little nonplussed for a moment and then rallied. 'A pageant? Well yes, I did mention the idea some time ago.' It had been two years ago, in fact, and nobody had shown the slightest enthusiasm. 'I'm sure it would be quite appropriate. Britain Through the Ages – the development of our nation. Yes, it has possibilities.'

'Especially as relating to Devon,' the doctor said gently. 'I think that was your idea, wasn't it? The people of our county who have done so much to put Britain in the forefront of the world. People like Drake – a local boy, indeed – and Raleigh. I'm sure there are many others.'

'I don't believe it was her idea at all,' Felix whispered to Hilary. 'He's just handing it to her on a plate.'

'What does it matter, so long as she takes it on?' Hilary murmured back, and blushed as Mrs Warren turned her head to see who was talking. She lowered her eyes quickly and stared at her clasped hands.

Dr Latimer was speaking again. 'Well, that's excellent, Mrs Warren. I'm sure we can leave that in your capable hands.' He moved on swiftly, before Joyce could make a protest. 'Now, what other ideas can we come up with, I wonder?'

The silence was even deeper this time. It was clear that nobody else was going to take the risk of being manoeuvred into taking on some project without having plenty of time to think about it. The doctor waited a few moments until the silence became embarrassing, and then smiled. 'You're all busy thinking of ideas, I know. Well, let's have another meeting in – let's say a fortnight from now, shall we? And then we can really begin to make plans. A sequence of events throughout the summer, I thought, with the pageant as a grand finale.' He looked round the gathering. 'Try to bring a few more people along to the next meeting, if you can. The whole village is going to be involved, so it's only proper that as many as possible should be here right from the very start.'

He tapped the gavel again and leaned over to speak to Miss Kemp, the school headmistress, who was in the front row. The rest of the company looked at each other and began to scrape their chairs as they got up. A low hum of conversation started as they put their chairs back against the walls and left the hall.

Dr Latimer and Miss Kemp smiled at each other. 'Well,

that's started the ball rolling,' he said, pulling on a pair of thick gloves. 'They'll talk about nothing else for the next fortnight.'

'That's right,' she agreed. 'The real meetings take place in the pub or the village shop or at field gates. It's as if the four walls of the village hall stifle them.'

Felix, walking through the village with Hilary, asked, 'Why do they seem so sure? I didn't think anyone appeared at all interested in doing anything at all.'

'That's villagers for you,' she said. 'Won't say a word at any meeting that seems at all official, but the seed's been sown and as Miss Kemp said, the real meetings will be taking place at this very moment.' She glanced at the warmly lit windows of the Bell Inn. 'Probably in there.'

'A much more comfortable venue,' he grinned. 'I don't suppose you would like to go in with me and see?'

Hilary shook her head. 'Not tonight, I'm afraid. I've got some things to do at home. You'd better go on your own.'

'Another time, perhaps,' he suggested, and she looked at him and said, 'Yes. Perhaps.' They had stopped and she put out her hand for him to shake. 'Goodnight, Felix.'

'Goodnight, Hilary,' he said, and watched as she walked through the big open gateway and up the Barton drive.

Stella had been to the meeting as well. She walked back along the lane to Dottie's cottage and slipped through the door into the warmth of the living room. The lamp had been left burning low and she turned it up and sank into the old armchair in front of the glowing range.

Her first week at the school seemed to have gone quite well. There had been no new children starting after Christmas, so even the youngest knew where everything was and what should be done. They'd been primed by Miss Kemp to be helpful, and were eager to guide Stella through her first few days.

'This is where we hangs our coats. We'm not allowed to wear our boots in the classroom.' A row of diminutive Wellington boots stood on the cold stone floor of the lobby. 'The lavvies are outside.' A small girl with red curls led her out into the playground and into a lean-to building round the corner, where there were three cubicles, each with a wooden seat over the earth closet. 'It stinks,' the redhead informed her cheerfully, 'but we'm used to it and the nightsoil cart comes round every week. The boys have got theirs the other side of the door. You and Miss Kemp have got your own; we're not allowed in there even when we can't wait.'

Next she was shown the classroom. The 'babies' who had started in September at the age of five had low tables and small wooden chairs in one corner, while the bigger children had desks and benches. Stella had six 'babies' and a dozen older children, some of whom would go up into Miss Kemp's class next door when they were seven or eight. Altogether, there were thirty-eight children in the school, coming from outlying farms and hamlets as well as from Little Burracombe and Burracombe itself. When they were eleven they would take the 'scholarship' exam which would determine whether they went on to the grammar school in Tavistock or to the secondary modern.

'There's the blackboard,' her self-appointed guide informed her. 'You has to write our lessons on there, see, only the babies can't read. They play with beads and things. And you got to watch out for the boys. They'm proper little terrors.'

'You'm a fine one to talk, Janet Crocker,' declared a big, rough-looking boy with black hair and eyebrows, who looked at least nine. 'You gets into more trouble than anyone.'

The red-haired girl poked out her tongue at him and he put both thumbs to his temples and waggled his fingers, screwing up his nose as he did so. She gave a yell of fury and dashed at him, and Stella found herself having to stop a fight even before the morning had properly begun.

Still, after that they had settled down quite well and, determined not to give self-important little Janet Crocker the satisfaction of seeing them with beads, she'd been able to start the babies off with some paper to draw on while she set the bigger children a writing exercise. Then she went back to the babies with a reading book, and having looked over the various standards of writing started to form a kind of teaching plan that would cover all abilities.

As the days went on, she'd got to know all the children by name and was beginning to get to know their personalities. On the whole, they were pleasant, easy children but by Wednesday she had identified three potential troublemakers – Brian Madge, the big, black-haired boy, who looked nine but was in fact not yet eight, his arch-enemy Janet Crocker, who was bossy and never stopped talking, and a small boy who looked exactly like a cherub. Not that he'd actually caused any trouble yet, but Stella had learned to be suspicious of little boys who looked like cherubs.

She had enjoyed her first week, but she was glad it was Friday. Two whole days to recover and relax, and plan her lessons for next week! After school today, she and Miss Kemp had had a cup of tea together in the headmistress's tiny office and the older woman had told Stella that she'd started well. 'I love to hear the little ones singing, and you've taught them two new songs already. They like you.'

'Well, it's early days yet,' Stella said. 'They're nice children. And I'm learning the dialect quite well – I only had to ask Barry Stacey to repeat himself twice today.'

'You're settling in very well,' the headmistress said. 'You'll be part of the village in no time.'

Stella wasn't too sure about that; she knew how long it

took for strangers to become 'part of' a village. But the meeting this evening had made her feel a little more as if she belonged. She put some more wood on the fire and sat back in her chair.

The room was full of memorabilia from Dottie's life as a dresser in the theatre. Photographs and playbills lined the walls, many of them featuring 'her' actress, but there were other pictures too – sepia prints of ancient ladies in thick coats, with sticks, or family groups with everyone sitting up very straight and stiff, looking as if they were held in clamps. Stella remembered reading once that the early photographs took so long to expose that the sitters really were clamped, to stop them moving and blurring the picture. She got up to take a closer look at some of them, wondering who the people were. Members of Dottie's family, she supposed – grandparents, cousins and so on.

Nearly all the photographs had been taken before the war. There hadn't been much film to be had during the war, and the family photos seemed to stop in the late 1930s. There were a few of Dottie herself, with 'her actress', and then no more. Stella sat down again, feeling a little sad.

She had no photographs of her own family. Everything like that had been lost when they were bombed out. Babies had been born, grown up a little and then died, without any pictorial record being made of them. Her own mother, father and sister, and her baby brother – all no more than memories. There would never be any pictures of them to hang on a cottage wall, fading as the years went by but still there for someone to gaze at and wonder about.

The one picture that had been saved was the wedding photo of her parents, which her mother had always taken to the air-raid shelter with her when there was a raid on. But after that awful night when that second, fatal bomb had fallen, it had disappeared and Stella had never seen it again. She felt suddenly lonely, the grief sweeping through her once more as it had done so often over the years, and she wished she had it now, to look at and hold and weep over. It seemed so cruel that she should lose so much and not even have that one small thing.

She got up, put the guard over the fire, and went to bed so that Dottie should not come in from the pub and find her crying.

The bellringers were at their usual table in the pub, slaking their thirst with a pint of ale each. As it was their practice night, they hadn't been at the meeting but had sent Ted Tozer's cousin, Norman, as their representative. Dottie Friend was there too, leaning her sturdy arms on the bar as she chatted with the regulars.

'Well into the new year now, aren't we? And just think, ten years ago those awful Blitzes were just starting. My stars, when you look back and remember all that's happened in that time!' Her face sobered. ''Tis a good job us didn't know what was to come. And a good job us can't know the future now, either.'

'Now then, Dottie, don't be so gloomy,' Bernie Nethercott chided her. 'That's not like you. Little ray of sunshine you are, as a rule, so no more of that long face. You'll turn the beer sour.'

'Oh, I'm not being gloomy – I'm just saying, that's all.' Dottie straightened up and began to draw Ted Tozer's pint. 'Live for the day, that's my motto, and be thankful for what you've got. That'll be a tanner, Ted, if you please.'

'No, I'm paying the full round tonight,' Ted said. The bellringers normally operated by their own agreed rule, each to pay for his own drinks. 'Being the first practice night of the new year and all. And to thank the team for being such a good 'un.' He turned, his pewter tankard in his hand, and lifted it high. 'Here's to all of you – to all the good ringing you've done this past year, and to more of the same in nineteen-fifty-one. Let's see a few more cups and trophies in the tower, shall us? Especially the Bill Barnaby Shield – let's make this the year we get it back from Little Burracombe.'

The others responded with cheers and nods. They were a keen competition band, going round to all the other towers in the area whenever there was a ringing contest and, as often as not, coming home with a cup, shield or First Certificate to pin proudly on the wall of the ringing chamber. But the William Barnaby Shield had eluded them for the past two years now – an especially bitter pill to swallow when the ringer in whose memory it had been presented had been a past captain of Burracombe itself.

The two villages, Burracombe and Little Burracombe, standing on opposite sides of the river, had been locked in conflict for longer than anyone could remember. The rivalry was often friendly – on the surface, at least – but sometimes went deep, and there had been times when real feuds had broken out. The ringers of both villages were always ready to help each other out, should a band be needed to ring for a wedding or some other event, but when it came to the competition they were deadly enemies. And the fact that Little Burracombe held a shield that Burracombe considered belonged rightly in Bill Barnaby's home tower, was a real bone of contention.

'They only won it by half a fault last time,' Norman Tozer remarked, sucking his beer noisily through his bristly grey moustache. 'Us'll get it back come May, see if us don't.'

The other ringers nodded their agreement. Nathan Pettifer, Ernie Crocker and George Sweet had all been in the team for years, getting back to the tower the minute they were allowed to after the war, for most of which the bells had remained silent. There were a few younger ones coming along now, too – Tom Tozer, Nathan's son Roy,

Vic Nethercott who was away doing his National Service at the moment, and a couple of boys from one of the outlying moorland farms on the edge of the parish – but none of them were yet considered good enough to take part in a competition. The older men were jealous of their position and not likely to give over a rope in favour of some youngster who had only been ringing for two or three years.

'Tell you what I've been thinking,' Norman Tozer said suddenly. 'This Festival the doctor was talking about at this meeting I just been to – we ought to be doing summat for that. A special peal, mebbe even a competition. Put on a bit of bowling on the village green, that sort o' thing. What d'you reckon?'

'I'm not sure about a competition,' Ted Tozer said at last, speaking in his habitual slow, thoughtful way. 'Didn't you say Mrs Warren's getting up a pageant? Us ought to ring for that, get the whole thing off to a good start. But a competition . . . that'd have to be on a different day. Us couldn't have it on Pageant Day, 'twouldn't do at all.'

'Well, there's plenty more days in the year,' his son Tom said, speaking up from the end of the long wooden table. 'And from what Norman's been telling us, seems the pageant's going to be on August Bank Holiday. Us could put on our competition on the Saturday. And I tell you what – why not have a novice competition as well, for ringers that haven't ever rung in one? That'd give some of the younger chaps a chance.'

Some of the older men looked down their noses at this suggestion, but Jimmy Sweet, who lived with his grand-father George, nodded enthusiastically. 'I reckon that's a good idea. Me and Roy've been ringing a few years now, it's time we had a crack at a competition but you chaps won't ever let us.'

'Well, and don't it make sense?' Ernie Crocker demanded.

As a farmworker, Ted Tozer was his boss and Tom very nearly so, but in the ringing chamber he was any man's equal. 'If us wants to win the competitions, us has to put our best chaps in, stands to reason. And me and your dad and Bob and Nathan and Norman here have all been ringers twenty years or more. You never even touched a rope till three years ago.'

'And whose fault was that?' Tom demanded quickly. 'Hitler's, weren't it? Had to go off to war, didn't we? But we're pretty good now and I reckon that with young Roy Nethercott and Vic, if he was back from the Army, we could make a decent fist of it. Have to have one of you older chaps in as well,' he added, 'unless we could teach someone else in the time.'

'And that us'll never do!' Norman Tozer slammed his tankard down and glared at him. 'There's nobody on this earth could learn to handle a bell well enough to ring in a competition by summer. Make us all a laughing stock, that would.'

'Well, all right, so we'd still need one of you,' Tom shrugged. 'But that could be in the rules – maybe up to two experienced ringers, to keep things steady like.' He turned to his father. 'What d'you think, Dad?'

Ted sucked in a deep breath and folded his lips together, thinking. Then he glanced at his cousin Norman, whose dark face was still glowering, and made up his mind. 'I reckon we could think about it,' he said at last. 'We'll have a talk next practice, when us have had time to turn it over in our minds. There's a lot to think about, see – who to have for judges, how many certificates we gives out, whether to go in for a trophy as well . . . it needs a lot of deciding. But it don't seem too bad an idea to me. Not too bad at all.' He slid another glance at Norman. 'Anyway, we'd better drink up now and be on our way. It's getting on for ten and Bernie's wanting to shut up shop. He called out

126

for last orders five minutes ago.' He lifted his tankard again. 'And before we all goes our separate ways, I want to make another toast. A Happy New Year to all of us, and plenty of good ringing. Here's to the Fifties. Hope for the future.'

'That's right,' they agreed, and lifted their own tankards in response. 'The Fifties. Hope for the future.'

They stood up and took their tankards back to the bar, where Rose and Dottie would wash them and hang them on their hooks, to be kept for their owners' next visit. Then they made their way out into the frosty night and stood for a moment breathing the icy air and looking up at the stars.

'I tell you what,' Tom said to his father as they began to walk along the lane. 'I reckon things are going to start looking up a bit now. We've got over the war, almost, and this big Festival will show the world what Britain can do. Things are bound to be different now, Dad. There's going to be a lot of changes in the next few years.'

'Changes?' Ted said, stopping to light his pipe. 'Well, mebbe there will be up in London and places like that. But not down here in Burracombe. Nothing ever changes much in Burracombe.'

Chapter Twelve

'I've asked that young artist feller to tea,' Dottie announced one morning. 'Luke, his name is, Luke Ferris. I dare say you've seen him about the village.'

'Oh yes, I've met him,' Stella said, 'when I came for my interview. But I haven't seen him since then.'

'He've been away over Christmas and New Year – off to London, so I heard. He'll have friends there, being an artist. Anyway, he came into the pub a night or two ago and I thought he looked a bit lonely, so I asked him to come in this afternoon. You'll be here, won't you? I'll make some of my scones and there's still a piece of Christmas cake left in the tin.'

Stella looked forward to meeting Luke again. His welcome as she climbed off the bus on that October morning had given her a warm glow that had, she felt sure, carried her through the ordeal of the interview. Not that everyone else hadn't been welcoming too, but that first moment had been vital. And later, as she'd chatted to him at the top of the wood, she'd felt a sense of instant friendship – as if they'd known each other for years. She'd been vaguely disappointed not to run into him in the village during her first week or so back.

The infant class ended the afternoon at three-fifteen. Stella helped her small charges pull on their Wellingtons and wrap themselves in coats, scarves and gloves, and saw them through the door to their waiting mothers. She busied herself for a while straightening desks and tables and putting chairs neatly on top ready for Mrs Purdy to clean the floor, and wiped up some spilled water from the nature table, where someone had brought in a few early snowdrops and put them in a jar. The previous teacher hadn't been very interested in nature and there wasn't much to be put on the table in January, but Stella was determined that when spring came she would encourage the children to bring in any treasures they might discover. Miss Kemp had told her she could take her class out on walks too, on fine days, and she was looking forward to rambles along the lanes and through the fields and woods.

She heard the older children clattering their chairs and slamming down their desklids, oblivious of Miss Kemp's habitual instruction to do this quietly, and then they streamed along the corridor past her door. A few minutes later the whoops and cries of healthy young humans released into freedom after a whole hour and a half of incarceration sounded outside and then died away along the lane, and the headmistress's face, framed by its grey curls, appeared.

'Another day over. Really, to hear them you'd imagine they'd been tied up and chained to the walls for months! Not that I don't feel like that myself at times, especially on days like today.' She looked at the tall windows which were streaming with icy rain. 'I don't believe it's got light at all. Those clouds are sitting right on the rooftops.' She came into the classroom and settled down for a chat. 'How have you been? The little ones have been remarkably good, considering that they haven't been able to go out to play.'

'Oh, we've been doing all sorts of things. I read to the dinner children,' this was the way they referred to those who stayed at school for their midday meal, 'and when the others came back we did songs with actions, to give them some exercise. And then I let them do some painting, only it made a bit of a mess.' She glanced ruefully at the sheets of soaking paper she was gathering up as she spoke. 'They haven't quite got the idea of using just a *little* water.'

'So long as they were happy.' The headmistress gave her an approving nod. 'You've started well, Stella. The children have settled down and I can tell they like you. I think my class are quite jealous that they didn't have you when they were in the infants'!'

Stella blushed. 'I really do want to be a good teacher. I like children. I suppose it comes from being an older sister.'

'Are you?' Miss Kemp asked in surprise. 'I thought – the Home seemed to imply in their letter about you – that you were an only child.'

'I was, when I was there. But I used to have a sister, and a brother too, a baby brother. I lost them both in the war.'

'My dear, I'm so sorry! I didn't mean to pry.' The headmistress looked distressed. 'There are so many sad stories from that time. I still have a child in my top class who lost his father, and of course there are several whose uncles died. I didn't intend to bring back sad memories.'

'It's all right,' Stella began, but before she could say more, a clattering of galvanised buckets and brooms announced the arrival of Mrs Purdy in the lobby, and they heard an exasperated mutter.

'Just look at all this mud! I knew it'd be like this, with all this blessed rain, I knew it. A never-ending job this be, a never-ending job.' The cleaner, a thin, scrawny little woman with mousy hair scraped back from her pinched face and eyes like a sparrow's, appeared in the doorway, surveying the two teachers indignantly. 'I scrubbed that lobby clean yesterday and to see it now you wouldn't think it had been touched for a month. I don't like to question the Good Lord in all His ways, but 'tis almost as if He does it deliberate. Well, I suppose I'd better just clean it all over again.' She turned and stumped back into the lobby, muttering beneath her breath.

Miss Kemp looked at Stella and raised her eyebrows humorously. 'And we'd better make ourselves scarce, before we find ourselves being scrubbed clean as well! I'll see you in the morning, Stella.'

Stella smiled at her and pulled on her coat. She hurried through the village, hoping that nobody would stop her along the way, but the wet, darkening street was quiet. Lights were on in most of the windows and through some she could see children already sitting down to tea in a cameo of warm family life. A memory came back to her of her own childhood, before the first bomb had fallen – herself, her parents and sister in their pleasant home in Portsmouth and then, later, in the little terraced house where Thomas had been born.

She shook the memories away and opened the gate to Dottie's front garden. Through the small, square window she could see Dottie, setting out a plate of scones on to her round table and, already at the table, the figure of Luke Ferris with his lean dark face alight with laughter.

Stella pushed open the door and walked in.

'And then I had to come home,' Dottie said. She had been recounting stories of her time backstage in the London theatre with 'her actress' and the tea-table was strewn with photographs and playbills. 'Nearly broke my heart, that did, but family comes first and my dad needed me. She understood that, but I knew she didn't really want me to leave her, no more'n I wanted to go. We'd had such lovely times together. And she came back to Burracombe whenever she could, stayed at the Barton till the war started and it was taken over. She and Mrs Napier, the Colonel's wife, they were great friends, known each other since they were at school. She was a lady, you see, my actress was, a real lady, welcome in the best houses in the land. And then there was Maddy, of course. She came as often as she could to see Maddy.'

'Maddy?' Stella queried. 'Who was Maddy – a dog? I suppose it wouldn't be easy to keep a dog if you were in the theatre in London—'

'My stars, no!' Dottie rocked with laughter. 'Maddy weren't no dog! She was a little girl – my actress's little girl. Well, not hers exactly, but a pretty little thing that she took a fancy to and adopted. She brought her to me to look after. It wasn't safe in London, and she knew I'd love her like my own. And so I did.' Dottie took out a handkerchief and put it to one eye. 'The little girl I never had, she was. I knew I'd have to give her back in the end, of course. My actress would have liked me to go back to London with her and look after them both there, but I couldn't do that. I was settled here again by then, you see. I'd enjoyed being in London when I was younger, but after the war – well, I knew Burracombe was my place. I didn't want no more of the big city, especially not after all the bombing and such.'

'So Maddy lived here with you all through the war?'

'That's right, my pretty.' Dottie got up from the table. 'Now, I've chattered on long enough. Let's have some more tea, shall we? And look, there's more scones ready to go in the oven – take only a few minutes to bake, they will, and there's plenty more jam and cream to go with them.' She moved the kettle to the hotter part of the range and it began to sizzle at once. 'Don't tell me you'm not hungry – young folk are always hungry.'

'Well, I'm not going to deny that!' Luke said with a grin. 'Especially when it's your scones on offer. You're a marvellous cook, Dottie.'

'Go on with you, anyone can make a few scones.' But she looked pleased all the same, and Stella smiled at the young artist. He was looking better than the first time she'd seen him, she thought, his narrow face filled out a little and he wasn't quite so pale. He didn't seem to have had a haircut since they'd last met, but she supposed that was part of being an artist. They all seemed to want to appear unconventional in some way, as if ordinary clothes and hairstyles didn't go with artistic talent. Perhaps it was true.

Dottie went out to the scullery and Luke said, 'I've been looking forward to meeting you again. How have you been settling in? Do you like Burracombe?'

'Yes, I do. It feels like home already – even in the rain!' They could hear the wind in the trees outside, and the rain lashing at the windows. Darkness had fallen and Dottie had drawn the dark red curtains, enclosing them in a warm cocoon. Logs glowed in the range and Alfred was slumbering like a large mound of tabby fur in one of the armchairs. 'I'm so lucky to have a place like this to live, and the school's just the right size.'

'And what about the children? Are they little demons?'

'Some of them,' she acknowledged with a smile. 'But most of them are dears. And Miss Kemp's not at all like a headmistress – not the ones I remember, anyway. She seems to understand the children. She doesn't let them get away with anything, but she's very kind.'

'Sounds as if you've known some tartars!'

'One or two,' she agreed. 'The teachers at my school were very strict. And how about you? Are you comfortable in your cottage up in the woods?'

'Pretty well – as long as a tree doesn't fall on me!' He tilted his head towards the window as a particularly strong gust of wind rattled the pane. 'I've had a good look at all those near me, though, and they look pretty sturdy. I get plenty of fresh air, anyway, and that's important for me – I've had TB, you know.' Stella nodded, remembering that the vicar had told her this. 'And Uncle Basil and Aunt Grace make sure I get a good meal at least once a week.' He

133

watched as Dottie opened the oven door and took out a tray of scones, risen to twice their size and golden-brown on top. 'And I sometimes get invited to the most delicious teas!'

'Go on with you, you'm nothing but a flatterer,' Dottie scolded, but she was flushed and smiling. 'Charm the birds out of the trees, you would.' She slid the scones on to a flowery china plate with fluted gold edging and put them on the table. 'Now, you help yourselves to cream and jam, and don't give none to Alfred, he's getting too fat as it is.'

'Never mind if *we* get fat, then!' Luke said, taking one of the scones and dropping it quickly on his plate. 'Ow! They're hot!'

'Come from a hot place, didn't 'em,' Dottie retorted. She seemed to enjoy bantering with the young artist. 'And you won't get fat, young things like you. Always on the go, the pair of you – you up there in the woods and Stella here with all those little tackers in the school keeping her on her toes. You need good food inside you.'

There were just three scones left when Luke finally announced that he thought it was time for him to go. He eyed them regretfully and Dottie found a bit of greasproof paper to wrap them in and put them into his hand as he stood at the door. He gave her his warm smile and then looked across at Stella.

'It's been good to meet you again. Why don't you come for a walk on Saturday? I'll show you some interesting bits of the moor.'

'Oh yes, I'd like that. Shall I bring some sandwiches?'

'I'll make some pasties for you both,' Dottie offered. 'And there's an old Thermos flask in the cupboard, so you can take some tea as well. You'll need a hot drink if you'm going on the moor.'

'I won't argue with that,' Luke said. 'If your pasties are

as good as your scones, they'll be worth walking for. Thanks, Dottie. But what about your meat ration?'

'Well, it'll only be a bit of mince and some potato and swede. But if you'm bothered about it, you can get a joint at Bertie Foster's one day and bring it round for me to cook for Sunday dinner for us all. Then us'll be square, see. Brisket makes a lovely pot roast.'

She saw Luke off into the darkness and came back to gather up her photographs. She replaced the framed ones on their hooks and put the albums back in the cupboard by the fireplace. Then she stood for a moment stroking the slumbering cat and looking into the glowing embers.

Stella was already clearing away the tea-things and didn't notice the satisfied smile on her face.

Val Tozer was walking down the farm lane when she heard the footsteps approaching. It had stopped raining but was too dark for her to make out who the other person was until they were face to face, and then she stopped abruptly.

'Val!' Luke exclaimed. 'What are you doing out here?'

'I suppose I'm allowed to walk along my own village street,' she retorted. 'What are *you* doing?'

'I've just been to tea with Dottie Friend.' He hesitated. 'Look, Val, I haven't been around because I spent Christmas in London . . .'

'Did you? I can't say I noticed.' She began to walk on.

He fell into step beside her. 'Where are you going?'

'I'm going to work, not that it's anything to do with you.'

'To work? At this time of day? It's nearly six o'clock.'

'I'm on the night-shift at Tavistock Hospital. I'm a nurse, in case you've forgotten.'

'I haven't forgotten,' he said quietly. 'I haven't forgotten anything. Val, I want to talk to you—'

'And I've told you that *I* don't want to talk to *you*.'

'Maybe not,' he said, his tone hardening a little, 'but you

can't ignore the fact that I'm here. Look, can't we just talk to each other in a friendly manner? Why are you so angry with me? It's all a long time ago now, and I never understood what went wrong anyway.'

'I was *engaged*, Luke!'

'I know,' he said steadily. 'But that didn't seem to stop you falling in love with me.'

Val drew in a deep breath and quickened her pace. 'Go away, Luke.' Her voice was trembling with anger. 'Go away. Leave me alone. I've nothing to say to you. *Nothing.*'

He started to speak again, then stopped. They walked along side by side for a few moments. She said, 'It's no use, Luke. You might as well go back to your cottage.'

'But how are you getting to Tavistock? There's no bus now.'

'I'm walking to the main road. I can catch the bus there.'

'Couldn't someone have taken you? It's pitch dark and freezing cold. Your father's got a car, hasn't he?'

'Yes, and he's also got fifteen cows to milk. It's only a mile or so, for goodness sake. I've walked it more times than I've had hot dinners.'

'Well, I'll walk it with you if you don't mind.'

'I do mind!'

'I was brought up too much of a gentleman to let a lady walk along dark lanes on her own. You don't have to talk to me if you don't want to.' He waited but she said nothing and he sighed and said, 'I won't talk to you either. I'll just walk beside you. You can even pretend I'm not here, if you'd rather.'

'I shall,' she said shortly, and they marched along the lane together in silence.

Overhead, the clouds had rolled away, leaving a sky sprinkled with stars. The wind had dropped but the air was colder now and Val thrust her gloved hands deep into the pockets of her coat. Her heart was thumping uncomfortably and she was very aware of the man at her side. Pretend he wasn't there? It was no more possible than flying. She felt misery flood over her and tears sting her eyes.

They were almost at the main road. A few cars pricked the darkness with their headlights. The bus was due in a few minutes and she could escape him, but even a few minutes seemed too long.

'Please, Luke,' she said, her voice shaking, 'please leave me alone.'

He turned in the darkness and searched the pale oval of her face. The anguish of her tone hadn't escaped him and he felt a pang of sorrow. It was an anguish he knew so well, for it had kept him awake for many nights in those early months; and the unexpected sight of her in the village, on that October day when he had first met Stella Simmons, had brought it knifing back into his heart.

'Val,' he said gently, 'don't push me away. Please. I know you were hurt – we both were – but it's so long ago, and I've never forgotten you.' He laid his hand on her arm and she leaped away as if she had been bitten. 'Val, *please*!'

'I told you, Luke – leave me alone!' The lights of the big double-decker bus came into sight round the corner and she stepped out into the road, waving. 'I don't want to talk to you, I don't want to *see* you! Just keep out of my way!'

The bus drew up beside them and she jumped on to the platform. Without looking back, she ran up the stairs to the top deck and the bus rumbled away. Luke could just see the back of her head as she sat down.

He stood at the side of the road, watching as the lights disappeared into the distance. Then he turned and walked slowly back along the lane to Burracombe.

Chapter Thirteen

Joyce Warren lost no time in getting together a committee to arrange the Festival celebrations in Burracombe. She co-opted the vicar, Dr Latimer, Miss Kemp, Hilary and Ted Tozer. All protested that they were too busy, but their protests were ignored and on Thursday evening they found themselves gathered together in the vicarage drawing room and furnished with new notebooks and pencils.

'I've asked Felix to be present as well,' Basil Harvey said, indicating the curate. 'He ought to be involved in as many village affairs as possible, and it will be useful if I can't manage to attend all the meetings.'

Joyce looked slightly aggrieved, but nodded and said, 'I hope you've all brought your reading-glasses. It's so annoying when people come to meetings without them and can't make notes.' All except Hilary and Felix produced their spectacle cases. 'Now, we're here to discuss the Festival of Britain. As you know, I'm organising a coach trip to see the Exhibition itself – in fact, I'm organising several. The WI will be going, of course, and I dare say the church will want a trip as well; some of the same people would like to be with both groups, so I suggest we join together on the same date and I make the arrangements for both. And what about the school, Miss Kemp? Would you like me to—'

'That won't be necessary, thank you, Mrs Warren,' the headmistress said with a smile. 'Miss Simmons and I have already discussed this and we'd like to organise our own outing. We shall, of course, need a few mothers to come along as helpers, and we wouldn't want to impinge on your arrangements. And some people may like the chance to go more than once.'

Joyce Warren moved her shoulders slightly in acknowledgement. 'I'm sure you'll have a very successful day. Now, as to the—'

The doorbell rang and the vicar got up. 'That'll be Miss Bellamy. I'll let her in.'

'Miss Bellamy?' Joyce asked. 'I don't think she was on my list.'

'No, but she was on mine.' Basil opened the door and the little woman came through, unbuttoning her ancient tweed coat and puffing with cold. Her bright little eyes surveyed the gathering and she plumped down on a chair beside Felix Copley. Joyce stared at her with hostility.

'I'm sorry, I didn't think you'd wish to be involved.'

'Of course I "wish to be involved",' Constance said, slightly emphasising the repetition of Joyce's words. 'Get involved in everything in this village. Always have – see no reason to stop now. Don't often have a big Festival. Got to make our mark.'

The vicar sat down again. Joyce opened her mouth, but before she could speak Ted Tozer said, 'Before us gets under way, I'd like to make a proposal.' They all turned and looked at him. 'I'd like to propose that we asks the vicar to be chairman of this here committee. We'm meeting in his house and it seems only right and proper he should be in charge.'

There was a murmur of agreement from all except for Joyce, who said, 'But the vicar has already said he might not be able to attend all the meetings. How can he be chairman?'

139

'We could have a vice-chairman for when he can't come,' Hilary suggested. 'I propose Dr Latimer.'

'That's an excellent idea,' Constance said, but Joyce hadn't finished.

'The doctor is just as likely to be forced to miss meetings as the vicar. Suppose there's an emergency in the village? He might get called away at any time.'

'That's a good point,' Ted agreed. He turned to Dr Latimer. 'How many emergencies did you have last year, Doctor?'

'Let's think.' Charles Latimer stroked his chin solemnly. 'There was the new baby over at Walker's Farm – and that time when Ernie Crocker fell off a haystack and broke his collar-bone – no, that was the year before. Oh yes, and Bertie Foster cut his thumb quite badly when he was jointing a bullock, but I don't think that was really an emergency, I just happened to be passing at the time and—'

Ted turned back to Joyce. 'There you are. I don't reckon there'll be many times when neither the vicar nor the doctor could be here. So do I have a seconder for vicar being chairman?'

'I really don't think we can ask the vicar to shoulder any more burdens,' Joyce began, but Constance Bellamy had already raised her hand.

'And I'll second Charles as well,' she said in her gruff voice, and Joyce, seeing the hands raised all around her, fell into a dissatisfied silence.

'I think we can declare the meeting open, then,' the vicar said. 'Now, as we all know, the Festival of Britain—'

'Excuse me,' Joyce said loudly. 'Don't you think we need a secretary? There'll have to be notes taken – minutes of the meetings – and I imagine there'll be a certain amount of correspondence. In fact, we probably ought to appoint a treasurer as well. If we're going to have formal meetings, with a *chairman* and *vice-chairman*,' she lifted her chin and gave them all a challenging stare, 'then we must do the thing properly, and have all the usual officers.'

'I'm not sure that having a chairman necessarily means—'

'Oh, let her do it!' Ted Tozer, having got his way, lifted one hand and flapped it a little, as if brushing off a fly. 'Let's have Mrs Warren for secretary if that's what her wants. Might keep her quiet if she'm busy writing it all down,' he added, not quite sufficiently under his breath for Joyce not to hear him.

The potential secretary glared at him. 'Is that a formal proposal, Mr Tozer?' she enquired in a voice of ice.

'If you wants it to be,' he answered imperturbably.

'Are you willing to take on the post?' the vicar asked her. 'I'm sure we'd all be very grateful.' His voice faded to a murmur of '. . . clear handwriting . . . letters to write . . . nobody better . . .' and Joyce, her lips pursed sulkily, hesitated, then shrugged her shoulders in acquiescence.

'Since you've asked me yourself, Vicar, yes. I'll be glad to.' The others could almost see her thinking about headed notepaper. 'And the post of treasurer?'

'Don't see why we need one,' Constance Bellamy said. 'Not going to be fiddling about with money. This is just to think up a few ideas, isn't it?'

'Oh no!' Joyce was alight again at once. 'No, certainly not. This committee will be co-ordinating the entire village effort towards our part in the Festival. We shall be in a position to evaluate any ideas for events and make sure that the dates don't clash. I'm sure every active group in the area will be wanting to do something, and without efficient co-ordination it could so easily descend into chaos – absolute chaos. And that being so, it makes sense for us to handle the financial side as well.'

'But surely the different groups will handle their own finances,' Hilary said. 'I mean, if the Whist Club want to hold a special drive, it won't be anything to do with anyone else, will it? Why should they need to ask a special committee?'

'In case the dates clash,' Mrs Warren said with exaggerated patience. 'They'll want the village hall, won't they? Suppose someone else wants it the same day?'

'Well, they'll just ask Mrs Purdy,' Hilary said. 'She's caretaker, isn't she? Doesn't she have a list of dates? Don't people always ask her? Anyway, I don't see what that has to do with money. They'll just pay her in the normal way, and people will pay to go to the drive. And they'll organise their own prizes, just as they do when they have a Fur and Feather. So I really don't see why—'

'Oh, for goodness sake!' Joyce cried. 'I never said a word about the wretched Whist Club! I'm sorry, Basil,' she said, subsiding a little, her face pink, 'but really, if you can't keep some sort of order we're never going to get anywhere. Now, are we going to have a treasurer or not?'

'Let's have the question coming from the Chair, shall we?' Basil said mildly. He looked around at the committee members. 'What do you think? Are we going to need a treasurer?'

Nobody spoke for a moment, then Ted Tozer cleared his throat. 'It seems to me, Vicar, there be two ways of looking at this. Either we don't need one, so there's hardly any work to do and it might as well be lumped in with the secretary's job, or else we do need one, and it'd be better to sort that out now than wait and find out. And it often *is* lumped in with the secretary's job anyway, so why not do that now?' He paused and they gazed at him, waiting for more. 'I propose the two jobs go together and Mrs Warren does 'em both – and now can we please get on with whatever it is we'm here for?'

'We'll have to have a seconder,' Joyce began, and Charles Latimer cut in quickly, 'I'll second that!'

'All in favour?' Basil asked, and they all nodded. 'Carried

142

unanimously.' Everyone drew in a deep breath of relief. 'Now, shall we get on with the business of the day – er, evening.'

'Yes, let's do that,' Ted said, glancing at his wristwatch. 'Pub shuts at ten.'

Hilary caught Felix's eye and they glanced hastily away again. The vicar's mouth twitched and he looked at the sheet of paper in front of him.

'First, we must thank Mrs Warren for preparing this agenda for us. I can see you're going to make a very efficient secretary, Mrs Warren. Item One – oh, there's *only* an Item One – is "Events".'

'That's right,' Joyce began eagerly. 'As I said just now, it's most important that whatever events are to be held should be properly co-ordinated. We need to contact the organisers of all the different groups in the village and find out what they plan to do.'

'I don't think many of 'em have made any plans at all,' Ted Tozer said. 'Only the ringers, anyway. That's the only one I've heard anything about.'

'The ringers?' She stared at him. 'You mean the bellringers?'

'Well, I don't mean the clothes-wringers,' he said. 'Of course I mean the bellringers. Talking about it the other night, us was. Thought we might get up a competition.'

'A competition?'

'Yes. Like the one we has every year for the Barnaby Shield. And all the others round about as well. There's the Lydford Trophy and the Walkhampton Cup and the Devon Eight – us can't go in for that, of course, since us only got six bells here in Burracombe – but there's plenty of others.' He looked at her with a touch of impatience. 'You must know about the ringing competitions.'

'If that's when the village is full of men from all over the county and the bells never stop ringing all day and the

143

locals can't get into the pub, yes, I do,' she said disdainfully. 'I'm surprised the vicar allows it.'

'It's tradition, that's why! Good old Devon tradition. Used to ring for money and prizes, but that was stopped since it didn't seem fitting in a church, and now us just rings for the trophy or a certificate. And that's what us thought us'd do for this Festival. Set up a special competition, and have a bit of bowling for a pig while it's going on, that sort of thing. Maybe a race over the moor. And we thought we'd have one for novices as well – youngsters that have only been ringing two or three years and haven't had a chance at a proper competition. That'd bring some more in.'

Joyce looked unconvinced. She glanced round the little circle. Hilary, the doctor and Miss Kemp were looking interested, Felix enthusiastic, Constance engrossed in a worn patch in her baggy skirt. She looked at the vicar for support.

'I think that's an excellent suggestion,' he said promptly. 'And what a good example the ringers have set by coming up with such a splendid idea so early. I think we must give them the prize for being quick off the mark. Now, do we have any other suggestions?'

'Well, if you'd given me a chance to speak,' Joyce said huffily, 'I could have told you that the Drama Club is planning a pageant. In fact, it was mentioned at the meeting the other evening, so I hardly think the ringers can be said to be first off the mark. I'm sure their little competition will be very successsful, and I'll certainly put it on my list.' She wrote in her notebook. 'The pageant, however, will involve the whole village. The children will play a large part, of course,' she turned to Miss Kemp, 'and I'll need to discuss that with you – but there will also be parts for plenty of other people. It will portray the history of Burracombe from the earliest times to the present day and I shall be

144

writing it myself. I see it as being the highlight of the celebrations.'

She gazed round triumphantly and the others looked faintly stunned. Basil said hastily, 'That sounds wonderful, Mrs Warren. You've discussed this with other groups, I expect?'

'Well – not as yet, no. I thought it more appropriate to apprise you of my intentions first.' Joyce looked slightly deflated.

Hilary bit her lip. She could feel Felix beside her, shaking slightly. 'I think it's a very good idea,' she said quickly. 'A real highlight, as Mrs Warren says. And it would be a good idea to have both these events quite close together – over a Bank Holiday weekend, for instance. The ringing competition on the Saturday and the pageant on the Monday, and something else in the church on Sunday. A flower display, perhaps.'

'August Bank Holiday,' Constance Bellamy interposed. 'Beginning of August. There'll still be plenty of blooms about. The Flower Club could look after that.'

'Certainly,' Charles Latimer said. He and his wife Marian were both keen gardeners. 'And if we put word round early enough, people will have time to make sure they plant appropriate flowers.'

Basil Harvey beamed. 'Excellent! We're getting on very well. A weekend of celebrations – our own Festival, in fact. And various coach parties, too – I think we could each look after our own, couldn't we? Or would it be more pleasant if all the various groups arranged to go on the same day? Quite a lot of people belong to more than one, and they won't all want to go more than once. Who would like to organise that?'

'Well, I was quite happy to do so, but if I'm to act as both secretary *and* treasurer, as well as writing and directing the pageant . . .' Joyce Warren said, as if she were

145

bearing the entire world on her shoulders. She let her sentence trail away and put on a martyred expression.

'I'll do that,' Hilary said. 'I'll see which dates people would prefer and suggest we get together to fill the coaches. But if some want to do it on their own, I think they must be allowed to.'

'I agree. I'll certainly want to run the school trip separately,' Miss Kemp said firmly. 'As I said before, I'll need a few helpers and they'll be too busy with the children to look at the Exhibition on their own account. And we'll have to have some time at the Fun Fair as well.'

'Oh, do you really think—' Joyce began, but the headmistress squashed her protest before it was out of her mouth.

'The children will enjoy both the main Exhibition *and* the Fun Fair. There are going to be all kinds of interesting displays there as well as the usual rides. It will be something for them to remember all their lives.'

'That's settled then,' Basil said with a touch of relief. He looked at his agenda again. 'Well, that seems to be as far as we can go this evening. A most productive meeting. Thank you all for coming.'

'And the date for the next meeting?' Joyce prompted him.

'Let me see – it's still only January. I don't think we need be in too much of a hurry, do you? Unless there's anything urgent to discuss or some new ideas are put forward ... but to my mind, a pageant, a ringing competition, a flower display and coach trips are probably enough.'

'Us could have a sort o' fair as well as the pageant,' Ted Tozer said. 'Games and such for the kiddies, and teas, maybe a stall or two. Us'll have finished haymaking then so us could use my field, the one by the church.'

'Capital! And it's something that all the different groups

146

can join in with. Let's meet again in a month or two and see how far we've got with our plans.' The vicar folded his agenda as a signal that the meeting really was over and they all stood up and began to look for their coats.

Hilary and Felix walked away together, and this time she agreed when he invited her to go to the Bell for a drink. Dottie welcomed them and they stood with Ted Tozer at the bar, telling her about the plans for the Festival.

'Well, I reckon us ought to do summat about that too,' she said, her bright eyes sparkling at the thought of the celebrations. She turned and called through to the other side of the bar, where Bernie was serving customers in the snug. 'Listen to this, Bernie, there's going to be all sorts of shindigs going on in Burracombe for this Festival they'm getting up in London. A big pageant, games in Ted Tozer's field, a special ringing competition with bowling on the green as well, flowers on display in the church and goodness knows what else. Reckon we ought to put something on too, don't you?'

'I'll apply for a special licence anyway,' Bernie said, fishing a glass tankard out of the large bowl of hot water kept behind the bar, and drying it with a tea-towel. Bernie could never simply stand and talk, he always had to be doing something else as well. 'That's because there's always something else to be done,' he would say if anyone remarked on it. Now he said, 'All they ringers'll get a thirst on for a start.'

'Yes, but us ought to put on a bit of a show as well,' Dottie urged. 'Get out the flags, plant up a few of they barrels with some nice flowers. Pretty the place up, like.'

For months now, Dottie had had her eye on half a dozen old barrels that Bernie had stacked round the back of the pub. They would look lovely out the front with some bright flowers in them, she had told him, but Bernie, who barely knew the difference between a dandelion and a daffodil, had so far resisted. 'Who'd have to do all the work?' he asked now. 'Lug them round the front and fill 'em up with soil, and water 'em in the dry weather. Me, that's who, and I got enough on me plate already.'

'Look, I'd do all that,' Dottie promised. 'You just bring 'em round and I'll see to the rest.' To Ted, she said, 'You'll let me have some of Barley's dung, won't you, my handsome? I'll mix it up with a bit of good earth and the flowers'll grow a treat. I'll ask Miss Bellamy for some of her begonias, she always has a good show in her window-boxes. Make a nice bit of colour, they will.'

'Make it look like a flower-shop, more like,' Bernie grumbled. 'It's a *pub*, woman, a place where decent hardworking men can come and have a drink and a bit of a jaw. Who's going to want to come into a place that looks like Kew Gardens?'

'They'd go into Buckingham Palace if the beer was good enough,' Dottie retorted. 'Don't you think so, Miss Hilary?'

'I think it's a lovely idea,' Hilary said, finishing her shandy. 'Thank you, Felix, but I'd better be going now. I promised Father I wouldn't be late back. Not that there's any reason why I should be,' she added with a laugh. 'There's not exactly a lot of night-life in Burracombe!'

She shook her head at Felix's offer to see her home, and left him in the bar with Ted and some of the other regulars. It was a cold, clear night and she walked briskly, listening to the occasional bark of a fox and the shrieks of owls as they hunted across the fields.

I wonder if we can get Stephen interested in helping with the Festival, she thought. Her brother's call-up papers had still not arrived and he was at a loose end, roaming about the house, reluctantly accompanying the Colonel as he attended to estate business, or visiting his friend Jeremy Boulding at Little Burracombe. For the past few days, he had been in London, staying with friends from Cambridge, and had given no indication as to when he'd be home again. He hadn't said anything more about emigrating to America, but Hilary had seen some books about the country lying on his dressing-table and didn't think he'd forgotten the idea. She'd taken one back to her own room, to read in bed, and could see why Stephen was attracted to it. The wide open spaces, the lakes and mountains, the freedom . . .

It wouldn't be freedom for me, though, she reminded herself. Stephen just wants me to go and do the things I do here. Be a housekeeper. Do his cooking and washing and ironing, when what I really want is something interesting to do, something with responsibility. Something that will let me use my brain.

But whether she went with Stephen or made another attempt at leading her own life, there was still one question that loomed large in her mind. Who would look after her father? And how could she bring herself to leave him to his loneliness?

As Hilary stared at the alluring pictures in Stephen's book, she realised that she could not simply leave the man who depended on her so much. He's given his whole life to us, she thought – to his family and his estate. He never ran away from his duties. And neither can I.

Chapter Fourteen

Saturday was bright and cold, with frost casting a white blanket over the ground and riming the fronds of dead bracken with glitter. A robin was singing on Dottie's holly-bush as Luke and Stella pushed open the gate to set out on their walk, and the puddles along the lane cracked with thin ice.

'I'm glad it's cleared up – I was afraid it would rain,' Stella said. She had put on her Wellington boots, with an extra pair of socks inside. She wore a dark red jumper with a high neck that she had knitted herself, an old pair of navy slacks and a brown corduroy jacket that had been given to the Children's Home by a group of women who collected second-hand clothes for the children. Her knitted hat was pulled down over her dark curls and the cold air was stinging her cheeks into warm colour. She marched along at Luke's side, taking two strides to his one until he noticed and slowed down, apologising.

'Sorry – I forget that my legs are longer than other people's!' He hefted his old Army knapsack on to his shoulder. Dottie had filled it with pasties, still hot from the oven, the last of the Christmas cake and a Thermos of hot tea. 'You know, these pasties smell so good I think we should make a start on them now, before they go cold.'

Stella laughed. 'We'd better get out of sight of the cottage first! Which way are we going?'

Luke opened the gate leading into Ted Tozer's field. 'I

thought we'd go up the hill and on to the moor. There are some interesting standing stones up there – must have been a settlement thousands of years ago. There's a beehive hut as well – have you ever seen one of those?'

Stella shook her head doubtfully. 'I've seen beehives. Is that what you mean?'

'No. It's a stone hut shaped like a beehive. They're very old and there are only a few of them known on the moor. Some of them have roofs fallen in, so they're more like a shallow depression in the ground with stone walls round, but the one up here is complete. I don't think many people know about it – I found it one day when I was first here.'

Luke climbed the steep slope easily, talking as he went, but Stella was soon breathless and paused to look down at the village, tucked into its valley. Up here, the air was clear and fresh, and she drew a deep breath and held up her arms as if to embrace the rolling fields and woods and the moors above. She caught Luke's eyes on her and felt herself colour a little. 'It's so lovely, isn't it? I'm glad we came.'

'So am I,' he agreed, then said conspiratorially, 'Shall we have one of these pasties?'

She shook her head at him. 'I think we should at least wait until we're actually on the moor. Come on, I've got my breath back now.' She pulled off her hat and thrust it into her pocket, then plunged up the hill ahead of him, her dark curls springing out around her head. Luke watched her for a moment, then followed. After a few minutes, they emerged through a gateway on to the open hillside and paused again.

The moor stretched away before them, rolling towards the high tors. A rough track wide enough for a horse and cart ran along the contour, with sheep-tracks branching off to climb gently away through the bracken. A few sheep grazed nearby and in the distance Stella could see a group of Dartmoor ponies.

'Pasties!' Luke exclaimed, and they found a large, flat rock and sat down side by side, using their hats as cushions against the cold. Luke opened his knapsack and took out a tin box.

'Look how many she's given us. It's a good job we're starting early, we'd never manage them all otherwise.' He held the box towards Stella and she took one of the pasties. It was golden-brown, still warm, and when she bit into it she found that the crust was crisp and delicious, with just the right amount of rich gravy soaking into it from the meat and potato mixture inside. Luke closed the box and wrapped it in a spare jersey to keep the rest warm.

'I knew my old Army knapsack would be useful,' he remarked, biting the end of his pasty.

'You were in the Army? Was that during the war?'

'Mm.' He chewed for a moment before going on. 'I was a war artist. I wasn't painting pretty pictures – I had to go and draw things that were happening. Unpleasant, horrible things sometimes. It's a way of keeping a record, you see. Film can be damaged before it can be developed, or the photographer can run out, or something can happen to his camera, but an artist can usually keep his drawings safe. Or even do them again, if necessary.'

'You mean you couldn't actually *do* anything – you just had to draw what you saw, whatever it was.'

'That's right,' he said. 'It wasn't easy, at times. Seeing people being bombed or fighting battles – being wounded, dying even, and not being able to do a thing about it. But that was my job, you see. To draw. Make records of what went on. God knows what happened to all those drawings,' he added a trifle bitterly. 'I just handed them in and never saw them again. I suppose someone's got them, somewhere.'

They sat in silence for a while, finishing their pasties. The village lay below them, a cluster of buildings with the church tower rising from their midst. The sun had melted most of the frost but here and there, in shady places, the ground was still white. High in the pale blue sky, a large bird hovered on outspread wings.

'A buzzard,' Luke said, tilting his head back to watch it. 'See how it soars higher and higher, in a spiral. It's using the thermals.'

'It hardly needs to use its wings at all,' Stella marvelled. 'Why does it go so high? It surely can't see its food from up there.'

'Ever heard the expression "eyes like a hawk"?' Luke asked, grinning. He stood up and took her hand to haul her to her feet and they began to walk on along the track. 'So what happened to you in the war, Stella? You must have been quite little when it started.'

'Yes, I was.' Stella thought for a minute or two before answering any further. It was a complicated story, and she didn't want Luke to feel sorry for her. 'We were bombed out,' she said finally.'Twice. The first time, we were in the shelter so we were all right, but our home was smashed to smithereens. The second time . . . ' She hesitated. It was still not easy to talk about what had happened. 'Well, we'd been in the shelter but we were going over to a neighbour. She'd come to fetch us – me and my mother and sister and baby brother. My mother went back to the house for something and the bomb fell while we were on our way across the road. Muriel and I were all right, more or less, but Mummy and Thomas were killed. Everybody said they couldn't have known a thing about it,' she hurried on, hearing Luke's intake of breath. 'They were trying to help, of course, but I don't think it did help all that much, not at the time. We were just little girls and we could only think about ourselves.'

'That's awful,' Luke said quietly. 'What happened to you

after that? Where was your father – or had he been killed before then?'

'No, he was in the Merchant Navy. He was away at sea. We went and stayed with another neighbour – Auntie Jess, we called her, she was a lovely person and she looked after us really well. And when Daddy came home, she suggested that we should go out and stay at the same place as her two boys. They were evacuated, you see, to a village in the country. And that's what we did.'

They walked on in silence. After his first reaction, Luke didn't attempt to express any further condolences, and she was grateful. Even after all this time, Stella still found it difficult to talk about her loss, and sympathy made it even harder. After a while, he said, 'Don't tell me if you'd rather not, but what happened after that? You said the other evening at Dottie's that you'd been in a Children's Home. That's an orphanage, isn't it? So was your father killed as well?'

'Yes,' she said. 'His ship was mined. So then there was nobody to look after Muriel and me – we had a granny but she was in hospital – and we were both taken away from the village. I went to one Children's Home and – and Muriel went to another one.'

He stared at her. 'You mean they *separated* you?'

'Yes. They thought it was best. They said we wouldn't get adopted if we were together – not many people wanted older children anyway, and nobody would want two sisters. And they said we'd settle down and forget more easily if we were apart.'

'But you must have seen each other sometimes – you must have written to each other.'

'No,' Stella said. 'I didn't know where Muriel had been taken and I don't suppose she knew where I was either. I never saw her again. I don't know where she is.' Her voice trembled suddenly and then broke. 'She could be dead too, for all I know,' she said, and burst into tears.

'*Stella!*' Luke stopped and pulled her into his arms. He held her against him, his long fingers stroking her shoulders and hair as she sobbed against his chest. 'I'm sorry,' he murmured. 'I'm so sorry. I shouldn't have asked – this was meant to be a happy day. Oh Stella, you poor little love. I'm sorry – I'm so, *so* sorry.'

'No, don't, it's just me. I didn't mean to do that – it just suddenly came over me.' She drew away from him a little and felt for a hanky. He kept his arms loosely around her as she wiped her eyes and blew her nose, then she smiled up at him rather shakily and said, 'I'm all right now. Sorry to make your jacket all wet.'

'It doesn't matter.' He looked down at her gravely. 'Look, if you'd rather go back . . .'

'Oh no! No, let's go on. I'm all right. Really.' She pushed her hanky into her pocket and brushed back her hair with a determined gesture. 'I didn't want to spoil the day, I'm sorry.'

'You haven't. And I'm the one who ought to be sorry.' He smiled his wide, slightly wicked smile and added, 'Now that we've both said sorry more than once, we'll leave it at that, shall we? And I promise I won't ask any more questions.'

They began to walk on along the track. The air was still, and on a holly tree nearby a robin was singing, as if spring had already arrived. The sheep moved across the ground to the side of the track, their heads down as they munched the short winter grass. After a bit, Stella said, 'Actually, I think I'd like to talk about it. I never have much, you see – they didn't want me to at the Home. I suppose it was all part of their idea that if nobody mentioned it I'd forget. But you don't forget having a family, even if most of them have been killed. And you don't forget you've got a sister somewhere.' Her voice shook once more and Luke took her hand and held it warmly in his.

'I'd like to find her,' Stella said. 'I think about it a lot, especially now that I've finally left the Home. I don't know where she is or where to start, but it would be so lovely to find her again. I want to know she's all right.'

'Was she older or younger than you?'

'Two years younger. I used to look after her – well, I thought I did.' She laughed a little. 'The big sister, you know! I was so upset when they took her away. I knew she'd be missing me, and I didn't think anyone could look after her as well as I did.' She was silent for a moment, then said, 'I hope she found nice people to adopt her. I hope she's been happy all these years.'

'Are you sure she was adopted? After all, you weren't, were you? If you could just find out which Home she went to—'

'Oh, I was adopted,' Stella said quickly. 'At least, I was fostered first, but they wanted to adopt me. And then she died suddenly, the woman who would have been my mother. And the man didn't think he could manage on his own. I don't think he wanted a child as much as she did, anyway. So I went back to the Home and that was that.' She paused, then said, 'They were very good to me there, you know. It was a good place to be – I mean, if you have to be in an orphanage at all. We used to go to a local school and I did well there, and they let me go to the local grammar school and stay on after I was fourteen. Even when I was too old to be in the Home, they let me stay on, in return for helping with the little ones. I was an assistant nurse then, but Matron knew I wanted to be a teacher and she helped me to go to college and let me go back during the holidays. Otherwise I'd have had nowhere to go. I couldn't have done any of it without her.'

'I suppose you were lucky in that respect,' Luke said.

'Oh, I was. I know that. If anyone could be said to have been a mother to me, after I lost my real one, it would be Matron.'

'Wouldn't she help you find Muriel, then,' he asked, 'if she's so helpful and so concerned? She must know how hard it's been for you, to be separated from your sister like this.'

'I did ask her once, just before I left to go to college. I knew her better then, you see, she'd taken an interest in me and helped me. But she just said all those records were confidential and after this amount of time it would be impossible to find out where Muriel had gone. She didn't know herself where Muriel went. When I was first sent there, all she knew was that I'd lost my family in the war. Nobody even told her I had a sister. And I wasn't old enough then to do anything about it.' She tried to explain to Luke what it had been like to be in a Children's Home during the war. 'We never got much chance to talk to people, you see. The nurses were all so busy and a lot of the children there were in just the same position as me. It wasn't at all unusual to separate families.' Once again, she paused and then added very quietly, 'Muriel might even be dead. I don't think I'd want to find that out.'

Luke was still holding her hand. He tightened his fingers around hers but remained silent. After a long time, he said, 'I've never lost anyone in that way, Stella, but I do know what it is to lose contact with someone you love. You never stop wondering. If there's anything I can do – if you'd like to try again to find her – well, I'd really like to help. I mean that.'

Stella stopped and looked up at him. The bright blue of his eyes was no more than a rim around the darkness of his pupils. His wide, smiling mouth was serious, the lips pressed together in a firm line. She felt the tears come to her eyes again and stepped forward to lay her head against his chest. He put his arms around her and they stood close and quiet.

'Thank you,' Stella said at last. 'I'll remember that. I'm not sure if I'm ready to try again, or how to go about it, but when I do, I'll talk to you. It would be good to have a friend to help.'

'And two heads are always better than one,' he said with a touch of humour back in his voice. He held her away from him and dropped a quick kiss on her hair. 'Now let's go on and find these standing stones. And then I think it'll be time to broach this flask of tea and maybe try another pasty!'

Chapter Fifteen

Val had come off night-duty and decided to do some shopping in Tavistock before going home to the farm. She had the weekend off and could go to bed for a few hours to keep herself going until her normal bedtime. Next week, she was on days again and would be able to come home every evening.

She walked down the hill to the town, feeling her heart lift at the view down West Street towards the church, with the moors rising beyond. The air was clear and bright, and she heard the mellow tone of the tenor bell chiming the hour. The streets were quiet at this time, with the shops just beginning to open, and Val went to the greengrocer for some fruit, and then to Pillar's, the newsagent, for the *Radio Times* and her mother's *Woman's Own* magazine. By then, Perraton's was open and she decided to have a cup of coffee before catching the bus back to the village.

It was gone ten when she got off the bus at the corner of the lane which led from the main Plymouth road to Burracombe. The local bus ran less often than the Plymouth bus, and Val enjoyed the walk on a morning such as this, after a night spent on the ward. She would be ready for bed when she arrived home, but would sleep all the better for the fresh air and exercise.

She strolled along, swinging her bag of shopping and letting her gaze wander over the rolling moors. The road sloped up gently before dropping over the rim of the

159

hollow in which Burracombe lay, and as she came within sight of the village she paused for a moment, leaning on a stone wall and enjoying the view of the cottages straggling between winding lanes, the church and pub, her father's farm and the Barton where her friend Hilary lived. She looked at the fields, still frosted after the clear, cold night, and the woods where the charcoal-burner's cottage was just visible through the leafless trees, smoke rising from its chimney.

Luke was there. Val felt a tightness in her chest and her pleasure evaporated. The thought that she might meet him at any time in the village brought a sharp pain to her heart; she wished that he had not come, or that he would go away. Why had he come here, to Burracombe of all places? Was it on purpose to torment her? It was possible, she reluctantly acknowledged, that he hadn't known she lived here – and even if he had, he would have thought she was married by now. But once he had realised it, shouldn't he have moved away? Shouldn't he, if he'd had a shred of decency, have left the village – left her in peace? I don't want him here! she thought furiously. I don't want him reminding me of everything that happened. I just want him to go away, so that I'll never have to see him again.

As she stood gazing towards the wood and the sloping fields, her mind swirling with bitter thoughts, she saw two people sitting on the edge of the moor. Her eyes narrowed as she realised who they were.

One was the new schoolteacher, Stella Simmons. And the other was Luke.

Val stared at them. A strange mixture of emotions struggled within her as she watched. There was the pain that always came with the thought of Luke, and the desire to push him from her thoughts; yet at the same time there was an unexpected annoyance at seeing him with Stella. So that's the man who says he still loves me! she thought scornfully, but followed this with a swift reminder to herself that Luke could not be expected not to make other friends, especially when she had told him so clearly that there could never be anything between them again. And he was only going for a walk, for heaven's sake! It didn't have to mean that he and Stella were anything but friends. The young teacher had only been in the village for a week or two, anyway – they hadn't had time to develop anything more.

She watched as they stood up and began to walk on. Luke was carrying a knapsack, as if they planned a long hike. They were looking at each other, obviously talking with some animation – and then, to her amazement, they stopped suddenly and Luke pulled his companion into his arms. She leaned against him, her face buried against his chest, and he stroked her back and her hair with both hands.

Val shrank back against the wall, her heart thumping uncomfortably in her chest. She wanted to look away, but couldn't. She could only watch as the two distant figures stayed still and close for several minutes and then, at last, broke away and walked on. They were holding hands as they walked.

Val pushed herself away from the wall. She felt sick and near to tears. I'll have to tell her, she thought. I'll have to tell that poor girl how dangerous he is. I can't let what happened to me happen to her as well.

She walked slowly down the hill, her pleasure in the morning gone. She felt tired and depressed, and wanted nothing more than to get into bed and pull the covers over her head.

Church flowers were always a problem during January, but Hilary had become an expert at making interesting arrangements. Today, she and Constance Bellamy had raided Constance's garden and entered the church armed with sheaves of evergreen foliage, hellebores and a few early camellias.

Felix was in the vestry. He peered out to see who was coming in and hurried out, beaming. 'Goodness, you look like the march of Macduff – I can hardly see you behind all that greenery. And flowers, too! I didn't think there were any about at this time of year.'

'They're Christmas roses,' Hilary told him as she laid bunches down on the chancel steps. 'And camellias from Miss Bellamy's garden – she's got an early bush. I'm going to put some on the altar and some more here and there to brighten up the foliage. And here's a bunch of snowdrops for the pulpit.'

'I'd offer to help,' he said, 'but my idea of arranging flowers is to stuff them into a jam jar and hope they're the right way up!'

'You'd better leave us to it, then,' Constance Bellamy said. She was already heading towards the vestry with the containers from last Sunday. She put the dying flowers into a galvanised bucket and tipped the stale water into the sink, then refilled the vases. All her movements were brisk and energetic. She brushed past Felix as they met in the vestry doorway and began to sort out the foliage, clipping it to the required length with secateurs.

'What did you think of the meeting the other evening?' she enquired as Felix hovered about, trying to help by picking up the bits and dropping them into another bucket. 'Your first experience of a village committee, was it?'

'Yes. I'd already met Mrs Warren, of course – she asked me to tea the other day. She's certainly very active in village life.'

Constance snorted. 'Likes to think she is! Got her finger in all the pies, that woman has. Ted Tozer's got her measure, though. *He* wasn't going to let her take charge.'

Hilary said, 'She will be more or less in charge, all the same. The secretary usually ends up running things, especially when the secretary is Mrs Warren!'

'Oh, that's all right,' Constance said. 'Nobody minds her doing all the work. We just don't want her swanning about the village as if she owned the place. Not that she won't do that anyway, whatever she's called.' She carried the vase of bright pink camellias to the altar and set them in the middle, where they glowed like June roses.

Hilary made a face at Felix. 'Miss Bellamy and Mrs Warren are sworn enemies,' she whispered. 'Miss Bellamy's family's been here for centuries, but Mrs Warren only came here when she got married. Her husband's a solicitor in Tavistock.'

'Well, we mustn't criticise. Her sort are often the backbone of the village. Love to spend their time organising things.'

Hilary laughed. 'Mrs Warren was her husband's secretary before they got married. I expect she organised him too. Still does,' she added. 'I shouldn't say this, but I've heard that he only goes to work to get some peace!'

They giggled together and Constance came back and looked at them suspiciously. 'What are you two finding so funny? Have I got my skirt tucked up at the back?'

'No, no,' Hilary assured her. 'It's nothing to do with you, really, Miss Bellamy. We were being rather naughty about Mrs Warren, I'm afraid.'

'That's all right, then. Mind you, it wouldn't be the first time. Went up to take Communion once and knelt down in front of everyone with my skirt tucked into the back of my knickers!' Constance picked up another armful of foliage and began to stuff it into the pedestal that stood in front of the pulpit. 'Good thing I'm not easily embarrassed.'

'I can't imagine that ever happening to Mrs Warren,' Hilary said, laughing. 'She always looks as if she's off to a wedding, even when she's only going down to the butcher's shop for a few chops.'

Constance sniffed. 'Puts too much importance on appearances, she does. You don't see me spending an hour every morning titivating! Too much to do.'

Felix and Hilary looked at each other again. Constance certainly didn't appear to have spent an hour on her appearance today. She was wearing a shapeless skirt and jacket of a rather murky green tweed and a bright yellow handknitted jumper that hung almost to her knees. On her head, as usual, was something that looked very like a tea-cosy.

'She once did wear a tea-cosy to church,' Hilary said to Felix after Constance had finished the flowers and stumped away, bearing the remnants to be added to the compost heap Jacob Prout kept in the corner under the yew trees. 'You could see the holes for the spout and handle. She knits them herself and I think she uses the same pattern for both.'

'She's a very good soul, though. Although I feel rather ashamed of the way we laughed at Mrs Warren. A man of the cloth shouldn't behave like that.' He gave her a sidelong glance. 'I'm afraid you're a bad influence on me, Hilary.'

'*I'm* a bad influence!' she exclaimed. 'Who was it who kept trying to make me giggle at the meeting the other evening? I'm surprised Basil didn't tell us he'd split us up.'

'I'm afraid my sense of humour does get the better of me at times,' Felix admitted, 'especially when someone's being pompous or self-important. But you're right, I really must learn to behave. I'll never be a bishop if I keep laughing at the parishioners.'

'Is that what you'd like to be?' Hilary asked curiously as she wrapped her scarf round her neck. 'A bishop?'

'It's what my father would like me to be. He *is* a bishop.' Felix disappeared into the vestry and came out without his cassock on. He was wearing a tweed jacket and grey flannels, and although his dog-collar proclaimed his status, he looked like any other lively young man out for a jaunt on a Saturday afternoon with his girl.

As soon as the thought entered Hilary's head, she felt herself blush. She turned away quickly and walked out through the old oak door into the January sunshine. Felix followed her and they stood for a moment looking out across the churchyard towards the green.

'How are you spending the rest of the day?' he enquired after a moment.

Hilary shrugged. 'I'm going home now to get my father's lunch ready. Then I'll probably go for a ride. What about you?'

'Got a few things to prepare for tomorrow, as I'm preaching at Evensong. Apart from that . . . '

Hilary turned and looked up at him. 'Don't you have any friends here? People you can spend your spare time with?'

'Not yet,' he said cheerfully, 'but I'm sure I shall have. Friends come to you wherever you live, but you do have to be willing to go halfway to meet them. You and I, for instance – I think we could be friends.'

'Yes,' Hilary said thoughtfully, 'I believe we could.' She smiled at him. 'Let's start now. Do you ride?' He nodded. 'Why don't you come for a ride with me this afternoon? And then you could stay for supper. We haven't got any other guests, I'm afraid. It might be boring for you with just my father and me.'

'It won't be boring at all.' He looked pleased. 'I'd like that very much. Thank you, Hilary.'

'I could ask a few others if you like,' she said. 'The new schoolteacher – that young artist who's living in the old charcoal-burner's cottage. I saw them going up on the moor earlier when I was on my way to the church. They looked quite friendly.' She thought for a moment, then said, 'On second thoughts, it might be a better idea to arrange something a bit further in advance – they've probably already got plans for this evening. I might get up a little supper-party next week, perhaps. I could ask Val Tozer as well – she's Ted Tozer's daughter and we're great friends, but she nurses in Tavistock so I'd have to find out when she's got an evening off. We'll soon get your social life going, Felix!'

'I'll look forward to it,' he said. 'But today, I'm happy just to go riding with you and come over to supper this evening. Thank you, Hilary.'

'I'll see you about two o'clock,' she said and walked away down the church path.

'I don't know about our Val,' Alice said as the family sat down to their midday meal. On Saturdays they always had sausages and mash with whatever vegetable was available from Alice's kitchen garden. Today, it was cabbage. The sausages came from Bert Foster, who made them himself at the back of his shop, and were meaty and full of flavour.

'Why, what's wrong with her?' Joanna asked, cutting Robin's sausage into small pieces. 'She seemed a bit tired when she came in, but she's been on night-duty, after all.'

Alice shook her head. 'She seemed more than tired to me. She was looking downright miserable – as if something had happened to upset her. I wondered if it was something at the hospital but she said no, everything was all right, nobody died sudden or nothing like that. And then she just brushed me off and went upstairs to bed. Wouldn't even stop for a cup of tea. And she wouldn't look me in the eye, neither. That's what worried me most.'

'Why d'you suppose that was, then?' Minnie asked. 'There's nothing she's ashamed of, is there? I can't imagine our Val doing anything she'd not want to tell us about.'

'No, of course she wouldn't. She didn't want me to see

how upset she was, that's why.' Alice offered the last sausage to Tom and he speared it with his fork. 'There's something eating her, and I just wish I knew what it was.'

'Well, you can't ask her,' Minnie said. 'She'm a grown woman now, Alice. She'll tell us soon enough if there's anything really wrong.'

'I don't know so much. I don't think she will.' Alice went on with her own meal, looking dissatisfied. After a moment or two, Jackie spoke in an injured voice.

'Well, if you've finished worrying about our Val, maybe you could think about me a bit. *I'm* upset too, and I don't mind telling you why!'

'Go on, then,' Tom said in a resigned tone. 'Tell us why. You've been dying to do it ever since we sat down.'

'Thanks very much! You're sure you don't mind listening, just for a minute?' Jackie looked round the table to make sure she'd got their attention. 'All right, then – I'm upset because Roy's got his papers.'

There was a brief silence. Then Alice said, 'His papers? You mean his call-up papers?'

'Yes, of course I do. His National Service call-up papers, just to make it absolutely clear.' Jackie's voice trembled a little. 'I wanted to tell you straight away, but you were too interested in our Val. He's going away, Mum.' Tears sprang to her eyes and began to trickle down her cheeks. 'Roy's going away.'

The family sat staring at her in silence. Tom rolled his eyes at his wife, who frowned at him. Ted looked faintly exasperated and Alice concerned. Robin, fastened into his high-chair beside Joanna, pointed his small fork at his young aunt and said, 'Jackie crying. Kiss her better.'

'It's not us she wants to kiss her better,' Tom muttered, and Joanna kicked him under the table.

'You see!' Jackie accused them all. 'You don't care. None of you cares about me.'

167

'Jackie, don't be silly,' Alice said. 'Of course we care about you. But you knew this would happen. You knew Roy'd be called up soon.'

'I didn't think it would be this soon,' she sniffed. 'I thought it'd be after the summer. We wanted to do all sorts of things together. We wanted to go to London and see the Festival.'

'Well, I expect you'll still be able to do that. He'll get leave. When does he have to go?' To be honest, Alice wasn't sorry to hear this news. To her mind, Jackie and young Roy had been getting altogether too serious. All that talk of an engagement, for instance! Alice hadn't even dared mention it to Ted. He'd have hit the roof. It would be a good thing if Roy was removed for a while, to let things calm down a bit.

'Next month,' Jackie said sullenly, obviously still disgruntled by the reception of her news. 'Less than three weeks. It isn't fair, Mum. The war's been over for years, I don't even see why men have to do this horrible National Service.'

'Because it's their patriotic duty, that's why,' Ted said sharply. 'Because we don't want to be caught napping like we were last time. We need our Armed Services, ready to go wherever they're needed. And you might remember, young woman, that there *is* a war going on – the Korean War. And our chaps are going out there just the same as—' He caught his wife's eye on him and trailed off into silence, while Jackie stared at him in dismay.

'Korea? You don't think he'd be sent there, do you? Oh Mum,' she turned to her mother, her face white with real distress, 'Mum, he could be killed!'

Thank you, Ted, Alice said silently, giving her husband a look before she turned back to her daughter. 'Now, don't you worry your head about that, my flower,' she said as comfortingly as she could. 'I don't suppose young Roy'll be sent out there, not for a minute. Why, it stands to reason he'll need to be trained proper and that takes time. He'll be safe enough, don't you fret.'

'Well, they sent blokes out in the last lot with only a few weeks' training,' Tom said, cheerfully oblivious of the effect of his words. 'Some of the young 'uns who joined our lot were barely out of school. At least Roy can handle a gun – quite a good shot, he is.'

Jackie stared at him and then burst into tears and jumped up from the table. She ran from the kitchen and they heard her feet on the stairs. Alice looked at both her husband and her son with vexation.

'You two! Don't you have no feeling at all? Upsetting the poor maid like that. Now we've got both of them crying their eyes out. I don't know why you men don't have more sense.'

'Come on, Mum,' Tom said. 'You've been worrying that she and Roy were getting too thick ever since New Year's Eve. I'd have thought you'd be pleased he was called up.'

'I am, but you didn't have to go talking about Korea, and what they did last time. It's your fault too, Ted. You brought it up. She was bound to be upset about him going away but she didn't have to have ideas like that put into her head. Next thing we know, she'll be asking to get married.'

'Get *married*?' Ted threw down his knife and fork. 'Now, that *is* a stupid idea! She'm nothing but a little maid still.'

'She's old enough to get married, all the same. She's already told me that she and Roy reckon they're engaged.'

'Engaged? I've heard nothing about this.'

'No, because I told her there was no point in mentioning it. I said you wouldn't hear of it for another two or three years at least. And what do you think she told me? She said that she and Roy had promised to marry each other, and that made them engaged, whether we like it or not. I wouldn't be a bit surprised if he hasn't bought her a ring and all. She's probably got it on round her neck now, on a bit of ribbon.'

Ted looked at her. 'You ought to have told me this, Alice. I'm her father. I've got a right to know.'

'Well, maybe I should have, but I was hoping it would all come to nothing – especially if Roy got his call-up. But now you've gone and put ideas into her head about Korea there's no knowing what those two silly children will do. We don't want no trouble brought to this house, Ted.'

'Hold on a minute,' Tom said. 'She's only just told you that Roy's been called up, and you've got her halfway down the aisle already, or else left holding the baby—'

'Tom!' Alice said sharply. 'We'll have none of that sort of talk, if you don't mind.'

'Well, that's what you meant. And it wasn't me who started all this.' Tom pushed away his empty plate. 'Are we getting any afters today, or shall I just go out and start work again?'

'Of course there's afters. It's roly-poly pudding, same as it is every Saturday.' Alice got up and began to collect plates together while Minnie went to the pan that had been simmering all morning. 'Now, don't you do that, Mother, it's too heavy for you. I don't want you scalding yourself.' She took the pan over to the sink and fished the pudding out carefully with two large wooden spoons. It was wrapped in a cloth and she untied the strings quickly from each end and tipped it on to a large plate. Red jam oozed from either end and Tom smacked his lips appreciatively.

'That's the stuff to give the troops – oh, suppose I shouldn't have said that! Us'll be walking on eggs now, till we know young Roy's going nowhere further than Crownhill Fort, down in Plymouth. Come on, Mum, give us a smile,' he cajoled her. 'You know she'll get over it. She's only a kid – it's a nine-days' wonder, this "engagement".'

'I hope you'm right,' Alice said as she brought the suet pudding to the table and began to serve it into bowls. 'I just hope you'm right.'

Chapter Sixteen

Roy Nethercott wasn't the only one to receive his call-up papers. Stephen Napier's came at the beginning of February and he was pleased to find that he'd got his wish and would be going into the Royal Air Force.

His father was not so pleased, and made his feelings known as he and Stephen were on their daily walk round the fields. It was the first step in Napier's plans for Stephen to take over the estate when the time came, and although Stephen was well aware of this, he could think of no real reason not to accompany him.

'Thought you'd forgotten that nonsense. Still, I dare say I could pull a few strings, get you back into the Regiment—'

'*No*, Father! I want to go into the RAF. I've told you, I want to learn to fly. What chance would I have to do that in the Army? I'd be better off in the Navy – at least they've got the Fleet Air Arm. But I've been put into the RAF and that's where I want to be, so let's leave it at that.' His face was flushed. Sent to his father's school and then on to Cambridge, never wanting for anything that could be given him, he had never had to defend his own desires, and Gilbert Napier was a hard man to oppose.

Napier's face was reddening too. He glared at his son. 'Leave it at that? No, I will not leave it at that! I want to know what other ridiculous notions you've got in your head. For a start, what's all this about America?'

'America?'

'Yes, America! All those books I saw lying around in your room the other day when I went in to find that cigarette case you borrowed. Brochures about emigration.' The big, silver head lowered, like that of a bull about to charge. 'Don't trouble to deny it.'

'All right, I won't,' Stephen said after a pause. He opened the gate into the next field and waited for his father to go through before closing it again. 'I have been thinking about it. Some men at Cambridge have been talking about it. They want people like us over there, Dad. Mathematicians and scientists. They want people for all kinds of research – the sort of research I could do. It would be a new life for me – a worthwhile life.' He looked at his father, willing him to understand, knowing that he wouldn't.

Napier responded exactly as his son had known he would.

'You've got a worthwhile life here! You've got an estate to run!'

Stephen shook his head. 'No, Father. *You've* got an estate to run. I didn't ask for it and you never expected me to have to do it. Baden would have made a good job of it, but I—'

'Baden's not here,' his father said harshly. 'If he were, then maybe I'd think about this crackbrained notion of yours – only *think* about it, mind you – but since he's not . . .'

'Since he's not,' Stephen said in a quiet voice, 'I'm to give up any ideas I might have had about using my own talents. I'm to be a substitute – and not even a very good one.' He bent to pick up a stick that was lying close to the hedge.

Napier made a sound of exasperation. 'That's ridiculous. You've got a perfectly adequate brain, or so your professors seem to think – they gave you a first-class degree. Of course

173

you wouldn't be a poor substitute. You're quite capable of learning the job. You've grown up with it, after all.'

Stephen brushed his fair hair back from his eyes. 'But I don't want to do it. Doesn't that make any difference? You do it well because you love the estate and the life, and so did Baden. But I don't. Oh, I don't mean I don't love it in my own way – it's my home, after all.' He flung his arm out and gestured at the fields and the moors above. 'I think it's one of the best places on earth. But then, I haven't seen many other places, have I?'

'You've seen most of Europe! Spent the last six months gadding about when you could have been at home learning your job.'

'But it *isn't* my job! And Europe's still a pretty dismal place. There's a lot to do before it's back to how it was before the war.'

'And don't you think it's people like you who should be working to put it back?' the Squire demanded. 'Instead of running off to America, reneging on your responsibilities?'

'The responsibilities *you* think I have.' Stephen's own anger was beginning to show in his voice. 'Father, you never took the slightest interest in me until Baden died! I was the second son, the *spare* – bit odd, a bit wet, a disappointment. More interested in my books than in the estate. Not much good on a horse, not interested in going out hunting foxes and coming back plastered in mud, talking about the kill. You never, ever took any trouble to find out what I *was* interested in. You never bothered about what I did.'

'That's quite untrue! I always read your reports – and good reports they were, too. I gave you credit for that.'

'Except that you'd rather I'd been good at sport than maths. You'd have been better pleased if I'd been rugby and cricket captain like Baden than got the maths prize.'

'I accepted the fact that you weren't any good at sport—'

174

'I didn't like it! I liked different things.' Stephen shook his head and swished his stick at some grass growing from the bank. 'Oh, what's the use? You'll never understand – we just go round and round in circles. Look, the fact is that you knew perfectly well then that I wouldn't be any good at running the estate. It didn't matter because you had Baden, and he wanted to do it. And the only thing that's changed is that—' he saw his father's face and bit back his next words, then said more quietly, '—we haven't got Baden any more. And I'm as sorry about it as you are. He was my hero.'

'So why not do his job for him?' Napier asked passionately. 'Why not take it on as – as a *memorial*, if you like? It would be the finest thing you could do with your life, Stephen, can't you see that?'

Stephen shook his head. 'No, I can't. I can't see it as being that important. Father, the big estates have had their day. Oh, it may take years – decades – for it to happen, but they just won't be practical any more. Families like us are dying out. Elder sons have been lost and younger sons don't want to take their place. The expense alone is going to drive us into the ground. Maintaining these big houses, keeping armies of servants – it's just not going to be possible. People don't want to do that sort of work any more. Look at us – think of how many indoor servants we used to have, and how many we have now. Two or three, and none of them live in. And outdoors too – the gardens and stables, they're all getting run down. You know it's true.'

'We're still getting on our feet after the war,' Napier began, but Stephen shook his head.

'It's been five years now. Things have changed, Father. People won't go into service any more. Women aren't content to spend their time in the kitchen. Look at Hilary – she's miserable because she hasn't got a life of her own. She

175

wants a career, but since Mother died she's been trapped here, looking after you.'

'Trapped – Hilary? How can you say such a thing! She has more freedom than most young women of her age. It's marriage Hilary wants, not a career – a husband and children to look after. That'd soon put all these ideas about a career out of her head.'

Stephen said nothing. He walked along at his father's side, wondering if things would have been different if he'd been able to do this as a child. If Baden had never existed, or if he'd been the elder son, groomed for his inheritance, would he have felt differently then? Would he still have wanted to take a degree in mathematics and go into some kind of research? Or would he have accepted his fate, accepted the grooming that Baden had been given, and taken on his inheritance without ever knowing that he might have had a different life?

But it wasn't any use wondering all this. Things hadn't been like that, and he did want a different life. He'd been hoping that his National Service would open the door to it, that by the time he'd done three years, as a Regular, and become a pilot, his father would have realised and accepted the fact that he was never going to come back to the estate, and turned his attention to someone else.

Hilary, for instance.

Hilary was busy preparing for a supper-party that evening.

She didn't want to call it anything as formal as a 'dinner-party'. Her father had been invited to dinner at the doctor's house that night and it seemed a good opportunity to bring together a group of the younger people in the village for a relaxed evening. She'd asked her friend Val Tozer, and Stella Simmons and the artist Luke Ferris, whom she had seen together several times. Stephen would be there, of course, and his friend Jeremy. Three men and three women. It should be fun, she thought as she went about her preparations.

They were having pheasant casserole with mashed potato and greens, followed by stewed dried fruits and cream. It was easy to prepare, with little last-minute cooking, and they could relax over a couple of bottles of wine from her father's cellar. She'd asked his advice and he'd recommended a claret and gone down to fetch it himself.

'Are you sure?' she'd asked doubtfully. 'I remember you saying this was a specially good one.'

'Of course I'm sure. There to be drunk, isn't it? Good for young Stephen to play host once in a while – got to have something worth giving his guests.' He'd put the bottles on the sideboard and gone off, leaving Hilary looking after him rather wryly. So it had become Stephen's party, had it? Well, no doubt it was all part of her father's plan to entice his younger son to take over the mantle of the estate, but she had a strong feeling it wasn't going to work.

She laid the table in the breakfast room, which was nearer to the kitchen and cosier than the big, formal dining room with its vast table and silver candelabra, and the portraits of grim-featured past Napiers looking down. Enough to put anyone off their food, she thought, lighting the fire.

Stephen came into the kitchen as she was peeling potatoes, and sniffed appreciatively. 'Smells good. Anything I can do?'

'You can fill the log-basket.' He went off to do so and came back after a few minutes to sit at the kitchen table, looking pensive. Hilary glanced at him.

'What's the matter?'

'Oh, the usual. Father wants me to become the next Squire and I don't. And he's found out about America.'

'Well, he had to know about it sometime. The rest of the world found out when Columbus did.'

Stephen looked at her for a moment and then slowly screwed up a ball of newspaper and threw it at her. 'Very funny, I don't think.'

'Well, come on,' Hilary said, grinning. 'It's not the end of the world, is it? Columbus thought it was, of course, but we know—'

'*Hil!*'

'All right,' she said, coming over to the table and sitting opposite him. 'I'm probably over-excited at having friends round for the evening. Is he upset?'

'Well, what do you think? Of course he's upset. He thinks the estate's going to be broken up into little bits and sold the minute he's dead, and the Napier name will be lost and forgotten, and all because I won't give up my life to looking after it. Honestly, he reckons that just because the war's been over for five years we're going to go back to the old feudal ways, with serfs touching their forelocks and dozens of servants keeping everything spick and span. You wouldn't have to peel potatoes then, Hil. You'd be in the drawing room eating chocolates and reading ladies' magazines.'

'What an awful idea,' Hilary said. 'I may not enjoy peeling potatoes, but it's better than being bored out of my mind, which I would be if that's all I had to do.' She paused for a moment, her hands pressed together, and gazed out of the window. 'He's living in the past, isn't he? None of that's ever going to come back.'

'No, it's not. The trouble is, I don't think we've really decided what's going to happen instead. This Festival – it's a step in the right direction, showing people what *can* be done. It'll make a lot of people sit up and open their eyes. But there are still a lot who won't move forward, and I think it's people in places like this – farmers and old families with estates – who will be the slowest of all. They want everything to stay the same, but it can't. Not after something like a world war.' He drew in a deep sigh and gave her a hunted look. 'I never expected to end up running the Burracombe estate and I don't want to. I'd be no good at it. I'd ruin the whole place.'

'Of course you wouldn't! You've got a good brain and you know the way things are done. You could do it easily.'

'All right, I could. I could forget all the plans I've been making since I was a kid – all the ideas I had about making my own way in life – and just settle down to running the home farm and collecting rents from the tenant farms. And be a magistrate, like Dad, and Master of the Hunt when I don't even like riding, and stride around the village as if I owned it . . . *No.*' He thumped his fist on the table. 'It's not for me, Hilary. It wouldn't be right.'

His sister said nothing for a few moments. Then she stood up and went back to the sink.

'Well, it'll sort itself out one way or the other, I'm sure. In the meantime, we've got guests coming this evening and I want time to have a bath and get myself ready before they come. And Dad'll be wanting one too, before he goes to the Latimers', so if you're not to sit at the table smelling like a farmyard, you'd better go and have yours now. And don't use all the hot water.'

'All right,' he said, getting up. 'I know when I'm being told to shut up and go away.' He came over to his sister and leaned back against the draining-board. 'I meant what I said the other day, you know. I've got to do this National Service first, and I'm going to do three years so that I can be a pilot. But after that, I'm going to America – and if you want to come with me, I'd like to have you.'

'We'll wait and see, shall we,' Hilary said, poking the eyes out of a potato. 'Three years is a long time, Steve. A lot could happen before we have to think about that.'

Chapter Seventeen

The party gathered at about seven. Felix was coming in place of Jeremy Boulding, who had telephoned full of apologies to say he couldn't come after all. Hilary had shrugged off Stephen's disappointment and asked the curate. 'He's not at all stuffy,' she'd told her brother. 'Anyway, we've got to have another man.'

Val was first to arrive, wearing a new plaid skirt in soft heather colours and a pale blue jumper. She came into the kitchen through the back door, looking tired but determined to enjoy herself.

'I'm glad you could come,' Hilary said, testing the potatoes to see if they were cooked. 'When I rang to invite you, you seemed a bit flustered. I wondered if there was anything wrong.'

'No, nothing's wrong. We're quite busy at work, that's all. I'll take my coat through to the hall, shall I?' She disappeared, leaving Hilary looking after her thoughtfully. She knew her friend too well not to notice that brisk, over-casual tone.

'Sorry it was all rather sudden,' she said as Val came back. 'I didn't realise till this morning that Dad was going out and it seemed a good chance for a few of us to get together. Not that I can't have friends round when he's here, but he always wants everything so formal, and it seemed a bit hard on Stella to subject her to an evening with one of the school governors.'

'Stella?' Val paused with her hand on the door. 'You mean the new schoolteacher?'

'Mm.' Hilary opened the oven door and checked the casserole. The pheasant had been jointed and was simmering gently in a rich gravy with mushrooms, chicken stock and a glass of her father's port wine. 'I ran into her in the village the other day and we had quite a chat. She seems very nice and she hasn't met a lot of people yet. And I've asked Felix as well – the new curate, you know. And—' The doorbell rang and she shut the oven door. 'That's someone now. I'll go and let them in. Go in the little sitting room and sit by the fire, Val, and we'll all have a drink. Stephen's around somewhere.'

Val did as she was told. The sitting room was smaller than the main drawing room, and comfortably shabby. It was the room that had always been used for the family when they were on their own, and the furniture was big and old-fashioned, with sagging leather sofas and armchairs. Blankets were thrown over them, and the dogs had their baskets in one corner. Newspapers and copies of *Horse and Hound* littered a side table, and a small bookcase was filled with books on hunting, horse management and Dartmoor ponies. A copy of Crossing's *Dartmoor* lay open and face down on the top, and a map had been folded up beside it.

Stephen was in one of the armchairs. He looked up and grinned when Val came in, then jumped to his feet. 'Hello, Val. Sherry?' He went over to a trolley on which stood two or three bottles. 'Dry or sticky brown?'

'Dry, please.' Val had learned to enjoy sherry when she'd been in Egypt. At home, it would have been sweet or nothing. She thought briefly of those days, then pushed the memory away. She sank into one of the other armchairs and accepted the glass that Stephen handed her.

In the hall, she could hear voices – a woman's, light and eager, and the deeper tones of a man. Her skin tingled.

Hilary had said she'd invited Felix, but this didn't sound like the curate's well-modulated light tenor. The woman's voice must be Stella's. And the man's . . . ?

Oh no, Val thought in dismay. Please, no. I've managed to avoid him all these weeks. I can't spend a whole evening being polite to him here.

Stephen was saying something, but she barely heard him. She sat tensely in her chair and watched the door. In another moment it was open and Hilary was ushering the schoolteacher Stella Simmons into the room. And behind her, as Val had known he would, came Luke Ferris.

'Here we are,' Hilary said cheerfully. 'And Felix is coming too, he arrived just as I was shutting the door. So that's all of us. Steve, give everyone a sherry, will you, while I see to the potatoes.' She whisked out of the room, leaving the door open for Felix to come in. The little group stood awkwardly for a moment, and then Stephen broke the ice by moving over to the trolley.

'You all know each other, don't you,' he said. 'No need for introductions. Val, have you met Luke before? He lives in the old charcoal-burner's cottage.'

'I know.' Her voice sounded as dry as a dead leaf. 'Hello, Luke.'

'Hello, Val.' His look was questioning, as if to ask if they should acknowledge that they already knew each other, but she returned it blankly. *Just don't mention Egypt*, she begged him silently. *Just pretend we're strangers*.

She turned to Stella. 'How are you settling in, Miss Simmons? Do you like the school? Are the children behaving?'

'Oh, let's use first names,' Stephen broke in, handing Stella the sweet sherry she had asked for. 'I can't be bothered with all this Miss Something and Mr Something Else. Anyway, Stella's too pretty a name to be kept under wraps. It means star, doesn't it? A bright, twinkling star.'

182

'I think it does,' she said, blushing. 'I'm not sure if my parents knew that, though. I can't have looked much like a star when I was born.'

'Didn't Winston Churchill say that all newborn babies looked like him?' Stephen asked. 'I'm sure he was wrong in your case, Stella. Not that I've seen all that many newborn babies. None at all, come to think about it. Have you, Val?'

'Well, there was Robin,' Val said rather shortly. 'My brother's little boy. But he looked more like a coconut.'

'Is he in the school?' Stella asked. 'There's a Robin in Miss Kemp's class. I wouldn't say he looked like a coconut, but he's got ginger hair!'

'No, he's only two. It'll be three years before you have him. And he doesn't look like a coconut now. It was just when he was born.' She caught Luke's eyes on her and turned away. 'Come and sit down on the sofa, Stella, and tell me how you like Burracombe. Did you know the area before you came here?'

'No, I'd never been to Devon, although I lived in the country for a while when I was little. I was evacuated to a small village near Southampton. I lived in a vicarage, as a matter of fact,' she added, smiling at Felix who had taken the armchair nearby.

'A lot of big houses were taken over for evacuation,' Stephen remarked. 'This one was. It became a school of some sort – I know we had to move out to one of the bigger cottages. I didn't mind too much as I was only home during the holidays, but it must have been hard for my mother.'

'The vicarage I was in hadn't been taken over,' Stella said. 'The vicar still lived there, with a housekeeper. He had four children billeted on him – two boys, and my sister and me.' She stopped abruptly, then went on, 'He was a lovely man. He used to play games with us, and we used to sell him our sugar.'

'Sell him your sugar?' Val echoed, thankful that the subject had been changed. 'Whatever do you mean?'

'They had a black-market operation going,' Stephen said with a grin. 'Did he flog it round the village? Was it "brandy for the parson, baccy for the clerk" like in the poem we learned at school?'

'No, it was nothing like that,' Stella said, laughing. 'It was just that we all had our sugar ration and he gave us a penny for every teaspoonful he put in his tea. He had a very sweet tooth,' she added thoughtfully. 'In fact, looking back, I can't believe that anyone *could* like that much sugar in their tea. I think he probably did it just to give us some extra pocket-money.'

'He sounds a very kind man,' Felix remarked. 'As of course, he should be, considering his calling!'

They all laughed at this. Felix had left off his dog-collar tonight and was wearing a plain white shirt and dark blue jacket, with a maroon silk tie. His fair hair glinted almost gold in the soft light. He sat back in his armchair, sipping his sherry, looking like any other young man out for an evening with friends.

'I've never known another vicar like him,' Stella said. 'He was more like a little boy who'd never grown up. He'd make snowmen and have snowball fights, and play cricket or collect conkers – and the housekeeper used to tell him off for getting his feet wet, just as much as the rest of us!'

The door opened and Hilary came in. 'Supper's ready,' she announced. 'I hope you're all nice and hungry. We're having it in the breakfast room – I know that sounds ridiculous, but it's cosier in there.'

They followed her. Stella, who had never been in the Barton before, was somewhat over-awed by the spacious rooms and comfortable furniture. Having spent years in an orphanage, she was accustomed to large buildings and plenty of rooms, but she was also more used to utilitarian furniture, linoleum floors and bare walls or, at best, a series of notices, mostly admonishing. Here, the floors were of polished wood with Persian rugs, and on the walls were pictures – portraits or landscapes. Those in the hall were mostly oils, but when she went into the breakfast room she saw that the pictures here were water-colours, softer and more gentle.

The room was looking warm and cosy, with a good fire burning and the lamps casting a soft light. Deep red velvet curtains were drawn across the French windows that led into the garden. The square table was laid for six, with a large candelabra in the middle, and on the sideboard was an array of vegetable dishes and two bottles of wine.

Stella took her seat nervously. When Hilary had invited her to supper, she'd expected something more like her evening meal in Dottie's cottage – fish pie, perhaps, or cauliflower cheese. This looked like a smart meal, and she hoped she would use the right cutlery. She glanced at Luke, who had sat beside her, and he gave her a reassuring smile.

To Val, accustomed to meals round the kitchen table at the farm, it also looked formal, but she had been in the Barton dining room and knew that from Hilary's point of view this bordered on the casual. She saw Luke smile at Stella and wished again that Hilary hadn't invited him. Of course, Hilary didn't know that they'd met before – she had left Egypt before Luke had arrived. She was just being kind to a newcomer to the village. For the first time, Val wished she had confided more deeply in her friend. But I thought I'd put all that behind me, she thought miserably. I never expected to have to face it all over again . . .

Stephen was handing her a warm plate with two pheasant joints on it, bathed in dark, rich gravy. 'Is that all right for you, Val? There's more if you'd like it.'

'No, this will be plenty.' She began to help herself to

mashed potatoes and cabbage. 'Hilary, this looks lovely. You must have been slaving away all afternoon.'

'Well, I'm used to cooking a meal every evening,' Hilary said a trifle ruefully. 'At least it's a bit more productive than some of the other things I have to do.' Stephen began to make violin-playing gestures and hum 'Tell Me, the Old, Old Story', and she made a face at him across the table. 'It's all right for you. You're a man – you can do as you like.'

'Oh, can I! Not if Father has anything to do with it. If he has his way, I'll be trapped here in Burracombe for the rest of my life.'

'And aren't I already?' she asked with a sudden twinge of bitterness.

'You could leave,' he said. 'You could just walk out, the same as I'm going to do.' And as she hesitated, he added, 'Give me one good reason why not.'

'I had to come home when Mother was ill. You know that. You were still at school, Baden was dead – there was nobody but me to do everything. She needed me.'

'I know,' he said more gently, 'but she doesn't need you now, does she? And all Dad wants you for is a housekeeper. Why don't you do it, Hil? Why don't you tell him you want to live your own life, and just walk out?'

Hilary stared at him. Then she said in a low tone, 'I can't. You know I can't. He has to have someone, doesn't he? And it's not going to be you, is it – so what else can I do but stay?'

The others sat silent, listening to this exchange. Stella, embarrassed, stared at her plate. Luke's lips twitched. Felix said, 'Are you sure you want us to hear this?'

Hilary glanced round, as if startled to find that there were other people in the room. Stephen shrugged. 'Doesn't bother me. We're not talking family secrets. Anyway, it's practically all Hilary and I do talk about these days. I'm

186

leaving – I got my call-up papers today. I'm going into the RAF.'

An excited babble of conversation broke out at once, as if everyone was relieved at the change of subject. Patiently, Stephen answered questions on whether he actually wanted to go into the RAF and what his father thought about it. 'He hates the whole idea – wanted to get me into his old Regiment. But I want to learn to fly, so I've told him there's no go. I expect he's grumbling about it to the Latimers at this very minute, but he can grumble till the cows come home. I won't change my mind.'

'Well, there you are, then,' Hilary said. 'Isn't that just what I've been saying? You've got your National Service to do, and you can make up your own mind what to do after that. But I left my chance of a career behind when I came home to look after Mother. By the time she died, I was running everything here. What would Dad do if I left him now?'

'Well, he could employ a housekeeper. And a few maids, like we used to have.'

'Stephen, don't be silly! Why do you think we don't have them now? People don't want to do those kinds of jobs any more. We have Jackie to come in every day, and Dottie Friend when I need help with some cooking, and we're lucky to have them, but proper, live-in housekeepers are like gold dust. You can still get them, but some are better than others and then they don't always stay, and Dad would hate having to get used to a series of strange women. And with neither of us here, he'd be so lonely. How could I go off and leave him here all by himself, with just a housekeeper?'

'Well, I still can't see why you shouldn't be able to lead your own life, the same as I can,' Stephen said, and Val nodded.

'I agree with Stephen,' she said. 'It's not really fair, is it?

187

I mean, look at me – I'm nursing, I could be a senior Sister, even a Matron. And Stella here could end up as a headmistress. Look at the things you did in the war, Hil – there must be heaps of jobs you could do.'

Hilary shrugged. 'Well, maybe. Anyway, let's change the subject. It's horribly bad manners to go on about our problems in front of guests.'

When everyone had finished their casserole, commenting how tasty it had been, Hilary gathered up their empty plates and Val helped her carry them out to the kitchen. They brought in the stewed fruits and cream and as Hilary was serving them out she turned to Luke. 'How have you settled down in the charcoal-burner's cottage? Are you comfortable there?'

'Very,' he said, smiling at her. 'I've got a woodburning stove that I can keep going all night, and plenty of kindling just outside the door. I get my water from a spring in the woods, and I've even dug over a little patch to grow a few vegetables. With those and the odd rabbit that I find on my doorstep, I can be quite self-sufficient.'

'Better be careful what you say about rabbits,' Stephen warned him with a grin. 'Father'll have you up for poaching, and since he's the local magistrate I wouldn't give much for your chances!'

Luke chuckled. 'I meant it literally. I find them on my doorstep, neatly skinned and – er – emptied out. I'm pretty sure I know who puts them there, but I wouldn't want to get him into trouble.'

'Jacob Prout!' Hilary said. 'It's all right, Luke, old Jacob can do as he likes. He's immune from prosecution.' She turned to Stella. 'Jacob's the old man you see doing all the hard work around the village – hedging and ditching, sweeping leaves, clearing culverts . . . '

'Mending roofs and drainpipes,' Stephen said.

'Building sheds –'

'Mowing lawns –'

'Digging his garden –'

'Looking after the churchyard –'

'Digging graves –'

'Ringing the church bells –'

'And anything else that anyone wants doing!' Hilary finished with a laugh. 'Burracombe simply couldn't afford anything to happen to Jacob.'

'Oh yes, I've seen him,' Stella piped up. 'He's nice. I took the children out for a walk the other day and he was showing them all kinds of things in the hedgerow – the tiny leaves of primroses starting to come up, and some old birds' nests from last year, and even some frogspawn in the pond. They all know him.'

'Everyone knows Jacob,' Hilary said, and Felix nodded.

'He showed me the bells the other day. We went up the little spiral staircase into the bell-chamber and he told me how he has to keep an eye on the frames and the wheels, and grease the bearings so that they'll ring smoothly. He says the ringers are going to get up a special competition for the Festival.'

'Oh, the Festival!' Hilary exclaimed. 'Do you know, if I've had Mrs Warren round here or on the telephone once this past month, I've had her a hundred times. If she has her way, it'll be Burracombe that everyone comes to, not London! We'll put their Exhibition right into the shade.'

'What's being planned?' Luke asked. He turned to Stella. 'You mentioned something about the children.'

'Yes, they're going to be in the pageant. Mrs Warren wants all the different groups in the village to take part, and each one will represent some event in local history.' She spoke a little shyly at first, then more eagerly as she gained confidence. 'The children are planning to do Queen Victoria's Jubilee. We're going to borrow two horses and a farm-cart from your father,' she looked at Val, 'and dress it all over like a golden carriage, with some of the children in the costume of courtiers, and the others will be outriders on ponies or part of the procession. It's a lovely idea because they can all join in and they don't have to remember any words!'

'And who's going to be Queen Victoria?' Stephen asked curiously. 'Miss Kemp? She's not really the right size – Victoria was tiny, wasn't she?'

'No, it's going to be Miss Bellamy.'

Stephen spluttered with laughter. 'Constance Bellamy? You're not serious!'

'Yes, I am. She's ideal. She'll look just like the Queen when she's dressed in the right clothes. I don't know what you find so funny about it,' Stella told him severely.

'Neither do I, now I come to think of it,' he admitted. 'You're right, she's ideal. Especially when she's got that "We are not amused" look on her face!' Stephen chuckled again. 'I'm looking forward to this pageant more than I expected. Oh, damn! I probably won't be here.'

'You'll have to ask for special leave,' his sister told him dryly. She turned to Luke. 'We're putting on a craftwork exhibition in the village hall. Things people make, that sort of thing. The big Exhibition is all about what Britain is making and doing, so we thought we'd do the same. I wondered whether you might like to put in some of your paintings.'

'Oh, but he probably won't be here then either!' Val blurted out. They all turned and looked at her, and she flushed scarlet and looked down at her plate. 'I mean, I don't suppose he will be. He's only rented the cottage for six months. Or so someone told me,' she finished, wishing she had never opened her mouth. For the first time in the entire evening she looked across the table and met Luke's eye. 'You'll be going back to London soon, won't you?' It sounded almost like a plea.

Luke didn't answer for a moment. Then he said, 'Actually, no, I don't think I will. I've already talked to Colonel Napier about renting for a further six months. Possibly even longer. I like Burracombe and there's so much to paint, I don't know when I'll be ready to move on.' The words *if ever* hung in the air.

'There you are, you see,' Hilary said in a pleased voice. 'So would you let us have some of your paintings in our exhibition? They'd be such a wonderful addition to our other crafts.'

'What else will there be?' Felix enquired.

'Oh, heaps of things. A lot of the women do needlework – embroidery, making clothes, that sort of thing – or knitting. And some of the men do very good woodwork.'

'Jacob Prout makes walking sticks,' Val contributed, her voice still a little tense. 'He marks them out in the hedges when he's layering and grows them into the right shape. They take two or three years to be ready, and then he cuts them out and carves them and polishes them up. Sometimes he puts a sheep's horn on top for a handle. They're real works of art.'

'And Bert Foster – you know, Felix, the butcher – does wood-turning in his spare time. He makes lovely fruit-bowls. We've got one here, see, on the sideboard.'

'Yes. If anyone cuts down a tree he goes round to get some of the wood.'

'Well, Burracombe never ceases to amaze me,' Felix said. 'So much talent in one small village!'

'I think it's going to be quite an event,' Hilary said. 'And on the day itself, as well as the pageant, there'll be games and races for the children and a few stalls and sideshows – someone's got a coconut shy somewhere, and there'll be bowling and guessing the weight of the sheep, and all that sort of thing. On the Saturday there'll be the bellringing competition, of course. It's going to be a really big weekend.'

'All we have to hope for', Val said, 'is good weather.'

Luke glanced across the table and she met his eye again. She looked away quickly, but not before he said, 'I think I hope for even more than that. Don't you, Val?'

There was a tiny silence. She looked down, furious with him and hoping that nobody else had noticed. Then Hilary got to her feet and began to collect their plates.

'If everyone's had enough, I think we'll go back into the sitting room and have coffee. Unless you gentlemen want us ladies to be traditonal and retire while you sit over your port.'

'Good grief, no!' Stephen exclaimed. 'Much rather be in comfortable chairs with you girls.'

Val and Stella helped Hilary to carry the dishes out to the kitchen. Hilary gave Stella the coffee-pot to carry and then touched Val's arm.

'What's the matter?' she asked in a low voice. 'I've been watching you all evening. Something's upset you. Is it Steve?'

'Stephen?' Val looked at her in surprise and shook her head. 'No, it's not him. It's – oh well, I just wish you hadn't invited Luke Ferris, that's all. I don't like him.'

'Don't you?' Hilary asked in amazement. 'Why, he seems a really nice person. What don't you like about him?'

'I don't know. I don't trust him, that's all. The way he looks at people.' Val was floundering and took refuge in irritation. 'I just don't *like* him, Hilary – isn't that good enough?'

She walked stiffly through the kitchen door and back to the sitting room, leaving her friend staring after her. For a moment, Hilary felt at a loss. She had never known Val to behave like this. She had never known her to take an instant dislike to someone, especially someone as pleasant and likeable as Luke Ferris.

Shaking her head, she picked up the jug of cream and went to join the others.

Chapter Eighteen

Easter, coming towards the end of March, was a cold weekend and, to make matters worse, it was also the weekend on which Summer Time started and the clocks were put forward by an hour. On Easter Sunday, Stella woke to a damp, gloomy morning and heard the bells ringing for early service. She sat up and looked out of the window.

Dottie's garden was filled with spring flowers. Primroses clustered on the bank in a carpet of gold, spangled with purple violets. Daffodils filled the borders and there were still some nodding white hellebores beneath the bushes of azalea and rhododendron. Soon these would be out too in a glory of colour, but Stella hadn't been here last spring, so she didn't yet know what colour they would be.

She slipped down under the covers again. She and Dottie were going to the mid-morning service together, and then Luke was coming for Sunday dinner. Luke didn't go to church services but he had painted the grey stone building from a number of different viewpoints around the village. He had even got Basil Harvey's permission to paint inside, and had told Stella that this was one of the pictures he would show at the exhibition.

It had become accepted now that Luke and Stella would go for a walk most weekends, either on Saturday or Sunday, and that Luke would also come for dinner or supper on one of those days. Stella felt easy and comfortable in his company, and he was the one person she could talk to about her sister Muriel. After a few attempts to find out about her when she had been in the Children's Home, she had given up. Everybody there had lost their family one way or another, and the staff had made it clear to her that they expected her to forget. One had told her that sisters weren't anything to write home about anyway (a remark that had baffled Stella for a long time) and she hated her own sister and hadn't spoken to her for five years. After that, Stella had kept her sadness to herself and even Matron, who had become a friend, didn't know how much she still thought about and grieved for her little Muriel.

She won't be so little now, she thought, looking past the garden and over the roofs of the cottages opposite to the field and moors beyond. She'll be nearly nineteen. A young woman. I probably wouldn't even recognise her if I saw her. If she walked down the lane and knocked on Dottie's door, I wouldn't know her. The thought was such a sad one that tears came to her eyes and trickled down her cheeks on to her pillow.

Just then, Dottie knocked on the door and came into the room bearing a tray. 'Morning, Stella. I've brought you your breakfast in bed for a special treat. Why, whatever be the matter, my flower? You'm crying!'

'Not really,' Stella said, sitting up. 'Oh Dottie, you shouldn't have! I'm the one who ought to be bringing you breakfast in bed. You spoil me.'

'Well, 'tis time someone did.' Dottie arranged the tray on Stella's lap. There was a bowl of cornflakes, a pot of tea, a little jug of milk and two slices of toast with a small dish each of butter and honey. 'I don't suppose you can remember the last time you had breakfast in bed.'

'No, I can't, except when I was ill. And you had to be really ill in the Children's Home to be brought breakfast in bed. You had to be in the Sick Bay, and nobody wanted to go there – Sister was a real tyrant.'

Dottie's eyes softened. 'You poor little soul. Well, 'tis all over now and if I think you need a bit of pampering, I'll give it to you. Been looking tired lately. I reckon they children have been playing you up a bit.'

'No, they haven't. They're very good. It's nice to have a couple of weeks' holiday, though. Next term's going to be very busy, getting ready for the pageant and everything.'

'Oh yes, the whole village is getting excited about that. I will say that for Mrs Warren, she do get things going, though Miss Bellamy don't see eye to eye with her.' Dottie chuckled and moved towards the door. 'Now, us'll need to leave for the church about twenty to eleven, 'tis always full of an Easter Day. I've got a nice shoulder of lamb to cook for our dinner. I'll put it in the oven before we go and the potatoes are all ready to pop in soon as us gets back . . . You take your time now, have a nice lie-in.'

She closed the door and Stella ate her breakfast, gazing out of the cottage window and thinking how different her life was now. She only had a few memories from before the war – mostly a warm blur of the house in Portsmouth, she and her sister playing on the hearthrug in front of the fire while their parents sat in their armchairs listening to the wireless Mike Simmons had built, or chatting. Her father hadn't been there all the time, of course – as a Merchant Seaman he'd been away more than he'd been at home – but in Stella's memories he was always there. And so was Muriel, her younger sister, with her toy animals and the doll Princess Marcia from which she had never been parted, until the night of the bombing.

She and Luke had discussed endlessly how they could set about finding Muriel. Up by the standing stones that first Saturday, they'd talked about it and he'd offered to help. 'I know a lot of people in London. They might know where records are kept.' Stella had felt a warm rush of gratitude towards him then. And he'd been as good as his word and had come back from his next visit to London with a list of names and addresses. Stella had written letters, explaining her problem, and they'd been sent off. Some had written back, regretfully apologising for not being able to help, but one had thought he might know a way of finding out which orphanage Muriel had been sent to. Some children, like Stella, had gone to local council homes, some to church orphanages, others to Dr Barnardos. Using Portsmouth and Southampton as starting-points, it might be possible to find out where she'd gone.

Stella finished her breakfast and got out of bed. She took the tray down to the scullery and had her morning wash there. Dottie had already prepared all the vegetables and they were in their pans, ready to be cooked when she came back from church.

What a lucky little girl Maddy had been to stay here with Dottie during the war, Stella thought. What a shame it couldn't have been Muriel.

'I've had a letter from my friend,' Luke said after dinner. After doing the washing-up, he and Stella had gone out for a walk, leaving Dottie to have her Sunday-afternoon nap by the fire. Alfred was curled up on her lap, the picture of contentment, a knitted yellow mouse with purple stripes resting under one paw. The little room was cosy and warm, and Luke had remarked that the best thing about going out on such a day was knowing you could come back in again.

'A letter? You mean from the man I wrote to about Children's Homes?' Stella's face flushed with excitement. 'What does he say?'

'Well, it's not quite as encouraging as I'd hoped.' He saw her face fall and added hastily, 'But it's not all bad news. He says that a lot of records got lost in one of the bombing raids – the building they were kept in was destroyed. And if Muriel was adopted, they might not tell you anything anyway. I think it's kept secret.'

'Oh.' They walked on in silence and Luke glanced down at her and laid his arm across her shoulders. 'Oh,' she said again in a small, disappointed voice.

'It doesn't mean there's no hope,' he said gently. 'We can still keep writing to the different authorities to see if they have records of Muriel. And I thought we might put a notice in one of the newspapers too. The big ones, like *The Times* or *Daily Telegraph*, often have notices in them asking people to get in touch.'

'You mean, "where they will hear something to their advantage",' Stella said. 'I don't know, Luke. Anyone could answer that, pretending to be Muriel. I was thinking only this morning, she will have changed so much by now I might not even know her.'

'You could soon find out. There must be lots of things you would both remember from when you were little.'

'Yes, but Muriel's two years younger than me – she won't remember as much. And anyone who wanted to pretend to be her would only have to say they'd forgotten all that. People do, you know. If they've had horrible times they just push the memories away.' She thought for a moment and then said, 'I'll do it if there's nothing else left, but let's try writing to the authorities first.'

They were walking slowly, Luke with his arm still laid lightly across her shoulders, when Val Tozer came round the bend in the lane, mounted on her father's riding horse Tricker. They were face to face almost before any of them realised it, and they all stopped, Luke quickly removing his arm.

'Hello, Val,' he said pleasantly. 'Nice to see you. Where have you been hiding yourself? I haven't seen you since we had that wonderful pheasant casserole at the Barton.'

'I've been busy,' she said shortly. She glanced down at Stella. 'I hope you're well.'

'Yes, thank you.' Stella felt embarrassed, without knowing quite why. There was no reason why she and Luke shouldn't walk along the lane together, and his arm had only been laid across her shoulders in a friendly way. Perhaps Val felt it was unseemly behaviour for an assistant teacher even so. 'It was a lovely evening,' she added.

'Goodness me, I'd almost forgotten it,' Val said carelessly. 'I'm surprised you haven't gone away for the Easter holidays. You must need a break from Burracombe.'

'No, not really. It's nice to have a chance to get to know the area, and Luke's been showing me around.' For some reason, Stella still felt the need to explain their being together. 'We've been to all sorts of places.'

'Nice for you,' Val said coolly. 'Well, I mustn't keep this fellow standing.' She patted her horse's neck. 'Walk on, Tricker.'

They stood looking after her. 'How funny,' Stella said. 'She didn't seem very pleased to see us, did she? I thought she was such a nice, friendly person.'

'She is,' Luke said absently, and then turned to continue along the lane. Stella glanced at his face. He wore a strange, shuttered expression as if he didn't want to talk and, although she still had questions to ask about their search for her sister, she decided to remain silent for the time being. Luke too had moods, she'd discovered, and although he was never unpleasant, there could be a chill in his voice which she found upsetting. It was best to wait until he got over whatever it was that had disturbed him.

They were through the fields and out on the open moorland before either of them spoke. And neither Val nor Muriel were mentioned again that afternoon.

Val was rubbing down Tricker, watched by the Shires, who

199

had just enjoyed their Sunday off, when Luke came into the stableyard. She felt his presence before she saw him, and her skin prickled. Slowly, she straightened, turned and faced him.

'What are you doing here?'

'Val,' he said, 'I need to talk to you.'

'I don't see why. We've said all we need to say to each other.' She turned back to the horse.

'No, we haven't.' He moved a step nearer. 'Val, we've got to sort this out. We can't live in the same village, running into each other all the time—'

'So go somewhere else.'

'Val!'

'Well, why not? Burracombe's not your home. You're only renting the cottage. You could move away, easily. I wish you would.'

'But why?' he asked. He spread out his hands. 'Val, we never quarrelled in Egypt. I know we did wrong – we went too far – but it was because we loved each other. I thought so, anyway. I know I loved you.'

Val flushed and glanced round, but the yard was empty. The afternoon chores of feeding chickens and shutting them in the barn had been done, and her father and Tom were in the milking parlour. Alice and Joanna were indoors and Jackie was out somewhere with Roy Pettifer, who would be going away next week. 'Don't say such things,' she hissed. 'Go away!'

He stared at her and sighed. 'Val, what is it? Why won't you talk to me?'

'I've told you. I told you in Egypt that it was over. I should never have let it happen. And when Eddie was killed . . .'

'Yes,' he said. 'I'm sorry about that, I really am. Please believe me, Val, if he'd still been alive, if you'd been married to him, I'd never have—'

'What do you mean, *if* we'd been married? Of course we'd have been married!'

'I'm only saying that for one thing, I didn't even know you lived here, and for another that if you'd been married to Eddie I'd never have said a word. I mean that, Val. But you're not married. He isn't here. And you've still got your own life to live.' He paused and Val, her colour high, scrubbed hard at Tricker's sides. 'Hasn't there been anyone else at all?'

'That's none of your business!'

'Perhaps not. But don't you think I have any rights at all, Val? I love you. I've loved you all these years, and I'll probably love you for the rest of my life. Doesn't that give me the right at least to know if there's a chance for me? If there *is* anyone else, if you really don't have any feeling for me at all, then I'll leave you alone. Otherwise—'

'Leave me alone anyway,' Val said. 'Go back to your little schoolteacher.' She faced him again. 'Do you really expect me to believe you, when I've *seen* you with her? Why, even this afternoon, not two hours ago, you were walking through the village with your arm round her, for all to see! You're always together. You go walking on the moors every weekend – she told me that herself. And it's quite obvious that she's in love with you.'

'Don't be ridiculous! There's nothing between Stella and me – nothing at all. We're friends, that's all.'

'So why were you kissing her then?' Val demanded.

Luke stared at her. '*Kissing* her? I've never kissed Stella in my life!'

'I saw you!' Val cried. 'Up on the moor – the first Saturday in January. I'd been on night-duty and I was walking back from the main road, and I saw you going up towards the standing stones. You put your arms round her and kissed her. I *saw* you, Luke.'

There was a small silence. Then he said quietly, 'All

right. You did see what you obviously thought was a kiss. But it wasn't like that.'

'Oh no? So just what was it like, then? Tell me, Luke.'

He sighed. 'I can't tell you. It's Stella's business.'

'Oh, so you've got secrets!' Val knew she was sounding childish now, but she couldn't help it. She felt confused, upset, angry and let down. And she didn't know why she felt like this. I don't care about him any more, she thought, rubbing the curry comb hard over Tricker's side so that he whickered in surprise. I don't even like him. I wish he'd go away.

'Val,' Luke said patiently, 'Stella and I are friends, that's all. There are no *secrets* – not the sort you mean. It's just something I'm helping her with, but it's her business and I don't think I can tell you about it.' He reached out towards her. 'Look, Val, what's this all about? What *is* this idea you've got into your head about Stella, and why does it matter so much?'

'It matters because you keep saying you love me and I don't know why!' Tears streamed down her face and she shook her head angrily. 'Why do you keep saying it if it's not true? What are you doing to me, Luke? Why are you tormenting me like this?'

'Val!' He reached out and tried to grip her hands, but she lashed out at him, and turned away. He dropped his hands back to his sides. 'Val, I'm not tormenting you, I'm telling you the truth. I do love you. I always have. I imagine I always will.' He spoke a little bitterly. 'Do you think I *want* to feel like this? Seeing you, looking just as lovely as you ever did, wanting you so much and knowing that it's never going to come right between us. I know we did wrong in Egypt, but it all seemed so different out there, we were thousands of miles from home, and we fell in love. Don't shake your head like that – we *did*. I know you loved me just as much as I loved you. But you were going to be married and we couldn't do anything about it. I knew you couldn't let Eddie down. I knew you had to keep faith with him.'

'I didn't though, did I?' she said tonelessly. 'I *didn't* keep faith, and I *did* let him down.'

'It was only the once,' he said, and reached out again for her hand. This time, she didn't reject him and he took it in his and turned it over, stroking the palm with his fingertips. Val shivered but made no other response and after a moment he went on, 'It was something I'll never forget, Val, that one night. It was all I'd ever dreamed of. It's in all my paintings, you know. They might be of fields and woods and moorland, but the feeling behind them all is the feeling you gave me that night. The love and the joy. I've never regretted it. I never will.'

'You're lucky then,' she said bitterly. 'I've regretted it a million times.'

Luke looked at her. Her eyes were dark with anger and remorse. A sense of futility and despair flooded into his heart and he let go of her hand and stepped back.

'I'm sorry, Val. I didn't realise you felt so strongly. I won't bother you again.'

Val said nothing. She turned back to the horse and laid her face against his neck. Luke hesitated, wanting nothing more than to take her in his arms and comfort her, but he knew that she would rebuff him. After a moment, he turned away and walked slowly out of the yard.

Val heard him go. She didn't lift her head until she was sure he had gone. When she did, Tricker's neck was soaked with her tears.

Jackie was also out walking, with Roy Pettifer. They had roamed for miles across the moors, golden now with gorse in full flower, and were at the standing stones, high above the village. As the afternoon drew towards evening, the clouds had drifted away and the sun came out low in the west, throwing long shadows behind the great rocks.

'When gorse is out of season, kissing's out of reason,' Roy quoted, proving that kissing was by no means out of reason today. 'Oh Jackie, I do love you.'

'I love you too. I'm going to miss you so much.'

'I know. How am I ever going to be able to bear being away from you?' He nuzzled her neck. 'You'll write to me, won't you?'

'Every day. I just hope they don't send you to Korea. I couldn't bear it if you had to go and fight. Our Tom says they sent people to the Front after only a few weeks' training in the war.'

'I don't suppose they do that now,' he said. He ran his hand down her neck and touched her breast with his fingers. 'Jackie . . .'

'Oh Roy,' she said longingly. 'Roy, I don't know . . .'

'Please,' he said. 'Please, Jackie. We won't get another chance before I go. It'll be weeks before I get home again – months. Please.'

'I don't know,' she said again. 'Suppose something happens? If my mum found out, she'd kill me – and suppose I had a baby? They'd send me away, I know they would, and you wouldn't be here. We wouldn't even be able to get married. I don't know what would happen to me.'

'You won't have a baby, I'll make sure of that. It'll be all right, Jackie, honest. Please.' He drew her down into the shadow of the stones, his hands and lips urgent. Jackie could feel her body melting. Roy's pleas had been growing ever more insistent over the past weeks and she knew that she wouldn't be able to resist for much longer. Almost, she wished that the next few days were over and the decision out of her hands. I'd be safe then, she thought. I wouldn't have to worry any more.

Jackie's desire for Roy was just as strong as his for her, but always in her mind was the fear of pregnancy. Alice and Ted had told their daughters often enough that they must never 'bring trouble to the doorstep' and Jackie knew very well what that meant. The 'little bundle of joy' would be a bundle of misery and pain if it came out of wedlock, and it was the girl who suffered, especially if the boy didn't 'stand by her' and marry her. The whole thing could be smoothed over then and people would forget in time, but if Roy were far away in the Army – perhaps even in Korea – Jackie would have to face it all on her own.

'Nothing'll go wrong, maid,' he whispered, stretching out beside her and stroking her from neck to thigh. His hand strayed a little further, and she shivered and felt her last few shreds of resistance slip away. 'Please, Jackie. I love you so much. Please . . .'

Jackie lay beside him, her heart thumping. His body was warm and hard against her and she seemed to have no strength other than to return his kisses. The sky wheeled above them and the shadows of the standing stones were flung like blankets of darkness on the close-cropped turf. I can't stop him, she thought. I can't. I don't want to stop him. Oh Roy, Roy, *Roy* . . .

Both were quiet and a little subdued as they came down the hill half an hour or so later. Roy held Jackie's hand tightly in his and when they reached the farmgate they stopped and turned to face each other.

'Jackie,' he said, 'you know I love you, don't you?'

'Yes,' she whispered, her eyes meeting his for a second. 'I love you too, Roy.'

'You're not sorry, are you?'

'No. I don't think so.' But the fear was there again and he heard it in her voice.

'Nothing will happen, Jackie. It really won't. You'll be all right.'

'Yes,' she whispered again, her voice almost too small to be heard.

He hesitated. 'It was good, wasn't it? You liked it?'

'Yes.'

There was a slight pause. Then Jackie reached over to unlatch the gate. 'I'd better go in now. Mum likes us all to have supper together of a Sunday night.'

'I'll see you again, won't I, before I go away?'

'Oh yes, of course you will. It's not till Friday, is it?'

'No,' he said. 'Not till Friday.'

A few hours ago, Friday had seemed unbearably close. Now the week stretched ahead like a desert, and neither of them knew how to cross it. Jackie slipped through the gate and closed it. They stood on either side, looking at each other.

'Oh Jackie,' he said again, 'I do love you. I love you even more now. And when I come back again we'll get married. I'll bring you an engagement ring, whatever your dad says, and they'll have to let us get married. They'll *have to*.'

Jackie looked at him. He could see the fear in her eyes, the dread that they might have to get married before that, if only he weren't going to be too far away. He felt a great, heavy load on his shoulders and he didn't know how to shed it.

'Goodnight, Jackie,' he said at last, and reached across the gate to put his arms round her shoulders. 'Goodnight, my flower.'

'Goodnight, Roy.' She leaned closer and let him kiss her. They drew apart, looking at each other with a sadness that they hardly understood, and then Jackie turned and walked across the farmyard to the back door.

Roy watched as she went inside. He saw her figure silhouetted against the light, and presently he too turned away and walked slowly back to his own home.

Chapter Nineteen

With Easter over, preparations for the pageant began in earnest. Joyce Warren and Miss Kemp had been busy during the holidays, planning the schedule, and the committee met in the vicar's drawing room on the first Wednesday in April to discuss their progress. As secretary, Joyce read a detailed account of the discussion at the first meeting, most of which the others had forgotten and would rather not have been reminded of, and gave a brief report of the state of the finances. Since there were so far neither income nor outgoings, this didn't take long. She then prepared to reveal the plans that had been made so far.

'Perhaps Miss Kemp would like to tell us about that,' the vicar suggested. He had been quite grateful to Joyce for her lengthy note-taking, since it had given him a chance to recover his breath after dashing through the door at the last minute, explaining that he'd had to slip over to lock up the church. Joyce, however, had been displeased by his lateness and had given him a severe frown. He smiled back affably and turned a benign gaze on the headmistress.

'Well,' Miss Kemp said, unfolding a sheet of paper, 'Mrs Warren and I have been roughing out a few ideas. We thought it would be nice if Burracombe's part in the Festival were to stretch over the whole of the Bank Holiday weekend – that's the first weekend in August. I believe the bellringers are happy to hold their competition on the Saturday?' She glanced at Ted Tozer, who nodded. 'We thought the Craft Exhibition could be open in the village hall every afternoon – except Sunday, of course – and serving teas as well. And we could have the flower displays in the church all over the weekend, with a special service on the Sunday, and then the Pageant and Summer Fair, with games and races and so forth, on Monday.'

'That sounds very exciting,' Basil said. 'Plenty going on. Are we going to be able to man the village hall every day? There'll have to be someone on each stall, and a regular army of people serving teas.'

'That's no problem. Each group that has a stall will provide helpers, and the WI will look after the teas. We'll need some of the men to organise the field for the games and races. Oh, and we'll need prizes, of course.'

'The villagers are usually very generous with that sort of thing,' the vicar observed. He turned to Hilary. 'Will you be loaning your donkey for rides?'

'I should think so. He rather enjoys it. He loves the children and they give him far too much to eat. Could you suggest carrots, rather than sugar lumps, Miss Kemp?'

'I'll try. The mothers will certainly be pleased not to have to provide a donkey with sugar out of their rations.' She went back to her papers. 'We've been planning the pageant itself, too. Burracombe Through the Ages – from the Standing Stones through the Bronze and Iron Ages, medieval times, the Elizabethan Age, the Civil War, right through Victorian times to the present day. The children are very excited about it.'

'Will there be enough of them to do all that?' Felix asked. 'Stella – Miss Simmons – was telling us about your plans for the Victorian Jubilee scene, and I got the impression that the whole school was going to be involved. How will they manage the rest of the scenes?'

'They won't,' Joyce said before the headmistress could answer. 'Other village groups will be taking care of the rest.

209

It will be like a carnival, with a procession through the village, starting at the ford and ending on the village green where there will be country dancing and a maypole. I shall be in charge of the country dancing, of course.'

'Why "of course"?' Felix murmured to Hilary and she gave him a reproving frown. 'Because she runs the village folk-dance group,' she whispered back. 'Surely you knew that.'

Mrs Warren coughed irritably. '*If* I could have everyone's attention—' she began, but Basil Harvey interrupted her gently.

'Actually, I think it was Miss Kemp who was telling us about this. Are all the groups willing to be involved in this, Miss Kemp? There's a lot of work in organising these fancy-dress affairs.'

'Costume,' Joyce corrected him. 'Fancy-dress is for parties.'

'Costume, then.' He raised his eyebrows enquiringly at the headmistress.

'Mrs Warren and I are working together on this,' she said. 'We've approached the Whist Club, the Scouts, Cubs, Guides and Brownies – most of them are in the school anyway – the Gardening Club and the Young Farmers. Let's see, who else . . . oh yes, the Drama Club, the bellringers – that's right, isn't it, Mr Tozer? – the Mother's Union and the WI. We're hoping to portray seven ages or events, and there'll be famous personalities too, like Sir Francis Drake who lived so near here and did so many wonderful things for us, Queen Elizabeth herself, and some other famous Devonians like Sir Walter Raleigh, Captain Scott, the Pilgrim Fathers and Sherlock Holmes.'

'Sherlock Holmes?' Felix echoed in surprise. 'Was he a Devonian?'

'We were thinking of the *Hound of the Baskervilles*,' Joyce told him reprovingly. 'One of Conan Doyle's most famous stories. We're hoping that someone will loan us a dog.'

'Well, you can't have my Rupert,' Constance Bellamy said at once, and they all laughed at the idea of Miss Bellamy's dachshund trotting along beside Sherlock Holmes and trying to look like a ferocious hound. Although, as Charles Latimer remarked, he had once given the postman a nasty nip on the ankle.

'I'm sure you'll be able to have one of the foxhounds,' Hilary said. 'I'll ask my father.'

'And then there's a Queen,' Joyce continued. 'We'll have to have a Queen.'

'A Queen?' Felix queried.

'Like a May Queen,' Hilary told him. 'One of the little girls, with a couple of Princesses. They love it. And it isn't just for the day itself – they'll be Queen and Princesses for the whole year. They'll give prizes at the Christmas party – that sort of thing.'

'Oh yes, I see. So how are they chosen? A beauty competition?'

'Oh no,' Miss Kemp said, horrified. 'That gives the children quite the wrong idea. No, we choose in various different ways, sometimes by ballot with the whole village voting, sometimes by fund-raising – the girls all have tickets to sell, and the one who sells the most becomes Queen – but for myself, I favour choosing on character. The other ways depend too much on families and favouritism. I think being appointed Queen should be an honour that can be achieved only by the child herself.'

'I agree,' Basil said, and Constance and Charles Latimer both nodded in concurrence. Joyce Warren looked doubtful.

'Presumably that means that you would have the choice, or at least, the casting vote, since you know the children best. Don't you think that could be construed as favouritism as well?'

Miss Kemp looked annoyed. 'I don't think so. I try to run my school fairly in all respects.'

'Yes, but Mrs Warren does have a point,' Basil said. '*We* all know that favouritism wouldn't enter into it, but you know what parents can be like. Perhaps it would be better if we appointed a small sub-committee of judges – people who know the children well. You would be on it, naturally, and if I might suggest myself, since most of the village children come to church and Sunday School, and perhaps the doctor? He sees them all at one time or another.'

Miss Kemp inclined her head. 'I think that would be excellent.' She allowed herself a small glance at Joyce Warren, who didn't seem to know whether to be pleased or irritated. She had gained a point, but since she had no children herself and as little contact as possible with those who lived in the village, she could hardly propose herself as a judge of character.

The meeting ended after another hour, and they all went out into the twilight. The evenings were getting longer now and it wasn't dark until after nine. Felix and Hilary sauntered along the lane together and walked out to the end of the village, where the Burra Brook ran under a narrow stone bridge and made a shallow ford. There were a few trees there, scattered over a small green, and they sat on a fallen trunk and watched the water. Since their ride together in early January they had developed a pleasant friendship, and Hilary often invited Felix over to the Barton to help exercise the horses. A few times they had gone into Tavistock for dinner at the Bedford Hotel or to go to the cinema. They'd laughed at *Father of the Bride*, thrilled to *King Solomon's Mines* and wept at *Sunset Boulevarde*. At least, Hilary had wept. It had been too dark to see if Felix had as well.

'You can see a kingfisher here sometimes,' Hilary murmured. 'Just a flash of colour, like a jewelled necklace going by. And a dipper, too, bobbing on a rock in the middle of the stream.'

'It's a beautiful area,' Felix said. 'I've really fallen in love with it.' He paused, then said, 'This Festival's going to be rather fun, isn't it?'

Hilary nodded. 'Yes. It'll be a busy summer but I love these village events. They bring everyone together. Not that it all goes smoothly, mind you – there are usually a few tears before bedtime! – but generally it all works out pretty well, and we're glad we made the effort.'

'Will you be going on one of the coach trips?' he asked. 'There seem to be quite a few being arranged – the WI, the church, and the school outing for a start. I'm not sure which I'll be able to go on. Mr Harvey will be expected to go with the church group, of course, and we can't both be away at the same time – certainly not on a Saturday in the middle of the summer. Someone might want to get married!'

'Not with half the village away in London, surely. Still, it wouldn't do if the coach broke down on the way back and neither of you could be here for Sunday services.' She stretched her arms above her head. 'You're a bit like the Royal Family, aren't you – you can never go anywhere together in case something goes wrong.'

'And I should think that's the only resemblance you're likely to find.' They were both silent for a few minutes and then Felix said, 'Are you still wondering what to do with your life, Hilary? Now that Stephen's gone into the RAF and there's just you and your father, it must be rather lonely for you.'

She shrugged. 'I don't know what to do. Sometimes I feel as if I'll go mad if I have to stay here much longer, and then I realise how involved I am with the village and I don't see how I can ever leave. Look at tonight, for example – all those arrangements for the Festival. I really do enjoy all that, but do I want to be doing it for the next forty years? It would be different if I were married to someone who was involved in the village as well, but I'm not.'

'Well . . .' Felix began, but she went on without hearing him.

'I mean, like my mother, or Grace Harvey. Being married to the Squire or the vicar is a career in itself – there are things it's traditional for the wife to do. She's a person in her own right. But me, I'm just the Squire's daughter – the *spinster* daughter – with no real place of my own.'

'Is that what you'd like to be?' Felix asked. 'Married to a man who was involved? I rather thought you wanted a career of your own, something like the one you had when you were in the ATS.'

'Well, yes. That probably is what I'd really like. I know it's an awful thing to say, Felix, but I *enjoyed* the war. I enjoyed having responsibility and authority. It showed me all kinds of things I'd never dreamed of – things I could do, things I was capable of. It was like stepping out from the shade into the sunshine.'

'I expect a lot of young women found that too,' Felix said.

'I expect they did. And some of them were able to go on and discover even more about themselves.' She got up restlessly and wandered down to the brook. 'Well, there's nothing I can do about it. Father would have a heart attack if I suggested leaving now. And he's lonely too, you know, Felix. He's lost the two people who mattered most to him in the world – Mother and Baden. He's disappointed in Stephen, and there's only me left. I can't walk out on him now, can I?'

'No,' Felix said, coming down to join her. 'I don't think you can.' He stood for a moment as if lost in thought, then caught at her arm. 'Come on! Let's go back over the stepping-stones. First one to fall in's a sissy!'

Hilary laughed and followed him across the big, flat rocks that had been placed at the side of the ford. It was a game that children had played for centuries. Halfway across, her foot slipped and she gave a little shriek. Felix turned and caught her, holding her steady as she regained her balance. They stood still for a moment, close together on the stones, and then he let her go and stepped across to the bank.

They walked back along the lane in silence and said goodnight at the entrance to the Barton drive.

Stephen Napier and Roy Pettifer had departed for their National Service within a week of each other. Hilary, expecting Jackie to mope for a while and then cheer up, was concerned when the young housemaid seemed to grow more miserable. She decided to broach the subject one morning while they were polishing the dining-room silver.

'We had a letter from Stephen today,' she said cheerfully. 'He seems to be quite enjoying the RAF, even though they haven't let him anywhere near an aeroplane yet. How's Roy getting on in the Army?'

'All right,' Jackie said listlessly. She was pale and there were dark rings under her eyes.

'Does he write to you much, or doesn't he get a lot of time?'

'Oh, he writes two or three times a week. I write every night. He's got his mum to write to as well,' she said a little defensively, as if Hilary might think this not enough. 'Anyway, he's not much of a hand at writing letters, Roy isn't.'

'Neither's Stephen,' Hilary said with a smile. 'A few lines was all we ever got while he was at school, and we were lucky to hear at all when he was at Cambridge. I don't think men are very good at putting their thoughts on paper.' She waited for a moment, then said gently, 'You mustn't let it stop you enjoying your life, Jackie. You ought to be going out with your friends, not sitting at home every evening.'

'I don't feel much like going out. Anyway, there's not all that much to do.' She rubbed half-heartedly at one of Baden's rowing cups.

'There's the Country-Dance Club. There's usually a dance to go to somewhere on Saturday evenings. And aren't you in the Rangers?'

'I suppose so. I haven't been to a meeting for a while.'

Hilary looked at her more closely. 'You are all right, aren't you, Jackie? You're not worried about anything?'

The girl's head came up and she flushed. 'No. Why should I be?'

'No reason. I just wondered.' Hilary took the cup from her hands. 'Look, I'll finish this. Why don't you make some coffee? My father will be wanting one soon and I'm sure I'm ready. We'll have that and then do the vegetables.'

Jackie said nothing but went to put the kettle on. Hilary watched her and sighed a little. I hope they didn't do anything silly before Roy went away, she thought. It would be a dreadful pity if Jackie were to spoil her life at this stage.

Jackie knew all too well that she and Roy had been silly, and was even more anxious than Hilary that her life shouldn't be spoiled. She finished her chores in silence, and left as usual at four o'clock, but instead of going straight back to the farm, she walked in the other direction, along the lane and into the woods, where she found a log to sit on and buried her face in her hands.

We shouldn't have done it, she thought. It wasn't all that special anyway – it was cold and uncomfortable and there was a rock digging into my back. And I just felt like crying afterwards. It wasn't a bit like I expected.

And now there was this awful, nagging worry that, whatever Roy had said, she might find herself having a baby. She didn't know what he'd done to prevent it. He hadn't used anything – just pulled away from her rather quickly and roughly. She didn't know if he'd been in time or not. It had all been so hurried; they'd both been afraid they'd be seen, and they'd both felt guilty afterwards. She thought he might have been almost as disappointed as she was.

She didn't even know if he still loved her. Could he, after that? It didn't seem to matter now whether she loved him or not; all that mattered was whether she was pregnant, and whether he'd be able to marry her quickly if she was. Whether her mother and father would let them marry – and the thought of telling them brought her out in a cold sweat of terror – and whether Roy would even want to marry her.

Oh, it's such a mess, she thought. It's such an awful, awful mess, and no one can help me. Whatever am I going to do?

Chapter Twenty

'We need to choose the Festival Queen and Princesses as soon as possible,' Miss Kemp said to Basil as she came out of church the following Sunday. 'We may have to make new frocks for her and her attendants. There are two or three in the school dressing-up box, but they're beginning to look a little worn now.'

'Yes, and that means extra expense,' Joyce Warren chimed in. She had come out just behind the headmistress. 'Where is the money going to come from for all this? We didn't discuss that at all at the last meeting. In my opinion, it should have been at the top of the agenda.'

'I rather fear you may be right,' the vicar admitted. 'I suppose we'd better organise some fund-raising. I'd hoped that each of the different groups would finance themselves, and we could repay them from money raised at the Fair itself.'

'And there's another thing we haven't discussed,' Joyce said triumphantly. 'Entrance fees – charges for the side-shows. It all has to be taken into account.'

'Yes, yes, I realise that.' He glanced past her at the queue of churchgoers waiting to shake his hand and tell him what a lovely sermon he had preached. 'Perhaps we can foregather at some other time and go over all this. Meanwhile, I think Miss Kemp is right and the choosing of the Queen and Princesses is our first priority.'

'Excellent,' Miss Kemp said. 'I'll give it some thought and let you and the doctor have a list of my suggestions.'

She walked on. Joyce, who could think of no reason to insist on being involved in this, moved away as well, and Maggie Culliford, who lived with her husband and five children in a ramshackle cottage at the end of the village, took her place.

'Did I hear you say there's going to be a Festival Queen?' she asked eagerly. 'I'll enter my Shirley. Her'd look a real picture in a nice frock. Blue satin, that's what would suit her best. Would her be able to keep it after?'

'I don't think so. Miss Kemp's hoping that one of the dresses already in the school box will do. If not, new ones will be made but I expect they'll go in with the others afterwards. Unless the Queen provides her own,' he added without much hope.

Maggie's face fell. 'Oh, if it's Teacher has the choosing of 'em there'll be no chance for my Shirley. Miss Kemp don't like her, never has. Always picked on my Shirley, she has. Do you know what she said the other day?' Her voice was beginning to rise with indignation and Basil's heart sank. The Cullifords were known all over the village for their quickness to take offence and their ability to make trouble. Their cottage was an eyesore, the garden a heap of rubble and thick with weeds. Jim Culliford hadn't had a regular job for years but eked out a living by doing casual labour on farms all over the area. The children were dirty and poorly clothed, and Miss Kemp was at her wits' end trying to teach them to read and write, when they came to school at all. They only attended Sunday School just before the summer picnic and the Christmas party, and Maggie herself was only seen in church when there was something to be gained from it. He'd wondered why she was here this morning, and now he understood. News of the Festival

Queen had leaked out. Miss Kemp was right – the sooner the choice was made, the better.

Alice Tozer came out next, with her daughter Jackie. Basil smiled at Alice and looked thoughtfully at Jackie. She seemed pale, and quieter than usual. She caught his eye, gave him a wan smile and looked away again.

'Ted asked me to tell you he and the other ringers are going up to Lydford next Saturday, for the Barnaby Shield competition,' Alice said. 'There'll be a service in St Petrock's, of course, and tea in the Nicholls Hall. You'd be welcome to go along and hear the ringing and have a cup of tea.'

'That sounds very interesting. I'll try to go. Lydford hold the Shield at the moment, do they?'

'No, 'tis Little Burracombe, but you know they got woodworm in the frames and the deacon says they got to be repaired before they can do a lot of ringing there. They'm all right for Sunday services and practices, like, but 'twouldn't do for the bells to be rung all day. So they decided to have it at Lydford.'

'Well, it will be a nice day out,' Basil said. 'I'll make a note of it. And how are you, Jackie?' The girl was standing there with her head drooping, taking no interest in the conversation – quite unlike her normal bright self, he thought. 'I hope you haven't caught this nasty cold that's been going round?'

'I'm all right, thanks, Vicar,' she said lifelessly, and looked at her mother. 'Can I go home now? I feel a bit tired.'

'Yes, I'm coming now anyway.'

Alice waited as her daughter moved away and Basil said quietly, 'Are you sure she's all right, Mrs Tozer? She seems very downhearted. I suppose she must be missing Roy. They're very fond of each other, aren't they?'

'A bit too fond, if you ask me,' Alice said grimly. 'And if

220

there's anything wrong, she hasn't told me about it – but to tell you the truth, Vicar, I've been a bit worried this past week or more. She don't seem to have no energy and no interest. It's not like her. I just hope—' She caught herself up and shook her head. 'I dare say she's just moping, that's all, but the sooner she gets over it the better. She's too young to be mooning over one boy.'

'Girls, eh!' the vicar said with a laugh. 'I know all about it – I've got two of my own, don't forget. Right, everyone seems to have gone now – I'll go and tidy up in the vestry, if young Felix hasn't already done so, and then we can all go home for our Sunday dinner. Will I see you and Ted at Evensong, Mrs Tozer?'

'I expect so.' Alice said goodbye and then walked down the church path after her daughter. I'm going to have to talk to that young woman, she thought resignedly. If even the vicar's noticed how she looks, everybody else must have done so as well. But it's too soon for anything to be showing up yet, surely. When was it Roy had gone away – just after Easter. And it was only the middle of April now.

It wasn't too soon to be worried, though. And if ever a girl looked worried to death, young Jackie certainly did.

The William Barnaby ringing competition was a big event, drawing teams from miles around; this year, there were eighteen entries. Some came in the morning and some not until the afternoon, and ringing would begin at 10 a.m., when the judges were safely ensconced in their upstairs room at the Castle Inn, close enough to the church for the ringing to be heard, and after the times had been drawn from Bill Barnaby's old trilby hat, kept specially for this task. Each team would go into the church, sound three notes on the tenor to warn the judges that they were ready, then raise the bells from their resting position, ring the required changes, and lower them again. The whole thing took about twenty minutes and the judges would be listening for every tiny fault – such as two bells striking too close together, or too far apart. The rhythm had to be kept perfectly all the way through, so that the ringing sounded almost mechanical, and it was difficult to believe that there were men pulling the ropes and listening for the calls.

Little Burracombe, as last year's winners, got first pick from the hat in the afternoon and were to ring at four o'clock, immediately before service. Peter Tavy, Meavy and Walkhampton went before them, and the first team to ring would be Whitchurch, followed by Lamerton. After the service, and a tea of pasties and cake, would come Bere Ferrers, Lydford itself and Kelly. Burracombe drew the last time.

'Separated you two all right, then, boys,' the captain of the Walkhampton ringers said to Ted Tozer. 'One before tay, t'other last of all. Well, there'll be some good ringing to listen to the rest of the time, sure enough!'

'I'll have a pint off you for that,' Ted retorted. 'We'm taking the Barnaby Shield back home with us, where he belong, aren't we, boys?' The others laughed and nodded their agreement, and then fell silent as the first three notes were struck to announce that Whitchurch were ready to begin.

There wasn't much to do except listen while the ringing was going on, but as they stood around the churchyard and on the knoll of the old castle ruins, the ringers took the opportunity to catch up with all the gossip from the various villages. A new vicar at one, a new baby at another, the death of a respected ringer and farmer at a third. Several were planning their own celebrations of the Festival of Britain, and they were all interested in the Burracombe ringing competition. 'Us'll be along for that,' one grizzled old farmer said, leaning on his stick, 'but you could've had it on a better date – right in the middle of haymaking, us'll be.'

'Well, you can nip back home to carry on once you've rung,' said Ted Tozer, who had the same objection but couldn't see any way round it. 'So long as you'm here for the judging at the end.'

'Oh, us'll manage that,' the old man said with a wink. 'Got to be here to collect our prize, ain't us? And have a pint in the Bell to celebrate.'

'Don't count your chickens,' Ted warned, but just then the Whitchurch ringers came down the path and the Lamerton team went in for their session. All the teams had been practising the special peal – Kilkhampton Queen's – which had been chosen by the previous year's winners, and they'd also been allowed one practice at Lydford itself. A good many of the villagers had come out to hear the ringing as well, including one couple who were complaining loudly.

'Is this going on all day?' the man demanded furiously in a nasal accent. He had recently moved from a large city 'up-country' and ran a men's tailor's shop in Tavistock. 'I never heard anything so ridiculous! They've been at it since ten o'clock. We came here for peace and quiet, not to be hounded out of our own house by wretched church bells.'

'Nobody's hounding you out,' Ted Tozer said. 'And the bells were here before you come. Didn't you think to ask if they was ever rung?'

The man glared at him. He wore a new-looking tweed jacket, an open-necked shirt and a yellow cravat. 'Of course we knew they'd ring – on Sundays. We're even prepared to accept them ringing on Tuesday evenings, to practise, if they've absolutely got to. But we did *not* expect to have this noise inflicted on us all day Saturday. And that's not all. They've been ringing on other evenings as well, for the past three weeks. It's out of all reason.'

'It's a competition,' Ted told him. 'Us've all had the right to come here once and practise. It's in the rules.'

'Your rules, perhaps! Nobody gave *me* these rules. Why do bellringers have competitions, anyway? It's not a sport!'

''Tis our sport,' someone else joined in. ''Tis the finest way us knows of spending our spare time. Ringing one night a week, and twice on Sundays – why, you couldn't have a finer hobby. Good for your body, good for your brain, and you won't find a better fellowship nowhere than in the tower. And *most* people appreciates listening to it, too.'

'But not all,' the tailor's-shop manager said nastily. 'And not all the bloody day long.'

'Now, look here,' Jacob Prout said angrily. 'There's no call for that sort o' language. Bells is Church business and we'm all decent Christian churchgoers.'

'Well, you wouldn't think so,' the man said. 'Disturbing the peace like this. And I still don't see why you have to have competitions. I don't call that Christian.'

'Christians can have competitions, same as anyone else—' Nathan Pettifer began, but Ted interrupted him.

'There be a good reason for ringing competitions. Keeps the standard up. Keeps people interested. Devon ringing be the finest in all England,' he went on proudly. 'None of that "scientific" stuff they goes in for up-country, we sticks to good old call-changes. Devonshire as clotted cream, they be, the finest bell-music there is.' He lifted his hand towards the church tower, where the bells were just coming down at the end of their peal. A few of the listening ringers were looking at each other and nodding appreciatively.

The shop manager was unimpressed. '*You* obviously think so. Not everyone agrees with you. How long is all this going on, anyway?'

'Should be finished by eight-thirty,' Ted told him cheerfully. 'Nine at the latest.'

'Eight-thirty? Nine? You mean it's going on all evening as well?' The man's jaw dropped. 'Well, we'll see about that! I'm going straight round to the vicarage to complain.'

'Why not wait till the vicar comes here?' the Lydford captain suggested. 'He'll be along at half-four to conduct the service.'

'Service? What service?'

'Why, the one us always has at a competition. You know what a service is – a few hymns, some prayers and a bit of a sermon. Vicar's been looking forward to it. Learned to ring hisself once, he did, only he don't get much time for it these days. You come along then, I'll introduce you to him meself.'

The shop manager scowled at him, then turned on his heel and marched away, stiff with indignation. The ringers laughed.

'How long's he been in the village, then?' Nathan asked the Lydford captain.

'About six or seven months, and he's been nothing but trouble since the minute he arrived. First it was old Mrs Barrow's cockerel crowing early in the morning. "Well, when d'you expect them to crow?" she asked him. Then it was my cows, after I'd turned 'em out in the spring. Said they was snuffling and snorting round his back window all night long. "So why did you buy a house with fields right up to the wall?" I asked him. Now it's the bells. I dunno why people like him comes to live in a village, I don't really.'

'Don't reckon he'll live here long,' Nathan said, and the others laughed again. Townies who came to live in the country and then complained about country life got short shrift.

Towards the end of the afternoon, Felix arrived. The crowd was making its way into the church, ready for the service, but the Burracombe ringers were still outside, listening intently and flicking their eyebrows at each tiny fault.

"'Tis Little Burracombe ringing now,' Ted told him. 'And they ain't doing too bad neither, though it hurt me to say so. Best so far, any road.'

'They're the ones holding the Shield now, aren't they?' Felix asked. 'Mr Harvey sent his apologies, by the way. He's had to go and see Mrs Jessop, who lost her husband last week. I say,' he moved away a little, gazing down at the big, flat tombstone against which they were all leaning, 'look at this!'

The others glanced at him. 'Oh, that be the clockmaker's tomb. Well known, that be.'

'It's wonderful,' Felix said. He read the long inscription, cleverly likening the life of the watchmaker, George Routleigh, to that of one of his clocks or watches, and ending with the words:

He departed this life
Nov 14 1802
Wound up
In hopes of being taken in hand
By his Maker
And of being thoroughly cleaned,
repaired
And set a-going
In the world to come.

'What a beautiful inscription,' he marvelled. 'I wonder who wrote it.'

'George hisself, likely as not,' Nathan Pettifer said. 'Don't suppose no one else had the book-learning.'

'No, probably not. I wonder how much business a clockmaker would have in Lydford. It seems an odd sort of trade for a country area.'

'Not at all. Think of all they wonderful old grandfather clocks they made in Callington.' The bells sounded their final round and Ted turned to go into the church. 'Better get inside. Service'll be starting any minute.'

Lydford had been an important place in medieval times, Felix realised as he talked to the ringers over their tea of pasties and sponge cake provided by the Lydford ringers' wives. The castle, whose ruins stood next to the church, had been a substantial courthouse and prison, and the infamous Judge Jeffries had sat here. There had once been a mint, where silver pennies were made, and the Castle Inn had some on show. Although it was now a mile or more away from the main road, the village used to be on the main stagecoach route and had originally been built by King Alfred.

'What – the one who burned the cakes?' Felix asked, at that moment in the act of taking a slice of Victoria sponge from a passing plate.

'That's right.' The wife of the Lydford ringing captain paused and smiled at him. 'Us don't use his recipe here, though!'

The competition ended at last, with an almost perfect peal from Burracombe. When they emerged from the ringing chamber at the back of the church, all the others were seated in the pews, waiting for the three judges to bring their results. It had been a long day for them, locked into their little room above the bar, and they looked pleased to be outside again. They traipsed up the aisle and stood facing the churchful of ringers. The tension, which had been growing all day, tightened its hold on them all.

'Well, boys, you all know what we'm here for,' Bill Brimacombe said in his deep, gravelly voice. He was one of the most respected ringers in the whole diocese. ''Tis the Barnaby Shield, and before us tells the results I'd like to take a minute or two to remember one of the finest ringers and the finest gentlemen any of us is ever likely to know. Old Bill Barnaby were an institution in these parts. He started ringing when he was no more'n ten year old, far too young some folk might say, but he were a strong little tacker and determined to do well, and he had a good ear. That be vital for a bellringer, a good ear. He picked it up quick as you like, and by the time he were sixteen he were in the village team, and ringing treble as well. And didn't they win some competitions, back then! Well, boys, I won't go all through his life or we'll be here all night, and you knows it as well as I do, but let's just say he rung the bells every Sunday, come rain or shine, and 'twas only the war that stopped un, when no bells was allowed. But who was it struck the first note as soon as VE Day was declared? It were Bill Barnaby, that's who, even though he were eighty-five year old if he were a day. And he rung till he were eighty-seven, and darn near – beg pardon, Vicar – *pretty* near died with a rope in his hand. So that's why this Shield was give in his honour and that's why the team that takes it home can be proud to put it on their wall.'

He paused for breath and his audience gazed stolidly back at him. If applauding had been allowed in church they would all have clapped heartily, but such displays were frowned on and there was no other way, apart from a few throat-clearings and low murmurs of agreement, that they could show their appreciation. In any case, they had done that this afternoon and evening, by ringing to the best of their ability.

Bill Brimacombe, having regained his breath, looked down at the sheet of paper in his hand and continued, 'Well, boys, with no further ado as they say, I'll tell you the results . . .' He read the list in reverse order, giving the number of faults counted and any other remarks made by the judges. 'Tenor was too slow, spoiled the whole rhythm . . .'; 'Second clipped the bigger bells every

228

time . . .'; 'A beautiful peal once they was up, but the rise let 'em down . . .' Finally, he came to the top three.

'Fourth team: rung a fine peal, we didn't think 'twould be beat, thirty-four faults. Sixth team: like clockwork, pleasure to listen to, twenty-nine faults. But the best of all was the last team of all – hard put to it to make any marks at all on our papers but it come out at twenty-one faults.' Bill looked up over his glasses and beamed, and his fellow judge Les Wonnacombe stepped forward and announced what everyone knew by then: 'The winners of the William Barnaby Shield are Burracombe, with Little Burracombe second and Meavy third.'

They did clap then. Church or not, you couldn't not clap the winners, especially when they'd all rung such grand peals. Ted Tozer, red with pleasure, collected the First Certificate and Shield, thrilled to the marrow to be taking it back to what he and the others considered its rightful place, while the Little Burracombe captain conceded defeat with a shake of his hand before going up for the Second Certificate. Every team received a certificate, signed by the judges and with a picture of St Petrock's Church on it, which would be pinned on the ringing-chamber walls with all the others. Those who hadn't won were only slightly disappointed; they all knew the best teams deserved their honours, and there was always a next time. Practice made perfect – or, as Jacob Prout remarked, as near perfect as you could ever be, being human. And there was the Burracombe Festival competition to look forward to, and still time for a pint in the Castle Inn.

The only person who hadn't enjoyed the day was the manager of the gentlemen's outfitter's. But he was nowhere to be seen.

Chapter Twenty-One

'Well, who do *you* think would be the best choice for the Festival Queen?' Miss Kemp asked with more than a tinge of exasperation in her tone. She, the vicar and Charles Latimer had met in her small living room in the school-house to discuss the problem, and so far had not been able to come to any agreement.

'I know you don't like the idea of Shirley Culliford,' Basil said ruefully, 'but she's really a sweet little girl and it would give her such a boost. That family always seems to be at the end of the queue when anything good is being given out.'

'That's hardly fair! They don't take advantage of what's offered them. If Shirley came to school in a clean frock once in a while, or even if she came to school at *all*! She misses at least one day a week, you know, and there's always some excuse – her mother's ill, or one of the little ones has to go to the doctor and there's no one else to take her – it's endless. If we did make her Queen, there would be no guarantee that she'd turn up to the events.'

'Well, would that be so very dreadful?' Basil asked mildly. 'There aren't really very many, are there? The Christmas party and the Carol Service – and perhaps one or two other children's occasions. And I'm sure she would come, if only for the party itself and the chance to wear a pretty dress.'

'That's just what I mean. They're only out for what they

can get, the Cullifords. You must know that, Vicar. How often do they come to Sunday School? Only when there's a party or outing in the offing.'

'I know. But I'm always hopeful that with encouragement . . .' He looked at the doctor. 'What do you think, Charles?'

'I can see both sides. Miss Kemp naturally wants the honour to go to a child who really deserves it by her behaviour and natural comportment, while you would like to give encouragement to a child who really doesn't get very much and – who knows – might really blossom if she only had some trust shown in her. Of course a little girl like, say, Jenny Pettifer would make an excellent Queen. And the Nethercott twins would be delightful as her attendants. But I have to confess to a soft spot for Shirley Culliford. I don't think she's ever had a really pretty frock in her life, or one that wasn't handed on to her or bought at a jumble sale. It does seem a shame, somehow . . .' He let his voice trail off, pensively.

'Oh all right,' Miss Kemp said. 'I know when I'm beaten! Shirley Culliford it is, and when her mother starts to complain about the dress and the rehearsals – if the child ever turns up for them at all – I'll send her to you. Along with all the other parents who think it should have been *their* child,' she added with bitter emphasis.

'Dear me, Miss Kemp,' Basil said, 'I would never have thought you a vindictive woman.' The doctor laughed and Miss Kemp shook her head in an I-give-up gesture. 'Now, who do you suggest as Princesses?'

'The Nethercott twins,' the other two said in unison, and the headmistress added, 'At least we can make two dresses from a single pattern and know they'll fit. And you must admit they'll look charming.'

'I think they'll *all* look charming,' Basil said. 'Do you

231

think you've got dresses in the school box that will do, Miss Kemp?'

'There are those bridesmaids' dresses from Margaret Courtenay's wedding two years ago,' Miss Kemp said thoughtfully. 'They might fit the twins – but there's another thing: Shirley Culliford's a year older than they are but she's no bigger. If anything, I'd say she's smaller. Don't you think that it's going to look rather foolish, having a Queen smaller than—'

'No, I don't,' Basil said firmly. 'Remember Queen Victoria. She must have been smaller than almost everyone in Court. And Constance Bellamy is going to look exactly right, taking her part in the pageant. Our own dear Queen herself is quite petite, you know.'

'Yes, of course,' Miss Kemp said meekly. In truth, she was beginning to feel rather ashamed of herself. She had been so pleased at the thought of Jenny Pettifer – top girl in the school, clever, well-behaved and pretty as well – being Festival Queen that she had rather lost sight of other aspects. The vicar was right. Shirley had none of the advantages that the Pettifers, humble though they were, had given their children, and you never knew what miracles a little encouragement might work. Even if nothing came of it, it might be the only time in her life when that little girl had a chance to shine.

'I'll find a nice dress for Shirley,' she said. 'Dottie Friend may run something up – she's a marvel with a sewing-machine. It'll be all right, Vicar. Shirley will make a lovely little Queen.'

'Excellent,' he beamed at her, and the matter was settled. They discussed a few other items, and then the two men departed, leaving Miss Kemp alone in the schoolhouse with her ginger cat Dundee, wondering just how it had come about that she had been persuaded to give up her choice of neat, pretty little Jenny Pettifer in favour of the dirtiest little ragamuffin in the school.

And what are the Pettifers going to say? she wondered, fondling Dundee's ears before getting up to make her bedtime Ovaltine. They were as sure as I was that Jenny would be chosen.

The life of a village schoolmistress was not easy at times.

Shirley Culliford could not believe her luck when she was told that she was to be Festival Queen. Miss Kemp had, as usual, called the whole school together for morning prayers and after 'Our Father' and a rendering of 'All People That On Earth Do Dwell', with Stella at the piano, she asked them to sit quietly while she gave out the notices.

'As you all know, we're going to London soon to see the Festival of Britain.' The children wriggled and grinned at each other excitedly. 'We'll be going on a charabanc from Tavistock and some of your mothers are coming too.'

'My daddy's coming,' Ernest Crocker said loudly from the back of the room, and two or three others joined in. 'Mine is, too.' 'And mine.' 'Mine says he wants to but he'll be too busy on the farm—'

'Yes, and some fathers are coming as well,' Miss Kemp said, raising her voice against the hubbub that threatened to break out as the children explained to each other which of their parents was coming and why the other wasn't. 'And it's going to be a lovely day for everyone, but you must remember that London's a very big place and we've got to be careful not to lose each other. We'll all need to keep together.'

'Will we be going to the Tower of London?' Micky Crocker, Ernest's brother, asked. 'They cut off people's heads there. I'd like to see someone have their head cut off.'

'Micky!' Miss Kemp exclaimed, as some of the girls cried out in horror and the smallest Culliford burst into

233

tears. 'Of course we shan't see anyone have their head cut off. We're not going to the Tower – and anyway, they don't cut people's heads off now. Stop crying, Betty, he was only teasing. He's a very silly boy. Lend Betty your hanky, Shirley . . . Because she's your sister, that's why . . . Well, why haven't you got a hanky? Silly question,' she muttered beneath her breath. 'When did any of the Cullifords have a hanky? Here you are, you can have one out of the box.' She opened the shoebox which contained various articles of property lost and never claimed, including a few small and tattered handkerchiefs which she had washed and ironed for just such an emergency. 'Here you are – now, blow. Good girl.'

Order restored, she resumed her lecture on staying together while at the Festival of Britain. 'Now, we'll leave here at half past seven in the morning. I know that's rather early but London's a long—'

'We'm always up by six,' remarked Brian Madge. 'My dad has to be up for milking and my mum works for the doctor, so she has to get all the housework—'

'Yes, well, it's not as early as all that. I'm sure you can all be on the green by seven-thirty, with clean clothes on and your faces washed. We won't be taking any dirty children,' she could barely prevent her eyes from straying to the Cullifords, all present this morning for a wonder, but in their usual grubby state, 'and remember you'll need to bring sandwiches. And some money for ice creams.' She remembered the outing they had gone on to Exmouth once, when Pamela Briggs had taken a pound note and lost it the minute she got off the bus, spending the rest of the day in tears. 'No more than a shilling each, mind. That will be quite enough.'

'Us won't be able to take a shilling each, miss,' Shirley Culliford said. She had finished wiping her sister's face and returned to her own seat. 'My mum can't afford a shilling for us, not with having to pay to go on the charabanc as well.'

'I don't expect everyone will take a shilling,' Miss Kemp said. 'I just mean that nobody's to take more than that.' She looked at the little girl in front of her. Her frock was dingy, the colours faded from much use and washing. Her fair hair was tangled and looked as if it could do with a good shampooing. She quite possibly had headlice – it was some time since the school nurse had been to inspect them. Yet there was a wistfulness in her large grey eyes that Miss Kemp suddenly longed to take away. She wanted to see the child smile. I don't think I have ever seen her look really happy, the teacher thought.

'And now,' she said, 'I've got some very special news to tell you all. News that you've all been waiting to hear, about our own celebrations here in Burracombe.' The childen buzzed with excitement. We'd better take them out for a walk after this, she thought, to let off some of this steam. And drill in the playground wouldn't be a bad idea, either. 'You all know that the vicar, Mr Harvey, and Doctor Latimer and I have been talking about who should be Festival Queen. Well, we had a meeting last night and we thought very, very hard, and we've made up our minds.' She paused. Jenny Pettifer was already swelling slightly with pride and the others were looking at her. Oh dear, Miss Kemp thought, and went on rather quickly, 'And we've decided that the Burracombe Festival Queen shall be – Shirley Culliford!'

There was complete silence. The headmistress sneaked a swift glance at Jenny and saw her face pale, then flush bright red. Her friends turned to her and there was a confused mutter of, 'It's not fair – it should have been you! You're prettier than Shirley Culliford. It's not fair. Not fair – not *fair*!'

Shirley was sitting very still. Her face too had turned

scarlet. To her astonishment, Miss Kemp saw tears in the big grey eyes. They ran down her cheeks, making streaks on her dirty face. Her lips quivered.

'No, Miss,' she said. 'That's a mistake. I can't be Queen.'

'Why not?' Miss Kemp forgot the indignant mutterings of the other children and beckoned the trembling child out to her. Reluctantly, Shirley came, and the others fell quiet and stared at her.

'Now then,' Miss Kemp said, 'tell me why you think you can't be Queen.'

'Because I'm not pretty enough, miss. Jenny's much prettier than I am. Everyone says so. And nothing nice like that ever happens to us. Cullifords don't get good luck, my dad's always saying that.' She lifted the hem of her frock to wipe her eyes and remembered that she had a handkerchief tucked into her knickers. She fished it out and scrubbed at her face.

Miss Kemp glanced at Stella and saw the compassion in the assistant teacher's eyes. Stella would sympathise more than most, the headmistress thought, remembering the tumultuous childhood she'd been told about. There must have been times when she thought that luck never came her way. She had a brief sense of what it must be like to live without hope, and turned back to the piteous figure before her.

'Shirley,' she said, 'you must never, never think like that. Good luck can come to any of us, and nice things can happen to you just as much as to anyone else. And being Festival Queen is nothing to do with being pretty – although I happen to think that you're every bit as pretty as . . . as any little girl in the school.' It would never do to make a direct comparison with Jenny, and it wouldn't be true – Jenny was a particularly attractive child. 'We all have different ways of being pretty,' she went on, 'so we'll hear no more about that. And today, you'll be able to go home and tell your mother and father that nice things *do* happen to Cullifords. Because today, you've been told that you are to be Festival Queen.'

She looked down into the small, grubby face. Joy shone through the tears, lighting the large grey eyes like opals, and the trembling mouth had widened into the first real smile Miss Kemp had ever seen. Why, she thought, I do believe the child will look really lovely, dressed in a pretty satin frock and with a little tiara on her head. Or maybe flowers in her hair. And for Christmas we could . . . She pulled her thoughts back quickly to the present. There were still the two Princesses to announce, and the rest of the children to pacify, not to mention Jenny Pettifer's disappointment to deal with.

'We'll talk about it later,' she said gently to Shirley. 'Go back to your place now, and come and see me at playtime.' She might take the opportunity to persuade the child to wash her face in the mornings, and perhaps they could find her a clean, tidy frock to wear, just for school. 'Now, the rest of you, settle down and stop that chattering. I've already told you that the Festival Queen is a very special appointment – yes, I know your mum had an appointment at the doctor's, Henry, but that's a different kind of appointment – what I was saying is that the Festival Queen is nothing to do with being pretty, or all the girls would be Festival Queens. We had to choose just one. And because the Festival of Britain is all about showing the world how wonderful Britain is and how everybody has such a good chance of having nice things happen, we had to be very careful in our choice. And that's why we chose Shirley.' She paused, not at all sure that she'd made it clear, even to herself, but the children were nodding wisely. It seemed to appeal to their logic, anyway. Only Jenny Pettifer was still looking upset.

She continued briskly: 'Now, we have three more

appointments to make this morning – the two Festival Princesses, and one very special one indeed. An important position that we've never had in this school before.' She smiled at Jenny, so that she would know that this was something for her, then announced: 'The two Festival Princesses, who will attend the Queen at our pageant and on lots of other important occasions as well, will be . . .' she paused dramatically '. . . June and Helen Nethercott!'

The children burst into loud cheers. The twins, identical with their dark curls clustered over their heads and their bright brown eyes, were popular with everyone. This was largely because they were always into mischief and had the enormous and much-envied advantage of being able to pass themselves off as each other; this meant that their popularity didn't always extend to their teachers, but as the headmistress often remarked, there was no real malice in them, and which of us wouldn't have taken such a wonderful advantage? 'I know there have been plenty of times when I'd have liked to have a twin to share the blame!' she'd said once to Stella.

'And just before we start our lessons,' she said now, aware that they'd spent rather a long time on their morning assembly, 'I want to tell you about the other very special and important post. With such a busy and exciting term ahead of us, Miss Simmons and I are going to need a lot of help. Now, I know you'll all do your best, but we felt,' she glanced at Stella, who hadn't the faintest idea what was coming, since Miss Kemp had only just thought of it herself, 'we felt that it would be a good idea to have one of you as a special helper. Someone we can trust to take on some of the little tasks that we would have to do. We're going to have a Head Girl! And the Head Girl is going to be none other than Jenny Pettifer!'

'When did you think of that?' Stella asked later, as they

drank a welcome cup of coffee while watching the children dash madly about the playground. 'I had no idea!'

'Neither did I,' the headmistress confessed. 'It was only when I saw Jenny's face and realised how disappointed she was – but more than that, I knew the children would never accept Shirley unless I did something to mollify them. The idea of a Head Girl just popped into my mind, and thank goodness it did,' she added feelingly.

'You realise you're going to have to have one every year now,' Stella told her. 'And what about a Head Boy? I'm surprised nobody's thought of that.'

'Well, I expect they will, and I dare say we ought to have one anyway. I'd probably choose Ernest Crocker, he's a willing little boy and quite bright. As for having one every year, why not? It's another thing the children can strive for and another challenge to their skills. We'll give Jenny – and Ernest, of course – real things to do – some of the simpler tasks we would have done ourselves. And Shirley's so pleased to be Festival Queen. She really couldn't believe it, you know. Her little face lit up like a lamp.'

'I know.' Stella's own face grew pensive. 'What is she really like, Miss Kemp? It's a problem for me, not knowing the older children. The ones I have in my class now will be familiar all the way through school, but I hardly know yours, and I'd like to. I wondered if I could take them for lessons sometimes, or for nature walks?'

'That's a good idea. You need to know all the children, even though you're just teaching the infants. I was thinking this morning that a nature walk would be a good idea. We'll take the whole school out together.'

As the crocodile of children trudged through the village half an hour later, Stella looked about her at the high Devon banks, studded now with thick clusters of primroses and scattered with violets, and at the hawthorn hedges with their soft green leaves now fully broken from their buds.

They turned off the lane and into the woods, already touched with a sheen of azure from the bluebells that would be the next flowers to carpet the ground, and then went into Ted Tozer's meadow and gathered round the pond that lay in one corner.

'Them's tadpoles, miss,' Ernest Coker informed her. 'See, they've come out their jelly stuff – spawn, it's called – and they'll get legs soon and turn into frogs.'

'Or toads,' Henry Bennetts added. 'They might be toads, just as easy.'

Stella crouched down and peered into the pond. The water was full of tiny creatures – tadpoles, water boatmen, skaters, snails – and she wondered if the school had a microscope. At the training college, they'd looked at pondwater and she would like to show these children that there were even more fascinating plants and animals to wonder at than could be seen with the naked eye.

They moved on after a while and Stella heard the full-throated song of a blackbird in a nearby tree and the high, sweet notes of a skylark soaring far overhead.

'I don't know why they need to build an Exhibition in London to tell the world how great Britain is,' she said to her headmistress. 'All they need do is come to Burracombe. There can't be a better place on earth.'

Only one more thing would make her life perfect now – to find her sister, Muriel. But any hope of that seemed as far away as it ever had.

Chapter Twenty-Two

The Festival Is Yours Today.

Dottie put down her newspaper and beamed at Stella. It was 4 May 1951 and the King was to open the Festival of Britain. The day before, riding through cheering crowds in his carriage, flanked by trumpeters in silver, horsemen in scarlet and blue, and accompanied by his wife and daughters, the Duke of Edinburgh and Mr Attlee the Prime Minister, he had gone to St Paul's Cathedral for a service of dedication.

'There's pictures, look,' Dottie said, moving the milk jug and honeypot to spread the paper out on the breakfast table. 'All of them sitting in the front pew. The Princess Royal, the Duchess of Gloucester and Prince William, Princess Margaret – she's ever so tiny, you know, I saw her once close to, at the theatre – and the Duke of Edinburgh and Princess Elizabeth. She'll be Queen one day – it do seem funny, don't it! And there's old Queen Mary, Queen Mother she is properly, only they don't say so here, and the King and Queen themselves. Don't they look lovely!'

'The King made a speech, too,' Stella said, reading the report. '*"One hundred years ago, Queen Victoria opened the Great Exhibition in Hyde Park . . ."*'

'That was the Crystal Palace,' Dottie nodded. 'They moved it afterwards. I saw it burned down before the war – terrible sight, it were.'

'*"This Festival has been planned, like its great predecessor, as a visible sign of national achievement and confidence",'* Stella continued, running her eye down the column and reading out scraps here and there. *'"Dark clouds still overhang the world . . . yet this is no time for despondency . . . I see this Festival as a symbol of Britain's abiding courage and vitality . . ."'*

'Oh, what lovely words!' Dottie cried, wiping her eye with the corner of her apron. 'Oh, he do talk lovely. They say he's ever so shy, you know, and stammers, but I always listen to him at Christmas and I think he sounds a real nice man.'

'"We look back with pride and forward with resolution . . . I have been told of the pageants and displays which have been prepared throughout our countryside—"'

'That's us! Someone's told him about us! Oh, suppose he comes down to see our pageant! The King hisself, here in Burracombe!' Dottie clasped her hands with excitement.

'Well, it doesn't actually say he'll go to visit the pageants,' Stella said. 'I don't expect he'll have time to go round them all, but it's nice that he knows about them, isn't it? Look, it tells you here what they're doing today – they're opening the Exhibition on the South Bank at eleven and they're going to be there an hour and a half. The public will be able to go in at half-past two.' She turned the page. 'Here are some more pictures of them. A nice one of the King and Queen, and one of Princess Elizabeth and Prince Philip. And – oh, look at this one of the little boys – Prince Charles and Prince Richard. I wonder where Princess Anne was?'

'Home in her pram, I should think.' Dottie took back the newspaper. 'She's only nine months old, dear little blossom. Look at this – pictures of what it looked like on television. My stars, that'd be something, wouldn't it – to be able to sit indoors and watch it on your own television. I don't know that anyone's got one in Burracombe, do you?

242

They haven't even got one up at the Barton. Let's see what's on the wireless tonight.'

Dottie and Stella had fallen into the habit of scanning the newspaper each morning to decide what they would listen to that evening, if Dottie wasn't working at the pub. *The Archers* was a firm favourite now, although Stella was aware that the children at school – especially the boys – still missed *Dick Barton*. Tonight, on the Home Service, there was a programme about the Exhibition as well as the first concert from the new Festival Hall. Then there was *Letter From America*, which they didn't usually bother with since they preferred programmes such as *Family Favourites* or *Palace of Varieties* on the Light Programme. Dottie said the latter reminded her of her days in the theatre.

'Well, it do look lovely,' Dottie said at last, folding the newspaper. 'I'm looking forward to the outing, aren't you?' She had offered to come on the school coach to help with the children, and was going to bake a huge number of rock cakes to take with them.

The outing had been fixed for a fortnight's time, and the children were so excited they could scarcely contain themselves. Stella had set up a table in the corner of the infants' classroom and they had made cardboard models of the Dome of Discovery and Skylon, covered with silver paper carefully saved from bars of chocolate. The Thames was represented by a winding snake of grey paint on the hardboard base, and a start had been made on the Battersea Pleasure Gardens. Ernest and Henry had brought in some leafy twigs and stuck them around like trees, with a woollen cat's cradle slung between them for the Treetop Walk, and two of the other boys were trying to make a model of the Guinness Clock out of plasticine.

'We really needs to see it to make a decent job of it, miss,' Micky told Stella solemnly. 'We will be able to go there on the outing, won't we?'

'I'll talk to Miss Kemp about it,' Stella promised. 'The model's looking very good. You're clever with your hands.'

'Well, me dad's the blacksmith, miss. He lets me help him.' Micky brushed his hands together. 'I want to make a proper model of the clock – one that works. It does all sorts of things, miss. It's got the toucans and pelicans and lions and the seal with the bottle of Guinness on his nose, and a kangaroo and a crocodile, and the Mad Hatter from that story about the girl that fell down a rabbit-hole –'

'*Alice in Wonderland*,' Stella said automatically.

'That's right, her's only a girl but it's a good story just the same. Anyway, this clock comes to life every quarter of an hour, miss, and all these birds and animals goes round in a circle and does things, and I thought if I could get a good look at it I could see how it works and make one. My dad'll help with the iron bits.'

'Will he? I'm not sure you'll be able to make one that works,' Stella began doubtfully, but he nodded his head vigorously.

'We will, miss, you'll see. My dad does clocks as well, see, he knows all about them. So I needs to get there in good time to have a proper look at it. I might need to stop there all day.'

'I'm afraid you won't be able to do that,' Stella said firmly. 'There's a lot to see, and we'll be going to the Exhibition itself first. But I'll make sure we see the clock as well. If it's as good as you say, everyone will want to see it.'

Micky sighed and shrugged. He hadn't really expected that he would be allowed to stay and watch the clock all day. There would probably be other interesting things to see, anyway. The Emmett Railway – that was something else he'd heard about. Perhaps if he could get a good look at that, he and his father could build one of their own, right here in Burracombe. What a fine sight that would be, chuffing round the village green . . .

He went off to find some paper, his head filled with ideas he wanted to jot down.

'Val, tell me to mind my own business,' Hilary said, 'but is there anything wrong in your family? I wouldn't ask, but you and Jackie both seem so miserable lately. If there's anything I can do to help . . . ?'

They were sitting on the terrace at the Barton, large cups of coffee on the table between them. Val had brought over a few of her mother's flapjacks and Hilary had put them on a plate. They were made to Alice's own recipe, with peanut butter as well as the more ordinary ingredients, and were deliciously chewy. But despite this and the view of the gardens, burgeoning now with life and spring colour, Val was looking pale and unhappy.

'No, there's nothing the matter,' she said listlessly. 'I'm just a bit tired, that's all. Too much night-duty. And Jackie's still upset over Roy going away.'

'Are you sure that's all it is?' Hilary asked gently. 'It seems to me like more than just missing her boyfriend. She seems worried over something.'

'Worried? Why, what could she be worried about?' Val was staring down the expanse of lawn towards a stand of tall beech trees, tinged with the salmon pink of uncurling new leaves. Then Hilary's meaning seemed to strike her and she turned her head, her eyes widening.

'You don't think she could be *expecting*? Our Jackie?'

'I hope not, but it did cross my mind. She seemed upset as soon as he went away. Oh, I know she would be, but I thought then there was more to it than just saying goodbye to her boyfriend. Most girls have to do that anyway. They drift around the house in tears for a few days, and then they get used to it and start writing letters and going out with their friends again. But Jackie didn't seem to do that.'

'She was talking about getting engaged before he went

away,' Val said. 'In fact, she told Mum that they *were* engaged. She didn't say anything to Dad, mind – she knew he'd hit the roof at the very idea. My goodness, Hil, if you're right he'll blow the roof right off! What are we going to do?'

'I don't know that I am right. I just wondered – I'm probably being very unfair.'

'I hope you are.' Val shook her head. 'It certainly puts my problems into the shade.' She stopped abruptly and Hilary gave her a curious glance.

'There *is* something the matter, isn't there?' she said after a moment or two. 'Why don't you tell me about it, Val? You know it won't go any further.'

Val looked at her indecisively, then seemed to make up her mind. 'Oh, I don't know, Hil – I'm just feeling restless, I suppose. I don't seem to be going anywhere with my life. I mean, it's the same thing, day in, day out – going into Tavistock, coming home again. Night-duty, day-duty. It's a worthwhile job, I know, and it's better than working in a factory or a shop, but where is it taking me? Am I going to do the same thing until I'm old? Isn't there anything else?'

'What else do you want?' Hilary asked quietly.

'What I *had*!' Val cried, thumping the little table so that the cups and saucers rattled. 'Or what I *thought* I had – what I thought it would lead to. Marriage, my own home – children.' Her eyes filled with tears and she brushed them away angrily. 'I didn't want to do this, Hil. It's so selfish. I'm not the only one to have lost her sweetheart in the war. Look at you, you were just the same – never got as far as being married.'

Hilary was silent for a moment. Then she said, 'I'm not sure that I wanted it all that much.'

'What do you mean?' Val stared at her. 'Didn't you want to marry Henry?'

'I'm not sure. I thought I did, but in those days we just

246

did what we were expected to do, didn't we? Girls were expected to get engaged and married; if you were still single at twenty-four, you were on the shelf. Too old to get a man. And Henry was around at the right time – our families knew each other ... we were sort of thrown together. Everywhere I went, he was there too. I sometimes wonder whether it wasn't all arranged. It all seemed so suitable – his father and Daddy being such friends and having the same kind of estates and everything. To tell you the truth, Val, I don't even remember him actually proposing; we just seemed to drift into it.'

'But you must remember him proposing!' Val exclaimed. 'No girl could forget her proposal.'

'Well, there you are then. I *have* forgotten – so he can't have done.' Hilary frowned, as if racking her brains. 'There was a day when we were out riding – it was a hunt meet – and Henry took a bank too fast and fell off. I went over to see if he was all right and when he'd got up and brushed himself down he said something about taking care not to do anything like that just before the wedding. And when I asked him what wedding, he just said, "Ours, of course!" And I think that was the nearest he ever got to a proposal. I went home and told Mummy about it, and she was so thrilled, she wanted to announce it at once. She sent in notices to *The Times* and the *Daily Telegraph* and Henry gave me his grandmother's engagement ring – I gave it back to his parents after he was killed, it didn't seem right to keep it – and that was that. I never even accepted him, not properly; it was all taken out of my hands and I went along with it. I couldn't see what else to do. It was the way things were done, you see. People like me married people like Henry, and that was that. We were just thinking about starting the wedding preparations when he went off and got killed.'

'But you must have loved him, surely?' Val asked doubtfully. 'You must have been upset when he was killed.'

'I was upset, yes, of course I was. But not heartbroken. Not like other girls were. I could see the difference between them and me. It was then that I began to wonder if I really did love him. I never really thought about it, you see. I just assumed that I did. I'd never been "in love" so I didn't know what it meant. And I never have been,' she added with a touch of wistfulness in her voice.

Val reached across and touched her hand. 'Oh Hil, I'm sorry.'

'There's no need to be. At least I've never had my heart broken.' She shrugged. 'Maybe I'm not the sort to fall in love. But I can tell you something, Val: I feel the same as you do about life. What are we supposed to do with it, we single women? We can't just sit about and wait for some man to take pity on us and give us a "life". We need a life of our own – something to do that we can be proud of. At least you have that, with your nursing.'

'I suppose so. But I *was* heartbroken when Eddie was killed.' Val paused, then added in a lower tone, 'And I have been in love.'

Something in her voice made Hilary glance at her sharply. 'Well, of course you were. You were engaged to Eddie.'

'Yes,' Val said, staring at her hands. 'Yes, I was.'

They sat quietly together for a few minutes and then she got to her feet. 'I'd better go now. I promised Mum I'd help her in the garden – she's planting out a lot of seedlings. Are you going on any of the charabanc outings to the Festival?'

Hilary nodded. 'I'm helping Felix with the church one. Why don't you come as well, Val? There are still a few seats. See if you can have your day off then.'

Val nodded and walked off round the corner of the

248

house. A trip to London to see all the wonders of the Festival that the newspapers had been talking so much about would be something to look forward to. But as she strolled down the drive, thoughts of days out and trips to London faded from her mind as she recalled their conversation.

Hilary didn't seem to mind that she hadn't married or had children. But I do, Val thought. I mind a lot. I don't like being single. It doesn't suit me. And yet, with Eddie gone, and never having the opportunity of meeting anyone else, what hope do I have?

She thrust away unwelcome thoughts of a lean, pale face and dark blue eyes beneath a mane of black hair, and turned her mind instead to her sister Jackie. Suppose Hilary was right! Suppose Jackie was worried and frightened about having a baby. Too frightened to tell anyone about it; too frightened to ask for help.

I'll have to talk to her, Val decided, pushing her own anxieties out of her mind. I'll have to find out if it's true.

'I don't know,' Jackie said. She twisted away from her sister, but Val gripped her arm and pulled her back to face her. 'I don't *know*, Val – I wish I did! How can you tell? And how soon can you tell? I don't know about people, only about cows and sheep and pigs.' Her lips trembled and her voice broke into sobs. 'Oh, Val, I'm so frightened! I don't know what to do!'

'So you could be,' Val said flatly. All the way home, she had hoped against hope that Hilary was wrong – that Jackie would tell her there was no chance of her being pregnant, that she and Roy hadn't done anything wrong. It had been a relief to find her sister at home by herself and Val had made sure they wouldn't be interrupted by asking Jackie to come up to her bedroom. Then she'd asked her straight out what was the matter, and whether she thought she might be pregnant. She'd thought that Jackie would be furious with her for even suggesting such a thing. I wish she *was* angry, she thought now, looking at Jackie's terrified face. It would be better than this. 'You could be expecting a baby.'

'Don't say it! Don't say it out loud! I've been trying not to think of it. I thought if I didn't say it, it might go away.' Jackie caught the expression on her sister's face. 'I know it's stupid, Val, but you don't know what it's like. It's never happened to you.'

'That's got nothing to do with it!' Val said sharply, and then softened her tone. 'Look, Jackie, it's not going to go away but first of all we've got to be sure that there *is* a baby. When did you and Roy – I mean, when do you think it could have happened?'

'Just after Easter,' Jackie said dully. 'Just before he went away.' She sat on the edge of Val's bed, plaiting the hem of the bedspread between her fingers.

'So that's, let's see . . . about five weeks ago. Well, that's not long. Much too soon to panic, anyway. What makes you so sure? Didn't you take any precautions?'

'We didn't know it was going to happen, did we? *I* didn't, anyway. And I wished we hadn't, straight away.' Jackie's eyes filled with tears again. 'I thought it was supposed to be wonderful, but it wasn't at all – it was just uncomfortable and peculiar. I felt as if everything had gone, somehow. And I was worried all the time that this might happen.' She started to cry again.

'Jackie, we don't know that anything *has* happened. When should you have come on?'

'Three weeks ago. I've been hoping every day – but it's never happened. So I must be, mustn't I. But how could it have happened so quickly? We only did it once!'

'Once is all it takes,' Val said grimly. 'It doesn't happen gradually, you know. It doesn't matter if you take risks once or a hundred times, it's still only once that you fall.'

'Well, I wish we hadn't done it at all,' Jackie said miserably. She dropped the edge of the bedspread and looked at her sister. 'Val, you're a nurse, isn't there anything I can do? Something I could take? You know – to bring things on. I'm sure I've heard—'

'*No!*' Val surprised herself with the sharpness of her voice. 'Don't even think about it. It's a baby, a human being. You can't kill it.'

'It's not a baby, not really. Not yet. It's just a speck, that's all.' Jackie grabbed at her sister's arm and shook it desperately. 'Please, Val, there must be something! Don't you remember when I missed three times once, a couple of years ago, and Mum took me to the doctor and he gave me some pills and they brought on my period? Couldn't you get me some of those?'

'No, I couldn't.' Val could barely speak for the surge of emotions welling up inside her. Anger, bitterness, regret – and yet, beneath those, a deep compassion for her young sister, so frantic and bewildered. She must have been going through absolute hell over the past few weeks, Val thought, and fought down her anger.

'Jackie, I can't just steal medicines from the hospital. And it's dangerous, anyway. Women have died trying to do what you're suggesting.' She paused, then added, 'And besides, it's murder. It isn't just a speck, Jackie, it's a baby, and it's growing all the time. It's going to be a person and there's nothing you can do to stop it.'

Jackie stared at her. Her face was as white as a paper mask, and her eyes like huge black holes. 'I'll have to kill myself then,' she said hopelessly. 'Because if I don't, Mum and Dad will.'

'*Jackie!* That's a terrible thing to say. A *wicked* thing. You mustn't ever, *ever* say such things again, do you hear me?' Val took her by the shoulders and shook her angrily. Then she caught herself up again and held her sister more gently. 'It won't be as bad as that. I'll stand by you. These things happen, you know they do. It's awful at the time, but people get over it. And once the baby's born – well, you know what they say. Babies bring their love with them.' Her voice shook and she turned away so that Jackie wouldn't see her own tears. 'Anyway,' she added, 'I expect Roy will marry you. You wanted to get engaged, didn't you?'

'Yes, but Mum told me there was no chance that they'd let us get married before I was twenty-one. And Roy's only nineteen. Suppose *his* mum and dad won't give permission? Oh, it's all such a *mess*!' Her tears began to flow again. 'It's not fair. There's you been engaged but never got married, and me having a baby I don't want. Why does everything have to go wrong?'

'I don't know,' Val said quietly. 'I just don't know, but it's the way it is and what we've got to do now is face up to it. Now look, it's still early days – if you've been worrying yourself sick over what happened, that might easily have stopped your period coming. When would you be due again?'

'Next week, I suppose.' The girl looked at her with sudden hope. 'D'you really think I might be all right?'

'We'll just have to wait and see, but it can happen. And you're more likely to come on if you stop worrying like this. Try to put it out of your mind for a few days and see what happens.'

'*Put it out of my mind?*' Jackie stared at her sister as if she'd suddenly grown two heads. 'Well, it's easy to see *you've* never had to worry about anything like this, Val! It's on my mind all the time. I can't think of anything else. I've been *trying* not to think about it all these weeks and it just gets worse and worse.' She picked up Val's pillow and thumped it back on the bed. 'It's like being in a horrible trap all the time, and there's no way out. There's no way out at all.'

Val bit her lip. 'Jackie, if there was anything I could do . . .'

'There is. But you won't, will you.'

'I've already told you, I can't. Do you want us both to end up in prison? Look, I've promised I'll stand by you. If it has happened, you'll have to tell Mum and Dad sometime, and I'll help you. And then there's Roy.'

'What about him?' Jackie asked with a return to her old, listless manner.

'Well, he'll have to know as well, won't he! Isn't he due some leave sometime soon? Don't they get a weekend or something after the first six weeks? Hilary says Stephen's coming back the week after next.'

'Yes, he's coming back then too. But I don't even know if I want to see him again. I don't know what I feel about him now.'

'I expect you feel just the same,' Val said gently. 'You've had a nasty shock and you're worried and frightened. I expect you love him just as much, underneath.'

Jackie was silent for a few minutes. She picked at the bedspread again. 'Do I have to tell Mum and Dad yet?' she asked at last. 'Can't I wait a bit longer?'

'Well, I certainly wouldn't tell them until you know for sure. There's no point in upsetting them unnecessarily. But you do have to tell Roy. If you two have to get married in a hurry, he'll need to arrange leave. You don't want him being sent off to Germany or Korea or somewhere before you've had a chance to have a wedding.'

'Korea! You don't really think they'll send him there, do you?' A new fear sharpened Jackie's voice and Val cursed herself.

'No, of course they won't. I don't suppose he'll ever

leave the country. Now look, I can hear someone down-stairs – it's probably Mum, back from Tavistock. Go and wash your face and then have a lie-down on your bed. I'll bring you a cup of tea – I'll tell Mum you've got a headache. You don't want her to see you've been crying.'

She went downstairs. Alice had gone out again to feed the hens so Val was able to make the tea without answering questions. She stood in the big kitchen, waiting for the kettle to boil, thinking of what Jackie had said.

There's you, been engaged and never got married, and me having a baby I don't want. And: *It's easy to see you've never had to worry about anything like this.* And then the age-old cry: *It isn't fair!*

She's right, Val thought sadly, unable to stop her own tears overflowing and rolling slowly down her cheeks. It isn't fair.

Chapter Twenty-Three

The school outing was fixed for Whit Monday, halfway through May. It was a Bank Holiday and half-term as well. Burracombe School being a church school, the children had Ascension Day off too, but the vicar had vetoed any suggestion that they should go to the Festival then.

'We always have a service in the morning,' he told Shirley Culliford's mother. The Cullifords weren't church-goers and had little idea of the significance of the various dates, apart from Christmas and Easter which seemed to have more to do with presents and chocolate eggs than anything spiritual. 'It would be much too late to think of going to London after that.'

'A service?' It happened every year, and every year Mrs Culliford seemed equally surprised. 'Do my youngsters hev to go as well?'

'Those who go to school, yes. They must come to school just as usual in the morning and they'll all walk to the church together. Everyone else is welcome too. You could bring the little ones,' he added without much hope.

As expected, Mrs Culliford shook her head vigorously. 'I ent been inside the church since my Joe were christened. Makes me go all funny, it do. Well, never mind. Shirley can help with a few jobs round the place in the afternoon, look after the little 'uns while I goes to Tavi on the bus to get me hair done.' She touched her brassy yellow curls self-consciously. 'Need a new perm, I do.'

She went on her way, leaving the vicar reflecting that there always seemed to be enough money in the Culliford household for hairstyles and cigarettes, if not for clean, tidy clothes for the children. Still, young Shirley seemed to be taking more care of herself these days. Ever since being appointed Festival Queen she had come to school every day with a clean face and a not too dirty dress. She had made an apron in the weekly sewing class, with three strips of coloured bias binding sewn on to it, and her stitches were really neat. Mr Harvey seemed to have been right about her after all, Miss Kemp had admitted to Stella.

The day of the outing dawned fine and warm, with just a faint hazy mist to promise good weather. The children were on the green by seven-fifteen, clutching their lunchboxes and the macintoshes that Miss Kemp had insisted upon, and hopping with excitement. The mothers and fathers who had agreed to come and help were there as well, trying to keep their own children under control, and Hilary and Val had managed to persuade Jackie to come along.

'It'll do you good to have a day out,' Val had said. 'And you know how much you wanted to go to the Exhibition.'

Jackie looked at her dolefully but said nothing, and Val remembered that the Festival had been a bone of contention between Jackie and their mother. She'd wanted to go with Roy – and stay overnight. She and Alice had quarrelled about it on New Year's Eve. What a long time ago that seemed.

Still, Jackie had agreed to come on the outing, although she didn't look as if she expected to enjoy it. Her face was paler than ever, her eyes smudged with dark shadows, and she was looking thinner. Val glanced at her anxiously. I hope she's not going to faint on us, she thought. Maybe I shouldn't have persuaded her to come after all.

The charabanc arrived and everyone scrambled aboard. Miss Kemp had a list and stood at the front, by the driver, checking off all the names. The driver was from a neighbouring village and often drove the bus into Tavistock as well; he was a cheerful man who seemed to have an inexhaustible supply of jokes to entertain his passengers, but wasn't quite so good at finding his way on long journeys. Stella had been deputed to sit behind him with the road map and make sure they didn't end up in Glasgow.

'He can't be that bad,' she'd protested, laughing, but Basil Harvey had given her a wry look.

'He can. He took the Mother's Union on a summer outing to Castle Combe once and they finished up in Castle Cary! They enjoyed themselves, but the Castle Combe Mother's Union wasn't too pleased. They'd prepared tea in the church hall and had to take it all home again.'

'Well, I don't think he could miss London quite so easily,' she said, 'but I'll make sure he doesn't go wrong.'

Felix was coming too; he sat down next to Hilary in the other front seat. Val and Jackie sat behind Stella. Stella gave them both a friendly smile, surprised when Val returned it rather coldly.

The charabanc set off and the children immediately began to investigate their lunch packets. Miss Kemp, well used to this, walked down the aisle telling them to put the food away again. 'We'll eat it when we arrive. There's a long day ahead and you'll be hungry if you eat it now.'

'Please, miss, when will us be there?' one small girl asked. 'Only I forgot to go to the lavvy before us came out.'

Miss Kemp gave her a look of exasperation. 'I asked you all if you'd been. You could have gone to the school lavatories.'

'I don't like the school lavvies,' the little girl said. 'There's germs there.'

'There are germs everywhere, but Mrs Purdy keeps the lavatories nice and clean.' The headmistress realised that there was no point in argument and sighed. 'We'll stop at Moretonhampstead. You can all go to the lavatories there. Well, those of you that *want* to, then,' she added, forestalling further objections. 'You don't have to go, but we shan't be stopping again for a long time. You'd better make sure all the little ones go,' she added to Stella. 'It's excitement more than anything else. Most of them have never been so far on an outing before, let alone to London.'

The journey continued, with the usual brief stops for children who felt sick, and a few traffic hold-ups. Stella was almost as excited as the children. I wish Luke could have come, she thought, but he doesn't really have much to do with the village, and nothing at all with the school. I must get him to come in and give them a painting lesson one day.

Felix, sitting across the aisle, gave her a warm grin. 'Are you all right with that map?'

'I think so. I've never been to London myself, so I won't be much use when we actually get there. I just hope everything's signposted.'

'I might be able to help you there. I know London pretty well – my grandparents live there and I visit them a lot. They used to take me about quite a bit when I was a child. There've been a few changes since then, with the bombing, but I can still find my way about.'

'You'd better take over then,' Stella said gratefully. 'I was dreading sending the driver the wrong way.'

Felix came and sat beside her. 'It's quite easy, really. It's right in the middle of London, on the South Bank of the Thames, and the Battersea Pleasure Gardens are a bit further down.' They put their heads together over the maps, and Val took the opportunity to go and sit with Hilary.

'How's Jackie?' Hilary murmured, glancing back at the girl who was staring dully out of the window. 'Did you get a chance to talk to her?'

Val nodded. 'You were right. She's scared stiff she's – you know.' She glanced around, aware that some of the villagers and children had sharp ears. 'Hasn't she said anything to you this week?'

'I've hardly seen her, to tell the truth. I've been away most of the week. I went to see one of my VAD friends – the girl who became a stewardess on one of the airlines.'

'Oh yes?' Val said with interest. 'Is she enjoying it?'

'Yes, she is. She goes all over Europe – to Paris and Rome, places like that – and she has a lovely flat in London. She's been sharing it with two other girls.' Hilary hesitated, then said, 'One of them's leaving soon, as a matter of fact, and she's asked me if I'd like to take her place.'

Val turned her head and stared at her. 'You? Go and live in London?'

'Ssh!' Hilary begged her. 'Yes, why not? I might apply to the airline for a job, too. Or find something else to do. There must be plenty of jobs in London – in one of the big stores, for instance.'

Val was silent for a while, taking in the idea of Hilary going to live and work in London. 'I'd miss you,' she said at last. 'And what about your father? He'd be pretty upset, wouldn't he?'

'Yes, he would.' Hilary frowned a little, then added with a touch of defiance, 'But I can't spend my whole life looking after him, Val. I came home when Mummy was ill, but that was years ago now. It's not as if he lets me do anything interesting. I could do more to help him with the estate, but you know what he's like – thinks a woman's place is in the home. In the kitchen, in fact,' she added bitterly. 'But I want more than that.'

'I know you do. So are you really going to London? When d'you think it will be?'

'Soon, I think. Now I've made up my mind, I don't want to wait. I feel I've waited long enough already. In fact, I'm planning to tell him tonight, when we get back. It'll be a good opportunity, don't you think? He'll ask how the day went, and I can lead into it from there.' She looked at her friend, flushed and bright-eyed, more excited and happy than Val had seen her for a long time.

It's the right thing for her, Val thought. She really needs something more than running a house for her father. But what about me? All I've ever wanted is to run a house for a man I love, and have his children. And it doesn't look as if it's ever going to happen. Hilary's getting the life she wants. Jackie might be having a baby she *doesn't* want. And me?

She thought of the hot, bright days in Egypt; the star-studded nights; the work on the wards, nursing soldiers who had been brought in suffering wounds that seemed almost unimaginable now. And the young war artist with his dark blue eyes and wild black hair, that even Army discipline couldn't tame.

And then, as always, she thought of Eddie.

The Exhibition was everything that they had expected. From the moment they entered the seemingly endless streets of London and first saw the shape of Big Ben, familiar from the pictures Stella and Miss Kemp had been showing the children, it seemed as if the little ones would blow the bus apart with their excitement. They made their way slowly, following a long line of coaches and charabancs, with Stella and Felix giving the driver directions and the children chattering like sparrows. When they finally reached the big coach park, Miss Kemp had difficulty making herself heard.

'Nobody will be allowed off this bus until you've all quietened down and listened to me,' she said, raising her voice so that it penetrated to the back of the bus. 'That's better. Now, this is a big place and we don't want to lose anyone. Every helper has four children to look after. We shall keep in our group, but there are a lot of people about and we may get separated, so stay with each other and don't wander off on your own.' She paused and looked at her map of the Exhibition. 'First of all, we'll go to the Dome of Discovery and the Skylon. They're easy to see.' She pointed out of the window and everyone twisted and craned their necks. 'If anyone does get lost, go to the Skylon and wait for someone to come and fetch you. After that, we'll find somewhere to have our sandwiches and then we'll go to the Battersea Pleasure Gardens.' The children cheered. 'We'll have two hours there and I've arranged for you to have tickets for some of the rides. You'll be able to go on the Emmett Train and the Treetop Walk, and the Caterpillar. And you'll be able to see the—'

'What about the Rotor?' Henry asked in an aggrieved voice. 'I wants to go on the Rotor.'

'They don't allow children on the Rotor,' Miss Kemp said firmly, making up her mind not to go anywhere near it, 'but you will be able to see the—'

'What about the Big Dipper, then?' he persisted. 'My brother knows someone who's been on it and he says it's 'andsome.'

'You can go on the Cake Walk and into the Hall of Mirrors. And you can—'

'There's an 'Aunted 'Ouse as well,' her tormentor said. 'I wants to go in that. Full of ghosts and skellytons, it is.' He put both hands to the sides of his head and waggled his fingers, pursing his lips to make the eerie noise he believed ghosts and skeletons to make. 'Whooh. Whoo-ooh.'

'Henry, will you please be quiet!' Miss Kemp snapped, losing patience. 'You'll have tickets for some of the rides and you'll have to ask your helpers if you can go on any of the others.' Having neatly passed the responsibility to Henry's own mother, she went on, 'We'll be leaving at five o'clock sharp, and I'll tell you where we're to meet when we get to the Pleasure Gardens. Now—'

'Ain't us going to see the Guinness Clock?' came the disappointed voice of Micky, the blacksmith's son. 'I wanted to see that. It goes every quarter of an hour and there's all these animals—'

'Yes, of course we'll see the Guinness Clock,' Miss Kemp said. Micky had been drawing the clock and trying to work out its intricate movements in every spare moment for the past three weeks. 'That's what I was going to tell you when Henry kept interrupting me. We'll go to see that together, and then you'll be able to choose which rides you want to go on – with your helpers, of course. And it'll probably be a good place for us to meet at the end of the afternoon.'

'Please, miss,' said a little girl anxiously, 'will there be any lavvies here, only I don't think I can wait much—'

'Yes, of course there'll be lavatories. We'll find one now and everyone can go before we visit the Dome of Discovery.' The headmistress climbed out of the bus and there was a rush for the door. 'One at a time, *please*! Remember that people will be looking at you and thinking that Burracombe people don't know how to behave themselves. Show them what lovely manners you all have.'

The children obediently got off the bus one by one and formed themselves into a crocodile. Miss Kemp heaved a sigh of relief and said to Stella, 'They should be all right. We've got enough mothers here, and a couple of fathers as well. Nothing should go wrong.'

'Provided Henry doesn't go on the Rotor or the Big Dipper,' Stella said with a grin. 'He's the sort of boy who'd be right at the top when it got stuck. Trouble seems to stick to him like grass.'

'Well, his mother's come along as one of the helpers so it's up to her,' the headmistress said. 'So long as she gets

262

him out of whatever scrape he manages to get into before five o'clock ... Now, if you've all made yourselves comfortable,' she announced to the children who were returning from the lavatories, 'we'll start.'

From then on, the day was nothing but wonder, and the children would remember it all their lives. They filed into the darkness of the Dome and progressed through all the Zones, from Land, Earth and Sea through the Living World and Polar Zones with the Captain Scott displays and husky dogs, ending at Outer Space where they could see radio signals being sent to the Moon and a huge screen showing their return. The wheeling display in the roof of the Stars and Planets didn't impress them so much, since they could see a similar display on any clear night in Burracombe, but by the time they emerged blinking into the sunlight half the boys had made up their minds to be spacemen and the other half explorers.

The tall, silver cigar shape of the Skylon rose into the air just outside the Dome and they took turns to stand on the spot exactly underneath and stare upwards. Then they went down to the seats all along the riverside and ate their lunch.

'There's so much to see,' Hilary remarked to Felix, who had escaped from the Cullifords to come and sit beside her. 'It seems a shame to leave it and go to a Fun Fair.'

'Well, it is the children's outing,' he said. 'I expect the others will be more worthy – the Mother's Union and the WI. And then there's Mrs Warren's village outing, for anyone who wants to go again or didn't go on the others. I can't imagine that she'll allow us to ride on the Caterpillar or the Big Dipper!'

Hilary laughed. 'She might find herself over-ruled about that. Anyway, once we're here we can do as we like. Will you be coming up again, Felix?'

'Oh yes. Mr Harvey and I will both come on the Mother's Union trip, and so will Mrs Harvey, of course.

But it would be nice to come independently too, don't you think? It would be easy enough to come by train.' He looked at her.

Hilary knew she was blushing. She said, 'Yes, I suppose it would.'

'Would you like to do that too?' he asked. 'Come with me, for a day out by ourselves? No villagers around to watch what we're doing and start any gossip?' He grinned and one of his eyelids flickered.

Hilary felt confused. She liked Felix and knew that he liked her, but she wasn't at all sure that it went any further than that. She didn't even know whether this suggestion meant that he wanted it to. What's more, she wasn't even sure how much longer she would be in Burracombe, if she took up her friend's offer of a place in the flat . . . On the other hand, if she had moved to London, she could always meet him here.

'It depends when it is,' she said at last. 'I'm quite busy just now. Let's think about it after we get home.' By the time Felix suggested it again, she would have told her father that she was leaving. She quaked at the thought of the fury and disappointment that this announcement would create, and knew that she couldn't make any plans until things had at least begun to settle down.

'All right,' he said cheerfully. 'We'll look at our diaries . . . It looks as though the headmistress is getting the children rounded up now. It must be time to make for the Fair.' He gathered up the debris of their lunch and crammed it into his tin. 'I'm looking forward to this. It's years since I've been on a roundabout.'

'Now, that I don't believe,' Hilary retorted, screwing up her own paper bags. 'Didn't you go to the Goosey Fair in Tavistock last October?'

'Yes, I did, but I didn't have the nerve to go on anything. I'd only just arrived then, hadn't I, and I didn't want to shock the local populace too much. But this is different. This is the King's Festival and if he and the Queen approve, I think Burracombe should approve as well.'

'Even Mrs Warren?' Hilary asked wickedly, and he put his head on one side and pretended to consider.

'Well, perhaps not Mrs Warren. But she's not here today, is she? Today is just for the kids!' He gripped her hand and pulled her up beside him. 'Tell you what, let's escape Miss Kemp's eagle eye and go on the Big Dipper. We might even get stuck on the top!'

Hilary followed him, laughing. Felix was a nice man, she thought, dropping her rubbish into a litter-bin. And although he was a curate, he wasn't nervous or obsequious as some she had met, trying too hard to make a good impression. He behaved with an easy confidence, as if sure that everyone would like him. And most people did.

All the same, she wasn't sure that she wanted their relationship to go further than friendship. As she'd told Val, she'd never felt herself to be really 'in love' and didn't know if she would recognise it if it came along. Nor was she convinced that it even existed, except as a romantic dream.

I don't want to end up as a vicar's wife, she thought. I want a life of my own. I want to *do* something, before it's too late.

Val and Jackie had agreed to help look after the Nethercott twins and two other little girls. 'At least if we lose one of the twins, we'll have the other one to show people,' Val said with a grin, but her sister responded only with a small, dismal smile.

Val sighed and shook her head. If only Jackie could relax for a little while. Even if her fears came true, there was no point in being miserable all the time. Hang on, you're a fine one to talk, she told herself ruefully. You've been mooning about like a lost weekend for the past six years now.

As she sat in the charabanc, gazing out of the window at the countryside, at orchards full of apple trees in blossom and gardens filled with late spring flowers, she realised that her mood had begun to lift just lately. Ever since New Year's Eve, when her mother had persuaded her to go down to the village green to hear the bells and dance round the oak tree, she had felt less oppressed by her memories. It was as if a heavy black shadow had begun to shift from her heart.

Yet her remorse over Eddie hadn't changed. She felt as guilty as ever about the way she had treated him. The fact that he had never known about Luke didn't make any difference. Val had been unfaithful to him, and nothing could change that. And Luke's return to her life should have made it worse. It *had* made things worse, she told herself fiercely. Seeing him had brought it all back – the anguish of saying goodbye to Eddie, knowing that she might never see him again; the misery of living through the days, the months, the years of separation; the sudden rapture of a forbidden love, coming out of the blue when she was in Egypt, and the inevitable guilt. And, most crushing of all, the terrible remorse when she heard that Eddie had died of his wounds.

None of that had changed, and the few encounters she had had with Luke had all been angry ones. Yet they were the only times when she had been able to express her anger – anger that she felt with both him and herself. Never, until now, had she been able to speak of what had happened. It was like the release of a volcano, dormant for months and then suddenly allowed to erupt.

'Val, wake up,' Jackie said suddenly, and Val shook herself and turned, disorientated for a moment. 'I've asked you three times now if you want a toffee.'

'Sorry – I was miles away.' She took the sweet that her

266

sister was offering her. 'How are you feeling now? You haven't been sick or anything, have you?'

'No. When's that supposed to happen?'

'At about six weeks, I think.' They were talking in low voices, wary of being overheard even though everyone else on the bus was talking at the tops of their voices. 'It doesn't happen to everyone, though. I don't think it's much of a sign if you don't get it.'

'Thanks, that's cheered me up a lot.' Jackie stuffed the bag of toffees back into her pocket. 'Val, you haven't thought any more about what I asked you, have you? You know – about medicines and things?'

'No, I haven't!' Val's voice was sharp and she lowered it quickly. 'I've told you, it's dangerous and it's illegal. And don't go asking anyone else.' A sudden fear gripped her. 'You haven't done that, have you? You haven't mentioned it to anyone else?'

'No, I haven't, you don't need to fuss.' Jackie sat back and stared out of the window. In front of them, Felix was moving over to sit beside Stella to look at the map, and Hilary glanced round at Val. 'Go and sit beside Miss Napier,' Jackie said. 'I'll be all right. I just don't feel like talking any more.'

Val hesitated and then shrugged. 'All right, then.' She did as Jackie had suggested and settled down beside her friend.

Jackie leaned her head against the window and wished she hadn't come. She felt tired and uncomfortable and had a headache coming on. I ought to have stayed at home, she thought. This was supposed to be such fun. Me and Roy were planning to come up to the Festival together and see all the sights. And now he's gone away and it's all been spoiled. My whole life's been spoiled. And all for the sake of a few minutes that were just a big disappointment anyway.

I wish I'd never done it. I don't think I'll ever do it again.

Stella was enjoying herself. She knew all the children now and liked the way they clustered round her, peppering her with questions about London. They ignored her when she told them she'd never lived there – anyone from 'up-country' must know about London, they believed – and continued to ask her about the Tower, Buckingham Palace, Big Ben and whether she had ever met any of the Royal Family, especially the dashing Prince Philip.

'I think he's proper handsome,' one of the older girls said as they walked down to the lunch-spot beside the river. 'Princess Elizabeth's lucky. Just think, he'll be King one day – King Philip.'

'No, he won't,' Stella said. 'Princess Elizabeth will be Queen, but he won't be King.'

They stared at her. 'Why not, miss? Why won't he be King?'

'Because it's Princess Elizabeth who will inherit the throne. Don't you remember the lesson Miss Kemp gave us all about it a little while ago? She'll be Queen, because she's the King's daughter, but Prince Philip won't be King.'

'So who will be King?' one of the boys asked.

'Nobody. We won't have one.'

'Won't *have* one?' he demanded, outraged. 'How be us going to manage without a King?'

'I've told you, we'll have a Queen,' Stella said, suspecting that they were about to go round in circles.

'Well, I don't think that's fair. If a girl can be Queen, a boy oughter be able to be King, didn't un?' He turned to his friends but they had reached the picnic tables now and were more interested in their lunch-tins. Stella heaved a sigh of relief. The rules of accession were more than she could cope with today.

Felix and Hilary were sitting together, and the children had rushed for the wooden benches. Stella hesitated, looking for a space, and noticed one beside Val Tozer. Rather unsure of her welcome, after the cool smile Val had given her in the morning, she slipped into it.

'Hullo,' she said, opening her packet of sandwiches. 'It's a wonderful Exhibition, isn't it? And the children are having a lovely time.'

'Yes, they seem to be.'

Stella took a bite from a Marmite sandwich. Val was staring across the river towards the Houses of Parliament. Not far away, the Festival Hall was beginning a lunchtime concert, and in the Riverside Theatre Leo Sachs was presenting a 'Song Saloon'. The whole area was filled with life and colour, and the sights and sounds of people enjoying themselves.

'They're going to enjoy the Fun Fair too,' she said. 'Are you going to go on any of the rides?'

'Haven't decided,' Val said crisply, and got up. 'Excuse me.' She walked away briskly, leaving Stella looking after her blankly. Whatever did I say to offend her, she wondered. She seemed quite annoyed – almost angry. Is it because Felix Copley came to sit beside me? Yet as far as Stella knew, Val had no special friendship with the young curate. Perhaps she wanted one, and was jealous of anyone else who had his attention. Yet she didn't seem jealous of Hilary Napier, who had more of Felix's attention than anyone else.

I suppose the truth is that she just doesn't like me, Stella decided, and shrugged her shoulders. There was nothing to be done about that. She finished her sandwiches and turned to the little girl who had come to sit beside her. It was Shirley Culliford.

'Are you having a nice time, Shirley?'

'Oh miss,' the child said, her eyes shining. 'It's like heaven!'

Val felt irritated with herself for the way she had treated Stella. The girl had done nothing to her, and had gone out of her way to be pleasant. It was just that whenever Val saw her, yet another emotion stirred amongst all the other complicated feelings she was experiencing lately, and she didn't want to give it a name.

I know Luke said there's nothing between them, she thought crossly, leaning on the low wall to look down at the river, and it doesn't matter to me if there is. So why does it annoy me so much? *I* don't want him.

And you don't want anyone else to have him either, a small voice whispered inside her. *Ever heard of dogs in mangers?*

I just wish he'd told me what this stupid secret is that she's got, Val argued. If I knew that, I'd know if he was telling me the truth. What can it be that he's helping her with? Why can't he tell me?

And why, asked the little voice inside her, *don't you tell Luke* your *little secret?*

Angrily, Val turned away from the river. It wasn't a nice river, anyway – too wide, too turbid, too deep. She preferred the rivers of Devon, like the Tavy, rushing over rocks and between heather-covered banks and through woods and fields towards the Tamar, or the Walkham, dancing to meet the Tavy at Double Waters. Or the Meavy as it cascaded into the Plym at Shaugh Prior. Clear, sparkling streams where fish could breathe and you could see the dipper flirting its brown tail on a rock or diving into the water to run along the riverbed. I don't like London at all, really, she thought. This Exhibition's all very well, but I'd hate to live here, and I had enough of travelling during the war. I'd rather be at home where I belong.

She thought of Hilary's plans to leave Burracombe and

start a new, independent life. Could her friend really be doing the right thing? Whatever Hilary believed, she had been brought up to live in the country, on an estate. She liked that way of life. She enjoyed the hunting, the daily routine of the countryside, the rhythm of the seasons, the social life. Could she really adapt to living in a place like London?

Someone touched her arm and she turned to find her sister standing beside her, a strange look on her face. 'Val . . .'

'What? What is it?' She felt a spurt of alarm. 'You're not feeling ill, are you? You haven't got pains or anything?'

'No. *Yes!*' Jackie shook her head, half-laughing, half in tears. 'Oh Val, it's all right! *It's all right*! I'm not going to have a baby after all.' She buried her face against her sister's shoulder. 'There isn't anything to worry about. It was all a false alarm! Oh Val!'

At last the outing came to an end and the charabanc set off for home. It had been a long day and there was still a lengthy drive ahead of them, but most of the children were so worn out with the excitement of it all that they would probably sleep a lot of the way. Miss Kemp had arranged to stop for fish and chips, which would revive them a little, and then they would doze again. She just hoped they hadn't eaten too much ice cream and wouldn't start feeling sick.

'I shouldn't think so,' Stella remarked. 'Did you see the cost of those Eldorado Neapolitans? *Three shillings*! I didn't know an ice cream *could* cost that much.'

'There were cheaper cornets, but I agree they couldn't have afforded much, and I don't think any of them brought sweet coupons. I did see Shirley Culliford almost obliterated by an enormous stick of candy floss, but really that's not much more than sugary air. Anyway, they all seem to have enjoyed themselves, and that's the main thing.'

'They'll never forget it,' Stella said. 'It's been a wonderful day.'

The children were talking about it too as they slumped in their seats, almost overwhelmed by the wonders they had seen. They had all been on the Emmett Train and along the Treetop Walk, and most of them had been on the Caterpillar. Micky had had to be dragged away from the Guinness Clock, and Henry and Ernest had given their mothers the slip and were next seen on the Rotor, glued upside down to the wall as the centrifugal force whirled them around. They had then managed to get on to the Big Dipper, where Henry had been sick and ordered off by the man running it, and after that, more subdued, they had done more or less as they were told.

'I liked the Cake Walk best,' Helen Nethercott informed Stella. 'June and me couldn't walk properly – the floor kept breaking up. It were ever so funny.'

'And in the Hall of Mirrors we went all funny shapes,' her twin said. 'I were all long and thin, and Helen were short and fat with bendy legs.'

'Those were two different mirrors,' Helen added. 'But there was all sorts, and us didn't know which way to go some of the time.'

'I'm not sure I know which way to go now,' the driver remarked, overhearing this. 'Is anyone looking at the map? It was all right coming into London, everything was signposted, but there's nothing to tell us how to get back to Burracombe.'

Stella and Felix grinned at each other and returned to their duties. With only a few wrong turnings and views of some unexpected parts of London, they finally found their way out and on to the right road to Devon. They settled back in their seats and relaxed.

'It's been a good day,' Felix said quietly. He had gone

back across the aisle to sit beside Hilary. He glanced sideways at her. 'You've enjoyed it, haven't you, Hilary?'

'Yes, I have. It's done me good. Helped me to come to a decision.' She was sitting with her head back and her eyes closed, a small smile touching her lips, and Felix looked at her curiously.

'A decision? An important one?'

'I think so. Important to me, anyway.' She opened her eyes and smiled at him. 'I can't tell you yet. I can't tell anyone yet. I have to talk to my father first. But when I have, I'll tell you all about it.'

She looked out of the window. They were leaving London behind now and trundling through the green countryside of Berkshire. She thought of the life she wanted to lead, the responsibilities she yearned to take on, the skills and abilities she knew she possessed and so desperately wanted to use.

Dad will be furious, she thought. He'll hate it. He'll rant and rave and tell me I'm letting him down, especially now that Stephen's gone. I couldn't even have done this if Stephen had still been at home – it would have been like condemning him to a life he didn't want, just as I've been.

But she was sure that her father would come round eventually. He wouldn't want to alienate his children for ever. He would have to accept that life had changed, that Hilary didn't want to stay at home cooking his meals and running his house. That she deserved more.

I'll tell him tomorrow, she thought. I'll tell him first thing in the morning.

But by then, everything had changed.

Chapter Twenty-Four

'And you don't know how long he's been like this?' Charles Latimer asked. He let go of the Squire's wrist and looked gravely at the distraught young woman beside him. 'You didn't see him last night, when you came home?'

'No. He left a note saying he was tired and had gone up early. And I didn't wake up until after eight. I thought when I came downstairs that he must have gone out – then I saw the dogs were still there and obviously hadn't been fed, and I began to worry. But I didn't actually come up to see for another half-hour. The first one down sees to them and I thought he must have heard me open the door . . . It wasn't until nine o'clock that I really started to worry. He's always down by then. And then I heard him call out.'

The doctor moved away from the bed and Hilary followed him, still casting anxious glances over her shoulder. She lowered her voice. 'He was obviously in awful pain and he seemed so frightened – I've never seen him like that before. What's happened to him, Charles?' She looked at her father, propped up on a pile of pillows and slipping into a doze. 'What's the matter with him? He – he's not dying, is he?'

'No, no, certainly not. But I'm afraid he's had a heart attack.' He laid his hand on Hilary's shoulder. 'I don't think it's a serious one – more a warning.'

'A warning?'

'Try to understand,' the doctor said. 'The heart's a

muscle, like any other, but if it's made to work too hard it will be overstrained. Your father's heart obviously can't cope with the amount of work he's been asking it to do. He needs to cut down in several ways – on the amount of work he does, the burden of running the estate, and also perhaps in the way he eats and drinks. He needs to lose some of that weight,' he glanced at the big body, 'just to give his heart less to do. Pumping blood round a heavy body and forcing the muscles to carry extra weight is a strain in itself.'

'I thought he ate well,' she said remorsefully. 'He enjoys his food so much. And he's very active.'

'It's not your fault. And activity is good, it keeps the heart strong, just as it keeps any muscle strong. But as I said, this must be treated as a warning that he's doing too much. If you don't want it to happen again, things have to change.' He paused, then said gently, 'It doesn't have to be the end, you know. People do recover from heart attacks and live many more years. Try not to worry too much.'

'But how do they live?' Hilary asked drearily. 'As invalids, needing help for the rest of their lives. Father would hate that.'

'Not by any means. Let's not worry about that.' He glanced out of the window. 'I can see Val Tozer running up the drive. She'll be a help.'

'I rang her as soon as I'd rung you. I rang Stephen as well, at Coltishall. He's coming straight home. I was so frightened, Charles.'

'I know. It is frightening, when it happens. But you did all the right things, and he's going to be all right.'

'Does he have to go to hospital?'

'No, he can stay at home. I'll leave you these pills – if he has any pain you just slip one under his tongue and let it dissolve. I'll see that you get a supply, but it's mostly rest that he needs. It's vital that he has bed-rest for at least two weeks and then takes it very easy – and I really do mean *very* easy, just getting up for an hour or two at most to sit in a chair by the window for instance, not even coming downstairs for some time after that. You'll need help. I can let you have the names of some excellent nurses. Diet's important too.' They heard quick footsteps on the stairs. 'Ah, that sounds like Val now.'

Val came in and went straight to the bed, casting a professional eye over the Squire. Hilary caught at her hand.

'It's a heart attack, Val. Dad's had a heart attack.'

Val squeezed her fingers. 'I know. Don't worry, Hilary. He's a strong man. He'll get over this, I'm sure.'

'I hope so,' Hilary said. 'Oh Val, I do hope so.'

Val looked at her friend. In Hilary's eyes she saw nothing but anxiety and love for her father. There was no sign that she had even considered the implications to herself of a long illness.

She'll never get away now, Val thought.

Stephen arrived at teatime. He was stationed at RAF Coltishall in Norfolk, and came by train through London to Tavistock. Val went to meet him in her father's farm-truck and was waiting on the platform as he jumped off the train, looking unfamiliar in his RAF uniform and dragging a grey canvas kitbag.

'Val! How is he?'

'Not too bad. The pain's under control now but he's very tired. Sleeping quite a lot, which is a good thing.' She marched briskly across the station yard and climbed into the driver's seat. Stephen tossed his kitbag into the back.

'Thanks for coming to meet me. What about Hilary – how's she coping?'

'As well as she copes with everything else. Doctor Latimer's arranging for a nurse to come in. Your dad has got to stay in bed for at least a fortnight, for a start. And there's the estate business, too. Pity you can't be here.'

'Well, I can't, can I?' he said defensively. 'I'm on National Service now. Can't get a discharge just because my father's got to stay in bed for a few weeks. I had to make a pretty strong case for getting these few days off now – make out he was virtually at death's door. Mind you, the way Hilary was carrying on this morning, I thought he was.'

'So did she. A heart attack's not funny, Stephen.'

'No,' he said after a pause, 'I know it isn't. Sorry, Val. I didn't mean that to sound the way it did. Of course I'm worried about the old man. Look, what are his chances? You're a nurse, you must know.'

Val drove in silence for a few moments. They were on their way through Whitchurch before she said, 'I don't think it was a really bad one, Stephen. Doctor Latimer called it a "warning". That means he could have another one, and it would probably be more serious. They leave scars on the heart, you see. And if you carry on doing the things that caused the first one, you're obviously in danger.'

'What sort of things? What do you mean?'

'Just generally doing too much, I suppose, in lots of different ways. Your father's not a young man, Stephen, and he's been through two wars. I know he didn't actually fight in the last one, but he was there, taking decisions, having to see his Regiment go into action. And he's lost his wife and his eldest son—'

'All right, you don't have to remind me about that,' Stephen cut in. He frowned and then said, 'So you're saying that it's what he's done and what's happened to him that's caused this, as much as any actual disease.'

'Partly, yes. He needs to take things more quietly. Get some help running the estate – that sort of thing. And cut down on what he eats and drinks as well,' she added. 'Really, he's got to do all he can to take some of the load off his heart.'

Stephen stared gloomily out of the window. They were out of the village now and running through farmland before crossing the moor to Burracombe. The afternoon light was so clear that the rocky tors stood out in sharp relief. A buzzard soared high above and a crowd of lambs raced from one end of a field to the other.

'I don't know what I can do,' he said at last. 'I've already had my Service postponed because of going to Cambridge. I don't think I can get exemption now.'

'And you don't want to, do you?' Val said quietly.

Stephen sighed. 'I'm a selfish swine, aren't I.'

'No, I don't think so, not really. You've got your life to live too.'

'Yes, but Dad thinks I ought to live it in Burracombe. Run the estate, be Squire like he is – like Baden would have been.' He sighed again. 'This would probably never have happened if Baden hadn't been killed.'

'A lot of things would never have happened if people hadn't been killed. But other things would have happened instead. It's no good thinking like that, Stephen. What you have to think about is what happens next. If you don't want to – or can't – run the estate, who will? Not that it's any of my business,' she added. 'It's Hilary you've got to talk to.'

They drove on, not speaking again, and Val dropped Stephen off at the Barton. He hauled his kitbag out of the truck and stared up for a moment at his father's bedroom window. Once again, he thought, their lives were about to change. Already *had* changed.

He heaved his kitbag on to his shoulder and started up the steps to the front door.

Stephen wasn't the only one to come home that week. The day after the Squire's heart attack, Roy Pettifer arrived on his first week's leave and astonished his mother with his polished shoes and sudden ability to iron his own trousers.

Without even waiting to change out of his uniform, he hurried round to the Tozers' farm and asked to see Jackie.

'Why, hello, Roy,' Alice said, a slightly reserved note in her voice. Jackie seemed to have cheered up a lot since the outing to London and she had a very good idea why. 'My stars, you do look smart! And how d'you like being a soldier?'

'It's all right. It's been all square-bashing so far.' He didn't tell her about the misery of those first weeks, the shouting and swearing, the continual hard graft and the apparently stupid things they'd had to do, just to learn to obey orders. That was more or less over now, he hoped, and they'd go on to more interesting things. He liked using firearms, and he was hoping that his skill with engines would be recognised and he'd be put on to tank maintenance. The massive vehicles fascinated him and he longed to get at their insides.

'I'm afraid Jackie's gone up to the Barton. They've got trouble there – Squire's had a heart attack. Had to get a nurse in, and Jackie's working extra time to help out. Mr Stephen's home too. You'd better go home again, boy, and I'll tell Jackie you'm back when she comes home.'

'You don't know when that'll be?'

'No, I don't. She said she might even stop the night. Dottie Friend's round there too, helping with the cooking. But I dare say her'll have a few hours off sometime. I'll tell her, don't you fret.'

Roy turned away and trudged off through the yard. He felt disappointed and vaguely hurt by Alice Tozer's manner. He'd expected a welcome, an invitation to come in and have a scone or something fresh from the oven – someone was always baking at the Tozers' farm – but instead she'd been quite cool and given him no idea as to when he might see Jackie. It was a funny thing, but he'd noticed a coolness in Jackie's letters too, just recently, and

279

they hadn't been quite so frequent. He wondered what was going on and hoped her parents weren't putting her off him. He'd hoped they might get officially engaged during this leave.

He thought of their last proper meeting. The hour they'd spent up at the standing stones. It had been his first time as well as Jackie's and he thought he'd done pretty well. The memory of it had warmed him during the cold, lonely nights in Army camp, and it was all he'd thought about on the journey home. He wanted to do it again. He'd thought they'd do it again the first night he was home. And now he didn't even know when he'd see her.

Briefly, he remembered the Squire's heart attack. I suppose that means the old man will die, he speculated. Wonder what'll happen then. Anyway, whoever takes over, they'll still want housemaids. Jackie would still have a job.

When he reached home, his mother had a plate of scones ready, straight from the oven. He sat down and piled them with strawberry jam and cream, and ate four without stopping.

'We're going to have to have a talk, Steve,' Hilary said. She was pale and had huge dark rings under her eyes. Since discovering her father on the floor of his bedroom, gasping with pain, his eyes filled with fear, she had barely left his side. The nurse sent by Charles Latimer had urged her to get some rest, but she'd been unable to stay away for more than an hour or so and had then come back to sit beside him, holding his hand and watching his face. Even though he seemed to be sleeping peacefully, she'd been afraid to leave him.

Stephen's return had helped. Napier had been awake when he crept into the room, and his lips had moved in a weak smile. He'd lifted one hand and Stephen had gripped it in both of his. 'Hello, Dad.'

'Stephen.' The strong voice was barely a thread of sound. 'Glad you could make it.'

'You gave us a scare. But you're going to be fine now, Dad. And I can stay for a few days – enough to see you on the mend.'

A small shadow of disappointment crossed the white face. 'Only a few days? I thought—'

'Got to do my National Service, Dad – patriotic duty, you know,' Stephen reminded him, a lump in his throat as he remembered the arguments they'd had over his call-up. 'Can't get out of it now, I'm afraid.'

'Hm.' The grunt sounded almost like the Squire's normal sceptical reaction to one of his son's remarks. But the tired eyes were closing again and Stephen glanced across at his sister. She nodded slightly and motioned to him to join her by the window.

'He's just drifting in and out of sleep. Charles gave him some sedatives and I've got pills for if he has more pain. The nurse he sent seems very good – Pat Smith, she's called. She's having the Pink Room, so that she's nice and near. She's in there now, unpacking.'

Stephen nodded. He glanced again at his father, now sleeping, and hesitated. 'I might as well do the same, if that's all right with you.'

'Yes, of course. And go down to the kitchen – Dottie's there with Jackie; they're getting dinner ready but she'll give you something to be going on with. I think there's some cake in the tin . . .' Her voice trailed away as she sat down again by the bed and Stephen stood irresolute for a moment or two, then left the room. I don't really know what I should be doing, he thought, running down the stairs for his kitbag. What *does* one do at times like this? I'm not needed for the nursing or anything like that, and it sounds as though the kitchen's pretty well organised – not that I'd be much use if it wasn't! And I can't take over the estate because I've never been here long enough to know what's going on, and when I have been home I refused to take any interest.

In fact, he thought as he bent to heave the long, cumbersome bag on to his shoulder, I'm pretty useless all round, really. And as he climbed the stairs and went to his bedroom, he felt as if a cloud of gloom had descended upon him, crushing all the pleasure and satisfaction he'd felt during the past few weeks, and bringing with it a dread that the bright new world that had opened up before him was going to be taken away after all.

When Hilary told him again the next day that they needed to talk, he looked at her warily, noting the weariness in her face and feeling the dread sweep over him again. Yet he knew she was right. Baden, who would have kept everything together, was gone and it was up to them to decide what to do. Neither of them could escape the responsibilities that had been dropped on their shoulders.

'I know,' he said, 'and we'd better start now. The nurse is up there, isn't she?'

'Yes, and he's asleep again. She'll call us if she needs anything, so we'd better stay close by. Shall we go into the drawing room?'

They settled into two armchairs and Stephen handed her a glass of sherry. Hilary sipped it and leaned her head back against the cushions.

'You look worn out,' Stephen said.

'I'm all right. Just didn't get much sleep last night. And we had a pretty long day the day before, as well – at the Festival. Goodness, it seems years ago now.' Her voice quivered a little. 'I suppose it's shock too. It was so horrible, finding him on the floor like that. I thought he was dead, Steve.'

'I know. It must have been awful.'

'Then he started to gasp and cry out. He was clutching at

282

his chest with both hands, so I knew it must be a heart attack. I didn't know what to do, so I just pulled the pillows off the bed and wrapped the blankets around him and tried to make him more comfortable. Then I rang Charles and Val. Charles came straight away and gave him a pill, and we managed to get him back into bed.' She sat up, putting the sherry glass on to a small table and wiped her eyes. 'Sorry, managed to keep it back till now, but talking about it . . .'

'It's all right, Hil.' Stephen hadn't seen his sister cry for years, not even when she'd heard that her fiancé Henry had been killed. He got up and went over to pat her awkwardly on the shoulder. 'I expect it's good for you to cry. Let it out.'

Hilary sobbed for a few minutes, then pulled herself together. 'Sorry. I'll be all right now, I think. What are we going to do, Steve?'

'About Dad, you mean? Or about the estate?'

'Both. I know you can't come home, but something's got to be done. He's going to need nursing for quite a long time. Charles won't say how long – I suppose he can't. It's too early. But Dad's got to stay in bed for at least two weeks, and even after that he'll only be able to get up for short periods. It'll be months before he can do anything much at all. And Charles says he must never go back to doing everything he's been doing.'

'Things are going to have to change, aren't they,' Stephen said after a pause.

'Yes, they are. And we're the ones who are going to have to change them.'

'Don't ask me to be the one to tell Dad that,' he said wryly. 'It'll put his blood pressure straight up again. He's the one who makes the decisions round here, and a few weeks in bed aren't going to change that.'

Hilary sighed. 'I know, but surely we can do it gradually. If we can get things organised, so that he can see we're coping with it all, it'll be better for him than letting him start worrying. Because that's what he's going to do, and that's one of the things that Charles says are so bad for him.'

'All right,' Stephen said. 'So what's he going to worry about most? The house or the estate?'

'Well, the estate, of course. He knows I've got things in the house under control.'

'And you could have the estate under control as well.' He saw her startled look. 'You know you could, Hil! You go round with Dad, you know all the tenant farmers and they know you. They respect you, too, and they'd all rally round. I've always said you could run this place with one hand tied behind your back. Far better than I could, anyway.' He grinned. 'Mind you, even the dogs could run it better than I could!'

Hilary smiled faintly and picked up her glass again. 'That doesn't mean I could do it – or that Dad would let me. I can't just effect a *coup*, you know. It's still his estate.'

Stephen leaned forward. 'No, but now's probably the only chance you'll ever get to show him what you can do. Wouldn't it be better than just going on as you are, without any real life of your own? Well, wouldn't it?'

Hilary looked at him for a long moment. She took another drink of sherry. Then she said, 'I hadn't intended going on without any life of my own, Steve. I've been thinking a lot about that and I'd come to a decision. As a matter of fact, I was going to tell Dad about it yesterday.'

He stared at her. 'What? What decision?'

'I've been planning to leave home,' she said. 'I've been offered a room in a flat in London. I'd just decided to leave Burracombe and live my own life at last.'

Chapter Twenty-Five

Roy was waiting at the end of the Barton drive when Jackie walked home that evening. He stepped out from under the beech trees and she stopped abruptly. 'Roy!'

'Hello, Jackie.' He made to take her in his arms but she backed away. 'What's the matter, maid? Aren't you pleased to see me?'

'I don't know – I mean, it's a surprise, that's all. What are you doing here? I didn't know you were coming home this week.'

'You knew it was going to be soon.' He sounded sulky. 'Come on, Jackie, give us a kiss. I've been looking forward to seeing you again.'

'Sorry.' She lifted her face and let him kiss her, but drew away again as his lips grew more urgent. 'Don't do that! Not here – anyone could see.'

'You weren't so fussy last time,' he grumbled, dropping his arms. 'What's got into you, Jackie?'

'Nothing. I'm just tired, that's all.' She began to walk on. 'We've got trouble here. Squire's ill.'

'I know, your mum told me. But that don't make no difference to you and me, does it?'

'No, I suppose not.' But her voice was listless and he gave her a sharp look.

'What is it? What's the matter? You've gone cold. Don't you love me no more, is that it? Have you started going out with someone else, the minute me back's turned?'

285

'No! I haven't been out with anyone else. If you want to know, I've hardly been out at all since you went away. I've been too busy sitting at home writing you letters.'

Roy stared at her. This wasn't at all the homecoming he'd expected. All the way home, he'd pictured Jackie running into his arms, letting him kiss her, kissing him back. He'd imagined them walking along the lane together, their arms round each other's waists, climbing through the woods to the standing stones, making love again in the very same grassy hollow with the stars wheeling above and the scent of gorse and heather all about them.

He quickened his step so that he was in front of her, then turned to block her way. 'So what's all this about, then?' he demanded. 'What have I done to upset you? You're treating me like something the cat dragged in.'

To his dismay, Jackie burst into tears. She stopped, right in the middle of the lane, and put both hands over her face. He stood helplessly before her, feeling angry and hurt. '*Now* what's the matter?'

'You don't understand!' she wept. 'You don't understand at all, Roy Pettifer. There's poor Squire laying up there in his bed and nobody knows whether he's going to live or die, and I've been there all day doing whatever I could, and Doctor's been three times, and there's this nurse come from Plymouth wanting this, that and the other, and Miss Hilary all upset and getting Mr Stephen home from Norfolk, and only me and Dottie Friend to see to everything, and you turn up and expect me to be all pleased and excited and just as if I've had nothing to think about but you coming home. And I can't, that's all. I just can't.' She burst into fresh sobs and Roy put his arms round her awkwardly.

'I'm sorry, Jackie. I really am. I never thought of it like that.'

'You never think at all, that's your trouble,' she sniffed,

but she didn't push him away. 'Look, I just want to go home and go to bed, Roy. I'm tired out.'

'Well, will I see you tomorrow, then?'

'I dunno,' she said wearily. 'I promised to go back as early as I could. There's ever so much to do there.'

'I haven't got all that long,' he said. 'Only a few days.' His suspicions returned. 'You do want to see me, don't you?'

There was a lengthy pause. They were walking along the lane now, and approaching the farm gate. Jackie sighed and turned to him.

'I don't know what I want, Roy. I'm too tired to think about it. Look – I'll try to get out sometime tomorrow. I'll come round to your house, shall I? That'll be best.'

'All right,' he said doubtfully, and watched as she unlatched the gate. She went through and turned to say goodnight, and he said, 'Aren't you even going to give us a kiss then, maid?'

Jackie hesitated, then leaned across the rail and gave him a brief peck on the lips. 'Goodnight, Roy.'

'Goodnight, Jackie,' he said, and stood there while she crossed the yard and opened the farmhouse door. Then he turned away and walked off down the lane towards the pub. If there was nothing else to do, he might as well go and have a drink. There were bound to be a few old mates there.

Perhaps it was just that she was tired and upset. Girls were funny like that.

It was true that Jackie was upset, but it wasn't just about the Squire. It had certainly been a shock to answer the phone yesterday morning and hear Hilary's frantic voice asking for Val, and she'd gulped the rest of her breakfast down hurriedly and arrived at the Barton close behind her sister. She'd been on the go ever since, doing her best to keep things going without Hilary's instructions, deciding for herself what ought to be cooked for lunch and dinner, letting people in as news of the Squire's illness had permeated round the village. It had been a relief when Dottie Friend arrived to lend a hand, but Dottie had other commitments too, at the pub and in the doctor's house. She'd been a big help, but Jackie was the only one who was there all the time.

Yet, despite the anxiety and the rush of it all, Jackie had found herself – in a strange, scarcely acknowledged way – enjoying it. She had never had full responsibility before, never been expected to make decisions, and although just deciding what to cook for dinner wasn't exactly world-shaking, it made her feel grown-up and competent. She liked it.

What had really upset her was seeing Roy waiting for her at the end of the drive.

It's daft, she thought as she went through the kitchen with barely a nod to her mother and grandmother. I knew he'd be coming back soon. And now that I know I'm not going to have a baby, I ought to be pleased to see him. I love him, don't I? We were going to get engaged . . .

She stood at the window, gazing out at the twilit fields and the dark bulk of the moors, and repeated the words over to herself. *I love him . . . We were going to get engaged* . . . They sounded strange, like a foreign language she only half understood.

'Jackie! *Jackie!*'

The girl went to the bedroom door. Her mother was standing at the foot of the stairs, calling up to her. 'Jackie, come down here. Me and your granny want to know how the Squire is. You came in with such a rush, we wondered . . .' She looked closely at her daughter as she came slowly back to the kitchen. 'He'm not worse, is he?'

Minnie was in her chair by the stove. She looked

anxious, her eyes wide and her wrinkled lips shaking. Jackie felt ashamed; she should have known they'd be waiting for news.

'No, he's not worse. Miss Hilary says it'll be a few days before they know for certain he's going to get properly better, but she told me the doctor's pleased with him. And the nurse is looking after him, and Mr Stephen's there as well.' She paused. 'It do seem funny though,' she said, her own voice quivering suddenly. 'I've never known him ill before, and to think he could have died all on his own up there, laying on the floor . . .'

Her voice broke and she sat down suddenly at the table and started to cry again. Alice came over quickly and laid her arm across her shoulders, murmuring comfortingly. She looked at Minnie.

'I knew she were more upset than she let on. 'Tis a shock for a young girl. And they've been asking a lot of her too, these past couple of days.'

'I don't mind working extra time,' Jackie said tearfully. 'Miss Hilary's been good to me. I didn't even know I was upset!'

'Poor Mr Gilbert,' Minnie said sadly. 'Knowed him since he were a little tacker, I have. I used to be his nursemaid when he were a babby, pushed him in his pram many a time. I never thought he'd go before me—'

'Mother!' Alice said sharply. 'He hasn't gone at all yet, nor's he going to. Didn't you hear our Jackie just say he weren't no worse and the doctor's pleased with him? Don't upset her any more than she is already.'

Jackie lifted her head and wiped her eyes. 'I'm all right, Mum. It just came over me a bit sudden. I'll help you get supper ready, shall I?'

'No, you won't.' Alice looked at her carefully. 'You'm looking worn out. You go and have a lay-down while me and your granny sees to it. Oh, and there was something

289

else I meant to tell you. Young Roy was round here an hour or two ago. Home on leave, he is – come to ask for you. I dare say he'll be back sometime this evening.'

'I know. I saw him. He met me as I was coming home.' Jackie's voice was dreary as she got up from the table, and her mother and grandmother raised their eyebrows at each other. 'I told him I was too tired. I expect I'll see him tomorrow, sometime.' She went up the stairs and they heard the creak of her bed overhead as she lay down.

'Well!' Alice said in a low voice, lifting a pan of potatoes on to the top of the stove. 'And what do you make of that?'

'Same as you, I dare say,' Minnie said. 'She's had a fright. I think young Roy Pettifer's the next one due for a shock – and serve him right!'

Stephen Napier had had a shock too. He stared at his sister and then got up and poured himself a second sherry.

'You're not serious,' he said at last. 'Leave Burracombe? Go to live in London? *You?*'

'Why not?' she asked defensively. 'Don't tell me you just see me as a substitute for a wife and housekeeper too, because that's all Dad sees me as now – and I'm tired of it, Steve. I'm really, really tired of it.' Her voice shook a little and she held out her glass. 'I'll have another one too, please.'

He did as she requested, still looking stunned. 'But you're such a country girl, Hilary. You like everything about it – the farms, the moors, the hunting, everything. And you love Burracombe. How can you think of going to live in a place like London?'

'I haven't always lived in the country though,' she pointed out. 'Don't forget, I was in the Army. I had a high rank and a responsible job. I worked with some of the most important men in the war. I miss it. I miss the company, the responsibility, all of it. I miss being someone people think is capable. I suppose I miss the respect.'

'People respect you here,' he said.

'Do they? Do they really? Oh, I'm the Squire's daughter so some of the older ones still touch their forelocks or lift their caps as I pass by, but I'm not sure that's the sort of respect I want. It isn't the sort I've earned, is it? Apart from that I'm quite good at arranging the flowers in the church, and being secretary of the Mother's Union and WI, and I can't think of much else. It's not exactly what they'll put on my tombstone, is it, Steve?' She drank again. 'I'll have one of those fulsome tributes that you see on church walls – *She was a dutiful daughter, wise and gentle in her ways, and loved by all who met her*. Well, is that how *you'd* like to be remembered?'

'Well, since I'm not a daughter . . .' Stephen began, then caught her eye. 'Sorry, Hil. I know it's not funny. But there could be worse ways to be remembered, you know.'

'Worse than being a dutiful daughter? I don't think so.' She put down her glass. 'I'd better not drink any more of this. I'll have to go and sit with Dad again soon. Nurse Smith's being very good but she's got to have some time off.'

'I know. I'll do my share as well, while I'm here. I'm only sorry I've got to go back the day after tomorrow.'

'Oh, that's all right.' Hilary leaned back against the cushions. 'I suppose I'll just have to set my own plans aside until we see what's going to happen.'

Stephen looked at her and, for the first time, saw Hilary as a person rather than just the girl he'd grown up with and known all his life as his big sister. He saw a tall, slim young woman with fair hair worn in a loose page-boy style and tired grey eyes. She was nearly thirty, he realised, and had lost her chance of marriage when her fiancé had been killed

– yet why shouldn't she have another chance? Why hadn't some lucky man snapped her up long before this?

Perhaps she was right – she needed to get away from Burracombe, start a new life, find another circle of friends. It wasn't right that a woman like Hilary should moulder away in the country, doing all the things a married woman would do, yet not being married. It might not have been so bad if she'd never known anything different, but she had. She'd had a very different life during the war, and he wasn't surprised she missed it.

'Don't forget what I said about emigrating,' he said at last. 'It's still on the cards, you know.'

'And how long do I have to wait for that? Two years – three – while you finish your National Service? You might decide to stay in the RAF even longer. You might make it *your* career. And I'll still be stuck here, arranging flowers and asking Dad what he wants for supper.' She bit her lip and added more quietly, 'That's if *he's* still here.'

'Of course he will be!' There was an edge of panic in Stephen's voice. 'Charles Latimer says he'll be fine in a few months. He's just not got to do so much. He'll be all right, Hil.'

'This time, yes. But what if it happens again?' She met her brother's eyes. 'One of these days, it's going to be the last time.'

'I know. But—'

'And who do you think is going to have to take over?' He stirred uncomfortably and didn't speak.

'How do you think Dad will have made out his Will? You know what he's like. He won't leave this place to me, that's for certain.'

Panic flared in his eyes now. 'I don't want it – he knows I don't!'

'You'll get it all the same. He believes it should be left to the eldest son and now that Baden's gone, that's you.' She stood up and brushed down her skirt. 'But you've got plenty of time to play at aeroplanes before then, because it's not going to happen for a long time. Now I'd better go and take over from Nurse Smith. You'll come up when you've had your dinner, will you?'

'Yes,' he said in a deflated tone, sitting back in his chair. 'Yes, I'll come up then.'

Hilary left the room and Stephen sat and stared at the empty fireplace. He felt vaguely ashamed of his part in the conversation. It didn't seem fitting to be talking about what would happen when their father died, yet Hilary was right – it would have to be faced eventually. Neither of them could drift along as if Gilbert Napier would live for ever.

Some day, someone was going to inherit the estate, and it was almost certain to be himself. It wasn't something that could be tossed aside like an unwanted keepsake. He could stay in the RAF, he could emigrate, he could fly to the moon, but it would still have to be dealt with. The Barton was a major part of his life, whether he wanted it or not.

Stephen buried his face in his hands and groaned.

By the time Jackie came home from work the next evening, Roy was almost in flames with impatience. Once again, he was waiting at the Barton gates, and this time he wouldn't take no for an answer.

'I've only got a couple of days, Jackie. You've got to come with me.'

'Why?' She saw the look on his face and shrugged. 'Oh, all right, then. Where d'you want to go?'

'Anywhere, so long as it's with you. Anywhere nobody can see us.' He gripped her hand tightly and began to walk along the lane. 'I want to be with you. I want to kiss you properly. Don't you want to kiss me?'

'Yes,' she said without enthusiasm. 'Of course I want to, Roy.'

'Well, you might sound as if you meant it,' he grumbled. There was a short silence, then he said, 'How's the Squire, then?'

'A bit better, I think. No worse, anyway. I took a cup of tea in for the nurse today and he's all propped up on pillows. They're not letting him lay down at all. I don't see how he gets any sleep – I know I couldn't, if I was sitting up all night.' She waited as Roy opened the gate into the woods. 'I don't want to be too long, Roy, Mum's expecting me back for supper.'

'She'll know you'm with me.' He closed the gate again and glanced at her. 'You never used to be so particular about your mother, Jackie.'

'Well, maybe I've grown up a bit since then.' They began to climb the narrow path, twisting its way up the hill between the trees and moss-clad rocks. 'A lot's happened since you went away, Roy.'

'And what's that supposed to mean?' He stopped and looked at her. 'You *have* met someone else! You've been two-timing me!'

'I haven't! I told you, I stayed in every night and wrote to you. You know that.' She tried to pull her hand away but he gripped it even more tightly. 'Let me go, Roy. You're hurting me.'

'Well, you're hurting me, too. I thought you'd be real pleased to see me again and you've treated me like dirt. Like *dirt*. And you say you've been writing to me every evening – well, all I can say is, you must have been doing something else as well, because the last week or so you haven't written more than a line or two any night. What's been going on, Jackie? Don't you think I got a right to know?'

Jackie looked around. They were well above the village now, almost at the edge of the moor. Not far above them were the standing stones, encircling their grassy hollow. If there was one place she didn't want to go, it was to the standing stones.

'All right,' she said, sitting down on a rock cushioned with moss. 'I'll tell you.' She waited as Roy sat down beside her and then turned to look at his face. 'I thought I was going to have a baby.'

There was a long silence. She saw Roy's face change – first with shock, then with dismay, a shiver of fear, and finally with a puzzled kind of relief. 'You *thought* you were? So you're not, then?'

'No. But I didn't know that until this week – when we were in London. It's been awful, Roy. I didn't know what to do. And I couldn't tell anyone – not till Val asked me, anyway.'

'Val? Your sister? You mean she knows?'

'Yes, and I think Miss Hilary does as well. But never mind that, it was you I ought to have been able to tell and I couldn't because you weren't here. I didn't know what to do,' she said again, reliving the terror of those weeks. 'You don't know how awful it was.'

'Well, it must have been. But if you're not – well, everything's all right, isn't it? And I promise it won't happen again.' He stroked her arm. 'I've got some rubbers – you know, French letters. We can get them on the station so I brought some with me. It'll be all right next time, Jackie.'

'Next time?' She turned her head and stared at him. 'What are you talking about? There isn't going to be a next time, Roy! I'm never going to go through that again, never.'

'But if we use—'

'*No!*' She was on her feet, tearing her hand from his grasp. 'I've told you, Roy, I'm never going through it again, never. I don't care what you use, I'm not taking any more chances.' She stared down at him. 'D'you know what would have happened to me if it had been true? My dad would have turned me out and my mum would probably have died of shame. Nobody would ever have spoken to me again. I'd have had to leave the village and I'd probably have had to give the baby away. And what could *you* have done about it?'

Roy jumped up too. 'I could have married you, of course! That's what we want to do anyway, isn't it? I know our families wouldn't have been best pleased, but they'd have got over it, and they'd have had to let us get married.' He gripped her hand again, his eyes shining. 'Jackie, think of it! We could get married – we could just tell them—'

'No!' she shouted again. 'No, we couldn't! I'm not telling lies and having everyone look at me and waiting for me to get fat. And what about when I *don't* get fat? What are we supposed to say then? And anyway,' she turned her face away, then turned back and looked him in the eye, 'I don't want to marry you, Roy. I wouldn't marry you if you were the last man on earth.'

The silence this time was so intense that Roy felt as if he could hear the moss growing on the rocks at his feet. He kept his eyes on Jackie's face, unable to believe what he had just heard. The world seemed to sway about him and he heard his blood roar in his ears; then it steadied and he realised that he felt sick.

'What do you mean?' he whispered at last.

Jackie took her hand out of his. His fingers seemed to have no strength in them. 'What I say. I don't want to marry you.' Her voice was quiet too, and tired, as if by shouting at him she had used up all her energy.

Roy shook his head. 'I don't understand. Why not? What have I done wrong? Jackie, we love each other. You don't mean it – you can't.'

'I do. I don't want to marry anyone. Not if it's going to be like this – all this trouble. I'd rather be single, like our Val.'

'All what trouble? I told you, it won't happen again.' He reached for her hand once more. 'Jackie, you said you loved me.'

'I thought I did.'

'You mean you don't any more? But I still love you!'

'I can't help it,' she said. 'It's not just the baby, anyway.'

'So what is it? What have I done?' He returned once more to his old suspicions. 'There *is* somebody else!'

'There's *not*! How many times do I have to tell you? There's nobody else and I don't suppose there ever will be.' She started to walk back down the path and he grabbed her arm again. 'Let go of me, Roy!'

'Not until you tell me what this is all about.' All his anxiety and disappointment came together in a flash of real anger. 'I got a right to know, Jackie! If it's not somebody else, and it's not anything I've done, and it's not the baby that never was, what the hell *is* it?'

'There's no need to swear,' she said. She stopped again and drew in a heavy sigh. 'All right, then, if you must know, it's what we done. You and me. What you wants to do again.'

'What we . . .' For a moment, he didn't understand what she meant. Then a painful flush swept up his neck. 'You mean when us went all the way? Up at the stones?'

'Yes.'

'But – but what's wrong with that? Oh, I know us shouldn't have, and I know you've been worried and upset – but there weren't nothing *wrong* about it, not really. It's just doing what comes naturally. Everyone does it. Even your mum and dad must have done it, or you wouldn't be here now.'

'Don't talk like that!' she flared. 'I know all that – I'm not a kid. But I didn't like it, that's all. I didn't like it and I don't want to do it again, and that's all there is to it.' She began to walk down the hill again.

Roy stood bewildered for a moment, then caught her up. 'What do you mean, you didn't like it? You wanted to do it as much as I did.'

'So I might have done, but I didn't know what it was like, did I? Now I do.'

'But it was marvellous. I thought so, anyway.' His voice was bemused, the anger gone. 'You don't really mean that, do you?'

'Yes, I do.' She turned and faced him again. 'It was uncomfortable. There was a rock sticking into my back, and it hurt. And you hurt me too. I didn't like it and I don't want to do it again, and if that's what being married is all about, I'll stay single.' She walked on again.

This time, Roy didn't follow her. He stood very still, rejected and humiliated. He thought of the times he'd relived that magical experience by the standing stones, under a twilit sky. He thought of the promises he and Jackie had made to each other, the plans they'd made, the life they'd meant to lead. He thought of the excitement he had felt on his way home.

She couldn't mean it. It didn't seem possible that she no longer loved him. It didn't seem possible that she hadn't felt that magic too, that it had been something uncomfortable and even painful for her.

He watched her go down the path and through the gate. He waited for her to turn and look up at him, but she didn't. He put his hand into his pocket and felt the little packet there, the packet that should have enabled them to love each other safely, without any of the worries Jackie had suffered over the past few weeks.

Then he turned and walked up the hill again. He found his way through the gathering darkness to the standing stones and their hollow, and he lay down on the grass alone and stared up at the wheeling stars.

Chapter Twenty-Six

Val spent as much time as she could at the Barton, but her duties meant that she could spare only an hour or so each evening. About a week after the Squire's heart attack, she hurried up the drive to find Hilary walking on the terrace. She ran up the steps and Hilary turned to look at her.

'Hilary! Whatever's the matter? You look as if you've been crying.'

'Oh, nothing.' Hilary shrugged and her mouth twisted. 'Or everything. Nothing new, anyway.'

Val stared at her. 'You're not making sense. What is it? Is your father worse?'

'No, he's still making good progress. Charles says if he goes on like this he'll be able to get out of bed and sit in a chair next week. Can you imagine, Val? Dad, sitting in a chair! It's as if he's become an old man all of a sudden.'

'Well, he's not a young one, is he?' Val said quietly. 'And he will get stronger, you know. The heart takes a long time to heal but in a few months . . .'

'A few months!' Hilary echoed. 'In a few months he'll be back to normal. And what about me, Val? Where will *I* be in a few months? What will *I* be doing?'

Val gazed at her helplessly.

'I'll tell you,' Hilary said bitterly. 'I'll be stuck here, the same as before. I'll be running the house and arranging the church flowers and doing all the things I've been doing ever since Mother died. I'm going to be doing them for ever,

Val. For the rest of my life. I'm *trapped*. I'm trapped all over again.'

'Oh Hilary . . .'

'It's true. I've known it all along really. I knew I'd never be able to leave and go to London. It was just a dream.' Hilary sat down on a bench and stared out across the wide lawn. Tonelessly, she said, 'I was a fool to think things could change.'

Val sat beside her and took her hand. 'What's happened? Tell me.'

Hilary sat without speaking for a few minutes. Then she heaved a sigh and turned to her friend. Her face was sad, as if she had just given up something that meant a great deal. She said, 'Stephen's gone back to Coltishall.'

'Oh.' Val didn't know what to say. 'But you knew he was going back. He only had a few days' compassionate leave, didn't he?'

'Oh yes, I knew he'd be going. But now that he has . . . We had a long talk about things – several talks, in fact. I don't think we came to any fresh conclusion but at least we've thrashed it all out between us. He's never going to come and take over the estate, Val.'

'No, I don't think he is. You knew that too, didn't you?'

'Yes, of course. He's made it clear often enough. But I suppose I thought, when Dad was taken ill . . . well, that it might have changed Steve's mind, made him think a bit more about it. Made him look at the place with fresh eyes.' She sighed again.

Val said, 'But it didn't.'

'No. It didn't make any difference at all. He really doesn't want to have anything to do with it. And he's right, I suppose – he wouldn't be much good at it. But would that really matter? There've been other Squires who weren't very good – look at our great-grandfather! He was terrible – wasted money, lost several farms gambling, let the house

300

and gardens run down, but when Grandad took over everything improved again, and by the time he died, the estate was back to where it had been before. It's keeping it in the family that's important, and Stephen wouldn't have been as bad as that. He wouldn't even have to do the work himself – he could just put in a good manager, like we had when Daddy was away during the war.'

'Who would cost a lot of money.'

'Well, yes, there is that. But it would be better than letting it all be split up, which is what he's talking about doing.'

'So what's the answer?' Val asked.

Hilary shrugged. 'We'll just go on as we are. I'll stay here and look after Dad and do whatever I can. At least I know enough about the estate to be able to take over most of the work he used to do. We won't need to think about getting a manager just yet. But I suppose that's what we'll have to do in the end.'

'And London?' Val ventured, hardly daring to ask.

'Oh, that's gone by the board. I've written to Katharine telling her it's off. She'll be able to find someone else for the flat easily enough.' Hilary looked up at the sky. 'So much for my dream of becoming an air stewardess and flying all over Europe. America, too. Oh Val, I'm sorry. You come to see me in your time off and all you get is moans and groans. I'm a selfish, self-pitying wreck!'

'You're not at all.' Val put her arm round Hilary's shoulders. 'What are friends for if you can't let off steam to them? Oh Hil, I'm really sorry about all this. I know I didn't want you to go away – that was *me* being selfish – but I'm sorry you can't. I know how much you wanted to have your own life.'

'Mm. Well, I suppose I just have to accept the fact that this *is* my life. At least I did have those few years when I

301

saw something more. If it hadn't been for the war, I'd never have had even that.'

'If it hadn't been for the war, a lot of things would have been different,' Val said quietly, and they sat together in silence for a while, looking at the lawns sweeping away to the beech wood and the moors above. 'Everyone's lives have been changed by the war, one way or another. But it doesn't necessarily mean they'd have been better.'

'We just can't tell.' There was a pause, then Hilary laughed and jumped to her feet. 'Listen to us, getting all philosophical! Come on, let's go indoors. Dottie's left a nice cold supper for us and Stephen brought up a bottle of wine from Dad's cellar last night. We never opened it, and I was going to put it back today, but I think we'll have it instead, don't you? Drown our sorrows?'

'Sounds a good idea.' Val got up and followed her into the house. But before she went in, she cast a last look at the view of the fields, the woods and moors, and wondered just how different her life would have been if it hadn't been for the war.

Eddie would still be alive, for a start. And she would never have met Luke Ferris.

Luke was sitting with Stella in the little orchard behind Dottie's cottage. The cherry-blossom was over but the apple trees were as white as snow, gently tinged with pink as if touched by the sunset. There were a few bluebells nodding their azure heads in the grass, and birds were busy dashing to and fro with their beaks laden with small worms and insects for fledglings or nesting partners. Stella followed their flight with her eyes, but she felt dispirited and watched them without her usual joy.

Once again, the search for Muriel seemed to have hit a brick wall. With Luke's help, she had written to everyone they could think of, but nobody had been able to come up with anything. The records of any orphanage that Muriel might have been sent to had been lost. There weren't even any records of where Stella herself had gone, and if anyone had been searching for her they would have reached the same impasse.

'So if Muriel's been looking for me, she'd be having just the same problems,' she said despairingly. 'I don't see what else we can do, Luke.'

'There may still be some way,' Luke said. He leaned back in the old wooden seat and closed his eyes, letting the warmth of the sun stroke his face. 'We could advertise in a newspaper.'

'Well, perhaps.' She turned her head and looked at him. His face had lost some of its winter pallor and was lightly tanned by the sun. Long dark lashes lay on his cheeks and she thought of the dark-blue depths of the eyes hidden beneath their lids. He was still thin, but not so gaunt as he had been when she had first met him last October. Burracombe suited him, she thought, just as it did her. The outdoor life, with so much of his time spent in the open air, walking the moors and painting, had completed his cure and he looked in perfect health. She wondered suddenly if he had any plans to go back to London, and felt a twinge of dismay.

Luke opened his eyes suddenly and stared at her. Stella felt her cheeks colour and turned hastily away. 'I was just going to ask you something,' she said at random, 'but I thought you were asleep.'

'No, just enjoying the warmth. What was it?'

'Nothing – I can't remember now.' Her colour deepened. 'It was probably about the newspaper idea. I don't know, Luke, I just can't see it working. We don't know which newspaper she reads or if she even looks at the Personal columns, or if she'd realise it was meant for her anyway. I mean, what are we going to say? "Have you lost a sister?" It sounds silly.'

'I do have another idea,' he said thoughtfully. 'I've heard that the Salvation Army looks for missing people.'

'I tried that, while I was still at college. They don't look for people who might have been adopted, and I'm sure she must have been, otherwise we would have found each other. I just can't think of anything else, Luke. I don't think I'm ever going to know what happened to her.'

At the desolate note in her voice, Luke turned and slipped his arm around her shoulders. 'Stella, don't give up. She must be out there somewhere. There must be some way of finding her. What about the woman you stayed with in Portsmouth – didn't you say she kept in touch with you?'

'Yes, until we were taken away from Bridge End. After that, we weren't allowed to write letters. At least, I wasn't . . .' She turned to him with a flash of hope. 'But *Muriel* might have been able to. Luke, you're a genius! All I need do is write to Auntie Jess! Muriel might have been going to see her all these years. I can't think why it never occurred to me before!'

'Hold on a minute,' he said, half-laughing, half-anxious. 'It's only a guess. It might not have happened that way at all. This "Auntie Jess" might never have heard from Muriel again. She might not even live there any more. All sorts of things might have happened.'

'Yes, I suppose so,' Stella said, feeling a bit flattened. 'But it's worth a try, isn't it. I can write to her. If she answered straight away, I might know by the end of the week. I'll do that, Luke. I'll write this evening and post the letter first thing tomorrow. Oh, wouldn't it be wonderful!'

Luke looked at her. Her face was bright and happy again, her eyes sparkling with excitement. He felt a rush of tenderness towards her and tightened his arm around her shoulders. She turned her face towards him and her lips parted in a smile of joyfulness. Without even thinking about it, he bent towards her and kissed her mouth.

'Oh,' Stella said faintly as he drew back again. 'Luke—'

'I'm sorry,' he said hastily. 'I didn't mean to do that. Don't be upset.'

'I'm not upset. I just didn't expect . . .'

'Neither did I,' he said. He hesitated, then withdrew his arm. His heart was thumping a little and he felt confused and uncertain. He said again, 'I'm sorry.'

'You don't have to be sorry,' she said. 'I – I didn't mind.'

Luke looked at her more carefully. Stella had never mentioned any boyfriends to him, never given any hint that she had ever had a relationship. For all he knew, this might be the first kiss she had ever had. He didn't know what she might make of it. Plenty of girls would treat it lightly, as no more than a kiss, a friendly gesture or something that might lead to more. He had a feeling that Stella was not like those girls. Stella would take it seriously.

He disengaged himself and stood up. 'I'm sorry – I'd better be going. I promised to start sorting out paintings for the exhibition. Mrs Warren's coming up to the cottage tomorrow to look at them.' He looked down at her and said gently, 'Don't worry about it, Stella. It was just that I felt so pleased for you – pleased that there's still a chance. Let me know when you hear from your Auntie Jess, won't you?'

He opened the gate and Stella heard his footsteps receding up the lane. She sat motionless, still feeling the touch of his lips on hers, and then she lifted one hand and touched her mouth with her fingers. The sun seemed suddenly to have grown very warm, the song of the birds was sweeter, and the colours of the garden much more vivid.

She got up and wandered slowly into the cottage to write her letter.

305

Luke walked down the lane, his hands in his pockets, his head down. He was angry with himself for kissing Stella Simmons. She was hardly more than a child, for all that she was a teacher. She had lived almost all her life in a Children's Home, leaving it only to go to college, which had probably been all women anyway. Not only was he almost certainly the first man to kiss her, he was probably the first man she'd ever had as a friend. He knew all too well how easily a girl like that could be swept off her feet.

And yet . . . And yet . . . He felt again that strange, warm tenderness and knew that he too had enjoyed the kiss. Her lips were soft and gentle, her body yielding towards his. And they were friends, with a pleasant, easy companionship that had comforted him through the cold, dark days of winter and through the bleakness of his relationship with Val Tozer.

Perhaps, he thought, he had loved Val long enough. She'd made it clear that she wanted nothing to do with him. He could live the rest of his life alone, wishing for something he could never have. Or he could turn his back and walk into a different future.

He was aware of standing on the brink of an abyss. He could let himself fall in love with Stella Simmons, or he could draw back.

What he could not do, *must* not do, was let Stella fall in love with him if he didn't mean to return her love. He could not ruin the lives of two women. Rather than that, he would have to leave Burracombe and disappear from both their lives.

The thought was a cold and lonely one, and he knew that it would not be simply the two women he would miss. He would miss Burracombe itself – the clustered cottages, the inhabitants with their different characters, some friendly like Dottie, others wary like Jacob Prout – and even he was beginning to come round, Luke thought with a smile. He would miss the companionship in the pub, the welcome he had been given at some of the farms, the solitude of the fields and moorland with its rolling hills, its rocky tors and hidden combes. He would miss the chime of the bells as they rang throughout the valley, and the mew of the buzzard as it soared into the sky, and the high, sweet singing of the lark.

All this was a part of him now. It was in his heart and his mind, and it went into his paintings. He did not know what he would paint if he left the village now.

He came to the gate to the woods and climbed the path to the charcoal-burner's cottage. In half an hour or so, Joyce Warren would be there with her ebullient presence, sweeping him along, commandeering his pictures for her exhibition, taking him over as she took everybody over.

Even she was a part of Burracombe. Even she was a part of what he didn't want to leave.

Chapter Twenty-Seven

Gilbert Napier continued to make slow but steady progress, and by the middle of June he was able to sit in an easy chair by his bedroom window, looking out over the wide lawns towards the beech trees and the moor. His first shock over, he was insistent that he felt well again, and Hilary was hard put to it to prevent him from getting up altogether.

'You've still got to go very carefully, Dad. You know what Charles said. As long as you're resting, you will feel better, but you mustn't put any strain on your heart. You mustn't even climb the stairs, so what would be the point of you coming down?'

'We could have a bedroom made up for me. What about the breakfast room?'

'Well, I'm using it quite a lot – it's cosier than the dining room.'

'The dining room, then.'

'Dad, you know we can't do that! That huge table – where would it go? And all the silver and everything.'

'So start eating there and let me have the breakfast room!' he barked, and Hilary stifled a sigh. There was no point in keeping her father upstairs to save him strain, if he were simply going to get himself all worked up about it. As well as physical rest, Charles Latimer had told her he must be spared any worry or anxiety. Yet she knew exactly what would happen if he came downstairs too soon.

'The next thing he'll be wanting to do is go to the estate

office,' she told the doctor next time he came. 'And then he'll start worrying about how things are being run there, and wanting to interfere. He'll want me to take him round in the Land Rover and before we know it, he'll be back working as hard as ever.'

'I rather expected this,' Charles said. 'He's used to being active – boredom will be his biggest enemy. I'll talk to him, anyway.' He went up to the bedroom, where Gilbert greeted him with a scowl.

'I hope you're going to make that girl of mine see sense. I'm perfectly all right now. What harm could it possibly do to make me up a bed downstairs? I could go outside – sit on the terrace, get some fresh air.'

'You seem to be getting plenty of fresh air here,' the doctor said, looking at the open window. 'I know it's frustrating, Gilbert, but you've got to follow the rules. You don't want another attack, do you?'

'Of course not! But—'

Charles sat down in the other chair. 'Believe me, Gilbert, this is the best way. Hilary's quite right when she says that if you come downstairs too soon you'll start wanting to go outside – which would be fine if you just stuck to the terrace, but you wouldn't, would you? You'd be wheedling or, more likely, bullying the poor girl into taking you to the office. Then it would be a trip round the estate in the Land Rover, perhaps dropping in to see some of the farmers. And you'll naturally want to discuss their farms with them, ask if they've got any problems – and before anyone can say Jack Robinson, you'll be back at work and heading for another attack. And the next one might not be a warning.'

The Squire sat silent for a moment or two, frowning. Then he said grudgingly, 'Well, maybe I would. But dammit, Charles, the work's got to be done. Can't let the place go to rack and ruin.'

'Is it going to? Hilary tells me she's putting in quite a bit of time in the office, and I saw her over at Whitstone yesterday when I looked in to see the old lady. She seemed to be getting along quite well with Stan Hodge and his son.'

'Hilary's got the house to run.'

'Dottie's helping out there, and young Jackie. You could always get more help in if you feel it's too much for her.' He paused. 'You trust your daughter, don't you?'

'Trust her? Of course I do! What sort of a question's that?'

'So why not give her her head? Let her take over the estate work for a while, just until you're fit again, and leave her to it. You can work your way back in gradually after a couple of months and take over again when you're completely fit. Mind you, you mustn't ever take on as much as you've been doing – that's what led to this first attack. But you and Hilary could work together.'

'And what about the house? I was thinking of getting a manager in for the estate, just for the time being. Then the girl wouldn't have to worry herself about it.'

'And where would you get a manager good enough to take over at a moment's notice but willing to leave again in a few months?' the doctor asked. 'It would be much easier for Hilary to find a housekeeper. And the business would be safe in her hands. It would still be in the family.'

Gilbert Napier sat silent, his face set in a heavy frown. Charles waited quietly, knowing that his old friend needed time to readjust his thinking. The idea of Hilary taking his place in managing the estate might need quite a lot of time.

'Think about it, Gilbert,' he said at last. 'At the very least, it means that you needn't make any big decisions just yet. Take the time to rest and get your strength back. But I do think Hilary needs a bit of help somewhere. She's rather a one-man band at the moment.'

'We've got this nurse woman. She does quite a bit.'

'She does the nursing work you need. That still leaves

the house, which Hilary was running before, and the estate which she's taken on. She's doing her work *and* yours, Gilbert. For heaven's sake, man,' he exclaimed, allowing his voice to become more emphatic. 'You can afford someone, can't you? And a housekeeper would be cheaper than an estate manager!'

'That's true.' The heavy face settled once again into a corrugation of frowns. 'Oh, all right, Charles, you win. I'll tell her to get a woman in for the time being. Maybe that'll stop you bullying a sick old man!'

Charles laughed. 'Sick old man indeed. You'll outlive us all – but only if you're careful.' His voice grew serious again. 'I mean that, Gilbert. You've got to take things slowly. It's too easy, when you feel well, to forget that there's a pump inside you which has been badly hurt and needs time to heal. You'll get tired anyway, and that'll tell you to slow down, but you've got to stop worrying about things as well. That's just as harmful.'

Napier nodded. 'All right. Point taken. I'll stay up here and play the invalid for as long as you think it's necessary. And maybe you'll come round and entertain the invalid now and then. Give me a game of chess, that sort of thing.'

'I'll be glad to.' The doctor got to his feet. 'Now I'd better be going. I've got other patients to see as well, you know, and most of them aren't so cantankerous as you. They do as they're told. Now, I'll drop in again tomorrow but remember – no going downstairs, and tell young Hilary to fix herself up with a housekeeper. It'll give Dottie Friend a break too – she's on the go all the time these days, either here or at the school or in the pub. I sometimes think there must be three of her.'

'She's a good woman.' Gilbert watched him go, then turned back to the window. So he was to be kept up here like a naughty child for another week or two, and Hilary was to take over the job he'd always thought he'd be

311

handing over to Baden. He sighed and then picked up a book the doctor had brought him. Reading in the morning seemed like the ultimate in decadence, but at least it took his mind off things.

When Hilary looked in an hour or so later, he was fast asleep in his chair.

'. . . And so Charles has persuaded Daddy to let me get a housekeeper so that I can concentrate on the estate,' Hilary told Felix as she arranged a huge bunch of roses on the altar. '*And* he's got him to agree to stay upstairs for at least another two weeks. He'll be allowed to do more and more – walk around, go from room to room – until Charles thinks he's ready for the stairs. And then he'll probably only be allowed on to the terrace. Charles is being terribly careful.'

'That's good,' Felix said, leaning back against the front pew. 'So you'll have a bit more time to yourself, then?'

'I don't think that's very likely,' she said with a grin. 'There are quite a few things that haven't been done since Dad had his attack. I'll need to go round all the tenant farms, for a start, and let them know what's happening and see if they've got any problems. And I haven't got the housekeeper yet – I suppose I'll have to advertise.'

'Perhaps someone will hear of it through the grapevine,' he suggested. 'You've only got to tell someone a piece of news before breakfast and everybody for miles around knows by lunchtime. I don't know how they do it.'

Hilary laughed. 'There's a lot more communication in the countryside than people think. We don't need telephones out here. Why, there's the man who collects the milk churns from the farm gates, there's the shepherd out looking over his sheep, the cowman in the fields, old Jacob Prout working in the lanes – it's a real network.'

Felix smiled, then glanced down at his hands before looking up again. 'I was hoping you'd be able to take a day off, now that your father's out of danger. I thought we might go out somewhere.'

'Oh.' Hilary didn't know what to say. She knew that he was growing fond of her but she still didn't really know what she felt about him. 'Well, that sounds nice,' she said doubtfully. 'But I'm not sure I can afford the time just now.'

'Can't you? It would do you good to get away for a day. You need a change. You're looking tired.'

'I am,' she admitted. 'And it would be nice . . . Tell you what, I have to go to Exeter one day – why don't you come with me? It's estate business, I'm afraid, but it won't take long and it's a nice drive across the moor.'

'Friday's my day off,' he said. 'Would that do?'

'It'll be fine.' They smiled at each other and Felix went off to the vestry while Hilary finished her arrangements. This was one job she had decided not to hand over, even though both Joyce Warren and Constance Bellamy had offered to take an extra turn. But Hilary enjoyed being in the dim, quiet church. Above her, the trusses of the vaulted roof ended in carvings of winged angels and at certain times of day the sun slanted through the stained-glass windows to light them with bright, jewelled colour. The ends of the pews were carved too, with animals and flowers which she loved to touch as she moved by them, passing her hand over the smooth wood and thinking of all the people who had done the same down the centuries. Members of her own family, many of them, for the Napiers had been in Burracombe since Norman times. This is why it's all so important to Dad, she thought. His own family, part of the village and the valley, part of Burracombe for as long as this church has been standing. This is why he doesn't want it to go.

She gathered up the debris and took the old flowers out to the compost heap in the corner of the churchyard. Jacob

Prout was there, tidying some of the graves. He straightened up as he saw her and gave her a nod.

'Mornin', Miss Hilary. How be Squire today?'

'Getting better, thanks, Jacob. It's a long job, though. Doctor Latimer says he needs to rest for some weeks yet.'

The old man nodded. He'd looked just the same all the years she'd known him, Hilary reflected, as sturdy as an oak tree and with a face that looked as if it had been carved from its trunk. It struck her that he could have been a model for the old Jack-in-the-Green figures one sometimes saw in old churches or on pub signs.

He said, 'My grandad were the same. Went down like a stone one December afternoon and spent the rest of his days in a chair. He liked being out in the sunshine, mind. Us used to put him outside of a nice morning and bring him in come evening.'

'You make him sound like a line of washing,' Hilary said. 'What did you do with him the rest of the time?'

'Sat in his chair by the fire, o' course,' Jacob said. 'He were an institution. Whole village knowed he were there and they used to beat a path to the door. Never short of company, my grandad, right up to the last.'

Hilary looked at him and thought of her father. He hadn't been short of visitors – as well as Charles, there had been Basil and Grace Harvey, Constance Bellamy, Miss Kemp and a few others – but she couldn't say that the whole village had beaten a path to his door.

'I don't think I remember your grandfather, Jacob,' she said doubtfully. 'When did he die?'

'My stars, you wouldn't remember my old grandad!' Jacob exclaimed, showing a mouthful of unlikely looking teeth as he laughed. 'Us lost he when I were a liddle tacker – why, I couldn't have been more than eight or nine, knee-high to a grasshopper, I were when we buried un. He'm over there now,' he said, nodding towards the far corner of the churchyard in such a manner that Hilary turned sharply, almost expecting to see the old man rise from his grave. 'Jacob Prout, same as me. Been there this sixty year or more. Ninety-five when he died. Ninety-five.'

'Goodness me,' Hilary said, trying to work it out. 'So he'd have been born – let's see, in about 1795! Good heavens!' She stared at Jacob. 'That's incredible. Why, who was on the throne then?' She racked her brains for long-ago history lessons. 'It must have been George the Third! Your grandfather must have been able to remember Queen Victoria's Coronation.'

'Went up to London to see it,' Jacob nodded proudly. 'Mind you, there was two more before that – George the Fourth and William the Fourth. Four different monarchs, my old grandad knowed. Four different monarchs. There can't be many as can say that.'

'My goodness,' Hilary marvelled. 'Just think of all the things he lived through. All the Napoleonic wars – why, he could only have been ten years old at the time of Trafalgar. Then there was the Industrial Revolution, the Crimea – the Boer War . . . he must have been like a walking history book by the time he died.'

'Not walking,' Jacob corrected her. 'He were in his chair by then, see.'

'I wonder if he could remember the Great Exhibition in 1851,' Hilary mused. 'The one that gave them the idea of having the Festival of Britain this year.'

'Oh, ah. He took my dad to see that,' Jacob said in a matter-of-fact tone, and bent to carry on with his work. Hilary stared at him.

'He took your father to London to see the Great Exhibition?'

'That's what I said, maid.'

'And you've never mentioned this to anyone?' Hilary demanded in an outraged tone. 'You knew we were getting

315

up a pageant and all sorts of things and you never said a word about it?'

He straightened up. 'But that were a hundred years ago. Nobody's interested in all that now.'

'I think you'll find we are,' Hilary said. 'I don't suppose you've got any souvenirs – pictures, books, that sort of thing?'

'Might have.' His mouth had tightened and she wondered if she'd offended him.

'I'd really like to see them,' she coaxed. 'We might be able to put them on display at the Fair.'

He said nothing for a moment, then shrugged. 'S'pose I could have a look.'

'Oh, thank you, Jacob. Shall I come round and see you in a day or two, when you've had time to look them out?' She had a sudden brainwave. 'Or maybe you'd like to bring them up to the Barton. I'm sure my father would like to see them too.'

'Squire?' He looked incredulous. 'What would he want to be looking at old stuff like that for?'

'Because it matters to him,' Hilary said. 'He loves Burracombe just as much as you do, Jacob. Don't forget, our family's been here for hundreds of years too, and he wants it to go on like that. Why, his grandfather – my great-grandfather – must have known yours. Our families have known each other for centuries. Think of that!'

Jacob gazed at her. She saw his face change as he grappled with the idea. The carved features seemed to soften and he nodded slowly.

'I dare say you'm right, maid. I dare say they did. In fact, one of my uncles worked in your gardens. I've heard un tell about it many a time.'

'There you are, then.' Another thought struck her. 'Jacob, there must be old pictures and letters and all sorts of things lying about in some of the cottages around here.

316

Wouldn't it be wonderful if we could collect them all together and make an exhibition of them. A Village History corner.'

'I thought this here pageant was supposed to be about history,' he objected, but she shook her head.

'That's *big* history. Things like Sir Francis Drake making the leats that supplied water to Plymouth, and the building of Dartmoor Prison for the Napoleonic prisoners-of-war, all that kind of thing . . . and I bet your grandfather remembered that too, but what I'm talking about is history right here in the village. Ordinary people and families who have lived here for generations. Trips to London to see the Coronation or the Great Exhibition, just as we're getting up trips to see the Festival now. I expect we've got some old photos too.' She was beginning to feel really excited. 'Jacob, it's a wonderful idea!'

He scratched his nose. 'Well, I dunno as I could put all that together, Miss Hilary. I mean, I ain't got the book-learning for that kind of thing.'

'No, but I know someone who has. And if you could just talk to people – get them to dig out their old keepsakes and photos and things . . .' She gazed at him. 'Would you do that, Jacob?'

He looked back at her and sighed. He'd always had a soft spot for Miss Hilary. She looked a lot like her mother, who had been, in Jacob's opinion, the loveliest lady who'd ever walked the village green. A crying shame it had been, someone like that dying so young.

'All right, then,' he said, bending to his work again. 'Won't do no harm to try, I suppose.'

Hilary threw her bundle of flowers on to the heap and went on her way. She was sure that Jacob would find sufficient memorabilia for a good display and she was equally sure that there would be plenty of old photographs and documents in her father's possession. She just hoped that he would agree to her suggestion.

Boredom, Charles had said, would be his biggest enemy. Perhaps sorting out old village papers and pictures would give him an interest, and perhaps when the villagers realised what he was doing they would beat a path to his door, just as their fathers and grandfathers had beaten a path to old Jacob Prout's cottage.

Chapter Twenty-Eight

Jess Budd, over in Portsmouth, didn't know where Muriel was. She wrote back to Stella at once, so delighted to have heard from her that Stella felt guilty at not having written before, and gave her some of her own family news. Rose was married and had a baby boy, Tim had done his National Service in the RAF and then joined the Merchant Navy, Keith was in the Royal Navy and Maureen was at the local Girls' Grammar School. Stella tried to imagine them all grown so much older, and gave up. I can't even imagine my own sister grown up, she thought sadly, and felt as if another door had been slammed in her face.

Dottie and Miss Kemp both knew of her search by now, and were sympathetic. 'It's such a pity when families are broken up like that,' the headmistress said. 'I don't know why they do it. Couldn't they have taken you both to the same Home?'

'Couldn't they have left us where we were?' Stella said. 'We had a lovely billet at Bridge End with Mr Beckett, and Tim and Keith Budd. We were as happy as anyone could be who'd lost both their parents and their baby brother. There was no need at all to take us away like that. It was cruel.'

'Yes, I think it was. And I'm really sorry you're having such trouble in finding your sister.'

Stella twisted her lips together and shrugged. 'Well, I don't know what else I can do. I think I'd better give up for the time being. We've got too much to do at school, what with the pageant as well. Have you seen the frock Dottie's making for Shirley Culliford? She's going to look really sweet.'

'A Culliford looking sweet?' The headmistress raised her eyebrows. 'Well, I must admit she's improved tremendously since she was chosen. The vicar was right. And she's quite a bright child as well, you know. I've never expected much from her before but she's doing really well in her writing and arithmetic.'

'Let's hope the others follow her example.' Stella had two smaller Cullifords in her class, each as tattered and grubby as Shirley had been. 'It looks as if Shirley finds keeping herself clean and tidy as much as she can cope with.'

'And her mother doesn't seem to have taken the hint, does she,' Miss Kemp agreed. 'Still, it's a big leap forward to have Shirley doing so well. We must be thankful for whatever mercies come our way.'

Hilary had been into the school to tell them about the exhibition of old village memorabilia, and the children were all pestering their parents and grandparents to turn out cupboards and unpack boxes of fading photographs. A few bits and pieces had already been brought in – Coronation mugs showing the faces of the King and Queen, and older ones with Edward VII. One boy had even brought in a mug with Edward VIII's face painted on.

'But he was never crowned!' Stella exclaimed when she saw it. 'We can't put that out.'

'How strange,' Miss Kemp said. 'They must have sold a few before he abdicated. I wonder if it's valuable, like the threepenny bits they minted.'

'You'd better take it home again,' Stella said to the disappointed boy. 'But look after it, won't you.'

The children had all gone home and Stella was tidying

the nature table when Luke popped his head round the door. She looked up with pleasure.

'There you are! I haven't seen you for days. I was beginning to think you'd left us.'

He came in a little awkwardly. 'I've been busy sorting out pictures with Mrs Warren, amongst other things. I wondered if you'd had a reply from your Auntie Jess?'

Stella's face clouded. 'Yes, but she hasn't heard anything. I'm not going to try any more, Luke. Not for a while anyway. It's just making me miserable.' She looked up at him. 'I've decided that this is where my life is and I've got to put the past behind me and make the most of it.'

He looked down at her and felt the tenderness sweep over him again. He wanted to pull her into his arms and kiss away the tears that were already filling her eyes. But that was all it was – a tenderness, a sorrow for what she had lost – and he was afraid that Stella would think it meant something more. He wasn't ready yet to let that happen and so he drew back slightly. As he did so, he caught the tiny change in her expression and cursed himself.

'I came to tell you I've got to go away,' he said with a rush. 'Oh, not permanently,' as her face dropped, 'just for a couple of weeks, that's all. I've got the chance of a space in an exhibition in London.'

Her face lit up. 'Oh, that's good. It's just what you've been wanting. You mustn't miss that. When will you be going? Can I help you pack up your paintings?'

'No, I've done that. I'm off tomorrow, first thing – catching an early train. Just popped in to tell you and say goodbye.' He hesitated, knowing that if their relationship had progressed as Stella thought it had, this would be the moment to kiss her. Damn it, he thought, I *want* to kiss her! But not in the way she'd like.

He stepped back a little. 'Sorry to be in such a rush – still quite a lot to do. As I said, I'll be back in a fortnight. I want to see some friends while I'm there too, and catch up with my family.'

He saw the look in her eyes and knew that she understood. I feel a cad, he thought miserably, yet all I wanted was to be friends. I still want that. I just don't want to hurt her.

'Yes, of course you must.' Stella turned back to the nature table and examined the glass accumulator tank which was full of tadpoles. 'Look, they're getting their legs now. We'll have to take them outside soon and put some stones nearby for them to climb out on.' She turned back and smiled at him, her eyes bright. 'I'll miss you. But I'm really pleased about the exhibition.'

'Thanks. I'll miss you too, of course, but I expect you'll be busy getting ready for the pageant. Jacob Prout was telling me about this history corner at the Fair. It sounds a good idea.'

'I think it is. We're getting all sorts of items from the children, and Dottie said she'd look out some old things as well. It's amazing how far back some of the families go, and they all seem to be absolute magpies, never throw anything away.'

He laughed, feeling more relaxed. The difficult corner seemed to have been turned. 'That's useful!' He settled himself on a corner of one of the desks. 'But you know, it really is amazing to think that if we could walk out into the village street and go back, say, three hundred years, we'd see dozens of people we recognised, just because the family likenesses go down through the generations. There'd be a Squire Napier trotting by on his horse, a Dottie Friend working at the village inn, a Bertie Foster in the butcher's shop, a George Sweet baking bread, and a Constance Bellamy living at the Grey House.'

'You're probably right. And there'd be Cullifords living in the end cottage, and a Jacob Prout keeping everything tidy – well, we know that because he started all this! – and a Ted Tozer farming the land with his horses. We're the strangers here, Luke.'

'Yes.' He looked thoughtful. 'And how long is it before we're part of the village? Of course, we need to get married first and have a family to start a new dynasty!' He caught her expression and slid quickly off the desk. 'Look, I'm sorry but I've got to go. Got a lot to do before I set off for the big city.'

'Yes,' Stella said. 'Well, have a good time, Luke, and I hope the exhibition goes well.'

'Thanks.' He paused for a moment, but Stella had turned back to the tadpoles. 'I'll see you when I get back, then.'

Stella murmured something and he hesitated again, then slipped quietly out of the door. Outside, he stood irresolute. Then he walked quickly away.

Stella stood very still, staring at the tadpoles. After a while, she straightened up and went to fetch her coat.

I made a mess of that, Luke thought as he walked along the lane. She's upset and disappointed. But it's better to do it now than let things go further and hurt her more. If only she hadn't been so hurt in the past. He thought of the big, sad eyes and the loneliness he sensed in her heart, and wished that he could be the one to take away her sorrow. If only they could have found her sister . . .

He was so deep in thought that he didn't even see Val Tozer when he turned a bend in the lane. They were almost face to face when he raised his head and saw her coming towards him. Involuntarily, he put out his hand and she immediately veered away.

'Val!'

She didn't stop. She was marching briskly, her eyes straight ahead. He tried again.

'Val, don't ignore me. Please.'

She stopped and faced him. 'What do you want me to say?'

He shrugged helplessly. 'I don't know. Anything. "Hello" would do, for a start. Val, I haven't seen you for weeks.'

'I've been busy. I've been helping Hilary – you know her father's ill, I suppose.'

'Yes. I went up there myself to see if there was anything I could do.' He looked at her and knew why he couldn't give Stella the kind of love she yearned for. 'Oh God, Val. We can't go on like this.'

'Like what?' Her voice was stony.

'Please,' he said. 'Come up to the cottage and talk to me. I'm going away tomorrow – I've got to go to London. I can't go without sorting things out between us.'

'There's nothing to sort out.'

'There *is*!' he cried. 'Val, you can't hide it from me. You're as miserable as I am. All right, I accept that we're never going to be together, you don't want that – but I will *not* accept that you've got no feeling for me. I know you have. I can see it in your face – it's in your eyes. It's all over you. Val, I know you as well as I know myself. Let's at least be honest with each other.'

'*Honest!*' she exclaimed, and turned her face towards him. He saw in her eyes a depth of pain that made him gasp, and he put out his hand again and laid it on her arm. This time, she didn't flinch away and he saw her eyes fill with tears.

'Come with me, my darling,' he said gently. 'Please. And then I promise I'll never bother you again.'

Val's head and body drooped. As if she had lost the will to resist any further, she let him lead her through the gate into the wood. Together, silently, they climbed the twisting path between the mossy rocks and the tall trees with their canopy of leaves, and came to the charcoal-burner's hut. Luke opened the door and they went inside.

'I haven't been in here for years,' Val said tonelessly, looking around. 'It hasn't changed much, except for the paintings.'

Luke's canvases and water-colours were everywhere, some hung on the walls, some stacked on the floor. There were two old armchairs by the fireplace and bookcases in the alcove. Oil lamps stood on the table and the wide windowsill. A bright rag rug – one of Dottie's – lay on the stone floor.

'Sit down.' He pressed her lightly into one of the armchairs. 'Would you like a drink? I could make tea.'

She shook her head. She seemed deflated, without spirit, and he knelt before her, looking up into her face, and took both her hands in his. She met his eyes and said wearily, 'Well? What do you want to talk about?'

'Us! What else? Val, we've got to get things clear between us. Why do you hate me so much? I know what we did was wrong, but we can't turn the clock back and we can't pretend it didn't happen. All we can do is put it into the past.' He stroked her hands. 'I told you last time that I still love you,' he said quietly. 'It's true. But if you want me to go away, I will. I don't want to make you unhappy.'

Val's head jerked up. Her eyes had lost their dead, dull look and were sparking with anger. 'You don't want to make me unhappy? It's a bit late for that, isn't it?'

'You weren't unhappy that night,' he said. 'You loved me then as much as I loved you. And ever since then . . .'

'Ever since then,' she said, 'you've been able to live your own life. You could forget about me if you wanted to. You probably did forget about me, until you came to Burracombe and we met again. Why did you have to come *here*?' she cried. 'Why here, of all the places in England you could have gone?'

'I don't know,' he said. 'Maybe we were meant to meet again. Maybe we're meant to be together.' His voice shook a little and he stopped, then went on steadily, 'I didn't forget you, though. What happened was something I'll always remember.'

'Oh yes,' she said savagely, snatching her hands away. 'You'll *remember*. But that's all you had to do, wasn't it – remember! I was the one who had to live with what I'd done. I'm the one who's had to live with the consequences.'

Luke looked at her. She had turned her face away and her expression was hidden beneath a fall of hair. A terrible suspicion began to dawn within his mind.

'Did – did Eddie find out about us?' he asked at last. 'Did you tell him?'

'Oh no! No, he never knew. He never had time to find out.' Almost inaudibly, she added, 'Thank God.' And then she whipped round, her face twisted with pain, saying, 'Don't you think that's a wicked thing, Luke? Don't you think it's terrible that I should be thanking God that my fiancé was killed?'

'Val—'

'But I do,' she whispered. 'I do thank God that he was killed before he found out. I even thanked God that my baby died too.' And she began to cry.

Luke stared at her, horrified, unable at first to take in the full meaning of what she had just said. Her crying tore at his heart. Great, painful sobs of anguish seemed to be forcing their way up from her throat, wrenching at her body, so violently that he was afraid they would tear her apart. He reached out again, then drew back, knowing that his touch was the last thing she wanted. Distractedly, he rubbed the back of his neck, unable to decide what to do. He couldn't torment her with more questions, yet now that she had begun to tell him the truth of what had happened,

326

he needed to hear the rest. He thought that she probably needed just as badly to tell him.

Val's sobs diminished at last, leaving her exhausted. Luke found a hanky and wiped her face tenderly, and she submitted to his touch. When her eyes were dry, he cupped her cheeks in both hands and said gently, 'Tell me about it, Val.'

'It was on the way home,' she said in a voice still thick with tears. 'Coming home from Egypt. It took us weeks and weeks, you know – we had to sail all the way round South Africa. I began to suspect after we'd been at sea for a fortnight. At first, I thought it was just the voyage, I thought it was sea-sickness. But I hadn't been sick on the way out, and besides it wasn't even rough. And then I realised what it was.' She raised her eyes and looked at him. 'I was scared stiff. I didn't know what to do. I couldn't keep it from Eddie and the family – everyone would know. Mum and Dad might not even let me stay at home. There was Jackie too, she was only ten years old. I didn't think I could even *go* home. But what would I tell them if I didn't? I'd been away nearly three years. How could I say I wasn't going home?'

'Oh Val,' he said. 'And I didn't even know.'

'There was nothing you could do. And we'd agreed it was over.'

'It wasn't, though, was it?' he said. 'It was never over for me. And with a baby on the way – our baby . . .'

'I never thought of it as "our baby",' she said. 'It was mine – and I was frightened to death of it. Oh Luke!' She began to cry again. 'It was my baby and I would have loved it, but I was *frightened* of it!'

'You were frightened of other people,' he said. 'Not of the baby. It was what other people would do or say that frightened you, and I ought to have been there to help.'

'Well, you weren't.' The anguish had gone from her voice again, leaving it flat and toneless once more. 'Nobody was there to help.'

Very gently, he drew her close. He felt the resistance in her body and then suddenly it vanished and she rested against him. He stroked her hair and shoulders and was suddenly reminded of the way he had held Stella, just like this, when she had told him about her sister. He would explain to Val, but not now. This moment was too important.

'What happened?' he asked at last. 'You said the baby died. Can you tell me about it, Val? What happened to our baby?'

'It was never born,' she said. 'I had a miscarriage. I didn't bring it on,' she added quickly. 'I was frightened and I didn't know what I was going to do about Eddie and the family, but I didn't do anything. I swear I didn't!' Her voice rose in panic and he soothed her again.

'It's all right, darling. I know you didn't. Were you ill – or hurt in some way? Tell me.'

'I don't know why it happened,' she said. 'I just woke up one night and I was bleeding. I told Mary – you remember her – and the other girls; you'd probably remember them too, there were half a dozen of us, all good friends, who'd been together in Egypt. They did their best but it wouldn't stop, and then the baby was born.' Her voice trembled and broke again. 'He was so tiny – like a little doll. I could hold him in the palm of one hand.'

'A boy?'

'I thought so. You couldn't really tell, he was so small, but I somehow knew it was a boy. I called him John. Little John.' She drew in a ragged breath. 'Nobody else knew. We – we gave him a burial at sea. We found a bit of flag and wrapped him in it, and the six of us went up on deck one night – they had to help me – and we said some prayers and put him over the side.' Once again, the tears came and the sobs shook her body. 'Oh Luke, it was like throwing a piece of rubbish over the side! We tried so hard not to make it seem like that, but that's what it was. Just a little piece of rubbish that nobody wanted.'

'It's not true,' he said. The tears were in his own eyes too, and his throat ached. 'He wasn't rubbish. He was our baby and we would both have wanted him. Oh Val, what a terrible time you've had. No wonder you didn't want to see me again.' He caught her against him. 'Oh Val, Val, can you ever forgive me for what I did to you?'

'We did it together,' she admitted. 'It wasn't your fault. I wanted it as much as you.' She paused, as if the admission had surprised her; as if she had never made it before. 'I felt so guilty. And it was all the worse that you didn't know – I had to feel guilty for you as well. And then, when I heard that Eddie had been killed, it was like a punishment. The worst punishment I could ever have had.'

'It was war,' he said quietly.

'I know. But he'd survived all those years, and to be killed then, when we would soon have been together again . . . oh, it seemed so cruel. And I really did believe it was my fault. I really did.'

'It wasn't your fault. He could have been killed at any time – you know that.' He was silent for a few moments, holding her against him, then he said, 'Do you think you'll ever be able to get over it, Val? Do you think there's any chance for us?'

'I don't know,' she said. 'I just don't know.'

'About Stella—' he began, but she cut him short with a gesture.

'Not now. I can't think about anything else now.' She moved away from him. 'I think I'd like to go home now.'

'I'll take you,' he said, and lifted her to her feet. They

walked down the hill together without speaking, and when he left her at the farm gate he felt as if dark clouds had gathered in his heart.

Chapter Twenty-Nine

'Well, that's a piece of good news!' Dottie laid down her letter and beamed at Stella over the breakfast table. 'My actress is coming to the Fair. She'm going to open it for us. Miss Bellamy suggested I might ask her, so I did, and she'm coming. Oh, it'll be good to see her again, her and little Maddy!'

'That's lovely.' Stella was pleased for her. 'How long is it since you've seen her?'

'Why, it must be two year or more. She used to come here a lot, you know, specially during the war. If ever she got a bit of spare time, she'd be down here to see us all, and Maddy of course when she were here too, and she'd have a rest. Everyone in the village knew her. They'll be thrilled to bits to hear she'm coming again.'

'Where will she stay? D'you want me to move out? I expect someone would give me a room, so long as it's not the Cullifords!'

Dottie laughed. 'No, my flower, there'll be no need for that. She'll stop at the Barton, likely as not. She knew the Squire and Miss Hilary as well, you see – a family friend she were. It'll do him good to see her again, too. She won't be here till the day of the Fair, more's the pity – she'm in Spain, making a film – but she'll be here in time to make her speech and all that.' She got up and began to bustle about clearing the table. 'I'm going up to the Barton this morning, to help Miss Hilary sort out some of they old papers and things Squire's been keeping all these years. She wants to make sure there's nothing that can upset the poor man, like pictures of Mrs Napier or Mr Baden. Then they'm going to make displays for the exhibition.'

'That'll be interesting.' Mention of the exhibition reminded Stella of Luke. She hadn't seen him since he'd called in at the school, and assumed that he must have left for London now. She sighed, wondering what had gone wrong between them. They'd been such friends and he'd been so helpful in her search for Muriel, that she'd begun to think it all meant something more. Obviously I was wrong, she thought, and now I've frightened him away and lost his friendship as well.

She set off for school. Preparations for the Festival were taking up a lot of time now and the children were getting very excited. Some of them had been to London again and come back with stories of the other exhibits they'd seen, or the rides they'd enjoyed at the Fun Fair. Micky was still working on making a clock like the Guinness one and had made several cardboard models. Shirley Culliford had started to wear her hair in plaits and continued to wash her face every day.

'If it encourages just one child to raise her standards, it could all be worthwhile,' Miss Kemp remarked dryly. 'Especially if it's a Culliford.'

Stella was teaching her infants' class some country dances. Jacob Prout had promised to make a maypole and Miss Kemp had said she could take two of the biggest girls into Tavistock one day to buy ribbons. They were making costumes out of existing garments – coloured skirts and blouses with puff sleeves for the girls, breeches and white shirts for the boys. Meanwhile, the bigger children were to act two short scenes about Francis Drake – one showing the famous incident on Plymouth Hoe, when he refused to break off from a game of bowls to go and fight the Spanish

Armada, and the other showing his return to Plymouth and being knighted by Queen Elizabeth. This had caused some dispute amongst some of the younger children.

'Can't us do when he threw down his cloak so the Queen could walk over a puddle?' Ernest asked. 'I wouldn't mind doing that. My mum's got some stripey curtains that would do for a cloak.'

'That was Sir Walter Raleigh,' Miss Kemp told him. 'And we've already got Geoffrey Martin to play Francis Drake.'

'Well, can't us do when Walter Raleigh threw down his cloak, then?' Ernest persisted. 'I've seen pictures of un. And there's bound to be plenty of puddles.'

'Well, thank you for being so optimistic about the weather, Ernest,' the headmistress said. 'Although I expect you're right. But I don't think we can do Raleigh as well as Drake. There are going to be lots of other things happening and we only have a little bit of time.' She saw his disappointment and said, 'I don't see why you can't dress as Raleigh in the procession, though, Ernest, if your mother doesn't mind making a cloak out of the curtains. Are they old ones?'

'Oh no, miss,' he said, cheering up. 'They're our best ones, in the front window. I'll go and tell her, miss.' He ran off and Miss Kemp turned to Stella with a wry expression.

'We'll be getting a visit from an irate parent any minute, asking why I sent Ernest home to say that she'd got to cut up her best curtains for fancy-dress costumes! Oh well, I dare say worse will happen before the whole thing's over. How are the dancers coming along?'

'Quite well, I think. I just hope they come for the last few rehearsals, after term ends.'

'Yes, that's the snag with putting on things in the holidays. Luckily, none of them are going away – not many do, in fact. What about you? Are you planning a holiday?'

'I'm going to stay with a college friend for a week,' Stella said, brightening at the thought of it, 'but not until after the Fair. I won't be leaving you in the lurch.'

'Good. Now, I want to discuss the plans for the Sports Day . . .' And the Fair was temporarily forgotten in plans for races involving sacks, eggs and spoons, and people with three legs.

Dottie arrived at the Barton to find Hilary sitting at the dining table surrounded by documents and photographs. The new housekeeper, Mrs Ellis, was now in command in the kitchen, with Jackie to help her, Pat Smith was still coming in during the day to look after the Squire, and Hilary was free to manage the estate and continue her part in village affairs.

'I don't want to give up too much,' she'd told Val. 'I like arranging the church flowers and helping with the Fair, but it's *so* good to be able to do something that demands a bit more initiative.'

She looked up and smiled as Dottie came in. 'I'm glad you're here. You'll know more of these people than I do. Look, I've sorted them into some sort of order – school photos, the football and cricket teams, WI outings and things like that. And there are quite a lot of the farms, look, with people sitting outside them. Do you know any of the names?'

'My stars,' Dottie said, running her eye over the fading pictures. 'You've got a collection here, and no mistake. Why, surely that's old Mrs Tozer, Ted Tozer's granny. She's been gone these past forty years – I remember her when she used to sit at the door with her spinning-wheel. Used to spin her own yarn, she did, from a fleece that Ted's grandad would give her, and she made all their jerseys from it. Dyed it, too.'

'Well, that's a nice piece of history, for a start,' Hilary

334

said, making a note on a piece of paper and putting it with the photograph. 'And who's this?'

'I don't know who that be,' Dottie said, staring at it. 'Don't look like none of the villagers to me ... Wait a minute, though. Isn't that the travelling salesman that come here a time or two, and put up at the Berrows' farm? Got a bit too friendly with their youngest girl, he did, and got her into trouble. They never saw him no more after that and the babby were born and grew up a bit wanting. They'm dead now, all of 'em.'

'Oh. Well, maybe we'd better not put that one in the Exhibition,' Hilary said, making another note. 'Now, here's an interesting one. It was taken here, you see — at the Barton. Outside on the terrace.' She handed over a larger print, less faded than the others, and Dottie took it and scanned it eagerly.

'Why, you know what that be, don't you?' 'Tis that school that was evacuated here during the war. Why, I knew every one of they little tackers. See that boy? Red hair, he had, and I never saw such a boy for getting into mischief, but a nicer little chap you'd never wish to meet. Now that one, the big one, he was different, a nasty piece of work, he was — and this one here, you'd think he was an angel straight from heaven, butter wouldn't melt in his mouth, but I wouldn't trust un further than I could throw un! And look, here's my little Maddy.'

'Really?' Hilary took the photograph back. 'My goodness, she changed, didn't she. She's quite a plain little thing there. I never really saw her as a child, I was away for most of the war. I only met her when she was about fourteen or fifteen.'

'Grew up a real beauty,' Dottie said with satisfaction. 'A real bit of village history, that be. I suppose you know my actress is coming to open the Fair?'

'Yes, I meant to mention it to you – we had a letter

asking if she could stay with us. It'll be good to see them again.' She looked at the picture once more and put it with the photograph of old Mrs Tozer. 'Yes, that must definitely go into the display. Now, Father's coming downstairs in a minute and he'll go through the rest with you. I've taken out all those I don't think he should see. Don't let him do too much, will you? An hour or so will be quite long enough, to start with.'

'Don't you worry about that, my flower,' Dottie said. 'Us'll have a high old time, looking through all these old pictures. Bring back a few memories, they will.'

'Yes, I'm sure they will. It's going to be one of the highlights of the Exhibition.' Hilary stood up. 'I'll go and bring him downstairs now. It's very good of you to do this, Dottie.'

'Bless you, 'tis a pleasure. I'll enjoy it. And I'll look after your father, don't you worry. You go off and do whatever you got to do. He'll be all right with me.'

Hilary smiled at her. 'I know he will,' she said. 'Everyone's all right with you, Dottie.'

Jackie Tozer was another one who felt all right these days. Her relief that she wasn't pregnant after all was so great that she had a smile on her face for everyone she met, and went about her work singing. It was her sister Val who seemed cast down.

'It's just like being on a blessed see-saw,' Alice complained to her mother-in-law. 'If it's not one, it's the other. There was our Jackie going about with her chin down to her knees – and you 'n' me have got our own ideas about why that was, Mother – and now she's bucked up and it's Val who looks as if she's lost a shilling and found sixpence. Between the pair of them, I don't know where I am.'

'I thought Val was picking up a bit,' Minnie said. She was sitting just outside the door, shelling peas, and Alice

336

was scrubbing a bowlful of new potatoes. 'After you persuaded her to go down the village with us on New Year's Eve, she seemed to be making a real effort. I thought she must have made a resolution.'

'If she did, she's broken it. She goes off to work in the morning without hardly a word and when she comes back it's straight up to the Barton to see Hilary. I don't begrudge her that, mind,' Alice added quickly. 'They'm good friends and Hilary needs a bit of company, what with her father being ill and her having to do all the work round the estate. But it don't seem to be doing our Val no good. She'm looking proper peaky.'

'Well, there's not much you can do about it, flower,' Minnie said. 'Her's a grown woman and got to make her own way. I've finished these peas now, if you wants to take them in.'

Alice took the pods over to the compost heap and then came back for the bowl. 'D'you know what I reckon, Mother? I reckon something's happened, and it happened all of a sudden. She were doing all right, looking a lot brighter, and then something changed. I'd dearly like to know what it is.'

She went indoors and Minnie closed her eyes and basked in the warmth of the late June sunshine. She understood Alice's worries – she'd felt the same way at times about her own children, Ted and his sisters Florrie and Maud. You could see there was something amiss, but unless they told you what it was, there was nothing you could do about it. You probably wouldn't be able to do anything if they did tell you. You couldn't sort out your own troubles, half the time, let alone anyone else's.

Grown-up children had grown-up problems, that was the top and bottom of it, and there was no sense in worrying yourself over it all. It would either come right or it wouldn't.

That was life.

Joyce Warren's problems also seemed to be getting worse. She was accustomed to things not going quite to plan, but there were moments when she thought the Fair and Exhibition were never going to happen. First, the boiler in the memorial hall had broken down, which meant that nobody could make tea. A few large kettles had been brought but they could only be boiled one at a time on the little stove and Joyce was frantic in case the boiler could not be repaired in time for the Fair.

'We'll be serving at least two hundred teas on the day,' she said after the next parish council meeting. The others had gone but she had managed to corner the vicar and was determined to make him listen. 'Probably twice that number. However are we going to manage?'

'It'll come in time, I'm sure,' Basil Harvey said soothingly. He had already suffered similar complaints from the Mother's Union, the Wl, the Whist Club and the Drama Group. 'I don't know why people can't bring a Thermos flask if they can't get through a couple of hours without tea,' he went on. 'There really isn't any need to struggle with stoves and kettles.'

'That's not the point. It's the Fair I'm worried about. Have you actually sent for the engineer, Vicar?'

'Of course I have,' he replied a little indignantly. 'At least, I think I have. I rang him on Monday . . .' He stared at her anxiously. 'I meant to ring him, anyway. I can't actually remember . . .'

Joyce tutted and rolled her eyes. 'I knew I should have done it myself! I'll ring him as soon as I get home.' She looked round the hall. 'And those chairs could do with renewing. I suppose it's too late to do that now?'

'It certainly is,' he said firmly. 'Anyway, if we're lucky enough to have fine weather I dare say everyone will want to be outside, and Miss Kemp says we can borrow the forms from the school. They're rather low, but at least everyone will be able to see what's going on.'

'And if we *don't* get fine weather?' she enquired, and he sighed.

'Then I don't suppose many people will bother to turn up, and the problem won't arise.'

'And what about the Exhibition itself? I'll need the hall for at least three days beforehand to set it up. Nobody will be able to use it during that time, and we must have the boiler in operation by then. I can't have men tramping in and out with muddy boots and spanners while I'm trying to organise the tables and the Art display. There's the bellringing competition on the Saturday as well. We've got to feed all those ringers. Where are we going to put them? Mr Tozer thinks there'll be at least sixty.'

'We could give them their tea in the church,' Basil suggested. 'There's plenty of room to sit there.'

'In the *church*? Did I really hear you say in the *church*?' She stared at him, scandalised.

'Why not? We can sweep up the crumbs afterwards. They have the announcement of their results in the church, after all. And we do break bread and drink wine there, you know,' he added with a twinkle.

Joyce was not impressed. 'I must say, Vicar,' she said in a tone so acid it could have dissolved metal, 'I never expected to hear you, a man of the cloth, speak in such a facetious way about your own church. I think it would be best if we forgot that this conversation ever took place. Do you know what they *eat* at these affairs?' she demanded, breaking her rule the moment she'd made it. 'Cornish pasties! The church would smell of them for days. Besides, we're having the Flower Festival in the church. We can't have a lot of great, clodhopping, muddy-booted bellringers stamping about amongst all our floral displays. Most of them are farmers, you know.'

'Most of them are churchgoers, too,' he murmured. 'And they do wear their best clothes for competitions.'

'Pubgoers, more like,' she retorted, ignoring the second part of his remark. '*I've* seen them in the Bell on practice nights.'

'Have you?' He looked at her with such innocence that she blushed and hastily changed the subject.

'Have you heard anything from that godson of yours? I wanted to go and have another look at his paintings, to make a final choice, and what do I hear but he's gone dashing off to London. Is he coming back, or is he going to let us down?'

'I'm sure Luke would never let anyone down—'

'Well, I hope you're right,' she snapped. 'Now, I'm sorry, Vicar, but I really don't have time to stand here gossiping. Some of us have things to do, you know! I'd better go straight home and ring up that boiler-man for a start – it's nearly nine o'clock, he should be at home, unless *he's* in the pub as well – and then I'll need to talk to Mr Tozer about the catering for the ringing competition. He told me his wife would see to it, but I haven't heard a word from her. I'd better go up to the farm first thing in the morning and see what she's arranging, if anything. Honestly, it sometimes seems as if I'm the only one who does anything at all around here!'

She marched out of the hall, leaving Basil Harvey staring after her, his mouth open. If only I were more quick-witted, he thought, I'd have reminded her that the ringing competition is none of her business and that Alice Tozer is sure to have everything well in hand. But no doubt Alice would make that clear herself. She could have quite a sharp tongue on her when she liked, could Alice.

Well, never mind, he told himself as he put away the

chairs. There were people like Mrs Warren in most villages and you had to admit that without them not much would get done. Bossy, impatient and high-handed, they nevertheless got things organised and, as a rule, quite successfully. He had no doubt that the Fair and all its attendant events would go off very well.

And do you know, he thought, standing in the middle of the floor with a chair in one hand, I do believe I did ring up the boiler-man. He said he would be here first thing tomorrow morning. Well, that will show Mrs Warren that she's not the only one who can get things done!

Gloating wasn't at all a suitable thing for a vicar to be doing, he chided himself as he closed the door, but even vicars are human.

Chapter Thirty

'Jackie!' Alice called up the stairs. There's someone down here to see you. It's Roy,' she added as her daughter emerged from her bedroom and started down the stairs.

'Roy!' Jackie stopped and half-turned to go back upstairs, but Alice's sharp voice stopped her in her tracks.

'Yes, Roy. And don't go dashing off upstairs and expect me to say you're not in. He's heard me call you, anyway. Whatever's the matter with you, maid? You used to be so thick!'

'Well, we're not now.' Slowly, Jackie came down the rest of the stairs. 'We just lost interest, that's all. Cooled off. I'd have thought you'd be pleased – you went on at me enough when I said we wanted to get engaged.'

'Yes, well, never mind that now.' Alice didn't really want to discuss the reasons why Jackie and Roy had apparently cooled off. 'He's here and he wants to see you. He's in the garden, wouldn't come in.'

Jackie went reluctantly through the kitchen and found Roy sitting outside on the bench where her grandmother often sat. He stood up when she came out of the house and she saw that he was in uniform. She looked at him.

'What are you doing home, then? There's nothing wrong, is there?'

'Depends what you call wrong,' he said. 'Come for a bit of a walk, Jackie.'

She opened her mouth to object, but the look on his face

stopped her and she followed him through the gate. They walked along the track for a short distance in silence and then she said, 'Well, come on then, Roy. How far do we have to go before you'll tell me?'

'I'm being drafted away,' he said briefly, and stopped to lean on a gate. His face was tight, his eyes shuttered. 'I'm being sent to Korea, Jackie.'

'*Korea?* But you've only been in the Army five minutes – and you're only National Service. Why are they sending you to Korea?'

'It's not just me,' he said impatiently. 'We're all going. You knew I might go there. We talked about it, remember? We wanted to get married before I went,' he added bitterly.

Jackie moved closer to him. 'Roy, I'm really sorry. You don't want to go, do you?'

'Of course I want to go! I might get killed – save me the trouble of doing it meself.'

'*Roy!* Don't say such things! It's wicked.' She put her hand on his arm. 'You won't get killed, Roy. You'll be all right.'

'Oh yes, and you know that, do you? There's a *war* going on out there, Jackie, a proper war. Just because we're not getting bombed over here doesn't mean it's not just as real as the last one. People are getting killed all the time – why should I be special?' He turned to her and she saw the tautness in his face. He looked thinner, she thought, and older too. Something had changed him from the bright apprentice and the eager lover to a man who feared what lay ahead.

'I didn't ask to be a soldier,' he said. 'I just wanted to be a mechanic. I'd like to work on tanks, I wouldn't mind doing my National Service on that sort of work, but instead they're going to make me fight. If I'd joined up as a Regular because I wanted to fight, I wouldn't mind, but I didn't. I don't even know what it's all about. I didn't know where Korea was till I looked it up in my school atlas.'

'Oh Roy,' Jackie said. 'I'm sorry. I really am.'

'And if that wasn't bad enough,' he said miserably, 'everything's gone wrong between you and me, and I don't know why that's happened either. I never meant to get you into trouble, Jackie. I just wanted to love you. I still do,' he added in a low voice.

She looked at him and felt her heart move. The tenderness she had felt a few moments before strengthened and she tightened her hand on his arm.

'Roy . . . I don't know what to say.'

'Just tell me it's not all finished,' he pleaded. 'Tell me we've still got a chance. You don't have to let me make love to you, if you don't want to. You don't have to be engaged to me. Just say you'll write to me, and let me write to you.' He looked into her face. 'Please, Jackie. Please.'

'Of course I'll write to you,' she said, her voice filled with tears. 'Not every night, like I did before, and I'm not promising to wait for you, but I'll write every week. I'll do that.'

'And I'll write to you.' He moved uncertainly towards her. 'Look, I know you'll probably meet someone else, but if you don't – if you haven't by the time I come home – well, d'you think there'll be another chance for us? Do you?'

'How do I know that? You could be gone two years!' Panic gripped her again, then she caught herself up and gave him a wavering smile. 'Look, I'm sorry, Roy, but what with everything that's happened I don't know what I think or feel any more. I just know that Mum was right – it's too soon. I'm too young. *You're* too young. I don't want to think about that sort of thing any more – not for a long time, anyway.'

'You might think different in two years' time,' Roy said.

'Well, we'll just have to wait and see, won't we. I've said I'll write to you, and that's all I'm going to say.' She looked into his face. 'It wasn't just your fault, I know,' she said more gently. 'I wanted to do it too. But it was all wrong and I don't want to do it again. Not yet.'

'All right.' He gave her a doubtful glance. 'Can I – would you give me a kiss, then, Jackie? Just one, to send me on my way? Please?'

'All right.' She reached up and touched his lips with hers, as lightly as a butterfly. He put his arms around her and held her loosely, and kissed her back. They stayed very still for a few moments and then he let her go and moved away.

'I'd better be going. I'm off in the morning. Goodbye, Jackie. Take care of yourself, won't you.'

'And you, Roy,' she said softly. 'You take care.'

He hesitated for one more moment, then turned and walked away. Jackie watched him, thinking that even from behind he looked different – more upright, more sure of himself. And yet he hadn't been at all sure of himself with her.

She felt a sudden fierce desire to call him back, to pull him tightly into her arms, to kiss him with all the passion that she'd learned with him during the long winter nights. And then he turned the corner and was gone.

When Jackie went indoors again, her eyes were damp and red. Alice and Minnie looked at her and then at each other as she went slowly back up the stairs to her bedroom.

'I do think her looks better for it, all the same,' Minnie said. 'They've patched it up, and it'll be a fair long time before anything else can happen. Got time to grow up, both of 'em.'

'And I can't say I'm sorry,' Alice remarked, sliding a tray of lamb chops into the oven. 'I can't say I'm sorry at all.'

Hilary started up the estate car her father had finally agreed to buy her only a month before his illness. Since taking over the estate management, she had been visiting all the tenant farmers in turn, telling them what was happening and talking over any problems they might have. They had all known her since childhood and welcomed her so heartily that sometimes she had difficulty getting away.

'You'll take a glass of my sloe gin, now,' one apple-cheeked farmer's wife urged her.' ''Tis full of goodness, won't do you no harm at all. Put heart into you, that will.'

'Gin, at ten o'clock in the morning? I don't think I'd better!' Hilary said. 'Thank you very much, all the same, but if everyone offers me alcohol I'll be rolling drunk by the time I get home.'

'A glass of home-made lemonade, then?' the woman suggested, and Hilary nodded gratefully. She followed her hostess into the kitchen and sat at the big, scrubbed table. 'And how's the Squire, then?'

'He's getting along very well, thank you, Mrs Barrow. Doctor Latimer's allowing him downstairs now and he's going through some old photographs and things for the Exhibition. I don't suppose you've got anything, have you?'

Hilda Barrow pursed her lips and shook her head. 'No, I wouldn't have anything of interest like that. Only a few old photograph albums and some old papers about the farmhouse. I suppose by rights they should be yours, but your grandfather gave them to my man's father when he took over the tenancy, and we've always kept them. 'Twouldn't be right to throw them away. They'm nothing to look at, though – all yellow and tattered.'

'Old papers?' Hilary echoed. 'Papers about the farm?'

'That's right. In an old envelope in our tin box. I haven't looked at them for years.'

'Do you think I could see them?' Hilary asked tentatively, scarcely able to believe her luck.

'Well, if you want to.' Hilda Barrow clearly thought this a strange idea. 'I'll fetch them down.'

Half an hour later Hilary left the farmhouse, her head reeling more than it would have done had she accepted the sloe gin, a large bundle of photograph albums and a packet of documents clutched under her arm. She had been almost afraid to ask if she could borrow them, but Hilda Barrow had pressed them into her arms.

'You take 'em, my blossom, if you think they'd be any good in that old Exhibition. 'Tis only some old maps and ledgers, and the ink's so faded you can hardly read them anyway. And there's nobody left now who even knows who the people be in those photographs.'

'But *you* know,' Hilary said.

'Oh, *I* knows, all right. They'm all my man's grand-parents and uncles and aunties, that's who they be. But there's nobody else to be interested.'

'But that's just the point,' Hilary said, gathering them together. 'People *are* interested. This is exactly the kind of thing we want for the Exhibition.'

Carefully, she put the packages on the back seat of the car and drove off. If she were to find such a treasure-trove in every farm she visited, they'd need the entire hall for the History part of the Exhibition alone. She hugged herself, thinking of her father's face when he saw them. Basil Harvey and Miss Kemp would be excited too, and even Mrs Warren. Nothing else as old had yet been found.

She was on her way home an hour or so later when she noticed Felix walking along the lane in front of her. She drew up beside him and leaned across to open the door. 'Like a lift?'

'Hilary!' His face lit up. 'What a nice surprise.' He ducked his head and folded himself through the door. 'I'm really out for the good of my health, but I'd rather ride with you. Where have you been?'

347

'Touring the tenant farms. I thought they ought to have a visit, to let them know what's happening. And I've found treasure!'

'Treasure?'

'Yes. Wonderful old photographs, and documents showing all the old field boundaries, with their names. "Twelve acre", "Holly Meadow", "Sticky Bottom" –'

'I don't believe the last one!' he protested, laughing.

'It's true – I'll show you. It refers to a rather muddy field low down in the valley. Really, Felix,' she added primly, 'for a curate you have a very naughty sense of humour.'

'Most curates have a naughty sense of humour,' he said. 'Vicars too, and probably even bishops. We're only human, you know.'

'Well, most of them don't let it show. And you should be more careful too. Suppose Mrs Warren heard you.'

'Ah, but Mrs Warren's not here, is she? Thank the Lord,' he added piously.

'Felix! Stop it.' Hilary tried to stifle her laughter, but failed. She gave him a wry look. 'You know, you're a bad influence on me – and you shouldn't be. I may complain to the vicar.'

'Oh, he knows what I'm like already,' Felix said, 'and he has quite a sense of humour himself, you know. Well, where shall we go now?'

'Nowhere. I've got to go home and see how Dad is. I left Dottie going through old photos with him. You can come with me if you like, and have a bit of lunch.'

'Do you think I should? I wouldn't like to intrude. And I've been very remiss, I should have asked after your father. How is he?'

'He's doing very well. Please come, Felix. It does him so much good to see a different face, and kind and pleasant as Dottie is, he doesn't really have much in common with her.'

'All right, then. If you put it that way. But I'll ask a favour in return.'

'What's that?' she asked cautiously.

'That you come for a walk with me afterwards. It's my day off and we haven't spent any time together since we had that day in Exeter. Which I enjoyed very much indeed,' he added, turning to look at her.

'So did I. All right, I'll come for a walk, but we can't go far. I'll need to be back by four, when the nurse goes off-duty.'

'And so you shall be, Cinderella. I shall make sure of it. So long as you don't want me to turn into a white mouse or something, to draw your carriage along. I don't think I could manage that.'

'You wouldn't have to. It was the white mice who changed, into footmen. And we're going for a walk, remember. I won't even wear my glass slippers.'

'I can't imagine why anyone would want to,' he said thoughtfully. 'Most uncomfortable, I'd have thought, not to mention being rather dangerous.'

'I've heard somewhere that it was a mistranslation from the French for "fur". Not that I'd wear my fur slippers to a ball, either.' She turned the car through the gateway. 'Really, this is a very silly conversation. I hope you're not going to twitter on like this at lunch.'

'Not if you don't either,' he said solemnly, and they were still laughing when Hilary drew the car to a halt in front of the steps and they got out.

''Tis all in hand, Mrs Warren,' Alice said. 'You don't need to be worrying yourself about the bellringers' tea. I always sees to that, along with some of the other ringers' wives. 'Tidn't nothing to do with the Fair, anyway.'

'Of course it's to do with the Fair!' Joyce's patience was being stretched thin and it showed in her voice. 'It's a special competition, isn't it? A Festival shield? Well, then, of course it's to do with the Fair, and as principal organiser I ought to know what's going on.'

'Well, that's as may be,' Alice said. She didn't like Mrs Warren much at the best of times, and she especially didn't like her poking her nose into things Alice had been doing for years with one hand tied behind her back. 'As far as I'm concerned, 'tis just a competition, same as all the others, and as Ringing Captain's wife I does the tea, and that's all there is to it.'

'Yes, but you don't understand,' Joyce insisted. 'The point is that you won't be able to use the village hall. We'll have the Exhibition in there. And handing out sixty Cornish pasties in the church is out of the question. You'll need to think about it and let me know what you're planning to do.'

'Oh, that's what you'm making all this song and dance about, is it?' Alice folded her arms. 'Well, that's all right, then. 'Tis all fixed up. We'll be using the tent.'

'Tent?' Joyce stared at her. 'What tent?'

'Why, the tent we'm putting up in Ted's field, of course. Didn't no one mention it to you? 'Tis a proper marquee. Miss Hilary offered it to us. Left over from when they had that Army camp over at the Barton. Nobody never come to collect it, so they've had it stored in one of their barns ever since. She mentioned it to Ted and he thought it would be a good idea, in case it rains. I thought you'd be pleased,' she finished, giving Joyce Warren a bland smile.

'Of course I'm pleased. It'll be a wonderful asset. But I'm rather surprised that no one thought to mention it to *me*. I'm only the one who's trying to see that everything's co-ordinated and works well on the day. Over the whole weekend, in fact. It would have been common courtesy, if nothing else.'

'Well, we knows that, and if you'd give me a chance

when you first come, instead of starting on at me about ringers' teas the minute you were over the doorstep, I'd have told you then and saved all this argy-bargying. It were only this dinner-time that Ted told me. He saw Miss Hilary this morning. So nobody else has heard about it, and you'm the first to know.' Alice met her eye and Joyce found herself stared out. She flushed and looked away.

'I see. In that case I owe you an apology. I'm glad it's all been sorted out. How will you boil the water?'

'Big camping stoves. The Army left them as well.' Alice caught the gleam in Joyce's eye and added quickly, 'They wouldn't be no use for the village hall. Got to be used outdoors, see, in case of fumes. Anyway, the boiler's getting repaired tomorrow, so you should be all right there.'

'Tomorrow?' Joyce felt as if she were completely losing grip. 'How on earth do you know that? I haven't been able to get through to the repairman myself yet.'

'Saw un this morning, when I were in Tavi. He said the vicar had been on to him and that he'd be out tomorrow.' Alice smiled again and took pity on the other woman. She might be irritating – a pain in the backside, her Ted said – but her heart was in the right place, and you had to admit she put in a lot of work on things like this. 'Now, why don't you sit yourself down for a minute, Mrs Warren, and have a cup of tea with me and Ted's mother? Just made some scones, she have, and there's our strawberry jam and cream to go with 'em. You looks a bit fraught, if you don't mind me saying so.'

'Well, I've got a lot of things to do, but – yes, a cup of tea would be very nice, thank you, Mrs Tozer.' She smiled at Minnie, who was sitting in her chair and watching all that went on. 'These scones look delicious. Will you be making some for the Fair and Exhibition?'

'I dare say I will. And for the ringers' tea, of course. It looks like being a busy weekend.'

'It does.' Joyce felt slightly faint as she thought of all that was to happen – the bellringing competition, even though that did seem to be under control, the pageant, the Exhibition and the displays on the green and in the field. And heaven knew how many scones and pasties and sandwiches and cakes were going to be required. 'I just hope it all goes well,' she said with feeling.

'Oh, it will.' Alice brought the big brown teapot to the table and set it down. 'We'm all looking forward to it, Mrs Warren. 'Tis going to be a good day. And nothing's going to go wrong.' She smiled again. 'There might be a few surprises, but nothing will go really wrong.'

Chapter Thirty-One

Term ended and Stella spent the last few days with her class, taking down drawings and maps from the walls, tidying desks and clearing the nature table. The tadpoles had long turned into tiny frogs and been set free near the village pond; the water from the accumulator tank had been tipped into the pond as well, so that the snails and any other pondlife in the weed could return to their proper home. The puss-moth caterpillars had pupated and could be left in their tin until it was time for the moths themselves to emerge. There were several discarded skins, which were borne off as treasures by Micky and Ernest.

Miss Kemp came in just as Stella was finishing the last of the clearing-up. The children had rushed out into the sunshine, shrieking with excitement at the prospect of six weeks with no school, and Stella felt rather like shrieking with them.

'Well, that's that until September,' the headmistress said. 'Except for the Festival weekend, of course. But that's only just over a week away, so we'll have a nice long stretch after that. You said you were going away, didn't you?'

'Yes, but not until the last week of August. I'll be back in time to think about the new term, and I'm hoping my friend might give me some ideas. She's teaching at a school in Oxfordshire.'

'That's good. You'll be able to swap experiences.' Miss

Kemp settled herself against Stella's desk. 'You are happy here, aren't you? You seem to have settled in very well.'

'I love it, I really do. The children, the school, the village – it's all I've ever wanted.' She gazed out of her window at the view of Dartmoor sweeping away above the village. 'I'd like to stay here for ever.'

'I can understand that,' the headmistress said, 'but you won't want to remain an assistant mistress all your life. And I'm afraid you've a few years yet to wait for my shoes.'

'Oh, goodness no, I didn't mean that!' Stella felt her colour rise. 'I suppose I'll have to move on at some time, if only to get more experience. It would be interesting to work in a bigger school, too. But not yet. I want to stay in Burracombe as long as I can.'

'I hope you do. You've fitted in very well – the children love you and the parents seem very happy. Now, I don't want to start talking about next term yet, but we will need to get together a few days beforehand to talk about the new intake. There'll be some new children starting, and amongst them are the Crocker twins.'

'Oh yes, the vicar mentioned them when I came to see the school and have my interview. I've seen them around the village too. They look rather sweet.'

'They do indeed,' the headmistress said a trifle grimly. 'But so do their older brothers. You won't know Joseph and Sam Crocker. They're quite a few years older – the twins were an "afterthought". Sam's doing his National Service now, and Joseph – well, the less said about him the better, perhaps. Anyway, we shall have to hope for the best. I believe there will be three other new infants as well, so you'll have your hands full.'

'There are five going up into your class,' Stella pointed out, and the headmistress nodded.

'That's right. But as I said, we don't need to discuss this now.' As she glanced around the classroom they heard the shuffling and muttering sounds that accompanied Mrs Purdy's arrival. 'If you're all finished here, why not come over to the schoolhouse for a cup of tea? I think we deserve it, don't you?'

Stella agreed, and they opened the door to find the school cleaner already getting out her brooms and mops. She looked round as they came into the lobby and gave a nod of bitter satisfaction.

'So that's another term finished with, then. At least I'll be able to get on with me cleaning in peace and quiet, and know that when I comes in things'll be same as I left 'em yesterday. I know children have to come to school, but I just wish sometimes they could bring a bit less mud and dirt with 'em. Well, you go off and enjoy your holidays. Some of us don't get the luxury. Six weeks!' they heard her say indignantly as she shuffled into the main classroom. 'And they say teaching's a hard job . . .'

The two teachers looked at each other and Stella laughed. Miss Kemp smiled too and said, 'I think school cleaners are a breed apart. They either love the children or hate them. But under all that grumbling, Mrs Purdy's got a heart of gold. And she's an excellent cleaner.'

They walked across the playground together. It was mid-afternoon and the sun was still high in the sky. Stella could hear the sound of children's voices, playing on the green or in cottage gardens. She heard the clip-clop of hooves and glanced over the fence to see Val Tozer passing by with her father's Shire horse, Barley. She remembered seeing them on her first day here, as she got off the bus and heard Luke Ferris ask if she were the new teacher, and she waved, then remembered Val's coolness towards her and was pleasantly surprised when she waved back.

Miss Kemp paused as she opened the door and glanced over her shoulder. She waved as well.

'Val Tozer. A nice girl. One of my first pupils when I

came here. Such a sad thing that her fiancé was killed. I hope she'll find someone else some day.'

They went inside and Miss Kemp put the kettle on. Stella looked out at the tiny back garden and sighed a little. The bright summer sunshine seemed suddenly dimmed.

We all seem to have lost something, she thought. Hilary and Val lost their sweethearts and I lost my family. And millions of other people lost their loved ones as well, and their homes and all they owned. But we all have to go on living. Some of them are lost for ever, and we can't go on searching all our lives.

Val had surprised herself by waving at Stella. She walked on down the lane, with Barley's nose rubbing at her sleeve as he plodded at her side, and thought about the young teacher. I don't know why I felt so jealous of her, she thought. Luke told me there was nothing between them. Yet that sight she'd had of them, standing so close together on the edge of the moor, had been easy to misconstrue, and even though Val had tried hard to put Luke Ferris out of her mind, his arrival in the village had been more disturbing than she would have expected.

You can't stop loving someone just like switching off a light, she thought. I had a terrible time after Luke and I gave each other up, but it wasn't fair to blame him for that. He didn't even know. She thought of the comfort she had found in his arms, as he held her when she told him about the baby. The sensation of coming home. And she knew that she still loved him; that she had never really stopped.

She hadn't been able to let Luke go to London without seeing him again. She had got up early next morning and caught the first bus to Tavistock, walking quickly up the hill to the railway station. Basil Harvey would be bringing Luke and the paintings in his car, and she wanted to be on the platform before they arrived. I hope to goodness the

356

vicar manages to get him here in time, she thought anxiously. I hope they don't arrive at the last minute . . . And just in case, instead of a platform ticket she bought a return to Okehampton and then ran across the bridge to wait behind a pillar on the opposite platform.

It was only a few minutes before the train was due, and she had begun to fear that Basil was going to live up to his reputation, when she saw the two men hurry on to the station, laden with their packages. I hope Luke's got a taxi waiting for him in London, she thought, watching as they scrabbled for money and bought tickets, then panted up the steps and across the bridge. By the time they reached the platform the train was pulling in and the two men said a hurried goodbye before Luke scrambled aboard. Val, thankful for her foresight in buying a full ticket, climbed aboard too and as the train drew out again she made her way down the corridor to where Luke was struggling with his paintings.

'Here,' she said as he almost dropped one, 'let me give you a hand.'

Luke straightened up and stared at her. The thin package fell from his hand. '*Val*!'

'Yes,' she said, and bent to retrieve the picture. But as she too straightened up she felt his arms around her, and found herself drawn tightly against his lean, hard body. The painting fell to the floor once more as they clung together. 'Oh Luke, I had to come. I couldn't let you go away again, not knowing. Oh *Luke* . . .'

Dottie Friend was standing at her gate as Val passed. Now that they had a full-time housekeeper at the Barton, she was able to spend more time at home, and she was busy in the garden, dead-heading roses and threading honeysuckle through a trellis arbour that Nathan Pettifer had put up for her. She gave Barley a fallen apple and stroked his broad, smooth nose as he munched it.

'I was going to come up to the farm to see you,' she said to Val. 'Saved me a journey, you have. Squire and me have finished going through all they old photos and things, and Mrs Warren's asked me to pin them all up on some screens for the Exhibition. I wondered if you'd give me and Stella a hand with it.'

'Yes, all right.' It'll be a good chance for us to get together, Val thought. I know I've been unwelcoming towards her. 'When d'you want to do it?'

'Well, us can't get into the village hall till next Tuesday, so us had better do it as soon as possible after that. When be you off-duty next week?'

'Wednesday should be all right. Morning or afternoon?'

'Let's make it the morning, then. That'll be a proper job.'

'I'll be there about ten.' Val smiled at her and walked on. Luke would probably be home again by then, she thought. And she felt a lightening of her heart, as though spring had made a return visit and life was about to begin once more.

The whole village was geared towards the last-minute preparations for the Festival Fair and Exhibition. In Ted Tozer's field, the big Army tent was erected and trestle tables brought down from the village hall. This caused Joyce Warren some consternation, as nobody had thought to mention this to her and the first she knew of it was when she met Nathan Pettifer and Norman Tozer hauling them up on to Ted's cart, with Barley waiting patiently in the shafts.

'What do you think you're doing with those?'

The men looked down at her. 'We'm taking them down to the field. We needs 'em there for the ringers, tea.'

'But I need them in the hall! What do you think we're going to display our exhibits on? Put them back at once!' Nathan climbed down slowly and faced her. 'Can't do that, missus. Boss'll have us guts for garters.'

'And I'll have your guts for garters if you don't! Put them *back*.' She looked round helplessly and saw Dottie Friend coming down the lane with Stella. 'Dottie, do you have any influence on these people? Can't you explain to them that we need the tables for our exhibits?'

Dottie looked at the two men. 'How many are you taking?'

'Dozen or so. We'm leaving a dozen there – Miss Val said that'd be all you'd need.' He gave Joyce an aggrieved look. 'I were going to tell you, but you never give me a chance.'

'Oh. Oh well, that's all right, then.' The woman turned to Dottie and Stella. 'We'd better go inside and get started. I gather Val Tozer's already here. I hope that young artist's going to be back in time to set out his paintings. I can't understand why he had to go rushing off to London at an important time like this. They've got exhibitions going on up there all the time . . .' She bustled into the hall, leaving Dottie and Stella to follow her and the men to finish their loading.

As Nathan had promised, there were trestle tables already up around the sides of the hall and Val was standing at one, sorting out a pile of photographs. Beside her was a small enclosure made of rather wobbly canvas screens. She looked up as the women came in and gave Stella a friendly smile.

'These are fascinating. Look, this is the Army camp that was in the Barton grounds, and here are some of the evacuees at the school that took over the house itself. And look at these, from the Barrows' farm! I'm amazed anyone even had a camera as long ago as that. This one must be from the turn of the century, at least. Look at the women's dresses!'

They picked through the photos, exclaiming over them and deciding where to display them. Stella started to read some of the tattered documents.

'You know, someone ought to put all these into a book,' she said. 'It would be a lovely record to have. *The Book of Burracombe*, with lots of photos and documents, and people's stories written down – all the things we've been hearing while this has been going on.' She looked up, bright-eyed and excited. 'Don't you think so?'

'I do,' Val said. 'It's a wonderful idea. You ought to do it, Stella. You're the one with the education.'

'Oh, I couldn't! People don't know me well enough – I'm still a stranger here. It would have to be someone they'd trust and could talk to. You'd be the one.'

'Well, perhaps we could do it together. I could collect the stories and you could write them down.' They looked at each other with enthusiasm. 'Look, when all this is over, why don't you—'

A sudden commotion interrupted her words and she turned to see what was happening. The door was open and someone was struggling in backwards, evidently trying to get a large, flat bundle through without dropping it. Val stared and then put down the document she was holding and ran across the hall.

'*Luke!*'

He turned, and as he saw her coming towards him, he laid his bundle of paintings down on the nearest table. Then he held out his arms and she ran straight into them.

'*Well!*' Joyce Warren exclaimed, and drew herself up very straight.

'Oh, look at that,' Dottie Friend said, her round face beaming with pleasure. 'Isn't that lovely!'

Stella stared at them. Then she turned away and picked

up a photograph at random, studying it intently. Her face paled.

'Stella, my flower! Are you all right?' Dottie was at her elbow, her face anxious. 'You're not upset, are you, maid? He's a lovely man, I know, and you're good friends, but you can see there's something proper special there. You mustn't take it to heart.' She looked more closely at Stella's white face. 'Stella?'

'It's not that,' Stella said breathlessly. 'It's this photo-graph.' She held it up so that Dottie could see. 'Where is it? Who are all these children?'

Dottie fumbled for her glasses. She held the photo up to catch the light from the window, and then a smile broke out over her face. 'Why, it's the little evacuee children that were up at the Barton. It were taken over by a school, you know – well, us always called it a school, but it were more of a Home, really. Poor little tackers that had lost their mums and dads in the war. And look, here's Maddy – the little girl my actress adopted and brought to live with me.'

'Maddy?' Stella almost snatched the photograph away and stared at the child Dottie was pointing at. '*That's* Maddy?'

'Yes,' Dottie said, beaming at the photograph as if the sight of it brought back happy memories. 'That's her. It must be almost the only photograph there is, because you know we couldn't get much film during the war. Why?' She looked at Stella again. 'What is it? You look as if you've seen a ghost.'

'Not a ghost,' Stella said, and her eyes filled with tears. They spilled down her cheeks and as Dottie stared at her in dismay she shook her head, laughing and crying at the same time. 'Not a ghost at all. Dottie, it's Muriel – my sister! That little girl is my *sister*! My sister, that I've been looking for for years and thought I'd lost for ever. Oh Dottie, I've been searching so hard, and you knew her all the time. *She lived with you during the war.*' She sat down suddenly on one of the hard wooden chairs and put her face into her hands. The others noticed what was happening and came over in concern, Luke and Val still holding each other's hands.

'What is it? What's the matter?' Val asked. She looked at the others, bewildered and concerned. 'She seemed so happy a few minutes ago. What's happened to upset her?'

Dottie turned her head and looked at them.

'She's not upset,' she said. 'She's not upset at all. She's just found her sister, the one Luke's been helping her look for all these months.' She put her hand on Stella's shoulder and spoke directly to her. 'And what's more, my blossom, you'll be able to meet her soon, because when my actress is coming to open the Fair, she's bringing Maddy with her!'

Chapter Thirty-Two

The day of the Fair dawned at last. Stella woke and stared at her bedroom ceiling, hardly able to believe that it was finally here. She stretched under her sheets and thought over all that had happened since she had seen the photograph of her sister in the village hall.

She still found it amazing that she was actually living in the same cottage that Muriel had lived in. It seemed incredible that Dottie had known her and looked after her and yet, even though she had known Stella was looking for her sister, never realised there could be a connection. Yet it was understandable. There had been hundreds, perhaps thousands, of children orphaned during the war, and many more put in Children's Homes. And for some reason, although the village had known that the children at the Barton were in a Home, they always referred to it as a 'school'.

And then there was the change of name. By the time Dottie met her, Muriel had been known as Maddy for two years. They had changed her name at the Home because there was another Muriel of the same age, and when the actress had adopted her, she had decided to keep it. She told everyone that the little girl's name was Madelaine, Maddy for short, and Muriel herself had never corrected her.

'Didn't she ever say she had a sister?' Stella had asked wistfully, and Dottie shook her head. They were back in the cottage then, for Dottie had said Stella had had a shock and needed a rest and a nice cup of tea. What she had really meant was that Stella needed to get used to finding her sister at last and to ask questions and, now that they were home and the tea was made, she settled in the armchair facing Stella and prepared to answer those questions.

'I'm afraid she didn't, my flower. I did ask her once about her family and she said they were all dead.' She saw the pain cross Stella's face and added, 'Maybe they told her that at the Home – who knows? They did some funny things during the war, but they usually thought they were doing them for the best.'

'How could they believe that?' Stella burst out. 'How could they think that telling a little girl that her whole family was dead could be for the best, when it wasn't true? It was cruel! Separating us at all was cruel.'

'I know, my pretty, but we don't know their reasons, do we? Maybe she was grieving so much that they had to tell her that. You can get over a death – eventually – but 'tis hard to get over losing someone when you know they're still alive somewhere.'

'You don't have to tell me that,' Stella said bitterly. 'I've spent all these years grieving for Muriel, but I wouldn't rather have thought she was dead.' She looked at Dottie. 'Did – did she seem to grieve?'

Dottie sighed a little. 'I couldn't really say that, flower. She was just a little girl, wasn't she? She were only ten year old when she come to me, not quite eleven, and she'd been in the Home for two years then. I never knew exactly what had happened to her before that. We all thought it were best not to ask her too much – remind her, like. It was best that she put it all behind her.' She looked apologetically at Stella and Stella reached over and patted her hand.

'It's all right, Dottie. You did what you thought best, and you didn't know about me. And I know you'll have given her a good home. She couldn't have been with anyone better than you.'

Dottie's eyes filled with tears. She sniffed and rubbed her nose, and said gruffly, 'I only did what were right. And she were a sweet little maid, Maddy – still is.'

Stella was longing to see her sister. They were in France now, the actress and Muriel, but on the day of the Fair itself, they would be here in Burracombe. *After all her desperate searching, Muriel was coming to Burracombe – and she would have been coming even without my searching,* Stella realised. *All I had to do was wait, and she would have come to me.*

'Can we let them know?' she asked Dottie. 'Can you get in touch with your actress and tell Muriel about me?'

'I can't, maid. I don't know where they be. I had an address to write to before, so I could ask her about the Fair, but since then they've been travelling about, and I don't know where. Us shan't hear no more from them until they arrive.'

'So Muriel won't know I'm here? I'll be a complete shock to her.'

'A surprise,' Dottie said gently. 'A lovely, lovely surprise.'

'A shock, just the same, if she thinks I'm dead. We'll have to be very careful, Dottie.'

They sat quietly for a while, drinking their tea and thinking about what had happened. *I need time to take it all in,* Stella thought, *and if I need time after just seeing a photograph, how is Muriel going to feel meeting me in the flesh, with no warning at all?*

'She might not even believe me!' she said suddenly. 'She might not recognise me. Oh, *Dottie*!'

'Now, don't you start worrying yourself about that. She'll know you all right, and if she don't recognise you straight away, there'll be lots you can talk about, things you did when you were little, that only you'd know about. Anyway, we only see the differences in people for the first few minutes, when we meet them again. After that, we just see the things that are the same.'

'I hope you're right,' Stella said. And I hope Muriel likes me too, she thought. We've lived such different lives – me in the Home and now teaching in a tiny village, and her living with an actress in London and going abroad ... What is she going to be like after all that? What changes will there be?

She tried to keep her mind off the coming meeting by immersing herself in the Festival preparations. Almost everyone in the village was involved in one way or another, and she and Miss Kemp had arranged several last-minute rehearsals for the children. Jacob had put up the maypole, and they practised their dances, getting their ribbons so tangled at times that, as Constance Bellamy remarked, pausing to watch them as she gave Rupert his afternoon walk, you could have knitted yourself a Fair Isle jumper from them.

'I think they have,' Stella said, trying to unravel the brilliantly coloured strands. 'Honestly, there are more knots here than there are in a Boy Scouts' competition!'

The Drama Group was busy rehearsing too, and with the village hall now closed to everyone except those still putting up their Exhibition displays, the big tent in Ted Tozer's field was coming in very useful. On Friday night, however, everything had to be cleared out and the tables set up for the bellringers' tea. Alice Tozer and the rest of the ringers' wives were busy all morning, baking pasties, scones and rock cakes and setting the tables, while on the green Ted and Nathan were setting out bales of straw for the bowling.

The competition was to start at ten in the morning. It had been agreed that it would end with the last team at six, after the tea, and then the Burracombe ringers, who were not taking part in the competition itself, would ring a final peal. There were three novice teams as well, and Burracombe had been permitted to enter theirs, since it was their idea to set this up, although they would not be placed. The novices went first and the older ringers had to admit that they made a pretty fair job of it.

'Might let young Tom ring in the Barnaby next year,' Ted observed. 'He did all right on the treble. And young Jimmy, too, he rung that tenor as steady as a rock. Maybe they're right – us ought to give them a chance in one or two competitions.'

News was exchanged as usual, and everyone wanted to know how the men's outfitter's manager was getting on at Lydford. The captain laughed. 'Oh, he be leaving! Couldn't stand it no longer. Didn't you hear how he come into the church one day when us was ringing for a wedding, and started all his shouting and carrying on? Vicar told un a few home truths, I tell you! Told un he was never to come near the church again unless it were to pray at a proper service. I reckon that were enough for him. House went up for sale very next week.'

'Well, let's hope he don't come to Burracombe,' Ted said. 'Us don't want his sort here. Plymouth'd be the best place for he. City man, he is – likes the sound of traffic better than the sounds of cockerels and cows and good church bells.'

The new Shield was finally won by Little Burracombe. Ted Tozer presented it to his rival captain and they shook hands heartily in front of everyone. 'I'm pleased it's stopping at a Burracombe, if 'tis only the Little un,' he said, and they all laughed. 'But us'll get it back next year, see if us don't!'

By the time the ringers had all drifted away from the village after visiting the pub, and the women had cleared up in the tent, it was getting late. Val and Luke, who had been putting the final touches to his display in the village hall, walked home together under the pale twilight sky. They paused by the gate to the woods and leaned on it, watching the moon rise over the swell of the moor.

'It's all right between us now, isn't it?' he said at last. 'We've found each other again.'

Val nodded. 'I think so. But I still need time – it was such a shock to see you again after all these years. And then, thinking that you were in love with Stella . . .'

'I never was,' he said quietly. 'I like her very much – I suppose, in a way, I do love her – but more like a little sister than anything else. It seemed so sad, the way she'd been looking for her own sister all these years, and I wanted to help her. And all the time, she was going to find her anyway! It's so incredible.'

'I know. But I think she was falling in love with you, all the same.'

'That's why I went away,' he said. 'I couldn't let that happen. I'd already done so much damage to you. I couldn't have forgiven myself if I'd hurt another woman.'

Val leaned her head on his shoulder. 'You didn't hurt me, Luke. Everything we did, we did together. It wasn't your fault that Eddie died, or that I lost the baby, and it wasn't your fault I felt so guilty. I just couldn't face it all, and I took it out on you. Somehow, during the last few months, I've learned to take my own responsibility for it all.' She paused, then said quietly, 'Jackie thought she was pregnant a few weeks ago.'

'Jackie?' He turned and looked at her in astonishment. 'Your sister Jackie?'

'Yes. You know she's been going out with Roy Nethercott for a year or so now. They wanted to get engaged but Mum wouldn't have it, said they were both too young – and so they are. But then Roy got his call-up papers and was going away and – well, we can understand, can't we? It was all too much for them.'

Luke was silent for a moment. Then he said, 'Yes, we can understand. It's so powerful, isn't it? It puts everything else into the shade and nothing else seems important.'

'She told me she regretted it the minute it was over,' Val said. 'I don't think she even enjoyed it much. It was the first time for both of them, and they hardly knew what they were doing.'

Luke tightened his arm about her shoulders. 'I didn't regret making love to you,' he said quietly. 'It was the most wonderful thing that ever happened to me.'

'For me, too,' she said. 'I only regretted it because of Eddie. I never meant to let him down, Luke. I did fall in love with you, but I was engaged to Eddie, and I loved him too. I shouldn't have let it happen.'

'It's in the past,' he said gently. 'We can't alter that. But we can make the most of the rest of our lives.' They were quiet for a moment, then he said, 'But what about Jackie? You said she "thought" she was pregnant. Does that mean the same thing happened to her as it did to you? Is she all right?'

'Yes, she's all right. It was a false alarm. She realised it the day she went to London.' Val remembered something and added, 'I was so mean to Stella that day, you know. Jackie'd gone to the Ladies' – that's when she realised she was all right – and Stella came to sit beside me. I was rude to her. I still thought then that she and you . . . Honestly, I've treated her very badly.'

'Well, that's over now, too,' Luke said. 'You've made up for it in the past few days, and on Monday she'll have her sister back. And she's so excited about that, that she seems to have forgotten she might be falling for me, so that's OK! But is Jackie really all right? She must have had a bad fright.'

'She did. She told me about it in the end, and I felt so sorry for her – I could understand how she felt. Not that I could tell her that, of course.' Val was silent for a moment. 'I think she's got over it, though, and it's put paid to any ideas she might have had about getting engaged to Roy. She wouldn't even speak to him when he first came home, but she says now that she's agreed to write to him while he's away. He's going to Korea, you know.'

'So I heard. It's a bad business out there.' Luke shook his head. 'We've lost a lot of men, and some of them have been National Servicemen like Roy. We all thought that once the last war was over we could put that behind us, but it hasn't happened, has it? God knows where it will end.'

They stood very quietly for a while, watching the moon lift its head above the hills, and then he drew her closer and turned his face to hers. Their lips met in a long, tender kiss. He stroked her hair and face and kissed her again. Then he said huskily, 'You will give me another chance, won't you, Val? I know we've got a lot to talk about, and we need to get to know each other a lot better – we mustn't rush into things like we did before. But there's more time now. We can take it slowly.' He paused. 'If we can just be friends – that'll be enough, to start with.'

'Yes,' she whispered, and he saw the stars reflected in her eyes as she looked up at him. 'Yes, Luke, we can be friends. To start with.'

The sun was streaming through the yellow flowered curtains in Stella's room, casting stripes of golden light across her bed as she lay thinking over the past. Her memories had drifted further back now – to the dark days of the war, when she and Muriel and their mother had emerged from their shelter to find their house destroyed by bombs, the misery and confusion of the church hall where they'd slept until they'd been allocated the dismal little house in October Street, and the work their mother had done to turn it into a home. The birth of their brother Thomas during an air-raid, and then the second bomb, which had robbed her and Muriel of him and their mother.

There had been happier times, even then – the months they had spent with the Budd brothers, Tim and Keith, at the vicarage in the country, the visits their father had made to them there. And then he too was gone, and they had been swept up and parted. Why were people so cruel, Stella wondered, even when they meant to be kind? Why had it been considered better to separate her from her little sister? And why ever had they told Muriel that Stella was dead?

I'll never understand it, she thought.

It was time to get up. Dottie was cooking breakfast downstairs in the sunny kitchen, and Stella had promised to be at the village hall by ten, when the Exhibition was to open again. They had had a good many visitors on Saturday, when the bellringers had all taken the opportunity of some entertainment while the other teams were competing, and a lot of them had brought their wives too. Yesterday being Sunday, the Exhibition had been closed and the focus was on the church, with its flower displays. Both services had been full, and Hilary and her helpers had been congratulated over and over again on their arrangements.

Even when Felix had come to lock the church, Hilary had still been busy, checking over each urn and vase for dying leaves or petals beginning to turn brown. The last of the sunset was slanting through the windows as he came in, and she turned to smile at him.

'You must have finished by now,' he said, coming to stand beside her. 'They're perfect.'

'I want them to be perfect,' she said. 'Everyone's worked

so hard for the Festival, Felix, and it's all gone so well so far, but tomorrow's going to be the big day.'

'The big day for everyone,' he said softly. 'And I was hoping . . . I want to ask you something, Hilary.'

'What's that?' Her eyes were still on the flowers, but something in his voice caught her attention and she turned to face him. 'Felix?'

'I'd like you to make it a big day for me too,' he said. 'These last few months, Hilary, you've made such a difference to me. Coming into a village like Burracombe, a stranger from the other side of the country, well, it could have been so difficult. But you've eased my path. You've been a friend to me, a really good friend. And I wondered – is there any possibility that you might be more than that?' He paused as she gazed at him, and then said, 'I'm asking you to be my wife, Hilary.'

'Oh,' she said.

There was a long silence. Then she took his hand and led him to the front pew. They sat down and she turned towards him.

'Felix, I don't know how to say this.' She saw his face fall and added quickly, 'I've enjoyed spending time with you – showing you around, going riding sometimes, the day we spent in Exeter. It's been lovely. But with Dad being ill, and with my feeling so restless and dissatisfied with my life, I've never thought of anything else. I've been selfish, I suppose. I've never thought at all about how it might be for you.'

'But that doesn't mean there's no chance—' he began eagerly.

Hilary lifted one hand, and he fell silent again. 'I'm sorry, Felix, I think it does. I've been thinking a lot during these past weeks, since Dad had his heart attack. You see, what I've always wanted was something to *do* – something real and solid and satisfying. I thought I'd have to go away to find it – I even planned to leave home and go to London. But now, I think I've found it at home after all.' She paused and he saw the light in her eyes. 'Dad and I have talked about it and he's accepted at last that he's never going to be able to do all he used to do. He needs someone to help him run the estate – to take over from him – and I'm going to do it! He's going to hand over the reins to me. Burracombe Barton will stay in the family and a Napier will still be running it. And I know I'll be good at it – it's what I've always wanted.'

'But that doesn't mean you can't marry if you want to,' Felix said, and she shook her head.

'No, but you see, I don't think I do. I don't think I ever did, really.' She looked into his eyes. 'There *are* people like me, Felix, who stay single. It doesn't mean they don't want friends, though. I hope we'll always be friends. And that you'll find someone else – someone who'll make you a far better wife than I would.'

'I don't know,' he said a little sadly. 'I don't know if I will, Hilary.'

Hilary touched his cheek with her fingertips. 'You will,' she said. Then she got up and walked out of the church.

Felix sat for a long while in the front pew, with the colours of the flowers fading in the gathering dusk and their scent all around him. Then he too got up and walked out, locking the door behind him.

He felt as if he were locking away his heart.

Chapter Thirty-Three

By two o'clock, everyone was ready. The stallholders and those running sideshows were all at their posts, with coconut-shies, bowling for a pig, plant and bric-à-brac stalls, a plywood cut-out of a clown with holes for faces and hands, where you could choose a grinning Boy Scout to throw wet sponges at, and a display of woodcarving with Jacob Prout red in the face with pride and embarrassment behind a forest of walking sticks. Willy's, the local ice-cream maker, had sent a van to stand at one side of the field, and the ladies of the WI were all ready to serve teas in the big tent. There was a stage for the Drama Group and the Sunny Side Up children's dancing troupe to give their show, and a big arena fenced off in the middle for the Hunt Puppies and a demonstration of sheepdog skills. Over in another corner, Norman Tozer was preparing to shear a ewe, once everyone had had a go at guessing her weight.

Stella was in a fever of nervous impatience but was too caught up in the last-minute panics of the children to let herself worry any further. While Miss Kemp was making sure the older children were in their costumes and ready for the procession, she was dealing with a flurry of elves, fairies and pixies who were to accompany Shirley Culliford on her grand parade from the school playground to the village green, where she would be crowned Festival Queen. The Nethercott twins, in their Princesses' gowns and tiaras and clutching posies of flowers, looked as delightful and pretty

374

as everyone had expected them to, but nobody was quite sure about Shirley.

'I know she's improved a lot over the past term,' Miss Kemp murmured to Stella, 'but you never know with that family. Suppose her mother's decided to dye her hair and it's turned green? Or she put her frock on at home and fell in a cowpat!'

'Dottie will see that she's looking lovely,' Stella said. Dottie, having made the dress, had insisted on being the one to get Shirley ready. 'She'll be out any minute anyway, and then we'll see for ourselves.'

The rest of the grand parade had assembled as well. Ernest, wrapped in a cloak made (Miss Kemp was thankful to see) from an old curtain instead of his mother's best pair, made a splendid Walter Raleigh walking beside tow-headed Geoffrey Martin as Francis Drake. There were half a dozen Stone Age children clad in hessian sacks and carrying a large cardboard standing stone between them, and Micky and Henry had manufactured a very creditable replica of the Guinness Clock, which gave some of the other children the opportunity to dress as Mad Hatters, toucans and unicorns as they capered around the proud clockmakers. In the middle of all this was Constance Bellamy as Queen Victoria, her small sturdy figure clad in black, a stern expression on her face and with the burly figure of George Sweet in his best black suit and top hat as Prince Albert at her side.

The smallest children looked like a scattering of flowers, blowing in the wind, as they ran about ignoring Stella's instructions to stay together in one corner. Ted Tozer's trap was standing in the middle, covered in decorations, with Barley in the shafts wearing a large straw sunhat festooned with honeysuckle and rambling roses. In a few moments, the trap would lead the parade through the village, with Shirley in the place of honour on her throne (a kitchen chair wrapped in a red velvet curtain).

The school door opened and everyone stopped what they were doing to see the Festival Queen come out.

Shirley Culliford emerged. Her usually stringy hair was shining with cleanliness and hung in ringlets on each side of her glowing face. Her eyes were huge with excitement, and her face beamed with the biggest smile Stella had ever seen. She wore a dress of shimmering gold taffeta, and she carried a bouquet of summer flowers as proudly as if she were a bride – or, indeed, a royal Queen.

'Oh, my dear,' Miss Kemp said quietly. 'She looks perfectly lovely. Basil was absolutely right.'

The bells began to ring as the procession moved off, and all through the village the people gathered to cheer their very own Festival Queen. Stella, trying to keep her fairies and elves in order, found herself looking up at the clock and then searching the crowd with increasing anxiety. Dottie's actress still hadn't arrived. Suppose she was late. Suppose she didn't come at all.

Suppose there had been an accident on the way.

I can't lose Muriel again, she thought, with wings of panic beating in her breast. Not when she's so close. Oh, suppose she's decided not to come! Suppose she doesn't recognise me. Suppose she doesn't *like* me . . .

She felt someone grip her hand and turned her head to see Luke beside her, with Val on his other side. He smiled down at her reassuringly and her lips quivered as she tried to smile back. 'It's all right,' he murmured. 'It will be all right, you'll see.'

'Oh Luke,' she whispered. 'I can't believe it. I can't believe it's really going to happen.'

'I think it is,' he said, and nodded towards the end of the lane. 'I think this is her coming now.'

376

Stella felt her heart shake. The procession had reached the green now and Shirley was being lifted down, throne and all, and placed beneath the ancient oak tree. At the end of the lane, a large black car was nosing its way through the crowd. It stopped in the space reserved for it by the church gate, and a woman climbed out.

It was Dottie's actress – the famous Fenella Forsyth, who had entertained the Forces all through the war, who was a star of the London stage, her voice and beauty renowned throughout the world. Tall, slender and lovely, she had never married but she had once adopted a little girl and treated her like a princess. And that little girl had lived here in Burracombe; and she was Stella's sister Muriel.

As Muriel followed Fenella Forsyth from the car, Stella stood frozen to the spot. She could scarcely breathe. She watched, helpless, as her sister, dressed in the latest fashion and yet still, unmistakably, her little Muriel, smiled and waved at the people she knew so well. And then Dottie went forward and embraced them both, and murmured something in Muriel's ear, and Muriel looked past her and met Stella's eyes.

For a moment or two, they seemed to be enclosed in a bubble of silence. Even the bells had stopped, as if waiting. Then the cheers of the crowd, as Shirley Culliford was crowned Festival Queen, broke out and surged around them, and the two sisters ran across the green and fell into each other's arms. And, as they did so, the bells of Burracombe rang out once more, with joy in every note.

'Muriel!' Stella cried, feeling the years slip away as she hugged her sister against her. 'Oh *Muriel*!'

All Orion/Phoenix titles are available at your local bookshop or from the following address:

Mail Order Department
Littlehampton Book Services
FREEPOST BR535
Worthing, West Sussex, BN13 3BR
telephone 01903 828503, *facsimile* 01903 828802
e-mail MailOrders@lbsltd.co.uk
(Please ensure that you include full postal address details)

Payment can be made either by credit/debit card (Visa, Mastercard, Access and Switch accepted) or by sending a £ Sterling cheque or postal order made payable to *Littlehampton Book Services*.
DO NOT SEND CASH OR CURRENCY

Please add the following to cover postage and packing

UK and BFPO:
£1.50 for the first book, and 50p for each additional book to a maximum of £3.50

Overseas and Eire:
£2.50 for the first book plus £1.00 for the second book and 50p for each additional book ordered

---

BLOCK CAPITALS PLEASE

name of cardholder ....   *delivery address*
....   (*if different from cardholder*)
address of cardholder ....
....
....
....
postcode ....   *postcode* ....

☐ I enclose my remittance for £ ....

☐ please debit my Mastercard/Visa/Access/Switch (delete as appropriate)

card number ☐☐☐☐☐☐☐☐☐☐☐☐☐☐☐☐☐

expiry date ☐☐☐☐   Switch issue no. ☐☐

signature ....

prices and availability are subject to change without notice